KISMET

MADISON RYAN SERIES: BOOK ONE

D.W. PRICE

KISMET

PROLOGUE

The room was shrouded in shadows, except for the faint light that filtered through the gap between the curtains. She groaned, writhing, and twisting under the thin sheet that covered her body. Her voice grew weaker as she cried out for help. I moved closer, gently pushing away the damp curls that clung to her forehead, wiping the salty tears that ran down her cheek. My touch soothed her as it had before.

She was in danger again. I gazed at her, wondering what mysterious force or spell had linked us together. I cared for her — I knew for certain. Although, I thought I had left my humanity behind centuries ago.

The girl with the long wavy hair with eyes that matched the sea had stirred something in me, but I didn't dare to examine those feelings. All I knew was that I had made a promise to protect her. And I must keep that promise, no matter the cost.

CHAPTER ONE
HOMETOWN

After securing the clasp of my swimsuit, I slid into my shorts, grabbed a towel, and headed down the hall.

I noticed my father's office door was ajar and reluctantly poked my head inside. He was at work. He would be furious if he caught me in here. Yet, something edged me forward. I stopped in front of the Maps that adorned the wall behind the desk. My attention focused on the highlighted states marked with tiny red pins beside a black marker, which connected Alabama, Florida, and Georgia.

There were stacks of reports on his desk — pictures and notes of a missing girl that captured my attention. Shuffling through the files, I quickly realized she was one of three; their images were so familiar that I gasped and slung the photos back on his desk. My father had worked on similar cases over the years, only these disappearances were far too familiar, and a little too close to home. I squinted my eyes and focused on the images before me.

"They look like me." I mumbled. My hand went to my mouth to prevent any other thoughts from escaping.

I searched the files for clues to make sense of their likeness. Rebecca Miller, Sarah Jane Leighton, and Valerie Harris. My eyes widened, noticing the similarities. The victims were fifteen-year-old juniors in high school with complexions that mirrored mine, around five-foot-four inches tall, coupled with the fact that they all had long curly reddish-brown hair. With a pair of contact lenses, they all

2

could have been me. Shuffling through more of the papers, I noticed another girl — her clothes saturated with blood. Yellow and purplish bruises marked every inch of exposed skin. Why did I feel as though I knew her? Was she the girl from my dream last week? She looked so familiar. But there was no information about her, only the photos.

My finger slid across the photo, and in a strange unexplainable way I knew who she was. "Jennifer Stevens? Jenni? Everyone she knew called her Jenni, but she preferred Jennifer. She wanted to feel older." I said to myself, as more of her memories flooded my thoughts, a single tear traveled down my cheek and dropped onto my chest. I stumbled backward, dropping the stack carelessly on his desk, then hurried back to my bedroom.

Clutching my necklace tighter until the palm of my hand threatened to split open. I released the skeleton key, allowing the heaviness to hit my chest and sunk to the floor as if that would erase the images of those girls.

Once I regained my composure, and Jennifer's memories began to fade, I stood, and paced back and forth. I needed a swim, the only thing that could calm me down. The wood creaked beneath me as I took four steps at a time, although each jolt centered me. Finally, I hit the bottom landing; where my mom was watching television, perched on the arm of the sofa, duster in one hand, remote control in the other. She was watching the report of the disappearances.

Our local news anchor, Cyndi Newhouse, reported another missing girl, bringing the total to three from South Carolina. My brows furrowed as I considered the reports on my father's desk.

Why didn't Cyndi Newhouse mention the other girls? Or that the three missing girls in South Carolina were identical to the ones in my father's office, which would bring the total to seven, not three.

I watched as the life-size photos of the girls filled our flat screen. I forced myself to swallow as questions began assimilating in my head.

"Madison," I heard my mom say as she approached me. "You look as if you've seen a ghost," she teased, although I could see her concern. Her large golden-brown eyes saddened when they met mine. My mom's slender toffee-colored fingers fanned through her hair. She separated her wavy dark locks, which she did whenever her anxiety escalated. She went to the kitchen, and I mimicked her steps, stopping at the counter near the fridge while she continued around the center island.

"Another disappearance," I questioned, biting at my bottom lip.

"You know I cannot discuss your father's case," she ducked behind the island and returned a second later with a large cardboard box, which she placed on the counter. "Yeah, I know. It's strange that so many are missing, especially since they aren't reporting on all of them. They all look alike." My eyes narrowed, and I tipped my head to the side, studying her response. "Mom, I look like them. I look like those girls." She held up her hand to stop me from finishing as she waved a finger back and forth. "Madison, we are not having this conversation. I know that your nightmares have been getting worse," Yep. That shut me up.

She was right. The last few weeks were horrible. I awakened every night, consumed with an unexplainable terror. The four shadow figures had chased me, as far back as I can remember. Those shadow freaks no longer terrified me as they had in the past. That is not say that they don't still frighten me, because they do, only the recent nightmares are far more menacing, darker, and much more vivid. I felt a combination of fear for the missing girls, although the most frightening part is when I feel as though I am them. Their terror, every blow they incurred and the ripping sensation as someone or thing tore and ate them alive. I woke up every night for the past few weeks with my pajamas in tatters and screaming bloody murder.

"Sorry, didn't mean to upset you," she said softly, touching the side of my face with her warm palm. "Are you alright?" She asked. I nodded, still unable to form the words that would reassure her. She continued to study me. I knew that I had to say something.

"Fine, I'm fine." I managed. I shook my head, tipped forward until all my weight settled on the tips of my toes, and peered inside the empty box for a much-needed distraction. "Going somewhere?" I questioned, still trying to shake off the images of the girls. She placed another box on the counter.

"Madison, I wanted to wait until your father returned." She spoke. Her voice was cautious.

My chest- constricted. Had my father finally convinced her to send me away? He had threatened me with boarding school for majority of my life. Why would he send me away now? Why would she agree with him? I had been on my best behavior. Well, except for the occasional arguments with my father.

"We are relocating to Nirvana." She paused. "It's a quaint little town in Michigan." Her lips continued to move. Her mouth opened and closed; however, my mind refused to process her words. "I know you love it here. Nirvana will be a wonderful place to live, too," I caught. "Your father received the orders on Monday, and we have two weeks to be in place there. We have no other choice."

"Wait, you can't do this to me, it's my junior year." I stammered.

"I know," She shifted her eyes downward.

"I understand that you were hoping he would return. But unfortunately sweetheart, I spoke with his mother yesterday. She received a phone call from him a couple of days ago. She told me that he is never coming back," she stopped. "He said that you should stop calling." It felt as if my heart had stopped too.

"Why do you always have to mention him? My life doesn't revolve around Nic!" I wanted to scream, not because she was wrong. He had been my best friend for over twelve years. No, he had meant more to me than a friend. We had a lifetime of friendship, secrets, laughter, tears, and memories. Next to my mom there was no one I… my thoughts refused to continue.

"I know you miss him." She began. I jerked away from the counter. I was not going to have this conversation with her about Nic. She never could let things go. My mom, Miss 'Got to' fix everything, aka Elizabeth Ryan, forever the doting mother; she couldn't make this right. Nic was gone. To make matters worse, she was about to move us hundreds of miles away.

My feet padded across the kitchen tiles loudly. Okay, that was childish. What would come next? Would I hold my breath or fall to the floor, kicking and screaming? I stood in front of the patio door and stared out the window. I decided to have an internal tantrum instead. Even that felt exhausting.

"It's raining," I whispered as I slid the door open. The cool droplets began to coat my heated skin. I felt the warmth of my mom's hand on my shoulder. She ran her slim fingers through my tangled hair and gently wove the locks into a long braid that touched the waist of my shorts. She reached for my arm and removed the band I kept on my wrist to secure the braid.

"This is my home. How can you do this?"

"Home is where you are loved" was her typical and cheesy response.

"Why can't I stay here with Uncle Mike?"

"I wish we could debate this." She twisted me until we faced each other and gave me a stern look, which meant the conversation was over. "We leave on Saturday."

The front door opened, followed by heavy-laden footsteps, which sent my eyes over her shoulder. My father towered in the arched doorway from the living room to the kitchen. He was a large, well-built man, and his presence sometimes felt intimidating and scary. His blond hair was wet and tousled, and his black suit had dirt or blood; neither substance was unusual in his profession as a top criminal profiler for the FBI.

"Judging by the look on your face, I can assume that Beth told you about the move," he said from the entranceway. I nodded, afraid to speak because he would misconstrue my words and use them against me later. "Well, I think the move will do you some good," of course, he did. My father was older than my mom by fifteen years, forty-nine, and I knew that eventually the tables would turn, and I could ship him off to a retirement home in Nova Scotia. See if he likes daily threats of seclusion.

"She's concerned about this being her junior year," my mom explained.

"Why? She has no friends at school or on the island. The girl makes one friend in fifteen years; I believe it's safe to assume she won't make any in the next two years." Yep, that was my father, cold, distant, and deficiently lacking basic human emotions. The cold arctic air of Nova Scotia had nothing on him.

"Phillip, that's completely uncalled for," my mom's eyes flashed before she jerked around to face him.

"You know that I'm speaking the truth. You let Madison waste time with that damn boy and his dysfunctional family. He was worthless!"

"Don't talk about him!" I could feel my eyes beginning to burn. "You have no right to talk about Nic. You didn't know him. He was my best friend, no he was more than that to me," hot tears sprung from my eyes.

"Yes, you're right. Nic liked you so much that he left you at his prom and never looked back!" My father shouted. He tossed his cell phone on the table and walked toward me, but my mom stepped between us. "He was a worthless troublemaker, and look at you, groveling over the mutt!"

"I hate you." I lifted my chin to look into his eyes, refusing to back down.

"Madison!" My mom's hands flew to her mouth.

"I mean it, I hate that you're my," I was about to say father, but his hand hit the counter, and the glasses in the cabinets shook and rattled. I backed away from them and raced out the door and down to the beach.

I stopped to see if he was following me. He and my mom were arguing. I glanced back once more before diving in. My tears intermingled with the salt water and rain, as my body slashed through the waves. Once I was far enough away from the beach, I allowed myself to float, closed my eyes and I took a deep breath enjoying these precious moments of freedom, a brief pardon from the ironfisted rule of Mr. Phillip Ryan. I dipped into the water again, kicking my legs behind me. Every stroke took me further from the surface. My arms sliced the water effortlessly, curving, bending with the currents. The water felt like it was moving through me — soothing the tiny wounds left behind by his hateful words.

Something brushed against me. I glanced back to see a school of large striped bass. They swam by me, which evoked a much-needed smile. The bass dipped between my legs, near my ankles, and without thinking, I pointed to show Nic the school of fish, only he wasn't there. My father was right. Nic never cared about me. If he had, he would have never left without at least saying goodbye. I pushed away from the fish, headed to the surface, and returned to shore. A part of me wanted to continue swimming, but I reluctantly left the refuge of the water.

My father was sitting at the table on his laptop when I entered the house, a glass of wine in one hand, an unlit cigar pinched between his teeth. He looked up at me and scoffed. I disgusted him; there was no denying that. He called me a wild child because he believed I was uncultivated: a disgrace beyond hope, and like any untamed creature, I did my best to live up to that name. I learned how to drive motorcycles before my 14th birthday. Once, I snuck off to the ocean and swam the 15-mile distance to the lighthouse one foggy night, only to reach the shore and come face to face with Mr. Disgruntled aka my father and an agitated Coast Guard rescue team.

I recalled the way he would ruffle my hair when people were around. They saw his gestures as endearing. I knew better. He ruffled my hair the way one would a pet — I was his pet, or at least that is how he made me feel.

"You owe me an apology," his bark was crisp and firm, and his eyes never left mine. I never understood how his eyes softened whenever he looked at my mom and hardened when they met mine. His voice lost its roughness and became polished when he spoke to her, while he was coarse and heartless with me.

He loved my mom; however, to him — I was her defective

clone because although our features are identical, my mom was calm, with a loving mannerism. She was soft-spoken and even-tempered, and I was rough around the edges, "temperamental" was the word most would use. The physical difference that everyone noticed was our eyes. Her eyes were a light shade of brown, perfectly normal; however, mine were a vibrant shade of turquoise. I had to contend with the constant questions from friends and strangers alike, "Are your eyes from your mother's or father's side of the family?" "Why are they so light?" "Why do they look so freaky?" The questions and comments were relentless, although the open-mouthed stares bothered me more.

With both of my parents being the only child, there were no aunts or uncles, or cousins to compare myself to. All I had to rely on were the family albums, and even at an early age, it was easy to see my family had one thing in common, their large brown eyes. That is, except for me.

Over the years, I had guessed, like everyone else that saw us together, "Momma's baby, Daddy's maybe." There were times I prayed it was true, and my father was a greenish-blue-eyed man out there searching for me. He and my mom had a secret steamy love affair, and I was the creation of the love they once shared.

That may have been possible with someone other than my mom. She was madly in love with my father and is the sweetest, most trustworthy person I know. Another explanation could be aliens. They abducted her and inseminated her with their spawn, so I could someday take over the world. My glowing eyes communicate with them by sending signals to the mother ship.

If I were being honest, my eyes could be a little scary at times, their glowing coincided with my anger. The first time I caught a reflection of myself upset, I covered every mirror in the house with sheets.

"Madi," my father shouted and was now on his feet and standing in front of me before I had time to react. "Beth's not here to run interference!"

"I'm sorry," my words stung worse than the time I accidentally stepped on a yellow jacket.

"Now go pack!"

I stood there momentarily, wanting to see a trace of warmth in his eyes, a small gesture that told me he cared. But, instead, he waved his hand, dismissing me.

I slowly climbed the stairs, went to my room, and showered. Large boxes were beside my bed when I came out of the bathroom. I kicked the closest one across the room, knocking my lamp on the floor. My fingers gripped the skeleton key necklace for comfort as I crawled beneath the covers. I curled my legs up, tucking my body inward. The skeleton key remained wrapped in my tight grip until sleep finally claimed me.

I awakened to discover more empty boxes, bubble wrap, permanent markers, mounds of packing peanuts, a couple of rolls of tape, and a note from my father that read; you may leave this room when you finish.

The walls felt like they were closing in on me as I glanced around at the empty cardboard boxes. But I shoved them aside to clear a path and brushed my teeth.

After throwing on a T-shirt, shorts, and my favorite running shoes. I locked my door and climbed out of the window. My fingers gripped the windowsill tightly until my foot contacted the wood railing of the deck below. I peeked inside the kitchen to see my mom preparing breakfast; my father was sipping coffee from the world's best dad mug. That was a joke. At five, there was nothing that my father could not do. I marveled at how strong he was — now his strength frightened me — I swear when he is angry- he grows another five inches.

I leaped over the balcony railing, landing in a crouched position on the blanket of sand. I sprinted away from the house and ran down the street. Only the soft hum of a distant lawnmower broke the silence of the quiet street, still too early for people to be up and about. That made it the perfect time for me to go running. Ms. Richards's little Maltese, Patience, came rushing through her doggie door, barking like crazy. Patience's long white fur adorned with bright pink bows skirted across the ground. She hopped up and down in the grass. Patience was seven pounds of hatefulness and my archenemies. She used to chase me home when I was younger, nipping at my ankles once the thing punctured holes in the hem of my jeans. Ms. Richards installed an invisible fence when my mom threatened to call animal control. Patience could not leave her yard. I stuck my tongue out at her and increased my speed until her annoying yelps were no longer in earshot.

As I turned down McLeskey Lane, the beach came into view again — cut between the beach houses, stopping once I reached the large, chained link fence. Ignoring the brightly colored danger and caution signs, I crawled beneath. Once safely through, I headed up the rocky black terrain; my foot slipped again. The crashing waves drowned out the little voice in my head screaming for me to turn back. With the tips of my fingers, I positioned my foot sideways on a protruding rock and pushed myself upward. The process repeated until I reached the top of Raven's Peak — the highest point in Hatteras. The large black rock towered over the sea. No one was allowed to come here, although, at my school, this was a rite of passage. My father had forbidden me long ago, so I had not. Once I reached the top, I sat down to catch my breath, lying back on the smooth planes of rocks. Dark clouds hid the sun; however, that was no different from every day before. There was no way I would allow this dreary day to dampen this experience. This place was incredible, I thought to myself as I crept over to the edge and looked down. The waves leaped upward angrily as if warning me to back away. I flipped over, allowing my hair to fan out beneath me, imagining the waves licking at the ends. My eyes set on the grayish-colored sky before slowly shifting to my feet.

My hair danced around me as I stood on the edge. The tips of my running shoes no longer had ground beneath them. Gentle breezes swept past me, stirring a faint scent of sandalwood and sweet honeysuckle. "Goodbye, my friend," I whispered.

"Madison," someone said. I twisted to my left and then to my right, surprised to find myself alone on the peak. "Madison," the sound was more vivid. It felt as though a thousand butterflies had fluttered across my belly. I covered the span of my stomach with both hands, relishing the feeling that now coursed through me. A sudden wind blew, and I stumbled backward, nearly falling to my death, when something yanked me forward — I hit the hard rocky ground, scratching the palm of my hand and knees. A dark shadow breezed past me, leaving behind the most incredible scent; but a fraction of a second later, the smell and feeling dissipated.

CHAPTER TWO
RELOCATE

Saturday came and went; I threw another internal tantrum; we were about to move away from my home, the ocean, and any possibility that I might see Nic again. They refused to listen when I suggested that my staying with Uncle Mike would allow them time to focus on themselves. My father entertained the idea that was until my mom presented her counter, "If Madison stays, we all stay." She sure had a way of crushing my dreams. I had no voice in the decision that would alter my life.

I likened my parents to puppeteers, which would make me the puppet — thin, almost invisible strings manipulated my every move. They made the decisions, controlled my movements, and determined where I lived, slept, ate, and handed down punishments for any behavior that varied from their list of approved actions. They were more like wardens, and I was their prisoner— it sure felt like I was looking at the world through iron bars.

A strange feeling crept up, burrowing itself in the tiny hairs on the back of my neck, forcing them to stand on end. My stomach began to churn; for a second, I thought my lunch would resurface. And the movers were staring at me with their gold beady eyes. They were all dressed in the same navy-blue uniform shirt with dusty jeans and steel-toe boots, completing their look; they reminded me of the outdoorsy type — based on the caked dirt beneath their nails and overall rugged demeanor.

Something stood out to me as unusual. Was that the men all wore wide leather collars with identical wooden moon carvings that dangled from the center. Their hair variations of copper, and they looked like they had never heard of SPF 12.

The man named Jed, I assume, was the supervisor because he bossed the other men around. Jed must have seen me examining them because I heard him grunt something before, he closed the distance between them in four long quick steps to join me on the deck. His bright red curls coincided with the freckles sprinkled across his elongated face.

"Will this be going with you?" Jed's dark eyes watched me questionably; a slight hue of impatience helped darken his already sun-scorched complexion. He lifted the box, and I poked my head inside, where my childhood toys lay cradled. I had never played with my porcelain dolls, mostly because I feared damaging them, and three rag dolls usually adorned my bed. I riffled through the box to discover Tennessee, my knitted stuffed bunny. Carefully removing the bunny, I cradled him gently. Tennessee had seen me through sleepless nights, although no one knew where he came from. I awoke from a terrible nightmare to find Tennessee resting in my arms. His knitted sweater had begun to fray at the end, and one of his eyes dangled precariously. I would have to remind my mom to repair him.

The sound of Jed clearing his throat reminded me that he was still waiting for my decision.

"They all go with my things," I finally answered. Jed gave me a slight nod. His thick rubber soles left a black streak as he turned to join the other movers. There was something strange about the men — I had no clue what that was. However, I felt the need to remain cautious around them. That I heard my name at least five times in their conversation had me scrutinizing their every move. But one of the men caught me watching them and quickly hushed the others. He gave me a spiteful look before hoisting one of the larger boxes on his shoulder and ducking out of the house. The men had efficiently boxed, wrapped, taped, and loaded our lives onto two large moving trucks three hours later. My parents had agreed to keep the house for summer vacations, although something told me this would be the last time, I would set foot in my childhood home.

I focused on the back of my mom's head as my father locked the doors and barked orders to the movers. The pull to look back was far more challenging than I had expected — that glance left me feeling empty inside. Tears slipped from my eyes and gathered in the hollow of my neck. I put my earbuds in and turned-on *Alicia Keys*, '*Do Novo Adagio*' translated means '*Listen to Your Heart*,' well my heart was telling me that this move was a mistake. It took me a minute to realize this station was, SOOO not working for me, not when I wanted to roll out of the car and make a run for freedom, so I switched to something more upbeat.

We drove over eight hundred miles before the rain finally stopped; however, there were still another two hundred to go before we would reach Nirvana. My father refused to allow the movers to meet us at the house, which meant the trip would drag on forever. Adding to my misery was that he had to stop multiple times to ensure the men were cautious with his things. By things, I mean guns, bows, arrows, surveillance materials, and other gadgets.

"Phillip, I need to stretch my legs," my mom whispered, which we both knew was code for; she had to go to the bathroom. My father responded with a not-so-subtle grunt, which prompted an eye roll from me.

"Your eyes are going to get stuck like that," my mom teased from the front seat. She was staring at me in the mirror. I shifted myself out of view and popped my earbuds back in.

He took the first exit we came to and pulled into the nearest gas station. My mom hurried from the car and around the side of the building.

My father's phone buzzed, and he left the car before answering.

He was frustrated, judging by the angry scowl plastered on his face. I removed the earbuds and lowered the window. My mom joined him in the middle of the parking lot, and her smile quickly faded. Something was wrong. My mom looked overly concerned.

"Another one," I heard her say.

"No, two," my father's eyes met mine, and he dragged her further away. There were two more missing girls. I slid my phone open to Google and typed in recent kidnappings, and a flood of information began to upload. I backspaced and searched instead for teenage girl disappearances. An article on a possible serial kidnapper popped up — five girls are missing— the latest were from Cape Hatteras, South Carolina. Not to mention the two that aren't included in the count- so nine girls are missing. I scanned the images of the two newest victims. They looked identical to their predecessors — to me. The muscles in my throat tightened, and I found it difficult to swallow. The moisture in my mouth had vanished.

I closed my phone, hurried out of the back seat, and headed into the store. After grabbing two bottles of water, I joined the movers. Their drinks of choice were forty-eight-ounce cups of fountain sodas. I frowned when I noticed their mounds of nachos with cheese that oozed over the red and white paper bowls, hotdogs fully loaded, and chips, a stomachache in the making. What stood out about them was that their muskiness remained prominent despite the wafting odors of the hotdogs and nacho cheese. God, they smelled terrible — as the thought entered my head, the smell intensified. I heard sniffing, someone in the store agreed with me, and then I realized the sniffing was coming from behind me. A boy was standing close, and a large lock of my hair lay across his finger. His freckled nose wrinkled as if he wanted to consume the strands of my hair. My back met Jed's hard chest as I moved away from the boy.

"Sorry, Madi," Jed barked as he grabbed the boy by his collar and pulled him in front of me. Jed swiped his large palm across the boy's scruffy copper hair, and his face constricted to reveal a pain I understood. It was clear that Jed was the strange boy's father. He glanced up at me; shame washed his face. His nametag read Tobias, and he seemed anxious, which made me uncomfortable. Then, I noticed the small tattoo on his forearm— VHW. Strange. I thought to myself.

"Sorry about all of that," he looked down at his shoes, and I wanted to ask him why he was sniffing my hair, but his father had already shamed him enough.

"No problem, I'm Madi," I said, careful not to make eye contact with him.

"Yeah, I know," he gushed, which dared me a glance up; a scowl creased my brow when I realized he was staring at my chest. "That necklace, the skeleton key. I bet money it's from the Victorian Era." He said instead, and I felt a pang of guilt at my assumption that Tobias was creepy.

"You collect keys?" I tried sounding excited, but I was unsure if I did.

"No, history geek, my favorites were Georgian and Victorian Era," he laughed,

"Cool," I placed my water on the counter. The movers paid for their things and shuffled out the door, except for Tobias.

"That'll be three-forty-nine," the stringy-haired woman behind the counter said, folding her thick arms over her chest. I dug in my back pocket — pulled out three dollars; I thought I had a five. "Sorry, I need to get the change from my mom," I began, but Tobias's shaky hand extended a dollar.

"Thanks, give it back outside," I said, taking the money and handing the bills to the woman. She paid the difference.

"No problem. Seriously, I would put that necklace away if I were you. If it's real, it's valuable; I'm talking *about The Met* valuable."

"Never thought about it," I went to tuck it inside my shirt, only to realize that he was holding the skeleton key in his hand. When our hands touched, I felt a surge of something dark and dangerous. That notion would have been crazy a second ago; however, now, I believe it to be true.

"Let it go," I tried to snatch the skeleton key from his hand, but he held on tight.

"Take your hands off her!" The cashier thankfully intervened, and Tobias released the hold he had on my skeleton key. Quickly, I tucked the necklace inside my shirt and crossed my arms over it protectively. Tobias smiled. His eyes lightened until they glowed.

"You smell good," his words were thick, and his voice lowered as he stepped closer to me, inhaling deeply. I must remember to go with my first impression; this boy was a major creep.

"Gross!" I frowned, and he seemed puzzled.

"I wasn't going to hurt you," he wiped his mouth, and I gagged. A large hand appeared and pushed the boy into a rack of magazines; he stumbled but remained upright; the magazine and the tower of can sodas were not so lucky. They rolled across the floor, spraying everything in their wake. My father — he was pulsating with anger.

The cashier came thundering from behind the counter, ready to ream my father; however, she stopped short. His presence intimidated the woman. She began collecting the cans instead.

He reached into his back pocket and pulled two crisp one-hundred-dollar bills from his gold money clip and handed them to the woman. Her smile was submissive, as if pleasing him was her life's mission. He gave a subtle nod, and the woman hurried back behind the counter, arms filled with the busted soda cans.

His fingers quickly coiled around my wrist, yanking me through the aisle and out of the store.

"Let me go," I jerked my arm from his grasp, or he loosened his grip. Either way I was free again. My father crossed the parking lot in a matter of seconds. He was ranting at Jed. I heard him say, "Keep that damn boy away from my daughter!" Right before I slammed the car door closed. He continued to berate the man. His voice traveled into the car. Seconds later, he threw the door open and got inside; before he could shut the door, his eyes turned to me.

"Buckle your seatbelt and stay in the damn car! If you want something, Beth will get it for you!" he snapped.

"Not my fault Tobias was a necklace-stealing, girl-sniffing idiot! You hired him; you should be mad at yourself!" I dared.

"Stay in the damn car and stop presenting yourself to every boy that looks your way."

"Presenting, what?" Swear he was born in another era.

"Your body, and don't get me started on the way you dress, like some…" he stopped midsentence, although I was certain of how the sentence ended.

"That's disgusting!" I crossed my arms and threw myself back into the seat. He was wrong on so many levels that it wasn't funny. Me throwing myself on boys never happened, and there was nothing wrong with my clothes, jeans, t-shirt, and sneakers. If he thought this was provocative, he'd have blown a gasket at Hatteras High — except he never visited my schools. My father was an absent parent.

My mom came to the car, passing a bag of fast food and a cup holder with three drinks to my father through her open window. He reached over, opened the door, and passed the drinks back to me, all in one swift motion. My mom slid into her seat, all smiles until she saw us, her eyes questioning the mood in the car.

"Did I miss something?" her glance alternated between us.

"Beth, for God's sake, teach her how to behave around boys!"

"Madison," my mom snapped — to my surprise.

"I didn't do anything! Why did you bother bringing me with you?" I shook my head to prevent the surge of tears that were threatening to spill over. Him yelling at me; I learned to accept, not my mom.

"Trust me, if it wasn't for your mother…"

"Phillip, don't you ever speak to her like that again." There was no waver in her voice as she lifted her chin in defiance. "I'm not certain exactly what happened while I was buying the two of you something to eat, but you had better get it together!"

"Sorry, I lost my temper. Tobias wanted to make himself familiar with our daughter." My father shifted the car into drive, directing the movers to go ahead of him.

"He what?" She looked at me.

They talked amongst themselves about the incident in the store while I sipped at the drink, butter pecan milkshake, my mom allowed us momentary breaks from clean eating, and thankfully, today was one of those days. The shake was sweet, buttery, cool, and creamy, so thick that I could have used a spoon; only where is the fun in that?

I took another deep draw from the straw, slurping until the cheap plastic flattened.

I scanned my playlist, put the earbuds back in, turned the volume on blast, and rested my head on the door. There was nothing left to say; I was moving to a new town, away from everything familiar. If my mom wanted to help, she would need more than a butter-pecan milkshake; she should demand that we return to Hatteras or at least leave me there with Uncle Mike. I removed my necklace from inside my shirt, sliding the flat, heart-shaped crystal my father had given me aside, and traced my fingers over the intricate design of the skeleton key. The delicate carvings are bordered by diamonds; the center is encompassed by a diamond kaleidoscope. Truthfully, I had never wondered whether the gems were diamonds; the necklace was a part of me. So, I suppose in that respect, little 'Sniffer boy' was correct about the skeleton key's value because, for me, it was priceless, but "*The Met*, valuable." Yeah, right. I squeezed my eyes closed and kept them shut until they announced that we were home.

CHAPTER THREE
NIRVANA

I slid the legs of my jeans through the hanger and then eased the wooden rack over to make certain there was room for my black leather jacket.

The jacket I was wearing had seen better days. It used to belong to Nic and was old and worn, but that also made the material more pliable. Nic had given it to me about five years ago. He had gone through a significant growth spurt from five-foot-five to six-foot-two in just one year. I could almost feel him here, smiling down at me or cracking a silly joke. It was hard not to think about Nic when wearing this jacket, but I pushed those thoughts aside and got to work on the final box placing the books on the shelf of my reading nook, which was the best part of this old house, with all its large empty rooms.

My father planned to turn one into his office, a library, and a nursery; yep, they were trying to have a baby; I discovered that tidbit of information when I happened across my mom's stash of ovulating sticks. No worries, I only have three years left of my sentence, that poor kid would have to fend for themselves.

"I'm leaving now Madison." My mom's voice pulled me across the room. She and my father were attending a fundraising Gala, but unfortunately, since I took my time unpacking, I was not. He grounded me- and by 'he,' I mean my father, the man, the boss, and 'Mister-has-to-control-every-single-aspect-of-my-life.'

"Madison," she called once more.

I took the stairs four at a time, landing right in front of her tiny, manicured feet that she had squeezed into a pair of high-heeled, open-toed black pumps. Her long, wavy curls gathered high on her head and smoothed into place with diamond barrettes. She gave me a stern look that needed no words before replacing it with a smile.

"Please don't do that; I know how much you love hospitals, but let's try not to become so well-known with medical personnel in Nirvana," She knew there was nothing I detested more than hospitals. The most recent incident happened when my now ex-best friend, Nic, dared me to jump off the deck that was two stories high. He didn't think I would do it, but my broken leg showed him. They had to strap me to the gurney to keep me in the ambulance. I knew if my name were on any list, it would be to inform the paramedics to "please sedate upon arrival."

She flipped my hand over to place the list of emergency contacts inside. "You call me if you need to. My phone will be on the entire time. Sarah should be here soon. Remember to finish unpacking. I know this may be a huge request but try to avoid trouble while we are away…." Her extended pause caused me to look up. "Are you listening?" she asked, tapping her foot against the hardwood floor.

"Stop worrying about me. I'm the one that's going to be stuck here with a stranger when I'm more than capable of taking care of myself. Mom, staying here alone is not a big deal. I'll be eighteen in three years." The growing frown on her face told me I had gone too far.

My mom had assumed that I was oblivious that my babysitters all came strapped with Glock-9s and Taser guns. I discovered that truth when I was eleven. My father's profession put all of us in a certain amount of danger, and she was overly protective.

"We should take caution. You know your father's job is risky. But leaving you here will no longer be a problem if you continue speaking that way."

"Sorry, they say the truth will set you free," I teased.

"Yes, it can also damn you to hell or get you another day in your room," the lyrical sound of her laughter filled the air. I watched as she brushed away pieces of fuzz from the long dress that clung to her small, curvy frame. My father would be fighting mad by the end of the night, mainly because my mom could gain the attention of any man around her. The funny thing was she never tried. It was simply a matter of fact, not that my father believed her — suppose that was another trait he felt I had gotten from her — I thought about his reaction to my being friends with Nic or simply talking to Tobias. Sure, boys came around and tried to "hang out" — nothing came of it, so I assumed my weirdness was a boy-repellant.

"You're daydreaming again, aren't you?" My mom questioned.

"I'm sorry," a knowing smile spread across my face.

"You amaze me, Madison," she stared at me until I looked away, not sure why she was being so sappy. Then, she kissed me on the cheek and turned to leave.

"Love you, have fun!"

"I love you too," she responded before ducking out the door. The second she left, I turned my favorite Beyonce song up, playing it excessively loud. The windows in our living room rattled from the vibration. I jumped on the large sofa, pounding my fist in the air, dancing and singing along, until my foot landed between the cushions. I fell hard on the floor, right on my backside.

"Ouch, I guess you come in handy sometimes," I mumbled while rubbing my bottom. The phone rang, and I raced into the kitchen to answer it, still feeling a little topsy-turvy by the fall — I lost my balance and slid across the slippery floor. My hand knocked the handset off the receiver, and my body crashed into the wine rack. The bottles went airborne, hit the counter, and fell to the floor and wine splattered everywhere, drenching my hair and clothes. Two falls in one day. The likelihood of that happening until now was zero. I was usually agile, the changes in the air pressure here affected my sense of balance.

"Are you alright?" I could hear the concern in her voice from the moment the phone touched my ear.

"Yes, everything's fine; you just left; what could have happened?"

I wiped my face with the hem of my t-shirt, scanning the room and seeing the expensive bottles of wine shattered across the floor.

"Please stop running in the house and turn the music down," she warned. I glanced over my shoulder to ensure she was not standing there, quickly making my way to the living room to turn the music off.

"I'm fine," I said. If being a mother made you this on edge, I never wanted the freak-in job. Seeing what a handful I was, her friends told me, "You will get it back when you have children of your own." Well, I say to hell with that.

After changing my clothes, I went back downstairs to clean the mess, closing the door to the wine room where I tucked away the survivors. The doorbell rang as I finished mopping the floor.

"Can you give me a hand?" Uncle Mike pleaded as he struggled through the door. I took two bags from him before following him into the kitchen. "I've got everything we need for tonight," he exclaimed, taking graham crackers, chocolate bars, marshmallows, and high calorie treats from his bags.

"What are you doing here?" I asked, wondering what happened to the babysitter. Ugh, even thinking the word 'babysitter' made me want to gag.

"Is that any way to greet your favorite uncle?"

He was not my biological uncle but my father's partner and a longtime family friend. After training, they became partners and ranked among America's top criminal profiling teams. When I was younger, Uncle Mike would come to our house to meet with my father, although he stayed to hang out with me. He did everything I wished my dad had, built sandcastles, and went swimming with me.

"I can't believe you're here," I gave him another quick squeeze, so happy to see him. I felt as though I were going to burst.

"Your babysitter heard about your often reckless and impulsive behavior…she bailed. Something to do with rumors of you jumping out of windows still lingering out there," he winked.

"Well, whatever the reason, I'm glad you're here." I hugged his neck, eyeing him cautiously as my focus shifted to the bags filled with snacks, "Are you trying to get us in trouble?"

"I know Beth would have my head if she knew junk food was in her house, but she's not here, so I'm going to spoil my favorite niece," he said, as the smile spread across his face. I groaned while unpacking the sinful snacks. "O-M-G, relax; you're hanging out with your B-F-F on a Friday night," he exclaimed. I shook my head in disapproval and plopped down in a chair.

"We discussed this before I left Hatteras...and agreed that anyone over twenty-five should never speak that way," I explained again, knowing this was another phase. He would keep doing it until he became bored.

"Net-lingo begs to differ; it's for the older, but cool, generation to keep us in the loop," he said as if it were the absolute truth. I silently thought he had never been more wrong; if there were a hypothetical loop, it was — created to keep older people out of it.

"F-C-O-L" (For Crying Out Loud), C-Y (Calm Yourself), it's all E-M-R-T-W." He made gestures, giving me what his generation would call the peace sign. I dared not tell him that he just said (Evil Monkeys Rule the World).

He smiled, rubbing his coffee-colored hands together before pushing them through his thick black hair.

"Yeah, what do you say if we agree you never say that again? Then, I will selectively forget any of this ever happened," I teased, trying my best not to laugh.

"Madi, you are such an old lady," his large dark eyes gleamed as he tried to dig through my hair in search of white strands. I had never understood why he found this so funny. "There's a lot of wisdom somewhere beneath those massive curls." Yeah, I had heard that constantly. "Something tells me you've been here before," Uncle Mike blurted out, unable to hold back his laughter when I wrinkled my nose.

"Can I ask you something?" I pried, opening the box of graham crackers, and taking a bite.

"Yep," he sank into the kitchen chair, stretching his long legs before him.

"Were you able to find any of those missing girls?" I knew this question could meet the classified FBI wall he and my father often hid behind; however, I took a chance anyway.

"No, we're searching for them, gathering data, frustrating as hell," his answer surprised me. He looked up at me, and I noticed the dark circles beneath his eyes for the first time. Since the move, my father has been home more. I now understand that meant Uncle Mike had picked up the slack.

"Oh, and have you noticed that the kidnappers are choosing a certain type?"

"You said, one question," he shifted in the chair. "Madi, stop worrying; you're safe—no more talk of disappearances. I came here for a break," he stuffed one of the powdered-sugar doughnuts in his mouth.

"So, have you found my replacement auntie yet?" Uncle Mike's face brightened. He was rich, handsome, and funny, but his success did nothing for his personal life. He had recently divorced his wife of five years but didn't shed a tear. Uncle Mike represented himself in court, and his now ex-wife got the dog while he walked away with everything else.

"Hate to disappoint you, but that hot little teacher of yours back in Hatteras, Jessenia Diaz, has made her way to the top of my list," he nodded his head, as my eyes widened with surprise.

"You're dating my teacher; gross," I teased, wrinkling my nose in mock disapproval.

"She's not overly sensitive, or needy, and that allows me to work without…." Uncle Mike stopped mid-sentence, "Best we do not mention any of this to your mother. If she knew I was discussing my relationship with you, she'd have me charbroiled." He was right, of course.

"Enough talk about me. I know what will put a smile on that beautiful face! Get that motorcycle of yours and take it for a spin." I averted my eyes, popping a powdered doughnut in my mouth. "Don't ignore me; your motorcycle's hidden behind the garage."

"How did you know?" My teeth sank into the fleshy part of my lip.

"I'm the only reason you've been able to keep the damn thing; your father thinks the motorcycle is mine. I told him that Beth let me store it here- that I wanted to ride whenever I visited. Luckily, he didn't ask me to take it for a spin, or the truth would have come crashing down around us." Uncle Mike gave me a knowing smile.

"That does sound unbelievably tempting. It's not like my father has ever banned me from riding," my shoes were sitting by the backdoor, but my jacket was upstairs, so I hurried to retrieve them both. I opened the garage door and skimmed my hand against the wall to search for the light switch. A large cardboard box stood in the way, which took substantial effort to push to the side. I rolled the bike to the front driveway, jumped on the seat, and revved the engine. The streetlights blurred as I skimmed down the road. The streets were quiet; only the soft hum of my motorcycle broke the silence. I must admit that this place is beautiful. Instead of beach homes in Hattcras, there was a continuous stream of rich greens and browns, all the houses tucked safely behind towering trees. Taking a deep breath — a combination of sweet pine and the mustiness of damp earth tickled my nostrils.

I gripped the handles firmly, shifted gears, and the bike roared beneath me as I forced it to go faster; the blood rushed through my veins as the wind fanned my hair out behind me. It was like a force that propelled me forward, urging me to keep moving even when I wanted to stop. The speedometer needle quivered; the tires burned beneath me. That little voice inside me clearly said, "Turn around," but I ignored her, which would one day lead to my downfall. I raced toward town. My father will never know; I'll take a quick look around and make it back without anyone seeing me.

I parked my bike in the cover of the trees, blocks from the party, and hurried across the massive lawn. There were guests inside the house and in the backyard. The smell of gas and grilled meat engulfed the air as grayish smoke rose above the house. The song Pontoon was on blast, and I eased against the brick wall to see people dancing on the makeshift dance floor. I hid behind the tall bush by the side of the house and shifted onto my toes to peek through the large window. They decorated the grand room in red, white, and blue ribbons. I liked the idea that the guest could wear flip-flops and sundresses to the party outside or stilettos and semi-formal dresses like my mom's dress inside, although the music was the same. Funny, the younger crowd was dancing while the older crowd mingled, oblivious to the catchy tune.

My mom was the exception. She was tapping her foot to the beat with an occasional bob of her head as she spoke with Ms. Betty. My father could not be far behind. His voice sent my eyes toward the back of the room. His large arm was over Conner Whitman's shoulder like a proud father. Truth — Conner was everything my father could want in a child. The football team's star quarterback was intelligent, funny, and charismatic. He was also the only boy my father ever encouraged me to hang out with, which was strange.

I had met Conner a week ago at the mayor's home when we first arrived in Nirvana. The mayor hosted my father's introduction party. I remember standing outside, watching as my parents were ushered into the house. Unfortunately, it had started to rain, and I felt sick.

The rain was cold, and I had closed my eyes tight, trying to prepare myself to meet all those new people. When I finally opened them, a boy was standing on the porch. He had to be around my age. I wondered why he waited there in the rain but reasoned that the rain made him feel alive like it does for me.

"Do you need a towel?" he offered when I stepped on the porch. His blond hair framed a chiseled face, and his green eyes filled with concern. His muscular body reminded me of the football players at home, a quarterback, or a wide receiver. But truthfully, those were the only positions I knew. "Hey, it's not as bad here as you think." My eyes met his as the rain dripped down both of our faces.

"That's easy to say…this is your home with your family and friends." I sat down; my hands gripped the side of the porch.

"It can be yours too if you let it. My name's Conner; nice to meet you." He smiled and wiped the rain from his eyes.

"It sounds like a lot of people are inside." I grimaced at the thought of having to meet them.

"They are harmless. You should come in; city folks tend to get lost in this area quite quickly."

"I'm not a city girl, but I have lost my way occasionally." I glanced over at the large, wooded area.

"I'll go in first if you want me to; tell them to hold off on the introductory licking of the face." Conner's sarcastic smile widened.

"No, I will be fine; that's a common greeting in Hatteras too." I walked past him and reluctantly entered the house.

The large room was bursting at the seams, but my father appeared beside me and placed his hand on my back before leading me through the sea of people.

"What happened to your clothes? You look like something the cat dragged in!" His nose wrinkled in distaste, but I ignored him not that he'd notice.

"This is Ms. Betty; you've already met her son Conner, and that's Braden." My father was good with people; he could remember every word they spoke or the color of their clothes. So, for years, it was our game until I realized he would never lose.

"Hi, Madi," Braden said. He smiled and then jabbed Conner on the side. They exchanged glances with one another. The brothers looked like twins from a distance, but up close, not so much. Conner was taller and had small dimples on both sides of his face that deepened when he smiled. Braden's eyes were a darker shade of green, his nose straighter, and he had a pointy chin — his blond hair — sculpted into place.

My father elbowed me. "I'm sorry… it's nice to meet you," I managed before rubbing my ribs.

Ms. Betty came over and placed her slender fingers on my shoulder. She was petite with large, warm, green eyes and identical blonde hair. "We are so happy you moved here; I can't wait to spoil you! With a house full of boys, all my dresses have collected dust!" She was gleaming with excitement.

"Thank you." I smiled.

My walk down memory lane was — interrupted by my father's boisterous laugh. He slapped Conner on the back, and his eyes brightened. I stooped lower beneath the windowsill when Conner's eyes narrowed, and he looked right at me. My stomach began to squirm when the door opened; there was no time to escape.

"Hey, Madi," Conner yelled. I placed a quick finger to my mouth, then ran over and pulled him behind the bush. "Why all the secrecy?" he asked in a hushed tone.

"I'm not supposed to be here…so you better not say anything," I snapped.

He laughed, "Or what? Will you hit me with those little hands? Oh, I'm scared!" His teasing was getting on my last nerve.

"Stop it; promise you won't tell anyone I'm here."

Uncle Mike was expecting me back by now, but I wasn't ready to go home yet. I slowly peeked up over the edge of the window again. My eyes focused on the people dancing to the blaring music. I noticed large plates of food and children running circles around their parents.

"You know I got you. Why are you freaked? Your dad's cool," Conner's comment distracted me from the party.

"Yeah, as a cucumber, until you add me to the equation," I couldn't blame him for having that belief; most people did.

"Your dad is coming," Conner warned with a shove that nearly knocked me over. I dove behind the bush, my heart pounding in my chest. "Oops, my bad, it was a false alarm." He had the nerve to laugh. I reached between the bushes, yanking his feet from beneath him. Laughing when he hit the ground hard, I raced from the hiding place before he had a chance to retaliate.

"Madi!" a loud voice boomed over the music. My father must have seen me. I panicked and dipped into the forest, using the trees for cover. The sound of feet crashing through the brush sent me racing further into the darkness. Unsure of where I was going, surrender wasn't a possibility.

Suddenly overcome with an indescribable feeling that stopped me dead in my tracks. The loud voice calling my name faded out of range. The full moon cast a warm glow on the shadowy forest, illuminating the army of trees. My hands clutched my stomach to calm the butterflies swirling inside me. The further I advanced, the darker it became. Suddenly, I was no longer able to see anything. The overwhelming sensation was directing my every step. A gust of wind lifted my hair softly; I spun around quickly — nothing. My pulse began to race, and I struggled to breathe — time seemed to stand still. I stepped forward again, and the feeling evaporated. Although I wanted to follow, I knew I should not.

"Madi," the loud voice was closing in, only it didn't belong to my father. Uncle Mike flashed a light in my eyes, nearly blinding me.

"You're going to push Phillip over the edge!" he scolded, leading me out of the forest.

"There was someone back there!"

"Where's your bike?"

"Did you hear me? There was someone in the woods!" I looked back once more.

"What in the hell are you talking about? I was worried about you! I thought you would ride around the block, not a two-hour excursion. We need to beat your parents' home!" We raced across the massive lawn and jumped in his car.

"I'm sorry," I whispered, hoping my parents were not in one of the cars behind us.

When we pulled in front of the house, I felt relieved. My parents' car was still away. Uncle Mike stopped me when we stepped inside.

"If your bike's still there in the morning, I'll bring it by, and if not, you have no one to blame but yourself. I've defended you when Phillip says how impossible you are- I'm starting to believe he's right! How can someone so smart make such stupid decisions?" his eyes darkened.

"Uncle Mike," I swallowed as our eyes met, "Please, don't believe what he says about me," tears sprung to my eyes. "Please, I'll try harder," I dried my face with my hand.

"I'm sorry for yelling at you," he pulled me to him, "You scared the shit out of me," he leaned back to look down at me, "I love you, Madi, but I'm still mad at you right now."

I nodded and reluctantly went to my room — that was the first time he had been angry with me. Why didn't I turn around? I thought something was wrong with me as I climbed out of the window and onto the roof; the overhang shielded me from the rain, not that I would have minded. I folded my legs beneath, closed my eyes, and heard the rain hitting the tin roof.

This place felt foreign to me; the trees guarded our house like towering wooden soldiers. I was curious to know if they were to keep intruders out or me in.

My view of the ocean now consisted of lakes and small streams, none of which compared to the sea.

When I glanced over my shoulder, my mom was leaning out the window with her arms propped against the windowsill. I walked over and dipped back inside the room.

"Are you okay?" she asked, brushing the dirt off my jacket. "You know they are searching for the monsters kidnapping those girls. We learned tonight that there was another disappearance in Reed City, although they are certain the cases are not related. I'm not telling you this to frighten you; I want you to be extremely cautious. As for Mike, he was afraid something had happened to you. Take it easy on him. Helping us raise you was never part of his plan." She smiled.

"Ms. Betty will send her sons by tomorrow to pick you up for school. Your father doesn't want you driving alone until you're familiar with the area. I thought about taking you myself but didn't think you would appreciate my doing so, seeing how you're almost grown," my mom said teasingly. She kissed the top of my head before closing the door to my room. I crawled deeper beneath the covers, staring at the ceiling until my eyes would no longer remain open.

CHAPTER FOUR
UNFAMILIAR

After downing the whole glass of milk, I saw my mom pointing to the pitcher with more ice-cold liquid. I nodded, accepted, and finished the remnants of my pancakes. The only thing I loved more than my mom's blueberry pancakes were her banana pecan with warm maple syrup. The thought of those hot fluffy stacks of homemade goodness made my mouth water; however, my stomach would disagree. Two pancakes were more than enough to keep me satisfied until dinner. My mom knows I never eat school lunch, so she pushes breakfast every morning.

"Do you think I could drive myself today instead of riding with the Whitman brothers?" The question had barely cleared my lips when she raised her brow, stopping me.

"If teenage girls weren't disappearing every week, my answer would be yes. However, that is not the circumstance; I hope your father will find the person responsible for the kidnappings soon. Until that happens, you will not travel alone." She stood up and began removing the dishes from the table; I scraped off the gooey syrup and placed my plate into the dishwasher. Desperate to say more, having a license and not driving made no sense. Like going to the ocean and not swimming, maybe not as bad, but it was close.

"I know this move has been difficult for you, especially considering...." Only, she stopped herself and looked at me as if she understood and felt my pain. "I'm asking that you please try to make the best of our current situation," I wish there were a way that I could put a stopper on my emotions or at least pretend to be happy here for her. But, instead, my eyes went to the tiled floor as I slid my feet across them, trying to reign in the longing that I felt for home and, I'm being honest, Nic. He was what I missed most.

"Things will be okay here," which felt believable as I pushed away from the counter. I hugged her, grabbed my book bag, and headed out the door; I thought it best to wait outside for my ride. That way, she couldn't see the disappointment in my eyes. My father told me not to worry about the kidnappings; however, I believed he should have saved his speech for my mom. She was worried, and my sulking would only make things harder for her. So, I would plaster my happy face on and pretend.

The sound of a blaring car horn sent me running down the sidewalk, where Conner and Braden had jumped out of their car. They almost tripped over each other to open the door for me. I looked at them; I suppose it made sense that they dressed like opposites; Conner in his striped polo, baggy jeans, baseball cap, and sneakers, while Braden looked more as if he was going on an interview with J Crew; blue jean shirt, khaki pants, and coordinating boat shoes.

"Wow, face licking and opening doors; I thought my hometown was friendly," I said, lifting a brow.

Conner laughed as I got in the back seat. They exchanged looks back and forth at each other before stealing glances at me. I knew those looks because most boys in Hatteras never approached me. They were too frightened of Nic or had seen my father. Although the staring never ceased, the fact that the brothers seemed to share in the fascination made me a little uncomfortable.

"It's a little hot in here," I choked, removing my jacket, folding, and stuffing it deep inside my book bag; I leaned back in the seat as tiny beads of moisture gathered at the nape of my neck.

"I guess it's a little warm; the air is off," Braden said. He turned it on and rolled his window up. The cool air felt good against my skin.

"She's nervous," Conner offered. "Everybody's been calling us about you; they want to know your entire history; I didn't say anything." He turned to smile at me. "Well, not everybody, our friend Vaughn. But I bet you're nervous, right?" He said again.

"No, I'm okay," I lied; nothing felt right about this moment. First impressions have never been my strong suit.

We pulled into the parking lot of my new high school. It was a large building with smaller outer facilities attached to the side. There were picnic tables to the right. Braden explained that the gym was one of the small buildings and the cafeteria was the other as we exited the car. The tables made sense, considering the size of the structure. Being outside was part of my plans. Braden motioned for me to hand him my schedule, which I did. He ran his thin fingers up and down the page, squinting slightly before the lines in his forehead flattened, and he nodded his head as if recognizing the names.

"Your first class is English with Ms. Edwards, two doors down. After that, Mr. Thomas is your French teacher, and you have Mr. Brambleton for Government," Braden continued, listing off my schedule. Unfortunately, his voice faded after the first three classes, leaving me confused about why he was pointing across the hall. "I'll see you at lunch," he quickly descended the long corridor.

"Okay," I answered vacantly, knowing I couldn't keep the abundance of information this early in the morning. Suppose all high schools have the same typical cliché; jocks which Conner had made his way over to, the preppie crew, where Braden appeared right at home, a group of girls all dressed in pink were assessing every girl that walked by them. Oh, and then there was the peculiar group in the corner — they seemed a little intense but absolutely — beautiful. One girl gave me a dirty look and then stared at me — in that non-blinking sort of way, only the entire group seemed to have noticed me as the bell rang.

I pushed myself down the hall and into my first class, but repositioned my open book bag in my arms, a second too late. All my things tumbled to the floor, and I sighed, frustrated, as people began to snicker. I bent down to gather them and glanced up when a pair of black stilettos stopped before me. Her smooth copper complexion was flawless; it appeared as if a light film veiled her once-golden skin. Her thick wavy black hair pulled away from her face with a barrette.

"Don't pay any attention to them." The girl looked back at the two jocks, who seemed more than entertained. "Every year they grow physically, however strengthening their social behavior may take a lifetime." Her smile helped ease my frustration. "My name's Emma; it's nice to meet you, Madi." Her voice was softer than a whisper.

"How do you know my name?" I asked while picking up the rest of my things.

"Please, it's practically headline news when there's a new girl. You can sit beside me," Emma offered. I glared at the two jerks that were puckering their lips at me. "I'm sorry to say that they lack maturity and may also have some emotional issues." I couldn't help but chuckle at the amusing expressions on their faces as they realized she was referring to them.

Our class ended too soon; I sat there, trying to absorb the fact that we had a report due next week. Emma reached to help me with my bookbag, and her hand touched my arm. She felt like ice against my overheated skin. I jumped. She glanced down at her fingers, narrowing her brow, and examined her palm as if her hand belonged to someone else. "I'm sorry, you caught me off guard."

"No, I startled you," Emma said cautiously, then focused her bluish-purple eyes on me again.

"Are all of the teachers this intense?" I held up my notebook with enough assignments to last an entire month. The frustration was clear in my voice as I looked through all the work I was expected to do.

"I'll help you with your notes for English. Let me know if you need help with any other subject."

I mouthed the words, 'Thank you.' Emma smiled, "Can you come by my house Friday?"

"Yes, Friday is good," I said with too much enthusiasm. She handed me a piece of paper with her telephone number and address.

"Seven o'clock alright with you?" Emma asked as I gathered my remaining things and placed them inside my bag.

"That's fine with me," I responded as we left class together. Standing next to Emma made me feel more than a little ordinary. Her dress reminded me of those worn by stars in the classic Hollywood movies that I loved so much. It was black with a large white belt accenting her tiny waist, and she was wearing heels to die for; and I would if they were mine.

"You should try to relax; the vultures can smell fear from miles away." She smiled and adjusted the books in her arms.

"I'm cautious, not afraid." I looked around at the unfamiliar faces; even Ms. Anderson, my least favorite teacher from Hatteras, would be comforting now.

"Where's your next class?" Emma asked. I didn't realize she was talking to me until she took my schedule out of my hand. "You have Mr. Brambleton; his class is the door on the left. I'll see you later." Emma walked away before I had a chance to thank her.

When I entered the small room, I caught a strong scent of sweat and musk, the combination made worse by the blaring heat radiating from the vents. A large man sitting behind the desk didn't even bother to look up when he grabbed the slip from my hand. His salt-and-pepper hair needed a cut, as it hung in disarray around his face, which appeared larger due to his tight turtleneck sweater. Interestingly, he also wore a wool jacket when it felt like they had set the school's thermostat on 'hell.'

"Take the first available seat, ah, Miss Ryan," Mr. Brambleton's words were crisp as he glanced down at the slip.

I scanned the entire classroom until my eyes rested on Conner.

He was waving for me to come and sit beside him.

"Thanks," I said as I slid into the seat.

"No, thank you." He looked at me with those big green eyes and smiled, leaving me no choice but to smile back. Government class went by slowly. Mr. Brambleton's monotone voice seemed to drone on forever. I couldn't help but feel excited when the bell finally rang.

"Okay, what's next?" Conner asked.

"French," I said as I handed him my schedule and bag so that

I could open my locker, but the stupid combination didn't work. So, I spun it again and tried 30-25-40, and thankfully, the lock popped open.

A tall, muscular guy was rummaging through his bookbag a little further down. He pulled out two books and tucked the bag inside the metal compartment; however, his eyes remained on me.

"Why is that guy staring at me?" I whispered to Conner as I turned away from the nosy student. My question brought a smile to Conner's face.

"You're hot," Conner replied. His excitement caused my frown to deepen.

"Stop it," I lifted my brow, dismissing his comment.

"Blake Frederick, school asshole. His grandfather is the mayor; you met him. Blake is the outcast of the family, their dirty little secret," Conner said, "That's why he wasn't at the Labor Day party, oh but neither were you." He tapped his index finger on the side of his chin.

Ignoring Conner's jab, I glanced over at Blake again. He was now standing by the water fountain his gaze still focused on me.

"Why is he, their secret?"

"Not sure; it might have something to do with the fact the mayor's only daughter died while giving birth to him. She was away in college, no one even knew she was pregnant. Which isn't a big deal now, but I guess back then, especially with the mayor being in politics- his unmarried pregnant daughter would have been an issue. I heard that someone just dropped him off at the mayor's office, after delivering the news." He looked as if he wanted to say more but stopped when he noticed Blake approaching.

"You're Madi, right?"

"Yeah," I stepped back; Blake was inches from me. His warm complexion complemented his piercing chestnut eyes and dark, curly hair. He wore a pair of faded blue jeans and an Oxford shirt with a vest.

"I'm Blake. I wanted to say," he started.

"Come on, Blake. Let's go to lunch," the group leader commanded as she came to stand beside him. Her small entourage swiftly joined her. All three were incredibly beautiful, and their skin was radiant. The tallest forced a smile as she linked arms with Blake. She had a high, tight ponytail, and her white teeth complemented her flawless porcelain skin. The group disappeared through the cafeteria doors.

"Who were they?" I asked, annoyed by the utter contempt on the girl's face, the second time today that she had given me a dirty look.

"Bitches," Conner said bluntly. "The ponytail is Bria. The other two are Peyton and Lindsey. They follow her around." He added.

"They were rude," I said.

"Yeah, I don't think they're going to be your new best friends, so I'd stay away from them," Conner said before leaving to go to his locker.

When I walked inside the cafeteria, all eyes turned to me — the new girl. I made my way straight to Blake's table. Bria was sitting next to him. She and Lindsey were laughing as I approached, while Peyton appeared indifferent.

"Hi, Blake, right?"

"Yeah," he reluctantly smiled up at me.

"My name's Madi," I said as sweetly as possible before glaring at Bria. Blake looked up with an expression that said, "I don't want to be involved in what's about to happen."

Bria jumped from her seat to face me. Blake's hand locked onto her wrist to reseat her, but she jerked her arm away.

"Stay the hell away from him. He belongs to me!"

"Oh, he's missing his sold sign," I knew that was pushing it, but she had rubbed me the wrong way.

"Not going to tell you twice!" her threat seemed creditable. She looked as if she wanted to kill me as if my breathing annoyed her. Bria was so beautiful and yet ugly to the core, cold, heartless. My anger now matched hers — I could feel it bubbling to the surface.

"What are you?" I tipped my head to the side, uncertain why I asked her that question. Something felt wrong here; I narrowed the space between us.

"Get the hell away from me, freak!"

"Leave her alone, Bria." The order came from Emma, who was now standing beside me.

"The bitch needs to go back to where she came from. She doesn't belong here!" Bria yelled, moving quickly to face Emma. The two stood eye-to-eye. Emma didn't need to say another word for Bria to get the message; the she-devil turned to leave.

"We know you're not who you say you are," Bria said before she walked away, and the other two girls were right on her heels. Blake stayed at the table and shrugged when Bria looked back to see if he was following.

"Is your girl crazy?" Blake teasingly asked Emma, as if I were not standing beside her.

"No, pissed off," I answered for her and forced myself to calm down as Emma gave Blake a resentful look and ushered me out of the cafeteria.

"I'll make a mental note not to ever get on your bad side," she joked before leaving me for her next class.

By the end of the day, I had convinced myself to focus on the positive. I had already met a new friend and was excited to share my news with Conner and Braden. I walked across the parking lot, the books heavy in my arms. After struggling with the door handle, I tossed them into the backseat before climbing inside.

"I met a nice girl today!"

Neither seemed interested; they were too busy arguing about who got the most phone numbers. Secretly I wondered if this would be a daily occurrence, then quickly realized the odds were not in my favor.

"What's your friend's name?" Conner continued to scroll through his new numbers.

"Emma!" I blurted out with far too much excitement.

"There are at least twenty girls named Emma at our school," Conner replied, turning in his seat.

"Emma Hayden, she's going to help me with my reports. Two of them are due by the end of the month."

"Emma Hayden, huh, wow, that's interesting," Conner's voice dripped with sarcasm.

"You must have her confused with someone else," I remembered how kind she had been. "Do you know her?"

"Not personally, thank God," Conner responded. The two boys exchanged glances.

"What do you mean?" I slid closer, trying to understand the reason for all the secrecy.

Braden looked at me through the rear-view mirror, "Emma lives here with her brother. They moved here about three years ago to the outskirts of town. I heard she lives alone; no one has ever seen him. She claims he travels for work. One of the teachers filed a protective services report when we were in the tenth grade.

Sherriff Hilton investigated, but nothing happened; her brother showed up. Trust me; there is nothing sweet about Emma. Everybody at school hates her. She walks around like she's the greatest thing ever created." "With those weird eyes, the girl freaks me out," Conner added. They had to be wrong. Emma was friendlier than anyone I met today, especially that witch, Bria. And so, what if she wasn't all perky and bubbly? I was never a fan of those personalities. Conner twisted farther around in his seat. "You should stay clear of her too, Madi," he muttered, and Braden agreed. I shrugged my shoulders. Hatteras High had taught me that teenagers could be vicious; you either keep a low profile or grow thicker skin.

"Will there be more drama tomorrow? We want an advanced warning," Conner said, waving one of his fingers in my face.

"That sounds about right."

We pulled in front of the house as Conner leaned over the seat. "You need to be careful, that's all I'm saying," his warning was overly cautious, "I will buy a cross to protect you when she comes over or a stake to drive through her heart. You're much too pretty to sacrifice!" he yelled.

"What would your mother say if she heard you?"

"She would say, 'Protect the virgin sacrifice!'" Conner contorted his face.

My first week continued to be extremely busy, and not only had I spent time hanging out with Emma, but also Blake. Yep, Blake and I are now friends. We had fun, and he was nicer than I previously believed. His laid-back personality was what I liked most about him. We talked about the snobs and jerks that gave everyone a tough time, and as I unleashed my frustration about Bria's nasty attitude, he reminded me that he and the witch were exclusively dating. Blake and Bria, yeah, that makes no sense at all. I felt terrible at first; he laughed and agreed that she was sometimes more than a handful. As I ranted, Blake convinced me that not every person at Nirvana High was a spawn of the devil. He was right because I had met other people at school throughout the week. My mom was both shocked and ecstatic when I told her— I couldn't blame her; in Hatteras, I had one close friend, and here I had four, well three for sure. I still had not decided about Braden.

CHAPTER FIVE
DINNER GUEST

A s my mom drove my father's Porsche up Emma's circular driveway, I couldn't help but admire the grand entrance in front of us, shrouded in darkness. The car effortlessly made its way up. Felt as if we were entering a fantasy world — the graceful thin branches of the Weeping Willow trees swept across the hood of our car. I leaned forward, tilting my head upward as we broke through the canopy, and the landscape opened dramatically. Lush greenery blanketed the landscape; deeply twisted vines draped the wrought iron gates of the multiple balconies. Emma's home was — constructed beautifully with architectural columns and rich red and grey bricks that paved the curved walkway and continued up the porch.

"This place is incredible," I said as she parked in front of Emma's house.

"Southern mansion recreated in Eastern Michigan, bold, to say the least," my mom snipped.

"Well, I love it; it reminds me of the large estates in South Carolina," my defense of Emma's enchanted home caused my mom's brows to gather until the two nearly touched. She wrinkled her nose in distaste. I watched as she examined the house more carefully before shrugging off her obvious displeasure.

"Madison, you must be home before your father wakes up, no later than 6:30; come in quietly," she said firmly. It had taken me months to convince my mom to allow me to stay over Emma's. I was not planning to mess up this opportunity. I folded my hands in my lap and listened to her instructions carefully. "Your father would never have agreed to this; I, on the other hand, believe you could use a friend like Emma." I nodded and kissed her cheek before ducking out of the car. She waved, and I turned to see Emma standing in the doorway. Once inside, I was amazed by the sheer size of the beautiful rooms. An enormous chandelier teetered in the center of the vaulted ceilings; everything seemed larger than life here. All the woodwork was deep mahogany, with gleaming cherry hardwood floors and large oriental rugs adorning the floor in rich colors. The deep red tapestries, accented by rich shades of cream, exemplified what I believe a southern mansion would look like, including the sweeping staircase on either side of the foyer.

I followed Emma up the staircase, admiring the expensive paintings that lined the walls. The second landing was darker with natural lighting from the windows at the end of the hallway; only the overcast skies supplied more of a subtle silvery glow. The faint rustling of the curtains sent my attention to the window.

"That's strange," I said, stopping mid-stride as the familiar tug urged me to continue.

"Madi, in here," Emma opened the door to her room. I hesitated, wanting to know what was causing the butterflies to flutter across my belly. The feeling was intense and mesmerizing; I reached for the doorknob turning slowly, robotically. I stepped inside, and the smell of sandalwood and honeysuckle engulfed me, flooding my senses. "Madi," Emma said from the door of the room. "Madi," Emma's voice was so firm this time that the elevation of her tone caused me to jump out of the trance-like state. I glanced around to see that, in my daze, I had not only entered the room but had made my way to the oversized canopy bed and was now cradling a plush white pillow to my chest.

"Oh, I'm sorry," I stammered, hurrying off the bed, smoothing the indentions out of the plush white bedding. The room had distinctions of black, grey, and white clean-lined furniture — nothing like the downstairs.

"No problem," she appeared slightly uneasy until I joined her in the doorway. "You can keep the pillow," She teased, and I flushed with embarrassment — I uncurled the pillow from my arm and quickly placed it back on the bed. The fear of humiliating myself again compelled me to rush from the room. She closed the door and directed me toward her bedroom once again. I discovered that, unlike the other bedroom, her room personified Hollywood glamour; lush drapes streamed from her massive canopy bed, and varied colors of creams and lavender embellished the room's décor: large dressing area and vanity with a lighted mirror and cream bench trimmed in gold. I walked over to admire her gold brush and hand mirror, a bevy of fingernail polishes, lipsticks, eyeliners, and other image-enhancing products, none of which she needed.

"Wow," was all I could manage as I continued browsing her things until she tapped me on the shoulder and handed me a swimsuit and a thick cotton robe from her closet.

"I have a surprise for you; get changed and meet me downstairs." She pointed to the dressing room before ducking out of her room.

"Okay," I donned the white one-piece, surprised that it fit me perfectly, draped the robe over my shoulders, and gathered it closed. Emma was waiting by the staircase wearing an identical robe. We hurried down the stairs through the great room and out the French doors leading to the patio. The frigid chill in the air fluttered through my hair and slowly brushed my skin. "So, what's the surprise…" the question seemed to freeze in the frosty November air.

As Emma stepped aside, I couldn't help but be amazed by the stunning view. Everything was arranged perfectly, from the wrought-iron lantern scones to the oversized terra cotta pots filled with shrubs. The cream upholstered hacienda chairs were beautiful, and the blue and grey flagstone pavers led the way to a magnificent Olympic-size swimming pool.

"What do you think?" Emma asked as she entered the pool without splashing any water.

"Are you kidding? I've died and gone to heaven!" I screamed, stripping off the robe and joining her in the pool where she seemed at home; I smiled, knowing that was another thing we had in common. The heated pool was incredible. I poked my head above the surface, inhaling the icy air.

I glanced toward the house surprised to see a shadowy frame outlined in the window, "Who is that?"

"My brother," Emma laughed, although I wasn't sure why, "That was his room you were in," she continued.

"Oh, Conner said he never visits," I frowned when the masculine profile disappeared.

"Yeah, well, the blond gossips like a girl." Emma's annoyance was unmistakable.

"If you ask me, he- is- a girl," I twisted, shocked to see Blake kneeling by the pool, wading his hand through the water. He was only wearing a pair of black swim trunks, which meant he would be swimming with us. I looked over at Emma nervously, visions of my father showing up and hauling me off flooded my brain.

"Madi, I should have told you earlier," Emma splashed Blake as he slid into the pool with us, "This vagrant normally comes here to swim."

"It's not a problem," the words felt foreign as they escaped.

"My father would blow a gasket," I admitted.

"Good thing he's not here," Blake dove beneath the water, resurfacing with a mouthful of water he tried squirting at me a second later.

"That's gross!" I screamed before dipping below the surface. When I came up, Blake was swimming laps on the far side of the pool. He was fast but I'm faster. My inner voice challenged. Emma came up beside me, and we both watched Blake swim at a lightning pace from one end of the pool to the other. I narrowed my eyes as I watched him closely, "He's real," were the words that clung to my tongue. There are no pretenses with Blake. He was himself and didn't give a rat's ass who did or didn't like it — I respected that most about him.

Blake splashed water in our direction; Emma ducked while the blast hit me square in the face. I kicked water in his direction lazily.

Thankfully, Emma swam over to Blake, and the two disappeared beneath the water. On the other hand, I was still trying to ignore the pull I felt. Emma's brother, I wondered what he looked like. Why had I felt drawn to him? Why was he hiding in the room? He could've at least introduced himself. I climbed from the pool, oblivious to Emma and Blake arguing over which one won their mini race.

"Get back here," Blake yanked me beneath the water — it took me a second to regain my composure and knee him.

"Ouch," he grabbed his side before swimming closer to me. I continued to splash water on him. Emma joined in; that made it impossible for him to remain above the surface. "I give! I give," he laughed, tossing his arms in the air. "I have to go," his voice still light and filled with amusement, as he exited the pool.

He said a quick goodbye as we headed inside. Emma blasted The Kings of Midnight while we showered and changed into our pajamas. She ordered pizza; I had finished my second slice while she picked at the topping of her first. I reached for another piece, peeling the cheese, onions, and Italian sausage back and I stuffed the toppings in my mouth, laughing as sauce dripped down my chin. Emma shook her head as I discarded the crust. We stayed up late dancing and talking and mostly laughed until our sides ached, we crashed right before dawn.

My alarm went off, and I rolled out of the bed. I put on my sneakers and went in search of Emma. She was waiting in the foyer with keys in hand. During the ride to my house, we made plans to hang out again next weekend. Emma also clued me in on the school field trip. She explained that the seniors and juniors in the foreign language class had raised funds for a trip to Paris. I had seen the signs posted around the school and never thought of asking. My mom was weird about Paris, well, not so much Paris; her only daughter in Paris seemed to be more of the problem. Emma passed me the permission form. I should have returned it to her, but I stuffed it in my book bag instead.

My birthday and the holidays passed quickly, as did winter break. Emma mentioned the Paris trip again. I had two weeks at home to convince my mom that the trip would be good for me, only I chickened out. She would say no, and that I knew without question.

Today, I did something unthinkable; I gave my forged permission slip to Ms. Pettit, who oversees the school's foreign language department. She looked at me suspiciously when I used my credit card to pay for the trip, mumbling about how nice it must be to have money. I chose to ignore her condescending tone by plastering a larger-than-life smile on my face. Hopeful that my plan worked; I left Ms. Pettit's office.

I went to my locker to grab my English book, frowning as I stared at the note. *Madi #10* was — written on the folded sheet of paper, along with newspaper clippings. The missing girls had numbers written across their faces including Jennifer Stevens, "how would they even know about her? There were no reports about Jenni." I said in a hushed voice. As I glanced down at the numbered clippings again, the last one, a picture of me outside on the picnic table with a number 10 written over my head. I shoved the book back inside my locker. Tears sprung to my eyes as I ripped the note and clippings and slammed the locker shut.

I bolted down the hallway, not bothering to look at all the questioning eyes behind me. I ripped the jacket off as soon as I hit the large metal doors. Snow began to fall as the first tear trickled down my face. My pace quickened as I sped down the street with every step; I increased my speed. Running in the cold and snow can be a numbing experience. The snow was falling in clumps, making it even more exhilarating. I needed to block out the note — the words, those images, "You Are Next!" boldly written, "No One Can Save You!" I had no idea who wrote the note. However, the words played on my every fear. There had been nine kidnappings. Would I be next? That question kept me awake at night. I dreamt the cloak men were plucking young girls off the street as I raced away unhindered by their screams for help and into the arms of the man that protected me within my dreams. The wind at my back seemed to push me forward.

Slushy snow now covered the road, wetting my sneakers and socks; however, it did little to slow me.

I stopped to catch my breath before finally reaching home. My father had traveled to Reed City, and my mom had a doctor's appointment today, so the empty house meant that I did not have to explain why I had ditched school.

A hot shower soothed my aching muscles but did little to ease the deep fear inside me. Therefore, I kept busy, shampooing my hair again, allowing the conditioner to set, blow-dried, and straightening the normally curly locks until the silky strands rested at my hips. I organized my room, dusted, and did a laundry load. I placed a bottle of my mom's favorite wine, Hatteras Red, in the wine cooler, defrosted a pack of chicken breast, and began chopping cucumbers, tomatoes, and romaine for a salad. Then I rinsed the dirt off the potatoes, cleaning four, in case Uncle Mike returned with my father, and seasoned the cutlets with garlic and lemon. The phone rang twice — both numbers from the school. I erased both messages. They would both be angry. My hope was that my mom would make it home first.

A knock at the door unnerved me for a moment. I hesitated before answering, wondering if the school called the sheriff for students that went AWOL here. I went to my toes to look through the peephole, surprised to see the middle finger of Blake Frederick.

He was sitting on the rail, his long legs crossed in front of him, arms folded over his chest as if he were at home. I opened the door, scanning the area suspiciously, "I'm alone if that's what you're concerned about." He said calmly.

"No, wondering why you're here," I stepped onto the porch barefooted, which he seemed to notice. "Why'd you ditch?"

"Needed to get out of there," I retorted.

"You were crying," he stared out into the blanketed landscape. "No," I began, but he loudly scoffed at my denial. "Wasn't a question; you were crying," Blake went to his feet. I noticed for the first time that he wasn't wearing a jacket — he, too, had run from the school to my house.

"I didn't know you cared so much," I said, or that anyone except Emma and my teacher would realize that I wasn't at school.

"Bria told me what she did," The remorse in his eyes revealed the truth.

"She wrote the note." I knew that Bria didn't care for me, but damn. She had reached an all-time low, or maybe this wasn't as low as she could stoop.

"I guess everyone got a great laugh at my expense," my eyes filled with unexpected tears.

"Not everyone; I told her to back off," he said with more force than I had ever seen from Blake. He looked a little scary as his eyes darkened.

My body trembled as the words Bria wrote resurfaced. Those words for me meant that we would move, or my father would convince her to send me out of the country to keep me safe. They suggested I would never see Emma, Conner, or him again. We would move, and I would need to start over and try to find new friends. My thoughts were selfish — all those missing girls, and all I could think about was how their kidnappings would affect me.

"Stop crying," Blake yelled, making me cry harder. He patted my back awkwardly before enfolding me in the warmth of his arms. "Please stop," his voice had lost its edge, and I found it soothing. I nodded, leaned back, and wiped my face with my hands.

"She sees it, do you?" I sniffled.

"What?"

"That I resemble them," my voice cracked as I took in small gasps of air, trying to calm myself.

"Those girls that went missing a few months back, I guess, but that could be said about thousands of other girls," Blake's words made me feel only slightly better. "Look, Bria must have noticed that you favor them and used that to get under your skin. She has that effect on people, but she's going to leave you alone," he seemed to mull over his words for a minute before staring out into the distance.

"Glad you're not on the, get the freak out of Nirvana' campaign," a smile finally broke through the overwhelming sadness festering inside me.

"There would be no one left if we rounded up all the freaks," he teased, "Nirvana wouldn't be the same without you." Blake winked, and my smile broadened.

"Thanks for stopping by," I opened my screen door and stepped inside.

He nodded in acceptance before jumping over the rail and into my mom. She stepped back, and he caught her before she hit the ground. Blake looked apologetic as he helped her upright again; our conversation had become so intense that I missed her arrival and realized she had walked from the main road due to the snow.

"I didn't know you invited company for dinner," she said, making me speechless as she handed Blake her bags and breezed by me. I shrugged my shoulders as Blake gave me a curious look. He followed her inside, appearing intrigued by my mom. I watched from the doorway as he helped her unpack the groceries while she chatted about the snowstorm. The conversation came so easy for her, I thought as I closed the door and joined them in the kitchen. My mom smiled, seeing my prep work for dinner.

"Blake, does your grandfather know that you're here?" My mom asked.

"Ah, no, I should call him," he pulled the cell phone from his pocket and went outside. Once he closed the door, my mom turned to face me, her smile in place; however, her eyes were serious.

"We will speak of your playing hooky from school once your guest leaves. Change your clothes for a nice dinner; your father and Uncle Mike are coming." She waved me off, knowing that I wanted to argue that my clothes were fine, although she did have the advantage considering that I had ditched school. I rushed up the stairs, removed my sweatshirt, and put on my cinched-back plaid shirt, dark jeans, and tan boots. My mom smiled when I entered the kitchen this time. Blake was helping her with the table setting.

"There's my BFF," Uncle Mike yelled as he peeked through a crack in the back door. I ran to meet him, dosing him with kisses,

"Okay, okay, I promise to behave," his boisterous laughter filled the room. "What's up with my favorite niece?" He tilted his head toward Blake, and the insinuation caused my brows to bunch. We hugged before he pulled the chair out for me.

"I'm doing okay," I wrinkled my nose.

"I see," he winked, and Blake laughed.

"We're friends, Uncle Mike," I snapped at him.

My father entered the dining room, which mom had set with her expensive dishes. The thought of Blake as my boyfriend made me laugh a little. My mom seemed intrigued by him though — asking him about his childhood. She used the napkin to dab at her eyes when he told her he never knew his mother. I was wrong about her wanting to impress him for me. Instead, she was — equally captivated by him or his story. If Conner were my father's ideal child, Blake would have been my mom's. The two talked nonstop during dinner.

I toyed with my chicken until it became rubbery, sipping my water while pretending to listen. Until I realized my father was handing me something. I looked down; my throat went dry — every drop of liquid had dissolved, and my breath was strangling me.

"You want to tell me what this is," He whispered, his anger as he leaned into me.

"A field trip form," I forced myself to say.

"Show that to your mother, although she's already seen the form according to her signature." My father snapped, and Blake appeared uncomfortable. I passed the form to her. She sucked in air. Her eyes flickered with anger. Instead of screaming, she scooted back her chair and walked out of the dining room, her heels on the steps, followed by a slamming door. I was expecting her anger, but her sadness caught me off guard.

I opened my mouth to apologize, when his hand landed hard across my face, knocking me from the chair. A scuffle broke out. I eased myself backward, my back pressed against the wall as blood seeped from a cut on my lip. There was a flash of light and crashing, and my father fell on the floor a couple of feet away from me. Blake helped me as my father started toward me again — something stopped him, Uncle Mike? Blake? I couldn't see.

"Phillip," Uncle Mike bellowed, "What in the hell is wrong with you? Get a hold of yourself!" He shoved him back with more force than I thought Uncle Mike could, pushing him from the dining room before coaxing him onto the deck.

I ran from the house out into the snow — stood there for a while staring vacantly into the woods. Blake joined me there for at least ten minutes in the frigid air. His hand brushed across mine as he stepped in front of me.

"Madi, are you alright?" Blake asked.

"I want to be" was all that I could manage. "I never should have turned that form in."

"Why? Because your douchebag of a dad says so! Screw him!" Blake yelled; his body tensed, and I glanced back at my house. "If you ever need me," He touched my shoulder, and my entire body went from overheated to sweltering.

I eased away, "You should go."

"I will, but remember if you ever need me," he scuffed the snow with the heel of his boot. "Well, I'm here," Blake said in a matter-of-fact tone. His long strides had carried him to the forest perimeter before I could reply.

"Thank you."

"For what?" he yelled over his shoulder, "My awesomeness, charm, rugged good looks, well, you're more than welcome." Blake's playfulness at a time like this made me smile, which I quickly regretted when I reopened the tear on my lips. Tiny droplets of blood splashed onto the white snow, which I found both beautiful and disturbing.

The house was clean when I went back inside, with no evidence of what had happened except his handprint on my face and a small cut on my lip. Uncle Mike hugged me, apologizing for my father's behavior. I squeezed him.

My father tried to do the same when I started up the stairs. I shoved him away — his hitting me was nothing new. I had forgiven him, even when he forgot to apologize. He hit me in front of Uncle Mike — in front of Blake that was unforgivable.

"Madi, your father is trying to apologize," Uncle Mike said, which hurt me more than the slap. I lifted my hand and looked him right in the eyes. His seemed to be assimilating a strong defense to justify what just happened, but mine were filled with resolve.

"Phillip, he's Phillip to me, nothing more."

"Madi, you don't mean that. That's your father," Uncle Mike, forever the optimist.

"No, he's my mom's husband. I will never be the daughter he wants, and he will never be the father I deserve." My chest rose, making me feel taller as I faced him without wavering. "If you ever touch me again, I will tell her everything. We both know that she will never forgive you," my whispered threat must have resonated because Phillip stormed off. Uncle Mike stood there with a look of utter confusion on his face.

There was a moment as I lay in bed; the day's emotions gave way, tears dampened my hair, and I finally accepted the integrity of my words. I would never be the daughter he wants, and Phillip would never be the father I deserve.

The grayish-colored water caressed my feet. It felt nice here. I quietly watched the clouds dance across the heavens, forming into different shapes, then decided to explore my surroundings. Walking toward the opposite end of the beach, I stared at the distant cliff; it was magnificent. The edge expanded over the ocean like a protective arm, shielding the rest of its body from the crashing waves.

My nostrils flared. The scent was different here, like sweet and familiar. I gave the beach a complete once-over and saw someone standing in the darkness of the trees. I moved quickly toward the shadowy figure as the waves began crashing harder, compelling me to run with a greater sense of urgency. Then, out of nowhere, a strong gust of wind knocked me backward. Sand showered down on my body as I fell into the powdery substance.

I finally managed to return to my feet, but he was gone. My

frown grew as the waves began to recede, and the wind stopped its angry assault. It was as if they had a hand in his escape. I was half-tempted to resume my pursuit; only the feeling was gone. Something had severed the invisible lines that connected me to the man who stood in the shadows.

CHAPTER SIX
BREAKING DISHES

O nce inside the house, I removed my sneakers and placed them in the mudroom before heading to the kitchen. Spring break was only a week away, and I was more than ready for a break. However, the possibility of spending that time in the house made me shiver. Therefore, I remained on my best behavior. Phillip had ordered me to stay away from Blake. He said I lost one loser and didn't need to pick up another. Well, He got his way, sort of. Blake no longer came to my house; we spent time together at Emma's instead. Her house was way cooler anyway. Blake had a bullet to dodge too, — Bria. She detested me, and to be honest, the feelings were mutual.

I was going up the stairs to my room when soft, soulful music stopped me in my tracks. I turned around quickly and leaped down four of the stairs landing at the bottom that music was my signal that they were at it again — baby making. Gross. My stomach grumbled, and I figured the complaint had nothing to do with my mom and Phillip. I popped in my headphones and headed to the kitchen for a snack. I found a plate of leftover lasagna in the back, removed the aluminum foil, placed the lasagna in the microwave, and then poured myself a glass of milk. The mail was on the table, so I shuffled through it and noticed one letter addressed to me. I could not bring myself to pick it up. My eyes remained glued to the envelope until the microwave buzzer distracted me. I grabbed a fork from the drawer, put the now-steaming lasagna on the table, and ate. Even as I began

56

to eat the lasagna, my eyes never left the envelope. There was no return address. However, I knew the letter was from Nic. My nails repeatedly tapped against the wood table as I contemplated whether to open it. Nicholas Ramirez-Dubois had been my best friend for over eleven years; that all changed the night of his prom.

Nic showed up at precisely 7:30 with a corsage in hand. He placed the corsage on my wrist and locked eyes with me. I hugged him quickly and stepped back to admire my best friend. He was handsome, with smooth light-brown skin, loose curly chestnut hair, and hazel eyes, wearing a black tuxedo with a white tie and vest. He looked incredible. My mom's eyes filled with tears when she had us pose for pictures. She was like the paparazzi as she followed us to the car, still snapping shots. I was nervous about going with him because he had broken up with his girlfriend, Sheila. Tonight, should be fun if Sheila and her friends kept things drama free.

We entered the school auditorium to the sound of Maroon 5, and I swayed to the rhythm while Nic went to get a drink. They transformed the hall into 'Enchantment Under the Sea;' the stage was now a sunken ship where they had the photo op. Balloon-shaped dolphins and massive waves created the illusion of the sea. The metamorphoses astounded me; for the first time, I wondered if my prom would have this cool theme.

"Are you thirsty?" Nic held a small plastic cup brimming with a blue punch. I shook my head, no, and he placed the cup on a nearby table. His attention was on the dance floor; I saw Sheila grinding against an older guy, although her eyes never left Nic. Therefore, I had to assume that the R-rated performance was for Nic.

"You want to leave?" I asked, and he gave me an oddly confused look. "No, I want to dance," he pulled me in. I curled my fingers around his, surprised to discover they were damp. Nic's nervous demeanor tonight made me slightly uneasy. He was typically laid back and never allowed things to get to him. Suppose he was taking his break-up harder than I thought he would.

We were going to the dance floor when he looked down at me. The nervous look in his eyes made me feel a little anxious.

"What's wrong?" I stopped abruptly, and he turned to give me a nervous smile.

"We should talk about it later. Come on, let's dance."

We danced, for what felt like hours, laughing, and taking pictures. I could not remember a time I had this much fun. Our eyes met when the Kings of Midnights, Make Her Love Me, came floating through the speakers, one of the slowest songs on their album. Nic put his arms around me, and I put my head on his chest, he had a way of making me feel safe. I held him tighter, but he took a step backward. I looked up at him. "Did I do something wrong?"

He gave me one of the strangest looks, I had only seen it once after he had drunk too much, and his food was on the verge of resurfacing. He made a beeline from the dance floor with me trailing behind him. I found him on the side of the building with his face tilted toward the sky. He glanced down at me.

"You're scaring me," I managed. Nic leaned down; I thought he was going to kiss me — he did. We lingered there for a moment, and I took a small step forward. He stepped back and the shock brought my fingers to my mouth. My eyes went to my freshly manicured toes peeking through the strappy heels.

"Look, Madi, things between us have changed," he blurted out. "I like you," he said, so matter of fact that I first thought he was joking. Only, he was serious. "I know this isn't fair, but I had to tell you." He paused and swallowed hard as if he had ingested something painful, "This isn't working. I want to be with you. I shouldn't, but I do."

"I don't know what to say," I said, looking up at my best friend. He turned his back on me, yanking his fingers through his tight curls. My mind began to scream at me, "You're about to lose the only person that loves you! Do something! Anything, please!"

"I'm almost eighteen; you're only fifteen. I'm supposed to be looking out for you instead of wanting to be with you," Nic paced back and forth. His words cut through me, and I wanted to feel the way he did more than anything.

"Nic," I reached but he moved away as if my touch had injured him.

He clasped his hands behind his head, "Go inside, Madi!" there was an urgency to his tone that surprised me. I reached for him again, "Damn it, Madi! Go inside!"

"Wait, let's talk about this," I cried, my arms went around his waist and clung to him, when I noticed the tears flooding his eyes. "I never said no," I whispered against his chest.

"I know. I shouldn't have told you. It's just we never keep secrets and my feelings for you changed. I'm not being fair to you, or our friendship. I just need a minute." He thought I rejected him. "I'm okay." Nic said as he placed a soft kiss on the top of my forehead. I leaned back to look into his eyes and although I knew he wasn't alright, I let go. And he turned once again to stare out into the distance.

I returned to the dance and waited for him for what had to be hours, tears clouded my vision; when lights came on, and the chaperones started to usher everyone out of the building. I waited by Nic's car and searched the area for him; he was gone. When his car was the only one left in the parking lot; I called my mom to pick me up.

The following week, Nic's mom told me he went to stay with his grandfather until classes began and wanted me to know he could not see me.

My fork rattled against the table, pulling me from my walk down memory lane. My lasagna had gotten cold again, not that it mattered; I had suddenly lost my appetite. I placed the letter beneath my arm and dumped the lasagna and milk down the garbage disposal before going upstairs.

The music was no longer playing, thank goodness. My parents were now watching the evening news. I hurried past their room and into mine — slid the unopened envelope into my desk drawer, grabbed my book off the nightstand, and quickly immersed myself in the story.

Moments later, a door slammed, loud, angry shouting, and footsteps clambered down the stairs. The distant sound of shattered glass sent me from the room and down the hall. Phillip was picking up pieces of broken glass when a porcelain plate slammed into the wall next to him; another quickly followed.

"Have you lost your mind?" He rushed into the kitchen, where my mom was standing in her gown. She was sobbing loudly. I cleared the first landing, only to stop when she screamed at him.

"I want to leave this place! You didn't tell me that a girl is missing here too!" She went to her knees. "Why would you bring us here?"

"I didn't know," He joined her on the floor, enfolding her in his arms. "Beth, I will find them."

"We cannot stay here," she cried, struggling against his hold.

"She will be safe. I promise. I need you to trust me. Have I not protected you, protected her?"

Her sobs were now breathless gasps of air as Phillip continued to console her — my feet felt unsteady as I walked over to them; they looked up simultaneously. My mom had never appeared more fragile. She went to her feet, patted my hand, then turned away. I watched as she went to get the broom and dustpan, her body still trembling.

"What's going on?" There were broken dishes throughout the kitchen; not sure how I missed hearing the beginning of her tirade.

"Nothing, go to bed," Phillip's voice clipped with anger and frustration. He continued to watch my mom — unveiled fear settled in the crevices of his large brown eyes. Phillip was afraid that she would leave him. So, he held her tightly. I saw immense pain in his eyes when she pulled away. For the first time, I understood that as big and overpowering as Phillip was, my mom had all the power.

"Tell me what's wrong?" Again, I demanded with more determination, "Tell me!"

Phillip shifted to face me, and all traces of emotion vanished. He was afraid of losing my mom. I, however, was another story altogether. "You are not to leave this house alone; stay out of the woods," his eyes became soft again once they landed on her.

"You heard your father. It's not safe here," her voice sounded strained, and I knew she was again on the verge of tears. I hugged her and buried my face in her jasmine-scented hair. She needed this. I told myself, and so did I.

"Get some rest," she squeezed me once more, and I slowly

made my way back up the stairs, took a quick shower, and climbed into bed, where I lay awake for hours trying to decipher my parent's argument. A girl was missing in the area. I could only assume that she resembled me. My mom had never freaked out like that before. She never raised her voice — and she damn sure had never thrown dishes at Phillip. So, what in the hell was going on?

After my monthlong confinement, well except school, I received my pardon.

Conner, Braden, Ashley, and I decided to grab something to eat after a quick game of touch football. Ashley was one of the few friendly girls at school and Braden's new girlfriend. Her long, strawberry-blonde hair flowed loosely around her shoulders, making her bright blue eyes appear even more prominent. We drove to the diner and found one of the few empty booths. Conner's ears perked up when he overheard a couple talking about murders a couple of towns over.

"Aren't your parents going to Roanoke, Virginia, to meet about the murdered girls?" Conner asked.

"Wait, were they murdered?" my brows lifted, questioning.

"Yeah, thought you knew they found the bodies of some of the missing girls in Virginia."

"No, they never talk about his work," so they killed them. A girl was missing from the area. I wondered if she had gone to our school.

"The psychos removed all the internal organs; reports believe it's cannibalism, some sort of sadistic ritual or cult," Braden commented as Ashley, and I winced.

"That's some real Silence of the Lambs shit," Conner's excitement over the gruesome deaths was mindboggling. Ashley looked pale as she closed her menu.

"Uh, haven't seen that movie," I shot him a disturbed look.

"Conner, have you heard anything about the girl that went

missing last month?" My question stumped him briefly, or he was sorting through the information.

"Yeah, ah, her name's Joy," he gave me a quizzical look, slanting his green eyes as he stared at me.

"Do you know where she's from?"

"Here, she's a junior at our school," Conner was about to chomp down on his hamburger but stopped mid-bite; his teeth barely touched the large sesame bun. "She's sitting over there with her parents." He leaned in and whispered. I dared a glance over my shoulder, stunned by her appearance. Her skin appeared ashen; her cheeks sunken, and long, thick curly hair curtained her face. She must have felt my eyes on her because she looked up. When our eyes met — I jerked back around.

"Her name no longer fits her," Ashley chimed in, although she refused to look beyond her plate of fries. Instead, she dipped one into a pile of mayo, which almost made me gag a little. People did the strangest things with French fries, cheese, barbecue, mustard, and, I guess now, mayo. I'm not too fond of the way my mind bounces around- clearly the conversation was more important than Ashley's dipping choices.

"What do you mean?" I couldn't help myself.

"She used to be pretty; even your prince charming tried to date her," she gave Conner a daring look. "Sad, the police think that she was using a hallucinogenic because Joy was gone for over a month and didn't remember anything. A blob of mayo dangled from Ashley's lip, which distracted me from the conversation. Thankfully, she licked the thick glob off, and I could refocus again. Was Joy's disappearance connected to the other kidnappings? Even in her disheveled state, I could see the resemblance. Although they believed there were drugs involved. That had to be why my mom went with Phillip and Uncle Mike to their meeting if not.

"Well, my sources say that she showed up covered in blood. She told the police that the men had eaten the other girls. They were going to eat her too, but one of the younger guys helped her escape while the others were asleep." Conner continued to eat; I guess discussing cannibalism did not affect his appetite.

"Can we please change the subject," Ashley said, still looking ill. Conner shrugged his shoulders before sinking his teeth into his burger again.

I quickly calculated the kidnappings in my mind, reviewing the earlier news alerts, including Joy as a victim; I dug deeper into the recesses of my subconscious; they let her go, so maybe the kidnappers had stopped.

This revelation flooded me with relief — now they needed to find them — My parents and Uncle Mike met with the mayor today and planned to travel to Washington, D.C., next week to staff the kidnappings.

"Will you be staying with us while your parents are gone?" Conner gave me a wink that disturbed me more than his comment.

"Yep, I thought I would stay at my mom's friend Margaret's house. But, thanks to your mom, I don't have to. I'm surprised she didn't say anything to you."

"My mom doesn't like her husband, Daniel. She said he gives her the creeps." Conner said. "He was born here, and his sister lives in our neighborhood. They moved to California to work five years ago; we were all surprised that he and Margaret returned a week before you arrived, announcing they were married. She even helped him get a job at the auto repair station at the end of town," Conner explained.

"Swear you're weird; nobody should know that damn much about everything," Ashley said, causing us all to laugh.

Conner's ability to download and process information made him somewhat of a human computer. I agreed with his classmates from last year; they voted him 'most likely to become a reporter' during the previous year's poll. And the only introduction I had ever seen him give was when he met me; he knew everything there was to know about anyone who lived in this town.

"You can laugh all you want, but I'm the person you come to when you need information. Who always delivers the goods? I'll tell you who, me." Conner's voice was, muffled as he took another bite from his hamburger.

"Want a bite, Madi?" Conner dangled the disgusting burger in front of my face as I grimaced and leaned away. "I've seen you eat burgers before; you would have eaten mine if I hadn't returned from the bathroom in time. Your small size might have fooled me a month ago, but I'm on to you now," his smile grew.

"It's not the burger that grosses me out. I can't eat bacon." I wrinkled my nose in disgust — the smell mingled around us. Whenever I looked at a piece of bacon, the images of that poor pig filtered into my mind, and I started to feel sick. One of my strongest childhood memories was of the awful centerpiece at the banquet in Paris. My mom had recapped the night before, describing the beautiful decorations and entertainment, but the only thing I could remember was the dreadful sight in the middle of the table.

"You have got to be kidding me!" Conner wiped his mouth with a napkin. "Can you believe she doesn't eat bacon?" he asked Braden as if I weren't sitting beside him.

"I know — simply un-American; we should deport her!" Braden jabbed Conner before tossing a crumpled napkin across the table at me. Ashley excused herself to the bathroom, and Braden went to the cash register to pay.

"What race are you, Madi?" Conner asked once we were at the table alone.

"Human, last time I checked." It was interesting how it always came to this. "What race did you think I was?" The self-proclaimed, 'normal people' would ask about my ethnicity. I didn't know why they decided they were the normal ones, but I could see the way they watched me, wondering if I were even part of the same species.

"I would say bi-racial, but your mom looks mixed too. Braden thinks you're a swirl, part white-part black." In seconds, Conner had gone from 'cool' to 'jerk.'

"Wow, yeah, that's me!" I shouted and stormed out of the diner. I was so mad that slapping 'the hell' out of him flashed through my mind. I could tell my eyes were glowing as I stomped down the street, keeping my eyes on the ground until they returned to normal.

"Madi, wait, why are you so mad?" Conner raced to catch up with me. He could never understand that choosing not to share my ethnicity with him had nothing to do with a lack of pride because nothing could be further from the truth. The speculation over my race kept the other questions at bay, like my overly heated body, glowing eyes, and freaky connection with the wind and water. I was unsure what I was myself, and I couldn't explain the relentless nightmares that only gave me pieces of the truth.

Conner yelled. "I'm sorry. That was an idiot move; promise not to ask again." He was sincere. "I've got one more question for you," he smirked. "Where exactly did you think, you were going to go? Braden's our ride."

"Why do you think I'm so pissed off? We've still got a fifteen-minute walk to get to your house," I could feel my irritation with him lessen.

"Oh, I thought it was my being a jerk back there." His dimples deepened even further as he tried to fight back a smile.

"Yeah, well, that too."

CHAPTER SEVEN
LOCK DOWN

Margaret and Daniel arrived, and my mom embraced Margaret tightly. The two quickly engaged in conversation.

Phillip and Uncle Mike were outside on the deck smoking their cigars. Judging by the serious looks on their faces, I could only assume they were discussing the recent killings. Phillip had his hunting bow stretched across the table, cleaning supplies, and gleaming silver-tipped wooden arrows never did understand his reasoning for those. What difference does it make what type of arrow — I'm sure the deer could care less if the object that brought them death had a glistening silver tip. Uncle Mike leaned forward, tinkering with a giant crossbow, which meant bear hunting. I wrinkled my nose and tapped on the glass to get his attention. Phillip looked up momentarily, took Uncle Mike's crossbow, and returned to his polishing.

Uncle Mike came inside and gave me one of his famous hugs that lifted me off my feet. "There's my old lady!" Uncle Mike exclaimed as he spun me around the room. "How are you, beautiful?" he asked, putting me back on my feet.

"I'm great now that you're here." My smile brightened as I placed a kiss on the side of his face. "Where have you been?" I questioned, seeing how he had dropped off the map for weeks.

"Took a few refresher courses at your old school," he winked. I laughed when my mom slapped him on the back of his head. "What, you have a problem with me taking private Spanish lessons?" He sounded like a scolded child.

"You should be ashamed of yourself," she shook her head before kissing his bristly cheek softly.

"You," she pointed at Uncle Mike, "Behave yourself," before leading us to her guest. "I would like you to meet Margaret; we shared a dorm in college; it couldn't have been more than a year ago today," my mom joked. I, however, continued to examine the woman. Before today, I had only seen her in faded photographs. She made it easy for me to understand what people meant when they said, "College will be the best years of your life," because she looked nothing like her photos. The once bright-eyed, free spirit who had worn long, colorful skirts, loose blouses, and scarves no longer existed. She had traded them in for that awful orange business suit she was wearing. The jacket was at least two sizes too small and contrasted with her red hair. She had large, deep brown eyes, a pointy chin, and thin lips that all but disappeared as she drew them into a smile.

Someone touched my arm and looked up to see that Margaret's face was mere inches from mine.

"I'm your Auntie Margaret, and this is Daniel, my husband." She pointed toward the peculiar-looking man standing feet away. He approached us, and the closer he moved, the stranger he looked. His brown, greasy hair nearly covered squinty, dark eyes. He and Phillip were the same height, only he was thinner. Daniel's full, cracked lips formed into a smile, revealing a row of stained teeth. His face had dark streaks, and I was uncertain if the blemishes were dirt or his complexion. I reasoned that his unkempt appearance could have been due to his work at the auto shop, but my gut screamed, 'Dude's a filthy creeper. "Honey, this is my niece, Madi," Margaret said as he ogled me. Something in his eyes made my insides churn, like when I mistakenly drank a cup of spoiled milk. It was unsettling.

"Nice to meet you," I lied, holding my hand out. Daniel completely ignored my gesture and grabbed me tight in his arms, lifting my feet from the floor as he squeezed me. My earlier assumption was correct; it was dirt. There were streaks of white on his flesh where I had tried to push his arms away.

"You can call me Dan; all my friends do, and we're all family here." My eyes narrowed, and I heard Phillip scoff his disapproval. It was the first time we agreed on something.

"Have to steal her away for a sec," Uncle Mike tossed his arm over my shoulder and shuffled me away from Daniel.

We entered the kitchen, and he held out a bundle of envelopes; no, they were letters. The handwriting, I recognized; he pressed them into my ribs when I refused to accept them. "If you don't want to read your letters, fine, don't ever let Phillip see them." He pushed them into my stomach more forcefully and embraced me when Phillip walked by.

"Do you have to go with them?" I whispered, still unsure why Uncle Mike behaved so peculiarly; however, I knew his concern must be valid. His brown eyes widened as he stared unblinkingly at me. I knew that Phillip never liked him, and he hated that we were friends, although I never considered that he would harm Nic. Except something deep inside me would beg to differ — fragments of an argument — Phillip hitting Nic. So why can't I remember? Why are parts of my past so vivid that I feel I'm reliving them, while others are grainy, distorted pieces of a puzzle I could not solve?

Phillip glanced over at us before rescuing my mom from Daniel's embrace. She looked as relieved as I had when Uncle Mike saved me.

"Madi," Uncle Mike said, returning my attention to the letters. I nodded, rushed upstairs, and placed the stack beside the others. Nic's letters had become predictable — arriving every Friday. Why he sent them to Hatteras, too, was beyond me, not to mention a waste of his time. I closed the box — slid it deep beneath my bed and rejoined my family.

Uncle Mike was standing at the bottom of the stairs; he placed his arm over my shoulder, although he was miles away. I followed his gaze, which softly rested upon my mom. His eyes held such warmth as she and Margaret recounted their college days. Her laughter brought a smile to his face, brightened his eyes, and it was at that moment I wondered if Uncle Mike were here because of his job, his friendship with Phillip, or my mom.

"Madi, are you ready?" Phillip asked as he unlocked his arms from my mom's waist.

"Yes," I pointed to my suitcase by the door. Phillip nodded his approval.

I watched as their conversation went from the joys of college life to me. My mom handed Margaret a list of rules for me. I'm confident that I must remain in Nirvana topped the list. We never discussed the forged permission slip again. It was safe to assume I would not travel to Paris with my friends, other juniors, and seniors. Staying in Nirvana might have been tolerable if Blake were going to be here; he told me yesterday that he would catch night waves in Australia with Bria. My parents would be gone for a month, following up on leads about the men who kidnapped and murdered those girls. Phillip insisted that my mom join him since there were no other kidnappings. She had no valid excuse to refuse. Especially since Phillip hired a security detail to remain on standby, the first sign of trouble, they could swoop in to protect me. Yep, my first summer in Nirvana would officially suck.

"You never answered my question. Do you have to go?" I asked Uncle Mike.

"Sorry if there were any way I could get out of this, it would have already happened," he said as I leaned on him. "Don't worry; we'll solve the case and return soon." I knew Uncle Mike was trying to lighten my mood, but the way Daniel watched me left a sick feeling in my stomach.

"Alright, you try to stay out of trouble while we're gone," Phillip said. He ruffled my hair before handing me the suitcase.

"Okay," I managed to say, then quickly took the bag outside and placed it inside the open trunk. I slid into the back seat of Daniel's car cautiously.

"Madison, do you want to leave without saying goodbye?" My mom asked as she opened the door and climbed in beside me. "You know that I love you," she said, her eyes pooling with tears.

"I know, I don't want to say goodbye," goodbyes are so final, I thought silently before hugging her. "For the record, I love you more." She smiled and then walked back inside.

The couple came outside minutes later, jumped in the front seat, and headed home. We pulled in front of the weather-beaten house, faded yellow paint trimmed in red, the colors now blended, making it appear orange in areas. It would have been a beautiful home with a bit of care, I thought to myself.

"So, you're a daydreamer!" Margaret said flippantly. "Let's go!" Margaret tugged on my hand. The second I stepped out of the car; Daniel tossed my suitcase on the ground next to me — I took a deep breath and trudged up the sidewalk. Once inside the house, she dropped her enormous handbag on the table close to the door, kicked a worn pair of pumps across the floor, and plopped down on the sofa. "Your room is the first on the left; you have a bathroom to the right. That's as fancy as you're going to get here," she barked, and Daniel nodded agreeably, sitting beside her on the sofa.

"Thanks, you have a nice house," It wasn't a lie, although something was missing — warmth. I scanned the living room to find an oversized sofa, a loveseat, and a large recliner, all blue and grey plaid, with matching curtains. Margaret and Daniel had recently gotten married, but no photographs of the occasion, or little keepsakes or trinkets that gave homes that 'lived in' feeling.

"You're responsible for feeding yourself. Beth and Phillip aren't paying me enough to cook," she snapped. I nodded and hurried up the stairs.

When I opened the bedroom door, my jaw dropped in shock. The furniture was white, and the twin bed had pink pillows and a matching blanket. The curtains, knitted throw, and the area rug had all met the same fate. It looked like someone had thrown up a sea of pink vomit.

In the bathroom, nothing had escaped the pink demon. Of all the colors in the world, pink was the only one I hated. It was too girly for me. The only pink thing I owned was a pair of furry slippers. They were a gag gift from Nic, so I couldn't throw them away, although the thought had entered my mind. I put the suitcase in a chair by the window, telling myself there was no need to unpack.

During my last few days as a junior, I sat in the library to get a moment of peace. Usually, I would be outside at the picnic tables, but the weather forecast called for a thunderstorm. The winds had started to pick up speed in the morning, and the school had informed all students that they were not to go outside. I pulled my book closer to my face, willing myself to concentrate, when the tall, blonde-haired, blue-eyed girl came over.

"Hi, my name's Lauren," she introduced herself with a sickening level of perkiness.

"Yeah, we sit beside each other in Civics," I replied.

"What are you reading?" Lauren asked, eyeing my book, her voice irritating and whiney. It seemed like she unnecessarily drew out each word, which made it difficult to listen to her.

"*The Sacred Text of Heloise and Abelard,*" I managed to say.

"Oh, that sounds like fun," she exclaimed with a grin now covering her face.

"Yeah, if you can consider the tragedy of their love, fun." I grimaced when the words left my mouth. Talking to Lauren was comparable to my conversations with Suzy Sunshine, the doll Uncle Mike had brought me for my eighth birthday. I pulled the string once, and the damn thing never shut up; she rambled on for hours about how she wanted to be my "special friend." The doll's eerie smile and high-pitched voice annoyed me; tragically, two days after my birthday, she met a violent death. Maybe if she had kept quiet for a minute, she would have heard my warnings about the garbage disposal.

"My friends and I were wondering if you'd like to hang out with us tonight. We're going to see a movie at 8:00," she explained, glancing back at the girls waiting by the computers. The awkward silence between us should have answered the question — only she didn't move. I placed the book in my lap to look up at her and see that she would never give up. I gave in.

"I guess," I responded, hoping this wasn't an attempt to include me in her group.

When I first saw Lauren's clique, my first thought was that she and the other blonde-haired girls took part in a type of dare. I couldn't imagine anyone intentionally deciding to wear such clothes: pink shirts, white pleated skirts, and white shoes. The pink demon from my room at Margaret's house had visited these girls, too, and had no mercy when it invaded their closets. They also wore pearls and big, pink headbands that held back their huge, blonde curls. I later discovered their attire was more of a uniform; the girls enjoyed looking like Barbie's clones.

"Great! Can you invite Braden and Conner?" she asked, holding her breath.

Okay, now I was more than a little irritated. I should have known Lauren was up to something, or the girl would have never tried to acknowledge my presence. If Lauren was Suzy Sunshine, I was now a bobblehead doll, nodding slowly without conscious thought.

"You're the best!" Lauren said, cocking her head to the side with an 'I gotcha' smile. Then, she bounced down the hallway with her clan, leaving me with a sick feeling in my stomach.

After school, I returned to Margaret's house to change clothes and got ready. I secured my tighter-than-normal curls in a ponytail. One stubborn lock of hair refused to surrender, so I used my butterfly barrette to hold it in place. A car horn sent me down the stairs and out the door. I was surprised that Conner and Braden had already picked up Ashley and Lauren. Ashley was sitting in the passenger seat, which meant I would have to sit beside Lauren and Conner in the back. Lauren smiled when I slid in beside her.

"Hey, Madi, I tried to call you earlier. Tawny and Whitney decided not to come. They thought it would be weird to be the only one without a date," Lauren whispered. My eyes narrowed when I realized Conner and Braden had their arms draped over the girls.

Conner peeked around at Lauren, "Madi's fine, and she doesn't have a date," Conner added. I rolled my eyes at Mr. Obvious, now feeling even more uncomfortable.

"What movie are we going to see?" Lauren asked, scooting closer to Conner, if that were possible. When his fingers began twisting in her hair, I regretted my decision to come with them.

"*Alien Abductions*; there are supposed to be horrific death scenes," Conner exclaimed.

"I can't wait!" Lauren responded and moved Conner's hand to her lap. I shook my head and prayed that the hands of time would move faster.

"Madi, did you know Lauren loves scary movies?" Conner gushed.

"No, that is a surprise," I admitted.

"I love them! So does Ashley. Conner and Braden are coming to my house tomorrow to watch *Body Snatchers*. You're welcome to come with." Lauren's invite might have been more believable if it weren't for the pasted smile on her face.

"Got to study," I replied quickly.

We arrived at the Grandin Theater, and I could not get out of the car fast enough. Conner and Braden went to pay for the tickets while I waited with Lauren and Ashley. The two were engrossed in a conversation about which brother was cuter. I was lost in thought when I heard a familiar voice. Looking up, I saw Blake walking out of the ticket line.

"Hey, Madi, come to see what your peeps are up to?" he joked, pointing to the *Alien Abductions* sign behind me.

"No, yours," I retorted, glancing at the *Not, All Dogs Go to Heaven* poster.

"I guess that's funny," he said with a smirk.

"Hey, Blake," Lauren shouted, interjecting herself into our conversation in her normal squeaky tone. He gave her a slight nod, and she practically skipped away with a larger-than-life smile.

His eyes traveled over to Lauren and Ashley as they began to giggle. "They are the reason I would never date a freak-in' human," Blake explained, his voice agitated.

My eyes narrowed as I replayed the words in my head. "Wait! Did you say that you never date humans? So, what is this: 'Screw with Madi day'?" I questioned as I stepped toward him. Bria came around the side of the building, and I moved back as she approached him and linked arms.

"Why are you talking to her?" she sneered. Blake gave her a look that stopped her in her tracks.

"See you later, Madi." He gave me a head tilt, and I did the same although it looked cooler when Blake did it, he chuckled. Bria huffed, and he allowed her to drag him into the theater.

"You shouldn't talk to other girl's boyfriends, Madi," Lauren weighed in, and Ashley quickly agreed. They went to meet up with Conner and Braden, and I reluctantly followed them inside.

I ended up stuck between the two couples. The movie was frightening but not as scary as Lauren's desperate attempts for Conner's attention. Her foot must have kicked me ten times as she tried to lean closer to him. The other side of me was hardly any better. Lauren had said Ashley liked scary movies, but that was hard to believe since she had Braden's hand in a death grip.

After the movies, we went to the pizzeria on the outskirts of town and then drove around for a while. Conner and Lauren were all over each other and spent the entire time making out. Braden finally dropped me off at 2:00 in the morning. Margaret greeted me at the door, yelling, "Late night rendezvous with God only knows who, doing Lord knows what." She followed me up to the bedroom and continued her endless tirade about teen pregnancy, sexually transmitted diseases, and news articles she had read about sex parties. Her lecture drifted me to sleep, but it was a restless and dreamless night.

CHAPTER EIGHT
HAUNTED

I tried to think about something other than the Paris trip, which was difficult since everyone talked about nothing else—especially considering that I spent the morning watching Emma pack. I had not imagined this would end, with Emma going to Paris and me staying here, only that was going to happen. She offered to talk to my mom again, and I told her there was simply no convincing my mom once she had made up her mind. I would never know the reason my mom was so resistant to Paris. I did, however, know that doing so would hurt her, and I could not do that for fun. Emma dropped me off, and I reluctantly headed up the sidewalk.

I sat down on the weather-beaten porch contemplating whether to hang out by the lake near Margaret's house — it was still early, and although the forest looked inviting, I would explore later. I turned on the light and gasped when I saw Daniel standing in the corner.

"Where have you been?" he stammered, an enormous grin on his face.

"I told Margaret that I was going to hang out with Emma," I nearly made it by him when his fingers clamped down on my forearm. He reeked of alcohol and cigarettes.

"Run it by me next time, a young, little girl like you, running the street with those boys. I have been on that internet watching all the dirty things you kids are into," He could barely keep his balance, and I had to hold my breath to prevent breathing in his scent. "What kind of things do you like, Madi?"

That was the first time I wanted to change my name; how he said it made me sick. He ran his callused hand down my face.

"Is that you, Madi?" Margaret called from upstairs.

"Yes- yes, it's me," I stammered. Daniel's eyes darted toward the stairs, then back to me, and his grip suddenly loosened. I watched him stumble up the stairs. Their bedroom door slammed shut moments later. I exited the house slowly, afraid that Daniel might come back down. The floorboards creaked, and I held my breath until I was safely outside.

Once inside the forest, my worries seemed to fade away — the canopy created by the massive trees gave the whole place a feeling of secrecy and safety. Grayish-tinted light peeked through the trees illuminating the leaves, branches, and forest floor. I watched a couple of brown frogs jump from one puddle to another, their small slick bodies hitting the light at strange angles, highlighting the dark triangular mark between their eyes. I stepped around them, however, but crushed at least three beetles to avoid the frogs. "Sorry," I whispered, knowing they couldn't hear me, although I had hoped the gathering mounds of beetles around my sneakers would understand. A shuffle of my foot sent them scurrying away and me as well. The path opened as I neared the lake, and I quickly found the extended root of the Maple tree. The old tree understood me better than most humans. I rubbed my hand down the bark patting the massive trunk. As I leaned back, a shower of leaves floated down, and I smiled. "I feel the same way about you."

I rested my back on the trunk, contemplating whether to call my mom about the incident with Daniel. I thought about how happy she sounded earlier when we spoke. She told me they arrested the men who kidnapped and killed those girls. My mom was no longer on edge. Today, she sounded- giddy. She talked about the hotel's waterfall pool, manicures, pedicures, massages, and shopping. I was excited for her.

Then, she dropped the news that Phillip had scheduled an

appointment with the top fertility doctor in the country. That would require them to travel to Pleasant Grove, Utah. Well, once Phillip and Uncle Mike finished the business aspect of their trip. My mom needed to relax if she wanted to get pregnant; that was hard to do with me around. Daniel had technically frightened me, nothing more. I mean, he does have a creepy way of looking at me. The fact that he touched my face and grabbed my arm alarmed me. Phillip would dismiss Daniel's actions, and I would be at fault for blowing things out of proportion. My mom's trip to the fertility clinic would be on hold. I shook my head — my mom deserved this trip. That meant I would need to keep my mouth shut.

A ladybug landed on my hand, and I held it up to admire it. When I blew gently, it flew away. I watched it continue upward and disappear into the trees. "If only it were that easy," I whispered to myself.

I glanced down at the water. It looked refreshing and inviting, so I went down the mossy bank when my foot slipped, covering my backside in mud, and wiping it worsened matters. I bent down to the water to rinse the dirt from my hands. The sound of rustling leaves in the distance caught my attention. I paused, making my hands stiff in the pond so I did not ripple the water, twisting painfully slowly. After scanning the area and finding nothing, I crouched closer to the water to finish cleaning off the mud. The bush next to me began to move. I jumped up quickly, scrambled back to the maple tree, and braced myself.

Suddenly, two tiny cubs came pouncing out from the brush, and I shook my head at how paranoid and nervous I had been. The small cougars were too preoccupied with one another to notice my intrusion into their world. They had fuzzy tan fur with quarter-sized black spots and spiky claws that swiped at each other. One leaped onto the other and hissed playfully. I stepped backward, keeping my eyes peeled for the mother. Once I could no longer see the cougar cubs, I quickly turned and began running to put distance between the cubs and myself.

Something came crashing through the trees. I caught a brief

glimpse of the animal before powerful legs came pouncing down upon me and slammed me to the ground, and I felt the hot, intense breath against my neck. The weight of the mother cougar stifled my ability to scream, and the air squeezed from my lungs- she leaned back, and my heart caught in my throat. The enormous razor-sharp teeth were exposed, and a roar escaped from her dripping wet jaw, and everything went black.

My body felt relaxed, calm, and light. I floated off the ground; the clouds brushed against my heated skin as I drifted upward. "Madison," a smooth yet strong voice whispered. I desperately tried to push through the cloud, straining to see. My heart was racing with anticipation, and I began to panic as the cloud consumed me.

Margaret's banging on the door awakened me, and I stumbled out of bed, tripping over my sneakers. I grimaced; every muscle felt tight and ached like I had run ten miles in my sleep. But She busted into the room, causing me to jump back.

"I'm not sure what kind of things you kids are getting into, but you're going to stop it right now!" she scolded, waving her finger at me. I rolled my eyes at the deranged woman before going to the closet to get a T-shirt and a pair of jeans. She had finally lost all grip on reality, and I fantasized about someone, anyone signing her much-needed commitment papers.

"You're lucky I didn't call Beth last night when that man brought you home!" Margaret continued, stomping over to me, and ripped the clothes from my hand. She tossed them across the room, her face only an inch from mine. "It stops now! You are not going to see him again! Do you hear me? You had better not try that shit on me again!" Margaret screamed before leaving the room.

I had no idea what she was talking about — my head began to throb, and only fragments of last night surfaced, her creepy husband harassing me; and the two cougar cubs running away from them. The mother cougar, did she attack me? No, she couldn't have, or I would be dead. I strained to remember but hit a wall, and my memory refused to release another detail of last night. What man did Margaret believe brought me here? What had happened to me? I sniffed the scent of sandalwood and honeysuckle intermingled with my mango shampoo. No, there is no way.

The following week was grueling; my parents were in Utah, and Blake's in Australia with his emotionally detached girlfriend. Emma, Conner, and Braden were in Paris while they explored the City of Lights; I spent my days wandering the forest, and my nights were restless. This place was like watching paint dry in the winter — painstakingly slow and boring as hell.

I grabbed a bottle of water from the fridge to soothe the uneasiness in my stomach and then went upstairs to try to sleep once more, exhausted from tossing and turning. My eyes struggled to remain open, and soon everything became hazy.

I hurried down the abandoned streets; I could see the glistening lights of the Eiffel Tower ahead of me. I glanced over my shoulder for the men who had pursued me for as long as I could remember. They were nowhere in sight. I sensed danger was ahead of me; this time, my life was not in jeopardy— he was. The man that had saved me from my reoccurring nightmares — now needed me. Dread consumed my entire being and urged me to move faster. I reached a hotel, unable to see anything, but I knew he was there. My feet carried me swiftly through the long, narrow halls in search of the roof exit. I forced the large steel door open, and it slammed against the wall. He was standing on the ledge, and the wind was blowing so hard that it was impossible to reach him.

"I'm not sure why you're up here, but please don't do this!" I screamed as tears spilled from my eyes. "Please, I need you!"

My body jerked awake, drenched in a cold sweat. I glanced over at the clock. It was 3:00 in the morning. My heart pounded in my chest. I sprinted to the dresser for my small wooden box, frantically rummaging around for my credit cards. There was enough money on them to get me to Paris and back multiple times. With my passport and credit cards, my pulse felt a little closer to normal.

I opened my laptop, booked the next flight out, and then called a taxi. Quickly, I crept out of the house with nothing but my suitcase. The taxi picked me up further down the street, where I stood on the side, holding my luggage.

"You okay, Miss?" the taxi driver asked nervously.

"Yes, can you hurry, please?" I responded, dashing away tears as I worried about the man's fate on the ledge.

It took an hour to get to the airport and another two hours before I boarded the plane. My flight consisted of two significant layovers, the first at JFK and then at Casablanca. I rested my head on the wall beside me as my eyelids drooped. When I awakened hours later, airport security and bystanders were eyeing me suspiciously. My breathless screams for the man on the roof I knew was the reason. I sat there, trying to get myself together, when I heard the boarding call — I went to my feet and passed the people continuing to stare at me and down the long corridor. We sat idle on the runway for at least thirty minutes before the pilot made the "please be patient" announcement. Worry creased my brows as I imagined the entire country searching for me. The airport locked down, and travelers running around in panic. Then, they would see little me, escorted out by security. Madison Bailey Ryan, International Troublemaker. Forty-five minutes later and we were finally in the air.

I wondered if Margaret or Daniel knew — no, maybe not. If I were lucky, they would not think to look for me for at least a couple of days. I had spent the past week in that Pepto-colored room and neither checked in to make sure that I was still breathing. The only problem that I could foresee was my mom's phone calls. I would have to lie to her, and the thought of traveling to Paris against her wishes and ruining her trust and faith in me was awful; however, I needed to help him.

The sound of someone snoring awakened me. The man beside me had fallen asleep and decided my shoulder would be a good pillow.

"Ugh!" I wrinkled my nose in disgust and then pushed him off me. The warmth of my skin had left him red-faced and his shirt damp with sweat.

"Sorry," he managed to choke out; I would have forgiven him. However, this was the fourth time he had fallen asleep on me. Not to mention, there was an empty seat on the other side of him, but to avoid any more awkward touching, I stuffed my coat between us, and he had the audacity to scoff at me.

When I woke up hours later, the flight attendant had a seriously pissed-off expression. Her long, manicured nails tapped repeatedly against the seat.

"You must leave the plane now!" she snapped, first in English and then French. The irritation in her voice coincided with the mad-as-hell look on her face, and I suddenly realized that I was the last passenger on board.

"Sorry," I yelled over my shoulder as I hurried off the airplane. My day- had worsened. The airport was in complete chaos, and people bumped into me as they rushed through the terminals. I argued with airport security over my lost bag, which resulted in a traveler's check for clothes and a promise to deliver the bag ASAP. The fact that they snickered as I left their office-spoke volumes — my overnight bag was gone. I took a taxi to *Mercure Paris Voltaire Quartier Bastille,* where the senior class stayed.

Emma was surprised when the desk clerk called up to her room; she met me in the lobby seconds later, to my and the desk clerk's surprise. I teased that she must have grown wings and flown down the stairs. She insisted that I share her suite because no rooms were available at the hotel. The desk clerk handed me a key card, still cautiously watching Emma. She smiled, and he returned a nervous grin.

Immaculate, there was no other way to describe her suite. The living area was painted beige, with cream furniture trimmed in gold, high-back chairs sat in the middle of massive windows with curtains that swept the floor, a chair lounge, fireplace, gold wall scones, and fresh flowers were in crystal vases. As I continued forward, I noticed doors on either side.

"This is yours," She stepped aside as I entered my bedroom, well for the next few days. Shades of creams and rich reds were throughout the room. The bed was large enough for a family of ten, with lush high-back chairs, another fireplace, and beautiful paintings adorning the walls. "My room is cream and purple, although the layout is identical. You have a private bathroom and the kitchen you walked past when you came in," Emma said as I continued to admire the beautiful room.

"Thanks, Emma," I blurted out, and she beamed.

"You're welcome to everything, especially my clothes," She must have noticed I didn't have a bag. Emma ordered room service while I showered and changed into silk pajamas. The silk pajamas were soothing as I slid into the bed; I told Emma that she had ruined my love for cotton. She laughed as I snuggled beneath the covers to wait for my food. But, Exhaustion, the fluffy pillows, intricately woven sheets, and silk pajamas got the best of me, and I quickly fell asleep.

When the morning came, I buried my head deeper inside the pillow as the noise from the busy streets slowly filled the room. I reluctantly crawled from beneath the covers. It was my first full day in Paris, and my search for the man on the ledge was about to begin. If I found him, he could answer my questions. Why did I have such vivid nightmares? Why was this man in them? Why was he protecting me from the four-cloaked men? I wanted to know who this man was to me, and I needed to understand this because I could not get past the feeling that we were connected.

Last night's nightmare renewed my confidence because it revealed something that none of my other dreams had a face: his face.

I plopped down in a chair and kicked my legs over the arm. Emma must have left early that morning. There was a row of clothes tossed over the sofa. She laid them out as promised; I placed one of the sundresses on the bed and grabbed the city map off the table to scan the areas to search. The only problem was there were hundreds of hotels, and they looked the same. My frustration was at an all-time high as I climbed beneath the stream of hot water, allowing the powerful jets to massage my scalp and back. It came to me as I rinsed the remaining conditioner from my hair.

I had been going about this all wrong. Uncle Mike told me once when I went with him and Phillip on a hunting trip, "You cannot overanalyze things because that only gets in the way. You must feel." He sometimes said when he closed his eyes, it enabled him to refocus and find the prey. I remembered Uncle Mike twisting around, pulling back his bow, and shooting a swift arrow through a large buck's jugular. That must have been why I buried that lesson deep within my conscience.

I would have to clear my mind. My first vision when I stepped off the plane was the word 'Lafayette.' At the time, I thought that was his name; it meant something else. My hair whipped water droplets across the room as I hurried to Emma's laptop. I typed in 'streets with the name Lafayette,' but it was a quick dead end. When I searched for hotels with the name, I was surprised to find *Hotel Concorde la Fayette and hoped this was the* answer.

Three hours later, I stood in the hallway of the 33rd floor. My attempt to access the roof had failed, primarily because of the door chain, which triggered the fire alarm when I tried to squeeze through the small space. Security directed guest to the fire exits and out of the lavish hotel. I tried to sneak away to find another stairwell, hoping the door would open. Instead, an extremely rude firefighter grabbed my arm and escorted me outside. As I scanned the building for another opening, a familiar pull forced me to turn around. The butterflies settled deep within my belly, their delicate wings tingling my skin, followed by a tug. I glanced up, awestruck. As he walked past me, he had the same dark hair, a muscular frame beneath a tailored suit, and that intoxicating smell of sandalwood and honeysuckle. I followed him in a trance-like state down the busy street, wanting my limbs to cooperate and move faster. Unfortunately, my agility dissipated the moment he came into view. I stumbled down the sidewalk, bumping into people, oblivious of the raised pavements, and eventually losing him at 16 Boulevard Pershing.

"He's okay," I sighed, relieved as the words repeated themselves in my head. I stood there feeling comforted, knowing the man was alive and safe. A taxi pulled up at the curb, and I quickly jumped in.

As I looked at the busy people crowding the streets, I thought about my task for the next day. Seeing he was safe was the beginning; I still needed to meet him.

CHAPTER NINE

BEAUTIFUL DISASTER

T he muscles in my face had begun to ache from the smile that refused to narrow. This must be what beaming feels like, I thought to myself, because I swear that a light switched on inside me. The glow permeated through my veins, igniting every fiber of my being. I held my hands out to see if my fingertips were glowing and then laughed at the ridiculous thought. The taxi driver gave me a sideways glance over his shoulder. He mumbled words in French so quickly that I could not translate. Finally, the taxi stopped in front of the hotel. I leaned forward to read the meter, rolling my eyes at the inflated cost, before handing him the Euros. As I exited the taxi, I noticed Conner, Braden, and others were leaving. Conner was heavily engrossed in conversation with Braden judging by the excited look on his face; he was talking football.

"Conner," I yelled, thankful my voice carried over the car horns and the stop-and-go traffic. I smiled when he looked up, happy to see a familiar face. He came over and gave me what he would have called a bear hug; he squeezed me so tight thought I heard my ribs crack. Thankfully, I wiggled free of his hold and straightened my dress. Lauren sucked her teeth and rolled her eyes; all that was missing was a hiss and her claws.

"I thought your parents banned you from Paris," Conner said.

His voice was full of excitement.

"We agreed to disagree," I admitted.

"What does that mean?" Conner pried as Lauren came within earshot of our conversation.

"Are we going or not?" Lauren interjected, and for once, I was thankful.

"Sorry, yeah," Conner said flippantly and then turned back to me, "Madi, we can hang out tomorrow unless you want to go on the night tour with us?" He was oblivious to the fuming Lauren standing behind him. I noticed that she elbowed Ashley to get her attention. They folded their arms upon their chests, scowling at me, and a touch of amusement spread across my face. That Ashley jumped aboard team Lauren and the Pink Squad was no surprise. Especially since she refused to respond to my texts or phone calls once Lauren and Conner became an official couple.

"Yeah, Madi, you should come with us," Braden added. I thought Ashley's head would spin off her neck by how quickly she turned to glower at him.

"Thanks; I already promised Emma we would hang out tonight."

"Hopefully, I'll see you in the morning if the Queen of the Damned lets you live through the night," Conner said. I rolled my eyes as he went to rejoin his group. Lauren linked arms with him, and they headed to the tour bus.

I left the hotel early the following day and caught the bus to *Hotel Concorde la Fayette.* After the previous day's incident, I thought it best not to go inside. Instead, I went to a small café across the street, hoping the man might appear. My confidence began to waver when I finished my second latté, and there was still no sign of him; I had ordered water when my body began to tingle from the roots of my hair to the tips of my toes. My eyes went instinctively to the window.

"It's him," I muttered, tossed Euros on the counter, and rushed from the building. For a second, I had complete sight of him, and it felt as if my heart would stop, but as quickly as he appeared, he vanished into the crowd again. I could feel the invisible cords tug at me standing on the sidewalk; I closed my eyes briefly to heed Uncle Mike's advice again — taking in the sounds around me. The buzz from cars zipping by splashes of water hitting the pavement, heeled footsteps, and busy chatter began to fade away. I opened my eyes and placed one foot in front of the other, following the sensation down the street.

"Are you lost?" an unfamiliar voice asked, shattering my focus. I turned to see a pale man with stringy brown hair and deep brown eyes, "Can I help you?" As he stared, a slow smile spread across his face.

"No, I'm fine, thank you," I stepped around him as the feeling returned. Every part of me needed to know this mysterious man. I spun to look across the street again when a car sped past and splattered my jeans with the dark, murky water. "Damn!" I looked down at my clothes and then back across the street, although I knew he was gone.

I jumped back from the curb as another car flew past, only to bump into a cranky old man. "Stupid American!" he yelled and continued to curse at me in French; droplets of saliva flew from his mouth. As I stepped away from him, my foot landed in the dirty, brown puddle, splashing the man with the murky water. I would have apologized, but he let loose another tirade of French curses. Yep, I had successfully pissed him off.

A feeling of complete and utter aggravation washed over me— he was so close I clenched my fists. My eyes had to be glowing because I was officially mad as hell. I wiped the rain from my face and tried desperately to refocus as I pictured him. Was he merely a figment of my imagination? Was he a ghost that haunted my nights and consumed my days? The dream of him being in danger was the universe's way of screwing with my head. Whatever the reason, I needed to know him. Something deep inside told me if he were okay, then I would be too, and I needed to believe that. I walked back toward the hotel with my head still full of questions.

The man that had offered me help minutes before was about five feet behind me. I extended my stride and tried to move quickly when he touched my arm.

"My name is Giorgio," he spoke in English; however, his thick French accent was undeniable. He grabbed my wrist, and I jerked away from him. My movement was so quick I nearly tripped off the curb as a small, red car came speeding past.

"Don't touch me!" I screamed. I turned to keep walking when he did the strangest thing. He folded his right arm across his chest, extended his left, and bowed deeply at the waist. When he stood upright, there was a strange look on his face; I couldn't tell if it were a smile or a grimace — then decided, either way, it was creepy.

"I've cleared my entire schedule to show you the sights," he said as if my screaming at him had meant nothing — this man must think I bathed in 'stupid' this morning.

"Appreciate the offer, but no!" I hurried down the street before he could offer anything else. Shot another glance over my shoulder to find that he was still standing there with his dark eyes focused on me — luckily, a bus pulled up at a stop one block ahead, and I rushed to catch it.

What a weirdo. Who bows? As I entered the hotel lobby, I reasoned that this was not the 18th century. The elevator could not move fast enough. The Bellhop breathed a not-so-subtle sigh of relief when the elevator reached my floor.

After a quick shower and wardrobe change, I read the note Emma left on the table. It said she would be back later after visiting with her brothers. I wrote a quick, 'Okay, have fun,' and placed it back on the table before I headed out again.

Conner knocked as I reached the door. "Hey, we're heading to the bar down the block. Want to come?" I glanced over his shoulder to see Lauren and Ashley giving me the stink-eye.

"No, you go. I have plans," I told them. They all seemed surprised, which meant my loser status had escalated.

"Are you going with Emma?" Conner inquired.

"No, I'm going on one of those night tours," I responded, feeling like he was interviewing me again. I almost laughed at his inquisitive Sherlock Holmes impression. Conner was funny in that way; if there was a story, he wanted to be the first to know.

"The only night tour was last night," he retorted. I bit my lip and tried to think of a more convincing place I could be going so late at night.

"She can take care of herself! Damn, you act like you like her!" Lauren yelled in an irritated tone.

"That's not even a little funny!" I commented, looking over Conner's shoulder to make eye contact with Lauren. Unfortunately, my defense offended Conner, who stormed off with Ashley and Braden behind him. Lauren motioned for them to take the elevator without her.

"I don't care what Conner says. You're nothing but a manstealing bitch! If you think I'm going to let you take Conner away from me," Lauren ranted. I smiled right before slamming the door in her face. My mom taught me that if I didn't have anything nice to say, it was best not to say anything at all. Truthfully, slamming the door was the politest thing I could have done.

I left the hotel, ready to start my search again. Instead of taking a taxi or a bus, I wandered the local streets. Conner and Emma said we were staying near the best nightlife in Paris, so I figured I might have a good chance of seeing him nearby. The atmosphere on the street had changed. The flower carts were — packed up, and bar signs now illuminated the sidewalks. Drunken partygoers, who struggled as much with walking as I struggled with calculus, replaced the busy families. As I walked further, the crowds began to dwindle. Narrow alleys with shadowy entrances seemed to be the only thing ahead. The gargoyles perched atop the Gothic buildings gave me eerie feelings. The pungent smell of garbage and decaying flesh filled my nostrils, and I looked down to see a dead cat next to a dumpster. I used my shirt to shield my nose from the smell and continued down *Rue Richard Lenoir*, keeping my eyes peeled for any sight of the man. There was a group of men painting graffiti signs to the right. The shortest of the group shouted, "You look a little lost, tourist. You should book this site-seeing tour in my pants," as he grabbed his crotch and began to gyrate against his hand. Well, that was, the safest sex he would ever have — I scrunched my nose as the others laughed. Neanderthals, I scoffed silently and hurried around the corner and back near a populated area. My pulse slowed when I confirmed that the men had not followed me. I had barely caught my breath when a tall, skinny man bumped into me and yanked the purse. Emma had allowed me to borrow. I raced after him at full speed, maneuvering through the crowd.

I crashed into a man, although his body felt more like a wall, and the force propelled me backward; he caught me before I hit the wet pavement. I found myself in his arms with my body held tightly against his. "I'm sorry, he took my purse; it has all my documents and passports," I stammered as I pointed toward the disappearing figure. The man released his hold on my waist and ran after him so fast it was as if he were merely a blur. I followed them however found it impossible to catch up. Tears of frustration began to pool in my eyes, knowing that if my passport were lost, I would need to call my parents. They would kill me.

My thoughts of boarding school dissipated when the man appeared back in front of me in what seemed like seconds and placed the purse in my hand. I had to remind myself to breathe. My eyes were transfixed on the beautiful man as he stared down at me, and I found myself lost in his spectacular silver eyes. It was the ghost, but he was no longer a figment of my imagination — he was standing right before me. The thin white shirt clung to his strong arms, muscular chest, and sculpted abs. His hair was the color of night, and the wavy strands danced across his perfectly chiseled face. My head tilted to the side to admire his radiant bronze-colored skin.

He looked like a high-paid male model from the hottest magazines. Those eyes told me I couldn't have been more wrong; they were intense and almost dangerous. Although, fear was the furthest thing from my mind. My body reacted to his closeness, and I willed myself to relax.

"Are you alright?" I asked as images of him standing on the ledge washed over me. He appeared bewildered by the question. I watched as his thick brows narrowed, his silver eyes darkened, and his head tilted slightly as he stared at me.

"You should leave now. Never travel the streets alone; it's not safe for you to be out here," the seriousness of the man's tone told me more than the words he had spoken. This man — seemed concerned about my safety as I was about his. "Did you hear me? You are not safe here," he said with a forcefulness that should have moved me. Although my brain had not relayed that message to my feet, so I remained. We were standing close enough that if I lifted my hand, I could touch him, my fingers curled around Emma's purse instead.

"I've never felt safer in my life," the words streamed from my lips as he began to walk away. He turned and began to approach me again. My stomach felt as though someone had tied it in knots. His eyes urged me to flee as he brushed the stray lock of curls back from my face. He smelled wonderful, I thought to myself as he lowered his hand, leaving whispers of a fragrance that I suppose only belonged to him. I closed my eyes for a moment inhaling his scent until my lungs threatened to burst. My eyes shot open when I heard him say something in Spanish.

He lifted his hand again; the coldness of his fingers brushed gently across my cheek, "This place is not safe for you," he spoke in English as he took another step closer, sealing the space between us. The edge of his jacket touching me — the tips of his boots met mine — my hair swept around us, enfolding him in my curly tresses. He leaned forward, our scents intermingled, and my insides fluttered. "This place is not safe for you," he repeated. I closed my eyes again, waiting for his lips to touch mine. My wait was in vain. Even before my eyes opened, I knew that he was gone.

The rain that had begun as a fine mist developed into a downpour. Reluctantly, I returned to the hotel, completely unaware of the people as they raced by me to get out of the rain. I edged closer to the curb to keep them from bumping into me. When I reached the corner, my feet refused to move another step. The hem of my jeans up to my knees was now soaked with dirt, rain, and oil from the cars breezing through the busy city streets. I stood there, allowing the rain to shower down upon me. I loved the sound of the rain as the liquid reverberated off the sidewalk, umbrellas, cars, and me. My smile deepened as his words swirled around me, replaying them like lyrics to a beautiful song.

When I reached the other side, Emma was standing there. "Where have you been?" she questioned. She pulled me under her umbrella and guided me to the hotel. "I've been looking for you." The concern in her eyes brought me out of the spell the stranger had placed over me.

"Sorry, I was searching for, oh, I didn't get his name," I mumbled. "Anyway, this guy stole your purse; I was freaking out until the most beautiful man I've ever seen got it back for me," I managed to say.

"I'm not sure what you said, but from now on, please let me know when you want to come out at night. I'll come with you, or you can ask the blond brothers. They would follow you anywhere." Emma smiled half-heartedly. "You look a little pale. Are you sure he didn't hurt you?" She pulled her room key from her purse.

"No, not a single scratch," I replied. My smile began to grow as images of the man came to mind.

When we entered the room, there were two men near the window. Their eyes focused on something outside. Emma must have noticed the confusion that had suddenly replaced my dazed look.

"Madi, I want you to meet Austin," Emma said, introducing me to the man as he turned around. His muscular body was almost intimidating, although his smile was unexpectedly warm. Austin's features reminded me of someone else. He had wavy, jet-black hair and radiant bronze skin, although his most striking feature was his silver eyes. I knew it was rude to stare so openly at someone, but I found it impossible to look away.

"It's nice to meet you." I hesitated for a second and examined his familiar features' before I extended my hand.

"The pleasure is mine," Austin laughed as his cold fingers folded over mine.

"This is Lucas Michaels. He's an old family friend. He can be a handful at times, but he knows to behave himself," Emma said, giving him a determined look as she walked back to the window with Austin.

"You, my dear, are a breath of fresh air," Lucas whispered. He pressed my wet hand to his cold lips — which seemed to warm instantly. I eased my hand away when he began to inspect my fingers — most people were — taken aback by the heat that permeated from me. However, most were kind enough to pretend not to notice. Lucas continued to scrutinize me. He was leaner than Austin and inches shorter. Lucas's short brown spiked hair and eyes were darker than I'd ever seen, almost black. Aside from the hair, Lucas resembled Emma more than her brother did. He had a gorgeous complexion like hers, and as they stood next to each other, I thought about what a beautiful couple they would make.

"It's nice to meet you too," I said, blushing, before, I called over Lucas' shoulder, "I'm going to get out of these wet clothes." Emma nodded and then returned her attention back to the window.

"Can I help?" Lucas offered. I gave him a dirty look, which he only seemed to enjoy more, and felt as though his eyes followed me from the room.

I changed clothes slowly as I replayed the night's events. The way my body reacted when he held me. His silver eyes illuminated the night. I recited his words again as my subconscious formulated alternative endings to our meeting, all of which concluded with a kiss. The skin on my fingers and toes had more wrinkles than a Shar-pei when I finally left the shower.

After putting on my pajamas, I joined Emma in the living room, Austin and Lucas were gone.

"They could've stayed longer, Emma; it's not a problem." I sank down next to her. Emma shook her head. "What's wrong?"

"Nothing, hanging out with them was great," she admitted.

"You should go; I will be fine here."

"No, I made plans with them tomorrow," Emma explained somberly as she walked over to the window.

"Do they live here?"

"They are crashing at Annaliese's right now," Emma said. She had mentioned this Annaliese before.

"We could stay there instead of here; that way, you could see them every day," and this room is expensive.

"I wanted to stay in the city. But unfortunately, Annaliese lives an hour away, and I want to have fun with you," Emma said.

"What do you say we order room service and find a movie to watch?" I asked. Thankfully, she agreed to the movie — I grabbed pillows from my room, plopped down on the floor with the remote in hand, and flipped through the channels. Emma sat down beside me in her purple silk pajamas and high-heel slippers. I shook my head because, of course, Emma would have nothing less than high-heel slippers.

"I'm glad you're here," she said. She meant it, but something was weighing on her mind.

"Thanks for sharing your suite with me. And if all the guys here are as gorgeous as the one, I met tonight, I owe you big time."

"Madi, you have boys all over town that would love to date you.

You've never given them a chance, not even the blond brothers. What is it about this stranger you like so much?" Emma asked as her face lit up. I could tell this would be a better distraction than a movie. I prepared myself to tell her everything as I wiggled deeper into the pillow beside her.

"He reminds me of someone from my dreams, only it's more than that," I started.

"Tell me about this mystery man in your dreams," she urged as she gathered a pillow beneath her chin.

"I've always had vivid dreams and nightmares, but there's one that has haunted me for years. It always begins with me on an old cobblestone street. There are shops, flower stands, bakeries, and people with bright smiles but dark eyes. I continue, suddenly alone, on the murky, abandoned streets. Dead silence falls around me — then the sound of fast-approaching footsteps. Their footsteps get louder, closer — I see them — four men, their faces hidden in the shadows of black cloaks. They are after me — this I know instinctively — I run. The buildings begin to blur as I speed down the street. I turn left at the corner and cut down the alley. They run right past me only to stop a second later — their footsteps are approaching me again. My only thought is to run — that is when I feel him, like a guardian, he waits there in the shadows." I paused, "I don't know his name or why he's there, but the feeling of his presence is undeniable. That's usually when I wake up." My hands were trembling when I finished recounting the nightmare.

"You believe he's real?" Emma asked when I finished the sorted and unbelievable tale of my reoccurring nightmare.

"My earliest memory of the horrible dreams began in kindergarten, with slight deviations here and there. However, the man's protective presence and those angry cloaked men never changed. I know that he's real." I smiled at how ridiculous it sounded, even to me. Emma raised her eyebrows, "Don't look at me that way. The sadness in his eyes — I recognized. Something inside me wants nothing more than to be the reason he smiles," I continued, directing my gaze to the ceiling, "For a fraction of a second, there with him, it felt like the whole world stopped, and I could breathe." I looked back at Emma, half-expecting to see her eyes filled with laughter — surprised to see a veil of sadness instead.

"If you like him, you should find out more about him. Even if he isn't the one, you can have a little fun while you're here. You should live a little! You're in Paris; anything's possible!" Emma chided as she walked to the mirror and pulled her hair into a carefully sculpted ponytail. "I'm going to go with you tomorrow to be on the safe side," she added, clarifying that I would be wasting my breath if I tried to argue with her.

"I'll be fine; you go with Austin and Lucas; please don't worry about me," I reassured Emma as she reclaimed her spot on the floor. She nodded as she turned on the TV to flip through the channels.

I whispered his words again, allowing them to float over me like a cool breeze. Emma's laughter stopped me, and I looked up at her, embarrassed.

"Hey, if you taught me more Spanish, I would know how to say it right," I wrinkled my nose at her.

"Where did you hear that," her voice still filled with laughter.

"The man I met tonight, I'm not sure I said it right. Do you know what it means?"

"Yes," Emma leaned back and gave me her full attention.

"Tell me."

"He said, such a beautiful disaster," she could barely contain herself while I silently fumed.

"Sounded much more romantic in Spanish," I tossed a pillow at her.

"Yes, it does."

CHAPTER TEN
MUSE

Note to self — blue jean shorts on vinyl seats while riding on a non-air-conditioned bus — horrible idea; I came to that realization as I lifted my leg off the vinyl again, frowning as the thin sheen of sweat glued my legs to the seat like adhesive. Also, using the folded brochure for the *Musee d'Orsay* as a fan did little to combat the heat. The city was dreadfully warm, even with the cloudy skies. I felt confined on the overcrowded bus, and the humidity only worsened matters. However, there was no reason for me to complain.

Slowly lifting my sunglasses to massage my temples my guilt, a smidge of frustration and a healthy dose of exhaustion to boot — left my head pounding. *Last night I dreamt of my mom — the disappointment in her voice as I tried to plead my case about coming to Paris broke my heart. She ran out of the house and into the forest, and I raced behind her, calling out to her repeatedly. Only she disappeared, and I was alone in the bleakness of the woods. I awakened drenched in my own perspiration. After peeling out of the tattered and mud-streaked pajamas, I slid into the plush hotel robe. My heart continued to pound loudly beneath my chest, so I curled up in the chair and hugged my knees tight to my chest. And that was how I spent the rest of my night.*

"Are you okay?" Conner asked as he eased into the seat beside me. Lauren had moved to the front with the pink squad, a deep scowl developed on her face when she looked back at us.

"Yeah, I'm fine." The scripted words came from my lips as I

97

focused again on cooling myself with the makeshift fan. He sat there for minutes, green eyes squinting as they examined me. I tucked myself deeper into the seat, waving the fan vigorously; a small part of me felt guilty for ignoring Conner; however, I was too exhausted to deal with the drama that came with talking to him. Thankfully, Conner shrugged his shoulders and jumped back into his original seat.

My phone vibrated in my pocket, and I stood up to pull it out as the bus hit another pothole. My thighs slapped the vinyl seat, which gained everyone's full attention, thankfully; I was at least able to retrieve the phone before landing. Conner looked at me suspiciously, and I shifted to face the window.

"Hey," Blake's voice came through the phone grainy; I suppose one or both of our cell phone reception was to blame. "You get my messages."

"No, and hello to you too," I jokingly said as I flipped to the missed message on my home screen. Blake had sent me a picture of him night surfing. He was wearing a custom-made wetsuit on a glow-in-the-dark surfboard. "I am so jealous right now; thanks for rubbing it in! That looks like so much fun!"

"Madi, the water is incredible. I wish you were here. You would love night surfing!" His enthusiasm made me forget about the stifling conditions on the bus. "Enough about me. What's up with you? Does your mom know where you are yet?"

"No, I talked to her earlier. I hate lying to her."

"Hey, you know that the shit will get real when you return, right?"

"Yeah, but thanks for reminding me," I hope he noted the sarcasm in my voice.

"Make it count."

"I know your right…"

"Of course, I am," Blake said jestingly.

"Hey, Blake," I leaned forward until my forehead met the back of the seat.

"Yeah," he replied.

"Thanks," I gnawed on my bottom lip; there were so many things that I wanted to talk to him about, "I'll talk to you soon," was all I could muster.

"You bet," he hung up, and I forced my phone back inside my jean pocket. I eased my sunglasses back down the bridge of my nose to hide the tears in my eyes. It was beginning to rain, so I stuck my hand out the window, allowing the cool drops to soothe me.

I heard Ashley groan from the seat in front of me. "Do you have an umbrella?" she leaned over to ask. I glanced over my shoulder, puzzled because Ashley hadn't spoken to me in weeks. The closer Ashley got to Lauren's pink squad, the more like them she became. "Do you have one?" she asked again, "I don't want to get my hair wet."

"Sorry, I…"

"I should have known you wouldn't have one!" Ashley snapped before I could finish my sentence.

"You can share mine," Lauren offered as she sat down in the seat beside Ashley. "What were you thinking? I mean, look at her!" Lauren flipped a thick lock of glossy blonde hair, purposely revealing the deep red circular bruise on her pale skin. Oh, wow, I snickered under my breath, thoroughly amused.

The bus came to a stop; everyone jerked forward and then back again, and Lauren's head slammed into the leather seat.

"Karma," I chuckled softly. I eased into the aisle, only to find myself blocked when Lauren wedged herself in the middle to prevent me from moving forward. She remained there until everyone in front had exited the bus before she rushed up the narrow aisle. The battle between good and evil was waging war inside me; I punched Lauren in the face in one scenario. In the other scenario, I waited for the entire bus to empty before leaving, allowing me time to calm down. Good prevailed this time; I sat back down until they were inside the building. Lauren could keep her surgically altered nose, and her flawless skin would remain unblemished, at least for today.

As I stood at the entrance of the *Musee d'Orsay*, I thought about Blake's words, "Make it count," he was right; I needed to make the best of this time. My parents would ground me for months or ship me off somewhere, meaning I needed to enjoy every second here. *The Musee d'Orsay* should be incredible. I closed my eyes and took a deep breath before entering the museum.

When I found the group, the tour guide explained the sculpture *Nubians*, known as, The *Alligator Hunters*. I saw the African warrior, his spear aimed at the attacking alligator. A beautiful African woman perched to the hunter's left, gripping her two babies in fear. The group remained there; listening to the detailed history behind the sculpture, I was more interested in the paintings.

I walked down the long corridor to the gallery; excitement began to stir as the familiar feeling came over me with the distinctive tug that pulled me toward him. My stomach did a somersault, and I took a deep, ragged breath.

He's here, I thought to myself as I scanned the large room — nothing, but something deep inside me was urging me to search further, and I turned to rejoin the group instead. He came around the corner as I reached to tap Conner on the back — he was speaking with a woman, and I watched as she touched her thin-framed glasses, adjusting them on her nose. She was wearing a tailored business suit with a crisp white blouse. In her left hand, she held a clipboard and, in her right, a cell phone. She must have felt my eyes upon her because our eyes met, hers bright, round, and green, and she began walking toward me as if I were a long-lost friend.

The man stepped in front of her. He babbled in French. The one word I did understand was 'muse.' I reasoned that the woman could be his muse and then felt my heart sink at the thought. She peeked around his broad shoulders and shot me a quick smile before leaving. I stood there like an idiot, unsure of what to say. He was only a couple of feet away from me. My heart was racing, but my mouth felt paralyzed as I watched him walk in the same direction as the woman.

"Thank you!" I shouted impulsively. My words were so loud that people began to stare. And he turned and began to walk back toward me. I started to fidget and forced myself to breathe when he stopped close to me, our bodies nearly touching.

"You're welcome." The silkiness of his voice and how his intense silver eyes looked at me sent a shiver down my spine. "I see you left the purse at the hotel," he continued. He smiled — I locked my knees to prevent them from buckling. I continued to stare at him, unable to speak with him standing so close. He stood there waiting for my reply before he turned and disappeared around the corner.

Conner bumped me in the side, knocking me out of my trance and onto the floor. "Are you okay?" Conner asked.

"Yeah, I'm fine," I said, still dazed from the encounter. I replayed the conversation and realized this wasn't a conversation. My dream man had talked while I said nothing; what made it worse was that I let him walk away. If it were humanly possible to kick myself, I would have.

The tour guide was leading the group in the direction of the man. This was the one time I was okay with staying with the group.

"Why didn't you come with us? I thought you wanted to see the statues," Conner asked as we rejoined our class.

"No, I wanted to see the paintings," I said absently, "Conner?" I began, wanting to ask him if he saw the man, to assure myself that he was real. The feeling returned, freezing the question on the tip of my tongue. I looked over to see him in the corner. His silver gaze studied mine as if he could see through me. I stepped toward him and right into Conner. "Sorry," I braced the palm of my hand on his shoulder to steady myself. My stomach was not only doing somersaults but back flips and cartwheels.

"No problem," Conner said, and for a split second, I thought he blushed. So, I quickly removed my hand from his shoulder, tucking my fingers inside the pocket of my jeans.

Lauren motioned for Conner to rejoin the group, "Okay," he said agitatedly. Her eyes continued to burn holes into him from the front of the group.

"Sorry, Madi, I'll be right back," he said, racing to Lauren's side.

I glanced to the corner, but the mystery man was gone. 'How in the hell did he move so fast?' I fumed but reluctantly followed the group. The tour guide offered brief descriptions of the paintings.

Conner and the other boys began to laugh and crack jokes when we came to the painting *Orpheus' Lament*. The Greek musician lay defeated on a deserted beach. His arm was thrown back over his eyes in torment as he clung to the one thing he had left — his lyre. The words' loser,' 'pansy and stupid' sprung from the group. I shook my head at their immature comments, knowing they could not appreciate this man's anguish.

I stopped in front of the painting to admire the beautifully tragic piece as the rowdy group moved on. I thought to myself, I knew how the man felt. He had lost someone so important to him that he thought he couldn't go on, as I did. The memory of Nic's prom came streaming back, forcing tears to gather in my eyes. I felt incomplete without him, even now.

"Do you know the story behind this painting?" His silky voice made me smile as he approached and stopped beside me.

"Well, according to the myth, Orpheus was set to marry his love, Eurydice. Tragically, a venomous snake bit Eurydice on her way to their wedding. She died before reaching Orpheus. When he discovered Eurydice, Orpheus sang such a mournful song that the Gods wept and urged him to descend into the underworld where he could convince Hades to allow Eurydice's return." The man stepped forward slowly, and my pulse quickened as he shifted to look at me. "Orpheus played his lyre and sang for Hades so beautifully that Hades granted the couple a second chance. Hades ordered him to walk ahead of Eurydice to challenge Orpheus' trust in him, never looking back until they both reached the upper world. As they walked, Orpheus became nervous that Eurydice was no longer behind him. He turned to check, failing Hades' test, and seeing Eurydice disappear into the darkness forever."

"People believe that Orpheus should have died alongside Eurydice," I smiled up at him, feeling proud I had spoken more than two words.

"Orpheus may not have died physically with Eurydice; however, his life ended the moment her life did. His days consumed with grief and regret," his voice like a gentle melody. He shifted to the left, but my eyes remained locked on him.

"Regret," I questioned curiously.

"Yes, because he allowed his one true love to die. If he had never asked for her hand in marriage, Eurydice would have lived," he reasoned, shrugging his shoulders as if his explanation was common sense.

"You are implying that he wished their love never existed. Yet, he dared to love her," I managed. "Their love, although short, was not a tragedy; it was beautiful," Our eyes locked on each other, and a grin spread across my face.

"I believe you are a mythological romantic," he inferred, although I could tell he was impressed by my answer.

"Mythology is the basis of every great story," my words faded when he moved toward the window. I stepped forward, stopping before I got too close.

"So, you're not shy after all," he teased, and I laughed for the first time since arriving here. His nearness provided me with a sense of peace, calming me like the ocean's waves, and like the ocean, he invited me. "You smile, and it stops raining," he said as he gestured to the window. He looked back at me, and I slowly took one step closer — to assure myself that he was real. One more step, I thought, but the sound of laughter broke the trance-like spell.

His gaze rested on the group of boys Conner was with; they were now finding humor in the nude paintings. The woman he had been talking to earlier frowned. She then directed the tour guide to skip over a room with a closed door. The sign read, 'private collections.'

"What's in there?" I questioned.

"That collection is not ready for public viewing," he responded suspiciously. My eyes followed his back to the woman before she disappeared behind the door. When I turned back to look at him, he was smiling at me, and I couldn't help but blush. I bit my lip. "Get it together, Madi," I thought to myself.

"Are you an artist?" I asked, wondering how he knew so much about the museum.

"I dabble in paintings," he said modestly. I could have stared at him for hours; everything about this man appealed to me.

"Your paintings, are they part of the private collection? Can I see them?" I asked, trying not to sound overly excited. I looked back at the door to see a gorgeous couple come out. They looked at me and smiled. Why were they looking at me with familiarity? Had I lost my grasp on reality? Here I was, talking to a man that might not be real while being paranoid about people staring at me. I tried to shake it off, as my over-active imagination.

"You said the paintings weren't ready for viewing." My eyes narrowed.

"Special viewings are held for collectors only," he said defensively. He watched the couple leave before giving me his undivided attention.

"Perhaps I'm a collector," I said, lifting my chin and speaking in a laughable French accent — at least judging from the humor dancing in his eyes.

"You do not strike me as a collector; perhaps you would inspire a collection or an obsession," he whispered.

"What would you name that collection?" I teased.

"Whatever you desire," he said with a seriousness that almost made me a believer. "She Walks in Beauty," he offered, and the air hitched in my chest before exiting. I turned my gaze from him. The heat of his stare settled deep within me as I recalled the words of that poem, worrying my bottom lip. He recited the poem, and I breathed his words in, committing each syllable to memory. My heart swelled, and I shifted nervously onto my heels — tilted my head to the side when I noticed the woman again that he was speaking to earlier glance our way. She smiled before she ducked back inside the private room.

"Who is she?" I should have stopped myself, but I needed to know.

"She's the curator and a friend," he responded as his smile deepened. Again, the sparks of something that felt like dislike or jealousy flickered beneath my skin. 'Why did I dislike this woman?'

She seemed friendly. She is beautiful. If she had not been speaking to him — if she had not seen his paintings — or had so much access to him — then she would not have mattered at all.

I glanced at the door again, "When you said, 'dabble in paintings,' I can assume that was an understatement," I said, half questioning.

"Your group is leaving," he said. I turned to look at the group and realized that everyone was on their way outside.

"What's your name?" I asked, quickly turning back to him.

The question escaped my lips before I noticed he was no longer there. I sighed and reluctantly left the museum.

When I boarded the bus, I could hardly hold my excitement.

"Who was that guy?" Conner asked as I passed his seat. My delight bubbled over; someone besides me had seen him. 'He's real!' I thought, stopping myself from shouting it aloud.

CHAPTER ELEVEN
TANGLED WEB

I awoke to the sound of A Mother's Prayer, the ringtone for my mom that she chose. I scrambled out of bed and tripped over my twisted damp sheets before I reached the phone — silence. My mom's picture popped up on the screen a second later, right before Celine Dion could belt out another note — I answered.

"Hello," my voice was breathy, and I knew I needed to compose myself.

"Madison," she said, "Is everything alright?"

"Yes, I'm fine," well, that is true, I think, as I glared down at my torn pajamas. There were scratches on my arm and legs, and I touched them, my face frowning when I felt the puckered skin on my cheek. I went to my feet and checked the mirror, thankful there weren't any other marks.

"I called you last night twice, and Margaret, neither of you answered." My mom replied. I could hear the concern in her voice, and I felt a wave of guilt for the lie that I knew would be my reply.

"Margaret's phone has been messing up, missed calls or dropped, I think," I swallowed, and there was a bitter taste in my mouth. "My phone fell in the lake yesterday; I had to use the blow dryer to dry it out, sorry," that last part was genuine because I was sorry for having to lie to her. Once she learned the truth, I knew that she would never trust me again, and that knowledge brought tears to my eyes.

"You have to be careful in the forest Madison," my mom said, "I'm glad to hear your voice."

"Yeah, it's good to hear from you too. How are things going with the little bambino?" I asked.

"No news, is good news, or so they say, I'm not sure about," she stopped mid-sentence as if realizing it was me because she followed with, "What are you doing? I know that your friends are away right now. I hate that you are there alone. We should come home."

"No, please stay there. We still have six weeks before I go back to school. There will be time for us to spend together. Mom, I'm sixteen, you don't have to call me daily. Please enjoy yourself." I reasoned.

"Well, if everything is alright, I will call you Friday," that will give me four days before I will have to lie to her again. "Please be careful. Madison, I love you," she whispered, and hot tears stung my cheek.

"I love you more." I hung up quickly and sank to the floor. That conversation with my mom made it official, I, Madison Bailey Ryan, was a bold-face-liar. The stanza of the poem I used for one of my English assignments, 'Oh, what a tangled web we weave. When first we practice, to deceive.'

Emma called hours later to invite me on a shopping spree. I asked her for a rain check, and she made me promise that we would do something tomorrow. I agreed, and she hung up the phone. I took a long bubble bath, phoned room service, and ordered a fresh chicken salad on a croissant with pecans, grapes, and apples; my mouth watered at the thought. The person that took my order suggested a truffle-inspired cupcake. He said it was incredible. He was right; well, to be honest, everything was delicious. My chicken salad croissant was perfect, and I savored every delightful mouthwatering bite of the cupcake. The rest of my day went by quickly, too quickly. I spent it flicking through stations, painting my toe and fingernails. I even flat-ironed my hair; boredom was proving great for my self-care.

I raced down the cobblestone street as my mom's screams pierced through the still air; the urgency in her voice compelled me to move faster into the darkness. I paused briefly, smelled the air, and headed toward the forest. The scent of sweet jasmine belonged to my mom. As I trudge further into the woods, branches reach for me, slapping my face and tearing at my clothing, but I rush ahead. My mom was near, I told myself, moving closer. Her screams subsided, and I felt a warm breeze blow against my ear when she whispered, "Madison, you must leave Paris before the VHW discovers you." I shuddered as the ominous feeling overtook me.

"Who are they?" I cried back at her.

"Madison, leave now," my mom pleaded as her voice faded away.

A knock on the door woke me, but I lay there a little longer; I had dreamt of my mom again, and I thought that the problem with vivid dreams and nightmares is that they stay with you. They become a part of you. I could still smell the jasmine mingling in the air.

I opened the door to see Conner standing there in his sweats. We had talked about going running in the mornings but have yet to discuss a date or time, for that matter. Lauren skipped up beside him seconds later in her running gear. She was wearing a pair of white shorts and a pink tank top. I looked at Conner, who shrugged his shoulders. He had told me that Lauren hated to run. I knew she was joining us to keep an eye on me, the 'man-stealing bitch.' The thought was so ridiculous I almost laughed. I stuck my finger up, signaling for him to give me a minute — he nodded and draped his arm over Lauren's shoulder — I closed the door once they left the room.

I tossed on a pair of black shorts, a white tank, and running shoes, gathered my hair into a quick messy bun, did my stretches and jotted Emma a quick note.

I hope you had fun yesterday. We should go to the market later. I have so much to tell you!

M.

Conner and Lauren were already outside when I reached the lobby. It was still dark outside, although there was a silvery tint to the sky, signaling that daylight was near.

"Did you stretch?" I asked Lauren.

"Oh yeah, she stretched," Conner said as he elbowed Lauren lightly. She giggled, and I nearly threw up.

"We'll stay on *Rue Saint Martin*, and if we get separated, we can meet back here."

Conner nodded as he and Lauren started jogging down the street. Her stance was awkward, and Conner would be annoyed by the end of their run. Once my iPods were positioned and the volume was a satisfactory level, I raced down the close to abandoned streets. Sprinkles of people slowly made their way along the sidewalks instead of swarms. The traffic, however, remained heavy; cars buzzed past, and the taxis honked their horns every few seconds. I took a deep breath, increased my speed, and felt my heart rate accelerate, feeling a little closer to freedom each time my feet hit the pavement. Conner shot me an irritated look as I raced past him because he had to slow his pace for Lauren. The thrill of running excited me, and I pushed myself harder without hesitation down the empty sidewalk. The adrenaline pulsated through my veins, and I ran until my legs ached and refused to take another step. My pace slowed to a walk and my heart rate became steady as I explored the streets. When I reached a crossroad, a familiar sensation washed over me. He was close. I retraced my steps to the hotel and saw him crossing the street. He stopped right in front of me and smiled.

"You again," he exclaimed, his eyes brightening as they rested upon mine. "Where are you off to this morning?" he asked suspiciously.

"I'm running."

"We have taxis," he teased.

"Yeah, sounds boring," I tugged at the end of my ponytail. My dream guy smiled when I lifted my heels off the ground, and the man's eyes went to my legs. I thought they were my best asset, more dancers than runners' legs. I peeked from beneath my lashes; the look in his eyes remained good-humored, which meant at least — I received points for being entertaining.

"Are you going to the museum?" I questioned, seeing his

tailored grey Italian business suit. He must have a tailor in the city because I have never seen clothing fit this nicely on any man.

"Yes, for a meeting," his eyes flickered.

"Good to see you again," I said but frowned when I noticed him glancing down at his watch.

"Touché," he said.

"I'm going to *Marche d Aligre* around 2:00," I stammered, "Maybe we'll run into each other again."

"Perhaps," he responded as he brushed a stray hair from my face, shivers went up my spine, and I found it hard to stay balanced.

"I-I should go too," I stuttered once my words finally formed. My dream guy appeared thoroughly entertained — still scoring big-time in that department — I say to myself. "The market later if you're not too busy."

He nodded and continued down the street. I started back toward the hotel and found myself with renewed energy as I began to run again. The wind blew the wisps of hair around my face as I sprinted harder. I was about three blocks from the hotel when Conner and Lauren stepped out of a café. I slowed to a walk.

"Lauren was hungry," he looked like a toddler whose hands were elbow deep in the cookie jar. My breathing was heavy, and my face started hurting from smiling.

"I don't think she missed us," Lauren pointed out.

"No, I bumped into the man from the museum. I think we're going to meet up at the market," I said with too much excitement.

"You talked to that creepy dude from the museum again?" Conner's eyes narrowed suspiciously.

"If by creepy you mean gorgeous…then yes." I gushed, thinking about him, that suit, those amazing silver eyes, his smile.

"What is wrong with you?" Conner yelled — his tone bordered on anger.

"She's fine! Why does it matter to you?" Lauren snapped.

"I'm looking out for her! She doesn't even know that man's name!" Conner said. He was right; I should have asked for his name. I had at least three opportunities to do exactly that. I can't wait to see him at the market. He always makes me so anxious and thrilled! I hope I can talk to him without stuttering or blushing. It will be the first thing I ask him. If I can manage to say a whole sentence.

"You know these French men are only after one thing!" Conner added. I could almost see the steam rise above Lauren's head.

"I'll see you back at the hotel," my legs were in motion before he could respond.

I went to the room and searched for something to wear. The airline had found my luggage, only nothing felt right for today. I glanced over at the dresses Emma had hanging in the closet, biting my lip as I crossed the suite to her room and began to search through the expensive garments. The sound of the door opening pulled me from my browsing. Emma entered the room, her eyes glistening and skin aglow as if she had come from the spa.

"Shopping?" she teased.

"Sorry, I was going to call if I found something," I admitted while continuing to skim through the dresses, flowered chiffon frocks, embroidered silk cocktails, classic sheaths, far too many to choose from, I realized.

"Where are you going?" Emma asked with an inquisitive look on her face. Oh, right, she had no idea that I had not only met the mystery man. I had conversed with him, sort of.

"I'm meeting... him at the market," I did my best to sound nonchalant but knew I had failed miserably. Emma's eyes widened inquisitively; I could almost see the gears shifting in that cute head of hers. "We have to catch up; so much has happened." I said, "Come to the market with me today." I pleaded, hoping that Emma could meet the man.

"I'd love to go with you," she answered, "Would it be okay if Austin joins us?" She walked toward the door, and I followed her, wondering where she could be going since she had just gotten back.

"Yeah, that's fine," I said slowly. Emma swung the door open, and Austin stood on the other side. I wondered how she knew he was there because I hadn't heard a knock.

"Madi, it's nice to see you again," Austin said as he entered the room.

"It's good to see you too." I went to Emma's room, debating whether to dive into her closet again. Emma opened the door before I had a chance and pulled out a simple, white sundress. "Wow, that, well, it's perfect," my eyes narrowed trying to understand how she moved so quickly. I left the room to get ready.

When I returned, Emma and Austin sat on the couch waiting for me. "Stunning," a familiar voice said from the window, and I turned to see Lucas standing there. "I'm so glad I decided to join," Lucas added, and I blushed. He reached for the doorknob before I had a chance. "Damn, you smell good."

"Thank you, I think," I stepped into the hallway as Emma elbowed him.

"Ouch," Lucas gripped his side as Austin snickered and gave him a look that said, "You should've known better."

We exited the hotel and turned left for the market. Lucas and Austin walked ahead as we followed behind.

"So, you can wear dresses; you needed the right motivation," she teased, and I laughed because I had no defense.

"He is incredible, I saw him again a couple of times since we last spoke," I exclaimed.

"Well, any man that can inspire you to wear a dress, I have to meet," She continued.

"I invited him to the market, so hopefully, today will be the day," I practically skipped down the sidewalk.

We turned the corner, and my eyes widened as the crowded market appeared. The fragrant smell of strawberries, blueberries, and freshly baked loaves of bread captured my attention. The endless rows of fresh fruits and vegetables overwhelm my senses. Still, I remind myself that My Dream Guy was on his way, 'Stay focused,' I mumbled to myself, scanning the stands for my mystery man.

Emma and I chatted about everything; the weather, fashion, the market, and still, there was no site of him. So, I headed to the blueberry stand when they began to discuss the night scene and a couple clubs they should try. I thought the blueberries smelled incredible as I contemplated buying a basket.

"For the lady," Lucas said as he handed me the basket of luscious berries he had bought.

"Thank you," I accepted and pulled out five Euros to repay him.

"That was a gift," he said, refusing to take the money. The blueberries tasted sweeter here; I began to pop them in my mouth. I offered to Emma and Lucas, but they turned them down, and Austin wrinkled his nose in disgust. However, I continued to eat.

"We'll be back in a minute," Emma said as she grabbed Lucas' hand and dragged him around the corner.

"Uh, okay," I muttered, confused, but the two had already disappeared. Looking back at Austin reminded me of the man, and I surveyed the area again. 'Did he ditch me?' I wonder, 'Maybe traffic had delayed him,' I continue to reason.

"I can only imagine how exciting living in such a beautiful place must be. I would travel through all of Europe," I said to Austin.

"Well, Europe can become boring. I thought a quick change of scenery would break up the monotony so I visited the Leaning Tower this morning and found myself wishing it would fall." His voice filled with laughter. I laughed so hard that blueberries bounced from the basket, landed on the ground, and rolled down the street. He seemed pleasantly surprised by my reaction.

"Wait, this morning?" I thought about his comment. "You were in Italy this morning?"

"Yes, I travel fast," he said, winking at me. "One of my many guilty pleasures," he continued. His comment sounded more like a dare.

"I understand. My motorcycle goes fast." I gave him a sly look, and he shot me a surprised grin.

"We should ride sometime," he laughed, and I couldn't tell if he were joking.

"No, we should race, when you visit Nirvana."

"I believe you're serious," he said as he eyed me suspiciously.

"I'll try not to be all girly."

"There's nothing wrong with being girly," Lucas interjected as he and Emma rejoined us. "I have a nice little schoolgirl costume that would look amazing on you." My brow furrowed as I glared at him.

"I would hate to meet the kind of women who give you the impression that your behavior is either wanted or appropriate. If you have that costume, you should wear it for them. Your legs are long, and your features are far more feminine than most women." I scoffed.

"Uh oh, watch out. I've seen Madi when she's angry," Emma warned.

"I didn't realize you were so uptight; please forgive me," Lucas apologized. He appeared remorseful as he offered me his hand, but I refused.

"I'm just allergic to creepy," I retorted; Emma and Austin were both grinning as Lucas stared at me.

"Come on, Don Juan," Austin said to Lucas, "I think we've intruded enough for one day." Lucas winked before he and Austin glided away from the market and around the corner.

Emma turned to me, "Have you seen him?" she asked excitedly as her mouth formed into a smile — I sighed and looked around again before responding.

"No," I said as my shoulders slumped.

"What does he look like?" Emma said with a small plea.

My eyes gleamed as I pictured his gorgeous face and muscular body. "Well, actually, he looks," I began but stopped when a scream pierced the air. Emma and I both turned our attention to the direction the sound had come from. A small girl in a pink dress was sobbing as her mother helped her from the ground. The little girl took her mother's hand, and I noticed the blood oozing from the scrape on the girl's knee as she rose to her feet. The red stream trailed down her leg until it reached her white, frilled sock, leaving a small, circular stain.

"Aw, poor girl," I said, looking back to Emma, but she was nowhere in sight.

Emma's disappearing act lasted the entire night — she bopped into my room at around ten, apologizing for ditching me at the market. I, of course, had to forgive her when she said she had an emergency, although I knew that was a lie. 'Who was I to judge?' Besides, she had promised to make it up to me. Before our class tour, she suggested we go to a bistro blocks down from Notre Dame. Emma said the restaurant was unique, and I agreed to join her.

She was right about the restaurant, beginning with the deep red awning that read VIN des Pyrenees. Inside, postcards and memorabilia were decorated the walls; silently, I wondered about the story behind each postcard. A friendly woman greeted us at the door, weaving us quickly through the restaurant; she placed our menus on the table before gracefully disappearing. Emma lifted the checkered tablecloth to reveal a vintage wine barrel. My smile brightened as I studied the names written across the barrel.

"I knew you would love this place," Emma said as I continued to scan the room — it must have been one of the oldest restaurants in Paris.

"There is so much history here," I pointed to the chalkboard where the day's special was — written in French. The waiter approached the table and introduced himself as Francois. He gave us a subtle bow followed by a genuine smile as he handed us the menus — he seemed, charming. His dark eyes transfixed on Emma when he offered to read the specials in English.

"That won't be necessary, Francois," Emma said. She gave the waiter a friendly smile. His face flushed red.

"Madi, what are you getting?" she asked. She turned her attention to me as the waiter continued to gawk at her. I scanned the menu once more before responding. There were so many dishes that I found it hard to choose.

"The chicken and tomato salad," I said, "What about you?" I peeked over the edge when Emma didn't reply.

"No, thank you," Emma's mouth curved downward as she closed her menu and handed it back to the waiter before holding her hand out to take mine. "Two bottles of water," Emma added when I passed my menu to her.

"You're never hungry." My eyes narrowed as I noticed her staring out the window. "Would you rather go somewhere else?" I followed her gaze to see what she was staring at but saw nothing unusual.

"No, I will get something later." She scanned the room before looking back, her smile forced when the waiter returned with our water. I quickly opened mine and took a huge gulp.

Emma traced her finger over the checkered cloth. "What would you like to do after Notre Dame?" she asked, looking up at me.

"I'm not sure. We could go to the boutiques or the *Musee d'Orsay*," he might be there, or we could sneak into that restricted area. The waiter disrupted my daydream when he returned with my food.

I ate a fork full of salad and tried to understand why everything tasted better in Paris. The grilled chicken salad was my favorite dish, but it was as if I had never tasted it before. The fresh herbs, crisp romaine lettuce, sweet tomatoes, basil, and tender chicken were all good. Emma looked at the food with the same expression I had when my mom would serve Brussel-sprouts. She tried to hide her look of disgust as I continued to eat.

"Would you ladies like anything else?" Francois asked, directing his question toward Emma.

"That will be all, Francois," Emma answered.

The waiter smiled and bowed again slightly. "It was my pleasure." He put the check on the table and winked at Emma as he walked away. Emma grabbed the bill and smiled when she looked over it. She leaned across the table and handed it to me. Francois had written his telephone number on the back.

"You think he likes me?" Emma lifted one of her eyebrows, which made me smile.

"Are you going to call him?" I peeked at Francois from beneath my lashes. His eyes were still firmly planted on Emma. "He's perfect tall, dark, handsome, French. You should call him." My excitement caused Emma's eyes to brighten, but then she quickly shook her head.

"No, that would be a terrible idea," she said, placing the check back on the table.

"You were the one that said, 'You're in Paris; anything's possible!'"

I repeated her advice verbatim and pushed the half-empty plate away. We had a great deal of walking to do, and a full stomach would be painful. My eyes traveled to the check, then back up to her.

"I might call him," Emma reasoned. "He might have a brother. I've never gone on a double date before." She gave me a determined look as her eyebrows went up and down. I thought there would be no double dating unless Francois had a brother who was a tall, dark, silver-eyed stranger. Emma paid and stuffed the check into her purse before we left. We stepped onto the busy sidewalk and reached the intersection when Emma's phone rang. She spoke softly in French, then quickly closed the phone before turning to face me. She bit her lip.

"I hate to do this to you," Emma said as she began to back away from the curb. "I have to go, family drama," she said regretfully, and I knew she hated ditching me again.

"Do you want me to come with you?"

"No, we can hit the boutiques later," Emma offered.

"Yeah, of course, go. Let me know if there is anything I can do." Emma nodded, and I watched as she turned and disappeared into the sea of people.

CHAPTER TWELVE
COLLIDE

As I approached Notre Dame, I was mesmerized by the stunning landscape. The grass sparkled like emeralds in the sun, and the garden looked flawless. I marveled at the colorful stained-glass windows that shone like jewels, bells rang out in harmony, filling the air with music. Notre Dame was a masterpiece of beauty and elegance. The Gothic style was magnificent, and every feature was a work of art. I tilted my head to admire the towering arches before climbing the stairs to enter the sacred place.

I whirled around, feeling a surge of recognition. Could it be MDG? I scanned the crowd at the foot of the stairs, looking for his face among the strangers. I moved to the right, but the feeling faded; So, I turned left, hoping to catch a glimpse. He had to be here; I knew it; I faced the cathedral again and crashed into his chest. His arms came around me. I could feel his hands resting on my lower back.

"I'm sorry," I was too embarrassed to look up.

"There's no need to apologize," he said as he let me go and stepped back. "What were you looking for? Did you lose something?" he asked, tilting his head to the side.

"You," my response took him aback for a moment.

"You knew I was here?" He had a questioning look in his eyes,

"What are you?" he asked, appearing thoroughly perplexed. His question, while offensive, didn't sting the way it used to. My skin was thicker, and I had experienced years of questions about whom and what I was, which had desensitized me.

"What do you mean? I'm human like you, only not as…" unable to finish my sentence, although I wanted to say 'beautiful.'

"You are definitely more than human." His eyes seemed to look right through me.

I shuffled out of the way as a tour group moved toward the cathedral with cameras and maps in hand. Once they moved, his eyes met mine again, and I found it impossible not to smile.

"If we continue running into each other, I'll be forced to believe you're following me," he said, half-joking.

"I was about to say the same thing to you." My voice sounded breathy, I think, and my heart felt as if it were going to jump from my chest. He stepped closer, and his nearness all but consumed me. My legs went wiggly, and my eyes roamed his body freely. He flashed a smile, which caused the warmth to rise to my face. I suddenly remembered a crucial question.

"What's your name?" I asked.

"Jonathan." He stepped back, and I was finally able to breathe normally again.

"Do you have a last name, Jonathan?"

"Spenser, now that I have shared, it's your turn."

"I'm Madison, ah Madison Ryan, but everyone calls me Madi," I told myself to relax and to keep all stupid behaviors to a minimum.

"Would you mind if I called you Madison?" The words flowed out of Jonathan's perfectly shaped lips like a melody. I had never looked at anyone in this way before, and the idea of my lips pressed against his was suddenly the only thing on my mind.

"You're blushing. Why is that?" His hand reached out to me. The touch of his cool fingers upon my face nearly pushed me over the edge.

"It's hot out here." I bit my lip as the lie came pouring out. He looked at me through narrowed eyes and lifted his brow. I forced myself to look past him as another swarm of people flowed down the walkway.

"Has anyone ever told you you're not a convincing liar?" He gave me a half-smile and glanced down at his watch. The awareness that I would miss another opportunity to get to know him made me anxious.

"Am I keeping you from your tour?" Jonathan asked.

"I'd much rather stay with you," I said honestly, uncertain why I felt at ease with him; I just knew I did.

"Madison, it was great to see you again, but you better get moving." He turned to walk away; I caught his hand, feeling the chill and the strength of his fingers. My hand clamped around his wrist like a lifeline in a high-stakes situation. I couldn't let go. The puzzled look in his eyes showed me that I had made a mistake. But my fingers wouldn't release him.

"Sorry," I said, stripping my fingers from his wrist. "I was hoping you would meet me at the market. So, we would have a chance to talk," I bit my lip when he didn't respond. "I thought maybe," I dared a glance into his eyes and then quickly turned away as I tried to regain a shred of my dignity, "Oh my God! Why am I so horrible at this?" I asked myself.

"You're not," he said from behind me. I cringed and wanted nothing more than to dissolve. My eyes squeezed closed when he came to stand in front of me.

"Please tell me I didn't say that out loud?"

"If I say no, will you open your eyes?" he asked. I thought for a second and then slowly nodded my head. "Then no, I didn't hear you say a word." I opened my eyes to see Jonathan smiling at me. His lie made me feel a little better. "I owe you an apology; please forgive me; things were a little hectic yesterday. Allow me to make it up to you. If you're not going to the cathedral, there is a place that I believe you would enjoy."

"I would love to go with you," I said. He took my hand, and I tried to stay calm as his cold fingers wrapped around mine. We moved so quickly toward the street; I could barely gather my thoughts. He stopped in front of a black sports car and opened the door. He gestured for me to climb inside. The childhood lesson about not getting into cars with strangers disintegrated, and I slid into the seat without hesitation. My heart pounded abnormally fast inside my chest as he leaned over me to fasten my seatbelt. I closed my eyes as I tried to calm myself — Jonathan was already in the driver's seat when I opened them. The engine revved, and he smoothly pulled out into the busy street, aligning, and adjusting with the traffic flow.

I breathed in the crisp leather scent of the interior. My fingertips grazed over the stitching of the warm, black seat. Jonathan leaned forward and positioned the vents to blow cool air on me.

"Thank you," I said as the fans began to cool my flushed skin. "Do you live in Paris?" I asked one of the questions bouncing around inside my head.

"Yes and no. I travel frequently."

"Looking for things to paint?"

"You could say that."

"Do you have a wife or a girlfriend?"

"No, I'm quite single. How about you? You must have a boyfriend."

"I don't," I said. Jonathan gave me a skeptical look but said nothing as we weaved through the city streets. We drove for a while when he switched lanes, shifted gears, and pulled the car over. I looked around. It seemed wherever we were, people were leaving. "Where are we?"

"Saint-Jacques Tower," He leaned across me and pointed to the towering structure. My fingers itched to touch him. He was so close. He unfastened my seatbelt, and I began to fumble for the door, needing fresh air. As I pulled the handle, the door opened, with Jonathan standing on the other side. Had I missed something, I wondered to myself. I climbed out of the car, trying to understand how he moved so fast.

We started down the walkway; I stared in amazement at the tower that stretched into the clouds. There was a tall, iron fence with large trees planted around it. Their flowered branches draped over the top. The wind blew, and the sweet fragrance filled the air around us. A warm breeze caressed my skin, drawing my mouth upward into a smile. When Jonathan stopped, I shifted to look at him and realized he was pointing to the tower's peak.

"The tower was created in the 16th century, and this is all that remains of the Church of Saint Jacques de la Bouchiere, destroyed after the French Revolution." He continued down the sidewalk, and I struggled to keep up with his quick pace.

"Why do you believe the tower was saved?" I tried to move a little faster.

"Sorry." He slowed, and I felt relieved since we no longer moved at a marathon pace. "I'm not certain."

I continued to admire the tower as we approached the entrance. The few people still there were leaving, and the doors were chained. He took my hand and led me around the side of the building. That's when I saw the sign of the missing girl plastered on the corner of the gates. My eyes became fixated on her curly brown hair and light eyes; however, the date of disappearance bothered me the most. I knew that date — I moved toward the sign, but Jonathan touched my arm, distracting me. He noticed my preoccupation with the poster, although he did not comment; instead, he led me away.

"Are you as good a climber as a runner?" he stopped to ask. I tilted my head back, surveying the height of the fence.

"Yes, I thought the tower was closed to the public," I said, still distracted by the image of the missing girl.

I couldn't resist Jonathan's challenge. "Are you scared?" he taunted, and I grabbed the fence without hesitation. He was already on the top, waiting for me. He stretched out and pulled me up with ease. Then, he wrapped his arms around me and leapt back down. I was speechless at how we landed so gracefully.

We reached the building, and he turned to me, motioning for me to wait there. I watched as he disappeared around the tower and, seconds later, waved for me to follow. We crept inside through an arched entranceway, and Jonathan put a finger to what I imagined were incredibly soft lips, signaling for me to remain quiet. I held my breath and pressed my back against the wall as a stiff-looking security guard exited the tower to make his outside rounds. Jonathan took my hand, and we raced to the stairs; my gaze traveled up the never-ending staircase, which seemed to stretch toward the heavens. Jonathan took the first few steps as I followed behind. They appeared extremely unstable as they creaked and groaned beneath us.

"I promise to keep you safe." He must have seen the doubt in my eyes as I shifted my focus from him to the cracked wood; with a nod of my head, we continued upward. The top was in sight when he suddenly stopped. "Watch your step." Unfortunately, the warning came too late. My foot went right through the missing step. Jonathan's hand wrapped around my wrist, and instead of falling to my death, my body pressed against him. He placed his other hand gently over my mouth to muffle my scream. We remained motionless, my body molded to the intricate contours of his muscular frame; he was cold, ice cold, although the heat from my body seemed to warm him quickly. I glanced down, shocked to see the large opening where I could have fallen. He slowly let me go, and my feet settled on the same step he stood on. Jonathan interlocked our fingers and we continued upward.

He pushed the door open when we reached the top and closed the door behind us. I found it difficult to believe we were standing atop a tower. We walked over to the ledge, and I tilted my head to see the enormous gargoyle beside me. Perched over the city, snarling to reveal his sharp stone teeth. The gargoyle had the perfect view, and now so did I. All of Paris lie beneath us; miles away, I saw Notre Dame and, in the distance, the Eiffel Tower. I peered at Jonathan and noticed his eyes glued on my necklace as it dangled over the edge. When he reached over and touched the skeleton key, I reminded myself to breathe.

"You should be careful wearing such expensive jewelry in Paris. Was this a gift?"

"I can't remember." I tucked the necklace inside my shirt.

"You don't know who gave you that necklace?" His question caused my own curiosity to resurface. I had asked my mom a hundred times where the necklace had come from, but she never told me.

"My childhood memories feel like shattered pieces of glass. But my guess would be that it's a family heirloom that I put on one day and refused to take it off. So, they let me keep it. I used to be a little stubborn, or so I'm told." I hated not being able to remember. I looked straight ahead, not wanting to ruin this moment.

"Did the poster of the missing girl, upset you?" The question startled me, and I stepped back from the edge. He did notice. I took a deep breath and glanced away for a second before facing him again.

"She looks like me," I said, unable to prevent my voice from shaking, "They all look like me," I began, only to stop myself.

"Who looks like you?" Jonathan asked — his hand touched mine, and I looked back at him.

"That girl on the poster and the girls back in the States, ten including the girl on the poster of them, went missing; every one of them looked like me. They found them dead except for one. She claimed that a group of men abducted her and that she watched the men eat the other girls. Something deep inside me believes that I am the reason. That pain and guilt are so profound that it is difficult to share with anyone, including my parents, although I know I should. There's no one I trust enough to see that part of me," I managed.

"What part is that?"

"Every part," tears began to pool in my eyes, and I twisted away from him. "I'm afraid that they will think…" The clouds were getting darker. His eyes urged me to continue, and I wanted to share this with him. I pushed the hair back from my face and focused on the view below us. "They will think I'm crazy…Phillip, he's my father- would have the evidence he needs to send me away. Although, what I'm most terrified of is that the kidnappings will continue until," I inhaled deeply, smelling the metallic earthiness of rain right before it escaped the clouds. "If they are searching for me, they won't stop until they kill me. I would have preferred that they found me first."

"You feel responsible for the actions of others because these girls resemble you," his anger clear by the intense brightening of his silver eyes and sharp tone. "Based on what you've described, the kidnappers appear to have a certain type; most serial killers do," he said, and I wondered if he were right.

"What if," I began — he stopped me with the lift of his finger.

"Even if you are correct, which I'm not certain you are, everyone has a choice. Those men chose to kidnap, and they chose to murder. Therefore, the responsibility rests solely upon their shoulders," Jonathan said firmly.

My eyes brimmed with tears, and I squeezed them closed as the first raindrop fell upon my face.

"I love being outside, especially when it rains." My voice was whispery soft as I tried to distract myself from the sadness building inside me. I kept my eyes closed and focused on the rain as it pelted my skin, "There is something magical about rain; it cleanses the impurities from the world, from the soul. I love how the liquid caresses all it touches, creating new life while rejuvenating the old. It comforts me in a way that even I find difficult to describe. When most people race for shelter, I take my time." I open my eyes feeling the weight of my thoughts about the girls slowly dissipate, "The rain creates the most beautiful music as every single drop touches my skin. Sometimes, when it's quiet the rhythm whispers to me." My heart began to pound hard as he lessened the space between us. I imagine he must taste as sweet as he smells before blushing deeply.

"What does the rain say, when it whispers to you?"

"You're not alone. We are here with you. It's like a hug when you need it most, comforting and uplifting." I took a deep satisfying breath and glanced up at him.

"I want to kiss you." Jonathan inched forward; his lips were nearly touching mine. "Would that be, okay?" His fingers slid through my hair as he pulled me toward him, and his velvety soft lips touched mine.

"Yes," I breathed. My lips captured the sweetness of Jonathan's kiss; they were softer than I had imagined. I shivered as his icy hands touched the back of my neck. My fingers grabbed a handful of his rain-soaked hair to pull him closer. Our lips parted slightly, and I realized the rain was no longer the most comforting and magical thing I had experienced.

He leaned away and stepped back. "You kissed me," I said more to myself than to him as I wiped the rain from my eyes. He did taste sweet. I reasoned, like raspberry chocolate truffles, which happened to be my weakness. Like those delectable treats, I wanted more of his lips pressed against mine, more of his hands gently tugging my hair. However, the look of regret in his eyes prevented my thoughts from continuing.

"I shouldn't have done that," He reached over and took my hand, leading me toward the door, and my heart dropped. We started down the stairs. I jerked my hand away. My eyes searched his for answers, but he refused to speak.

"It's getting late," he said, extending his hand, I accepted, and we began to descend the staircase. I couldn't understand the reason he would be upset over a kiss…unless I sucked at it. The security guard was nowhere in sight when we reached the bottom of the tower and climbed back over the fence. I stole another look at Saint Jacques Tower as Jonathan took my hand and pulled me toward the car.

"The tower was beautiful," I whispered. Jonathan opened the door to allow me inside, my jeans were damp, and the material resisted my attempt to slide gracefully into the car. He did not have that problem when he eased into his seat seconds later; he glanced over at me when I began dabbing at my wet skin with the hem of my shirt. We stopped behind a large red tour bus, and Jonathan reached behind my seat and handed me a small towel.

"I thought you would appreciate this place. I often come here to think." His mood was improving a little. "There aren't too many places I can go in Paris that aren't overflowing with tourists." He glanced over at me and grinned.

"When I need to be alone, I head to the forest. It's the only place where I feel at peace. There are small streams close by where I like to read. The trees are as tall as the tower," I blotted the moisture from my face and passed the now-damp towel back to him. He wiped the water from his glistening skin, and I felt my insides warm.

"Do you enjoy living in Nirvana?" Jonathan asked. My eyes narrowed as I thought about his question.

"How did you know I live in Nirvana?"

"Your lighthouse keychain, the keys fell out of your purse," His answer left me even more confused — I looked at him suspiciously.

"The lighthouse isn't from Nirvana. It's from Cape Hatteras, where I used to live." I twisted in the seat to look directly at him. "How do you know where I live?" I repeated the question hoping he would tell me the truth.

"Your tour group registered with the museum. So, I assumed the lighthouse was from Nirvana." He laughed, and I furrowed my brow.

"Uh, that wasn't funny." I shook my head and wondered how he had gotten the information. I never registered for tours Emma did, and I went in her place. My eyes narrowed, as I realized he lied to me, but thought silently that, 'it takes one to know one.'

"I'm sorry, you're right. Please forgive me." His apology would have been much more believable if it weren't for the laughter in his voice. I began to study him, committing everything about him to memory. His bronze skin was luminous and contrasted against his black hair. I couldn't help but notice how well-built he was, his lean frame with muscles that looked carved of stone. Our eyes met, and I quickly looked away — those silver eyes made me feel things I knew had to be sinful. He was more relaxed since we left the tower. We stopped at a crosswalk, and he gave me a deep smile that made me nervous again.

"This may be a silly question, but here it goes anyway. What was it like?" I asked.

"That depends on what you're speaking of," he said. His smile widened.

"The kiss," I knew my face had to be beet red as his eyes focused on my mouth.

"It was incredibly sweet, much warmer than I expected, and softer than I could have ever imagined." He leaned toward me as if to kiss me again. A car horn began to blare behind us, and he pulled away. A sudden vibrating sound sent me to search inside my bag. I hoped it was Emma calling; I hadn't heard from her since earlier. As I pulled my phone out, I realized it was not mine but Jonathan's phone vibrating. He reached into his pocket and pulled out a small black cell phone. He silenced it before putting it back away. A part of me wondered if it was the woman from the art gallery.

"How is it possible that you're single?" I bit my lip the second the words left my mouth. He was a gorgeous, charismatic, wealthy artist living in one of the most romantic cities in the world.

"I travel so much that a relationship is out of the question."

"Oh, I see. I can't wait to travel, although I want to share those experiences with someone."

"Does that mean you're looking for a boyfriend?" I laughed when he asked the question and was half-tempted to ask if he was considering the position. "What's so funny?" he asked; there was a large grin across his face.

"I'm not searching for a boyfriend." That was as close to the truth as I could allow.

"You're not going to tell me why you're laughing?"

"It's something that my mom said once. Promise not to laugh." I tried to sound serious. He nodded his head as he pulled over in front of my hotel. "My mom told me that the women in our family aren't I'm destined for more than just a string of boyfriends. She said we must choose between fire and light; both are needed; however, one will burn, and the other will warm. One will shield, and the other will guide. She gave me the lighthouse keychain and told me to wait for the man that knows me from the inside out. The one I could trust to guide me through any storm." 'Strange that she chose my father to marry.'

He didn't find my mom's sentiment ridiculous. "Sorry, I have this habit of rambling sometimes. The basis of her advice is that I should choose wisely." My hands reached for the door, but he was already holding it open.

"You have an allure that is amazing." Jonathan's eyes locked on mine as I exited the car. "There's something about you that I find difficult to resist."

"That explains why you've been following me," I joked.

"I thought we agreed it was you doing the following," he replied.

I watched as he closed the door behind me and went to the driver's side. He slid into the seat. I bent forward as the darkly tinted window came down.

"Jonathan," I said, resting my arms on the door, "I'm going to the Jardin des Tuileries tomorrow morning around 7:00. I mean in case you want to bump into a pesky tourist."

"I will try." He smiled. I stood up when he drove off my fingers went instinctively to my tingling lips.

CHAPTER THIRTEEN
BLISS

My focus shifted from the view of the streets below — to the vibrating cell phone in my hand. It was day five in Paris and Margaret's patience was evaporating with each passing second. She called last night and left me at least three messages about how she covered for me when my mom called. Margaret was afraid that my parents wouldn't pay her if they discovered the truth — it was all about money for her, which made me wonder how she and my mom were best friends. I silenced the phone and tossed it on the bed. The easiest thing for me to do would have been to board the next plane and keep from digging myself into an even deeper hole, but I knew that the moment I got in the taxi to leave for Paris that it would come to this. I would have to face the consequences for my decision to stay here — Phillip's anger and my mom's irreversible disappointment. My time here was running out like tiny granules of sand sifting through an hourglass.

"I needed more time." My mom had spoken to Margaret last night, which gave me a couple of days before she would phone again. "A little longer," I pleaded to the heavens, because I hoped that would give me enough time to convince Jonathan of the possibility — of us. He was older, but not by much. He was no more than nineteen, if he could wait a little longer, I would be seventeen in three months, okay six months, but I would be heading to college this time next year. I knew that was a long time to ask a man like Jonathan to wait. He could have his choice of women. I frowned as that thought permeated in my subconscious. Well, he did kiss me, which had to mean something, my fingers went to my mouth as memories of my kiss with Jonathan came rushing back. The way his fingers felt in my hair as he pulled me close, I would always remember.

My cell phone vibrated again, and I quickly retrieved it from the bed. Blake had left me a text message, funny how he always seems to know when I need a laugh or a good talking too.

Madi, something tells me you are not enjoying yourself.
Come on girl, you're in Paris! Make that shit count…

Thanks, I think…lol I pressed send and closed the phone.

I collected my iPod from the bedside table, headed out the door — quickly crossing the hall to Conner's room, and gave the door an impatient knock.

My eyes narrowed when Lauren answered. She was wearing one of Conner's shirts and her hair looked an awful mess. Wow, she was making Paris count; something unfamiliar began to stir inside me, envy, not of Lauren and Conner of course, but of what I may never have with Jonathan. Would I ever open the door to his hotel suite wearing nothing but a smile and his perfectly starched shirt? "Conner can't go running. He's busy right now, but I'll be sure to tell him you came by," Lauren said with a smirk.

"Thanks," I said absently, walking away before she closed the door and then turned around quickly because I felt Jonathan nearby. He was leaning in the corner beside the elevator with one foot propped against the wall.

"Where are you going?" The silkiness of Jonathan's voice instantly relaxed me. He pushed off the wall and the look in his eyes caused me to fumble as I secured the strap on my iPod.

"Ah, running," I finally said, tightening the strap on my arm.

"I was hoping to take you to breakfast. That is, if you're hungry." He smiled, and my heart began to pound, as my eyes raked his pale blue shirt. He had left the first three buttons open, offering a glimpse of his muscular chest. I wondered if the shirt would feel soft against my skin, the thought fluttered through my subconscious and settled in my lower belly. "Are you hungry?"

"Starving," I blurted out and he lifted his brow as if to say, for food. I glanced down at my white tank top and black shorts and debated on racing back to the room to change.

"Don't worry, your clothes are fine. We're not going to a restaurant." I couldn't help but smile as I wondered where Jonathan was planning to take me. He shifted his gaze toward the elevator when it opened. "Does that smile mean yes?" he asked. I nodded excitedly, and the two of us stepped into the elevator.

We walked past the hotel until we reached his car. He opened my door and waited for me to climb inside. "Who's on your play list?" Jonathan asked as he leaned over me to fasten my seat belt.

"Trust me, you don't want to know. It's a melting pot, and quite embarrassing." He eased onto the leather seat — held his hand out and gave me an insisting look. I reluctantly went to setting on my phone and connected to his Bluetooth and pressed shuffle.

"I guess the truth will be revealed in a few seconds." He turned the volume up and smiled as the music of Kings of Midnight filled the car.

"Kings of Midnight are my favorite. I'm into the older stuff, but there are songs on the new album that are good." I reached over to turn the music up. His eyes remained on me, although he never spoke a word. "This has to be their best song ever!" My excitement caused him to smile again.

"Touché," the intensity of his stare caused me to look away.

"You've heard of them?" I looked back up at him as he nodded.

We continued down the busy street and I turned my attention to look out the window.

"Yes, I've been to a few of their concerts," he admitted.

"I'd love to go to one. Of course, Emma, my best friend, she would have to go with me. She loves the band too." Jonathan was silent. "Where are we going?" I finally asked.

"I told you, breakfast. However, it will be more like brunch by the time we get there."

"That's fine." I lifted my hair off my neck to cool myself.

"You're warm?" His eyes narrowed suspiciously, and he checked the air conditioner, to ensure that it was set to cool.

"I'm always warm." Our eyes met for a second, and my temperature rose even higher as tiny beads of moisture began to collect in the column of my throat. He turned the air on full blast, and I closed my eyes. The force of the chilly air lifted strands of my damp hair and caused me to shiver.

"How did you know what room I'm staying in?"

Jonathan smiled, "I asked the door man for room number of the pesky blue-eyed tourist from the states, slid him a tip and voila."

"Oh, really! And he thought of me." I laughed.

"Actually, I described your eyes as the color of the sea and told him that your hair is like the ocean waves." He looked at me as if it were the absolute truth.

"Oh," I squirmed in my seat trying to calm myself, before shifting my attention back to the window and saw that the streets were becoming — less congested. The tall skyscrapers and miles of concrete replaced by lush greenery and towering trees.

"What are you thinking?" Jonathan asked with genuine concern in his voice. My eyes met his before he had to refocus on the street. He turned the music off, prompting me to answer his question.

"I feel free here," I wanted to say, 'with you,' but didn't want to seem too weird, so I stopped myself. Instead, I sighed and focused my attention on the breathtaking scenery.

"Are you trying to escape something? Someone?" he asked.

"My mind itself, mostly," I admitted. "Moving to Nirvana was a drastic change, so was coming here, but even the change of the seasons affects me."

"So, summer bothers you. I will see what I can do about that." His voice was light and lifted my mood. the thought of twelve chilly months and the serenity that would come from frost covered landscapes, and crisp air brought a smile to my face.

"Winter is your favorite season. I would have imagined summer, since you love to swim," he said.

"There's nothing better than swimming in the winter. I love it." I wrinkled my nose, and his smile grew. His gaze remained on me until he motioned in front of us.

"This is Parc des Buttes Chaumont, the largest park in Paris," he explained, as he parked the car. My eyes focused on the steep cliffs that touched the clouds. He got out of the car first, and crossed in front to open my door, he helped me out, and then reached behind my seat to retrieve a wicker picnic basket. There was a plaid blanket folded neatly on top, which left me impressed. Did men do this? I knew Phillip held the door open for my mom, but he, well he is old. Most young guys hold the door open for one of two reasons, a sneak peek up your dress, or a sneak peek down your shirt — Jonathan had done neither. The girls at school rambled for hours about their dates, not once did anyone mention a picnic in the most incredible park. Chivalry wasn't dead, and perhaps today's knights drove black sports cars instead of armored covered horses. He was a romantic, and protective, that he proved when he rescued my purse, and again when he saved me on the stairs of the tower. "I see that you approve," Jonathan said, breaking my train of thought.

"Oh, yes, of course," I stammered, as I took in the scenery. He reached for my hand, as we entered the park. The endless gardens, inviting us into their sanctuary. The park was astounding, and I took a deep breath inhaling the aroma of freshly cut grass. Jonathan stopped right beneath a large elm tree, and I helped him spread the blanket over the damp grass before we sat down. He rested his weight on his arms as he leaned back, tilting his head toward the sky. His dark lashes hiding those incredible silver eyes. My eyes traced his perfectly symmetrical nose, chiseled features, and slightly full lips. He must have felt my gaze upon him because a slow smile began to grow on his face, and I quickly glanced away.

Jonathan unpacked the basket and offered me a slice of freshly baked bread. As he broke off a piece, I could see it was light and fluffy with a darker, crisp crust. He motioned toward a small wheel of cheese, and I nodded. His knife sliced through the cheese easily and he placed two triangles on my plate. I thanked him and took my first bite. The sharp taste of the cheese complimented the bread perfectly. My brow lifted when Jonathan poured a glass of red liquid and offered it to me.

"Juice," he said, smiling as he noticed my concerned look.

"Thank you," my face felt a little flushed. I took a sip, studying the glass for a moment. "Why is it that everything tastes so incredible here?" I asked. I ran my tongue over my lips before taking another sip of the delicious liquid.

"I'm happy to see you approve," he admitted.

"Aren't you going to have some?"

"No, it's too fattening," Jonathan joked. I held the baguette out for him, and he placed it inside the basket.

I giggled and I took another bite of cheese. My eyes continued to admire the park. It was far more beautiful than anything I had seen in Paris. Well, Saint Jacques Tower would forever be one of my favorite places too, I thought, but this tied for first place.

"This place is unbelievable," I said softly. "Thanks for bringing me here." I leaned my head to the side in amazement as a butterfly softly wavered over the blanket. It fluttered across my hand, tickling my skin. Its wings expanded to reveal deep shades of orange that contrasted with its black spots. My eyes widened when it settled on the tip of my finger, and I watched as the beautiful creature slowly wafted its wings. When my eyes met Jonathan's, again his filled with warmth that surprised me. He whispered something I could not understand. It took me a second to realize he had spoken Spanish.

"What did you say?" I asked.

"This park reminds me of home," he said in English.

"Where is home?"

"My brother and I were born in Soria, Spain. The city is known for beautiful Romanesque style buildings, but truly, the natural beauty is far more captivating. There is a park there, Alameda de Cervantes, where my brother and I used to play on our way to and from school."

His eyes brightened when he spoke about his brother. I imagined another Jonathan walking the Earth and Austin's image popped into my mind. That would be interesting, I thought to myself.

"We climbed these enormous elm trees, played in streams and fields nearby. I remember the flower gardens that my mother used to love visiting. My brother and I would play near the fountains, and often find ourselves in them, his fault, of course." He paused before continuing. "The people of Soria were always so warm and filled with laughter. Life seemed magical there, or perhaps I was too young and innocent to care about trivial things."

"Your home sounds like a beautiful place," I admitted.

"Yes, it is, and *Parc des Buttes Chaumont* is one of the few places that remind me of my past." He leaned back on the blanket.

"Where is your family?" I pried, and then wondered if I had asked too much.

"My family died a long time ago." His words spoken with a somber resolve, as he looked past me. The sculpted lines of his face tightened as if the question conjured up a terrible memory.

"I'm sorry." I whispered, as his sadness seemed to creep through me and settled somewhere deep inside somehow, I knew that my question had conjured up a painful memory. My eyes went upward as the storm clouds began to assimilate — darkening the already overcast sky.

"We should talk about something else. Tell me something about yourself." My attempt to get us both out of the solemn mood worked, and I saw his body relax again.

It would be easier for me to show you." His hand reached inside the picnic basket, and he pulled out a sketchpad and pencil. "You must remain still." His eyes pierced through me as he gave the instruction, and then turned soft as he smiled. The pencil began to move across the page in a swift, fluid motion.

It was almost shameful the way my eyes traveled the entire length of his body. The dark jeans outlined a pair of lean muscular thighs. His shirt showed off rippled abs as the thin material clung to his strong chest and broad shoulders. When I looked at him, a bronze sculpture came to mind.

He caught me off guard when he suddenly looked up. "You do know it's considered impolite to stare?" The teasing in his voice made me blush, his face now mere inches from mine. "You should behave yourself, Madison or, I'll be compelled to kiss you again," he warned. The smile on my face grew and I bit my lip, falling deeper into his silver eyes. They were like a snow-covered lake, and instead of swimming, I was drowning in them. I forced myself to snap back to reality.

"Show me," my hands reached for the drawing before I peeked at him from beneath my lashes. His hands remained clutched to the pad, and he leaned closer. My lips gently brushed against his before we both paused and allowed them to linger close together. Feeling his icy skin so near made me shiver, but within seconds, his lips touched mine. They were incredibly soft, and he tasted addictively sweet, my skin quickly flushed as my heart began to beat wildly with his touch. I slowly lowered myself back onto the blanket as he pressed against me. His fingers traveled down the sensitive area of my throat. Then as swiftly as the kiss started, he pulled himself up, leaving me lying with my eyes still closed on the blanket. My chest rose and fell as I caught my breath, and then I sat up to look at him. He gave me a teasing smile. I stared at him, wondering why he stopped our kiss. I had no experience when it comes to this sort of thing, but I would wager my trust fund that he was into me. Therefore, his reaction left me baffled once again.

"Here," he said, handing the sketch to me, "and now it's your turn to share." He nodded slightly, urging me to look down. I did. Awestruck that the drawing was like looking into a mirror. His illustration left me speechless and reminded me once again, of my resemblance to my mom, and for once, I felt as beautiful. He made me feel beautiful — made me look beautiful, because here on this paper I was my mother's daughter, no freakish turquoise eyes. I slid my fingers over the dark eyes and smiled.

"You made me, ah, look normal," I wanted to say.

"You are talented," this I spoke aloud, tilting my head to the side, looking over every detail of the sketch.

"Thank you, although you are a wonderful muse." He reached

out for the pad, and even though I did not want to let go, I released it, allowing him to place it back inside the basket.

"So, you're not going to share?" he asked impatiently. I knew he was waiting for my answer and debated if honesty was a wise move. He could run for cover to get away from me, but something told me he wouldn't.

"Okay, but no laughing. I told you before that the rain is one of my favorite things." He nodded, urging me to continue. "Well, there's more. I'm connected to the rain in a way that's difficult to explain." I paused. Jonathan was staring at me intently, but nothing about his face showed signs that he was contemplating an escape, or humor, which prompted me to continue. "When my best friend, Nic, left for college, it rained non-stop for three weeks." Again, I stopped to examine his reaction. Nope, he had not replaced his Italian boots with running shoes. Why had I revealed so much about myself to him? Instead of running, he leaned in closer. My brow furrowed as I tried to figure out if Jonathan had put some kind of weird spell on me.

"What are you thinking?" he questioned. He did not have the slightest bit of hesitation in his voice, and seemed to accept my secret without question, as if it were the most normal thing, I could've shared with him.

"That I could remain here forever," I admitted, before realizing the words had left my mouth.

"That wouldn't be a good idea, Madison." His voice was almost cold, and a second later, he was standing over me with his hand outstretched to help me up. I took his hand and quickly went to my feet. He reached down and folded the blanket, before taking the items back to his car. It gave me a moment to clear my head. There was a waterfall nearby, and I walked toward it, hoping it would distract me from the sudden change in his mood. The scenery was breathtaking, and I moved closer to get a better view. The water flowed through the wall made of stone, and the gentle sound as it rushed over the smooth rocks relaxed me. The liquid caressed everything in its path, including the mossy covered grass and the leafy vines. Jonathan returned to my side, but my eyes remained focused on the waterfall. I sat down on the bank, captivated by the streaming water as it trickled down. He took a seat beside me, and I twisted to look at him.

"I bet you're surrounded by tourists when you come here," I teased. My fingers brushed across the manicured grass. He laughed, and while I kept my eyes focused on the beautiful surroundings, I could feel that he was intently watching me. This had truly been the most incredible day of my life and soon it would be over.

Jonathan stood up then reached down to help me. His strong grip pulled me up, and he kept his hand locked with mine as we strolled down the sidewalk, and I delighted in the cool breeze that blew through the trees. As we continued through the grotto, I stopped and leaned back to see a remarkable, arched bridge that expanded across the river. The stone and mortar bridge gave the illusion that it was- carved from the mountain itself.

"It's named The Parc Buttes Chaumont Bridge," Jonathan said, "however, it's widely known as The Suicide Bridge." My eyes remained on the incredible structure — an uneasy feeling circulated through me.

Jonathan must have sensed my hesitation, because he pulled me closer and wrapped his arm around my waist. When we walked beneath the bridge, I felt the pain of those who had chosen death. My body ached as the loneliness they experienced on the ledge became my own. Then I thought of those who had turned around. It must have been difficult to search for a reason to live when the only feeling they had was hopelessness. I closed my eyes as their pain all but consumed me, my knees buckled, and I would have hit the ground if Jonathan hadn't tightened his grip. "Are you able to walk?" his voice pulled me out of the despair that was threatening to consume. I nodded.

"We should continue," Jonathan urged, as his cool fingers wiped the tears from my face. He ushered me from beneath the bridge and I could finally breathe again. His eyes filled with concern, but I quickly looked away. I dared a glance back and a sob escaped. This wasn't the first time, mournful feelings had plagued me, graveyards had the same effect on me, but this was information I decided not to share with Jonathan. I would need to space my secrets out, whether it be to keep him from running, or to entice him to stay. He held me close as we continued down the path. When the rain began as if on cue, he didn't say a word, but I wasn't surprised. Here was the proof of my secret, my strange connection with the rain. We walked together in silence as the cool rain drops eased my sadness and erased all traces of my tears.

Jonathan was the perfect tour guide. His knowledge of the area was endless, as he vividly described the details and history of everything we passed. An elderly couple strolled by us. A beautiful bouquet of fresh lilies was in the woman's arms — her nose buried deep in the white petals — her thin lips parted to reveal an incredible smile. The man draped his arm around her fragile shoulders. He gathered her closer and they strolled away oblivious of my intruding gaze.

"There's a vendor a few blocks over if you would like some flowers," Jonathan offered.

"No, thank you. I was…wondering about, their story. How did they meet? Do they have children? Grandchildren? Are they in love, is that even possible? Silly, huh?"

"Inquisitive, never silly," he whispered into my hair as his arms closed gently around me.

Our eyes locked and I stepped away, suddenly, "There is something that I would love to have," I uttered with far too much excitement. Jonathan nodded yes before he heard my request.

"Are you going to tell me what that is or would you rather I guess?" he jokingly questioned as we made our way from the park. "I would buy you anything," he said as if it were the absolute truth.

"I'd like the sketch that you made today." I wanted something tangible to remind me that this day wasn't a beautiful dream.

"The sketch, I offer you anything, and you want a sheet of paper."

"It was, a sheet of paper, like a diamond was once coal," I corrected him, "Now it's a Jonathan Spenser original." I raised a daring brow. He shook his head. The path circled around until we ended up back near the car. He placed the sketch in my hand, and then reached up and touched the side of my face.

"You make all of this a little too real for me," he whispered. My eyes narrowed as I tried to understand what he meant.

When he had safely buckled me in and climbed into the driver seat, he revved the car's engine. The car sped away so fast my hands instinctively went to my stomach.

"What did you mean; I make it real for you?" I asked.

Jonathan looked at the clock. "It's much later than I realized. I've got to get you back before you're missed." He was avoiding the question completely. I sighed deeply and rolled my eyes before directing my gaze out the window.

He was determined to take me back, and I was thinking that the day ended far too soon. Even the drive back seemed too short, and I found myself wishing for any reason for him to stay with me longer. I leaned over to kiss the side of his face, but he pulled me in further. His lips pressed into mine as his cool hand touched the back of my neck, sending waves of electrical currents through me. He reached up and gently stroked my damp cheek, before pulling away.

"Goodbye, Madison."

"Jonathan," I wanted to ask him when I'd see him again, instead I said, "We will see each other again, so this isn't goodbye. I'll see you later."

"Touché," his voice was filled with amusement.

I forced myself from his car and headed into the hotel as he drove away. I went to the suite filled with excitement. Today had been the sweetest day of my life and I would never forget a single second. I was about to call Emma when I heard a knock at the door. The steady beat sounded like Conner's knock, but I couldn't have been more wrong. The rhythmic knock belonged to the bellhop, and he was struggling to balance my bags.

"I tried to stop you downstairs." His voice was uncomfortably nervous. My eyes narrowed as I reached to take the bags from his arms. "I can place them inside the suite," he offered.

"Thank you, but I can manage." He gave me a frustrated look.

I lifted the bags from his arms and then quickly closed the door. Something about nervous men gave me goose bumps. I sat on the floor and began rifling through the packages when the door opened.

Emma stepped inside with a huge smile on her face. I was grinning from ear to ear, excited that I would finally have a chance to talk to her. My exuberant mood shifted when Austin stepped in behind her a second later.

"Hi Madi," Austin said. I suddenly felt guilty for not wanting him there. I was being selfish again. Emma should spend time with her brother, I reasoned silently.

"Hi," I continued to sort through the bag, and tried to prevent him from seeing the shame on my face.

"You shop as much as Emma!" He laughed and I did too, because we both knew there was no one that shopped as much as Emma did.

"She bought me all of this. I was about to thank her."

Emma poked her head around the corner. "I didn't buy you anything." She had a confused look on her face, but then shrugged before ducking back inside her room. I looked over the designer jeans all seven were my size, t-shirts, and dresses. I traced my fingers over a yellow peasant dress with white polka dots, and the hem would fall below my knees. The other was a black and white three-tiered dress. The elegant V-neck and thin spaghetti straps accentuated the empire waist. It was adorable and the cutest dress I had ever seen — I laid the clothes over the sofa. Who would have bought these for me?

"Emma," Austin said impatiently. He glanced down at his watch. "I'm sorry. We can talk later. I promise," Emma said before she and Austin rushed out the door.

I bit my bottom lip as I contemplated who could have bought the clothes, and then noticed a small package at the bottom of the bag. I opened the small gift and discovered a miniature Big Sable Point lighthouse; I would have recognized it anywhere. The beautiful black and white crystal replica brought a smile to my face. My mom had taken me to the lighthouse days after we arrived in Nirvana.

I finished unpacking my gifts, as my mind traveled back to

the conversation with Jonathan. Was he the one who had bought me these presents? I paced the room a little while longer before the desperate need for answers sent me back onto the street. The Hotel Concorde La Fayette was my destination. I had to see him again.

CHAPTER FOURTEEN
GRAVITY

I arrived at the bus stop just in time. The ride to the hotel went quickly, my mind distracted by thoughts of Jonathan and imagining our time together continuing. "Yes, I purchased the clothes and the lighthouse," he would admit. "And I've been thinking about what you said. Madison, please stay with me forever. I'm a fool for telling you it wasn't possible." I imagined him saying, as he would eagerly pull me into his room.

The bus jolted to a stop and my fantasy-filled head collided with the window. Damn it, I thought as I rubbed the bump and stood to walk off the bus. Determined to get answers and hoping that my dreams would become reality. Jonathan wanted me, or at least it felt that way when he kissed me. He also seemed conflicted about kissing me, clear by his pulling away. I knew that age was a large factor, but that wouldn't matter once I turned eighteen. We can at least explore the possibilities... exploring the possibilities with Jonathan that thought sent a wave of warmth across my skin.

I inhaled the musty evening air, which caused my nostrils to burn a little from the smell. I glanced around to see if I could find the offending odor seeing the discarded food along the curb swarming with flies supplied the answer. Composing myself, I pushed the large door open. The hotel was remarkably chic — well polished businesspeople with their leather briefcases — tailored suits, cell phones, and tablets were scattered throughout the lobby. Their faces showed traces of worry, while others appeared extremely relaxed, judging by the empty martini and wine glasses. I would imagine that they were a little tipsy. A couple glanced up at me as I walked by, their smiles made me feel uneasy. He reminded me of Stuart Townsend in the movie Queen of the Damned, not only in the features the look in his eyes, hunger. And she looked the singer Mya, golden brown skin, long wavy hair- could have passed for her twin. Both were giving vampire vibes, and I know that's not a thing and that I'm all worked up for nothing. There is no such thing as vampires, although Anne Rice's novels had me believing otherwise for years. The Aaliyah look alike licked her bottom lip, and smiled deeply, "Stop it Madi," I whispered to myself, and quickly moved by them. Stuart Townsend's twin left his seat and shadowed my steps, and I pretended not to notice as he stepped up to the counter beside me.

"I'm here to see Jonathan Spenser," I said to the staunchly desk clerk — he peered at me through tight dark eyes then outright ignored me to help the man. There was a hint of recognition on the man that I decided to call Stuart's face. I wasn't certain if Stuart knew Jonathan, or if he believed, he knew me. Something about his demeanor changed. His intense expression softened, as he stared down at me for a couple of seconds before he turned to address the desk clerk. Stuart ordered turn down service for his room, and a bottle of champagne before tilting his head slightly at me and rejoining the Mya look-a-like. They both looked my way perhaps because I was still staring at them and then they shifted their attention to one another again.

The desk clerk promptly informed me that he could not release information on hotel guests. I stayed in the lobby, eyeing the security guards and trying to think of a way to get past those annoying chains I had struggled with the last time I had broken into this hotel. My better judgment told me to go about this legally unless the desk clerk refused to see things my way.

I took a deep breath and tried to convince the clerk to phone his room. He seemed beyond agitated, but I was persistent. I could hear him muttering under his breath as he picked up the receiver and violently dialed Jonathan's room number, for which he received the sweetest smile that my lips could muster. The phone was ringing on the other end. It seemed like it rang forever as I looked back and forth from the clock on the wall to the receiver in the annoyed attendant's hand. The man slowly placed the phone back and returned his attention to me.

Mademoiselle, I'm sorry but there was no answer. I simply cannot help you any further," he said smugly — strange, sorry was the one emotion that did not register.

I stood there a couple more minutes, drumming the fine cherry wood desk with my nails, and glanced around the lobby once more. The Queen of the Damned couple gave me another creepy smile and I hustled toward the door. After a quick glance over my shoulder confirmed that the couple had not followed me outside- I could breathe again.

After waiting over twenty minutes for the bus, I tried to hail a taxi instead. That wasn't my smartest move. I was no more than a block down the street when the bus came and sped off before I could reach it. The word 'tourist' must be stamped on my forehead. People were staring, and two of them asked if I was lost. The second person to ask even offered me a ride. I had studied him thoroughly, not because I had thought about accepting, but because his offer struck me as unusual. He was only two or three inches taller than I was and appeared to be pure muscle. He could have been handsome if his face weren't contorted into a rigid scowl. His crimson-colored eyes were hungry, and he looked at me as if I were the main course.

He insisted on telling me his name was Liam. I saw the same tattoo that Tobias had on his arm, only Liam's was on his hand — VHW. I frowned because he smelled like the movers too.

Not only did the man refuse to leave me alone — he also had the audacity to move closer. His arm brushed against mine and I eased further away.

"You smell wonderful," there was a graininess tone to his voice, sounded like his vocal cords had been damaged, and his creepiness had escalated to pervert.

"Please leave me alone. I'm waiting for my friends." I lied. However, something told me that the lie was necessary. He shifted his body so that he was now in front of me. His scent smacked me in the face and caused my knees to weaken. He smelled as if he had used sewer water to bathe, rusty, metallic, standing water. The scent caused my stomach to churn, and tears sprung to my eyes. I stumbled backward, lifted my shirt to cover both my mouth and nose, as he eyed suspiciously. His foot slammed against the sidewalk so hard that I could have sworn the ground shook, or I still had not recovered from his smell. Liam was not tall, but with him now in front of me, and so close, he seemed to tower. My hope was that Liam did not understand English, so I repeated the words in French. He laughed, and I felt an icy coldness creep over me. I shivered as the man continued to cackle. His eyes were now dark and vacant as he looked down at me. I quickly turned away from him and started to speed-walk in the opposite direction. Liam's icy, cold hands wrapped around my right wrist, and he jerked me in the other direction. He began to pull me down the street. I tried to pull away but his grip — locked tightly around me. My left hand clutched onto his and I dug my nails into his cold skin. His skin was hard, and my attempts to scratch him failed.

He did not turn back to look at me. His gaze focused on moving forward. The people on the street seemed not to notice. They appeared to be, concentrating on their own path — their eyes straight to avoid involving themselves in the scene that was taking place. I planted my feet, although the rain made the sidewalk slick, and my feet seemed to glide across the cemented sidewalk. Liam ignored my efforts — tightening his grip like a boa constrictor; the more I struggled the tighter he squeezed my arm. I screamed so loud the sound vibrated in my chest. Finally, a red-haired woman passing by paused to inspect my situation. Her hands shook as she reached for her cell phone, fumbling to open the flip cover — Liam knocked the phone from her hand and gave her look that caused tears to spill down the woman's bright cheeks. She looked away, self-preservation her motive for not helping me as she quickened her stride. Her cell phone lay in pieces on the sidewalk — she walked right by them. Liam watched to make sure she kept walking — his grip loosened, and I twisted my wrist from his grasp and broke free. My feet were hitting the wet pavement faster than I had ever run before, as I raced through the city in search of anything familiar. Over my shoulder, I could see him running full speed behind me — the danger he posed — gave me the strength I needed to run at an even faster pace.

Suddenly, a hand came out of nowhere and latched onto my shirt — strong arms pulled me in, preventing my escape. With little effort, I was — tugged into a side alley. I twisted around, trying to thrash out of his arms. My punches contacted him, but it did more damage to me than him. His body was solid, and my hand was throbbing after each blow. "Let me go!" I hit him repeatedly. My hands began to sting, and I feared the delicate bones in my fingers would break.

"Madison!" I opened my eyes as his voice broke through my screams.

"Jonathan," his name escaped my lips as he loosened the tightness of his hold. He looked down at me, completely uninjured by my punches. His face showed both concern and frustration — tears began to pool in my eyes as I stared up at him.

"I told you not to wander these streets alone!" His teeth clenched tightly. The tears escaped and crept down my face, "Madison, please forgive my harshness," Jonathan said, brushing the hot tears that continued to flow from my eyes, like a faucet. "It's not safe for you to be out here." He continued to soothe, gathering me closer. I nodded and he stiffened, although this time he directed his anger towards Liam. The creep appeared feet away.

"She's mine!" Liam screamed. Jonathan turned to face him, easing me around until I stood behind him.

"You cannot claim that which belongs to another," Jonathan retorted. He stretched out his arms — hooking me behind me.

'What the hell!' I thought to myself. Neither of these men had claim over me, while I was content with Jonathan doing so, this was not the romantic place I had hoped it would occur.

"The girl was alone!" Liam's anger seeped through his words. I could see the red deepening in his eyes when he looked over at me.

"What does he want?" I whispered to Jonathan.

"You," His eyes stayed focused on the man.

"Okay, seriously...who in the hell says things like that? He wants me, so, people in hell want ice water; guess what, they're not getting it!"

I looked back and forth between Jonathan and Liam. Jonathan looked over his shoulder at me; giving me a look that said now was not the time to start ranting. He folded his fingers tightly over mine, and I must admit that during all the craziness I felt safe. Safe because something inside told me that Jonathan would not allow Liam to harm me. That knowledge allowed me to breathe a little more steadily, and summon the courage to meet Liam's sick, cold, and twisted stare. I stiffened my back and lengthened my neck to make myself at least appear taller.

"I said the girl is going with me!" Liam's eyes started to glow. I studied him without waver knowing any show of fear would only feed his sickness. Liam's anger centered once again on Jonathan. The muscles in his chest pulsated, hands tightened, and he shifted his weight until he was in a weird sort of boxing stance. That was all it took for Jonathan to pounce on him — Jonathan moved so fast that if I had blinked, I would have missed it. He grabbed Liam by the neck and slammed him into the brick wall. Liam's large body collided with the brick, sounded like a clap of thunder and I froze. A crack slowly formed up the side of the brick wall, traveling from behind Liam and up as far as I could see. Small fragments of the red brick fell at their feet and Jonathan held Liam against the building. Liam's thick legs and large feet dangled off the ground. Jonathan's attention remained on Liam; however, his order was undoubtedly — directed at me, "Wait across the street inside the hotel!"

This was surreal and I wondered if at any second, my alarm would go off and I would awake from this nightmare. Only this was my reality, a weird man was trying to kidnap me — I covered my mouth with my hands as a blood-curdling scream threatened to surface. Could he be the one that kidnapped all those girls — the girls that resembled me? If I were a little more courageous, I would demand that he tell me. Would he admit the truth? I mean there was still the possibility that Liam was a pervert that accosted tourist. The questions continued to circulate through my mind.

"Madison, get inside the hotel now!" Jonathan said with such force that I jumped. My eyes centered on the hotel across the street before nodding in his direction. I told myself that Jonathan needed me across the street so that he could focus on Liam — that was, the only way I could leave him. I turned quickly and began to run, dodging into traffic and in front of vehicles as angry horns littered the air. Once inside, I posted myself in front of the large window, bracing my hands against the sill. My eyes focused on the alleyway looking for shadows, movement, anything, however, saw absolutely nothing.

The building by the alley was still standing, despite the massive crack the two men had put in the side. How had that happened? How was that possible? I had seen fights before, however never with such damage. Nic and Bryce, a senior captain of the football team, had fought once. Bryce had slammed Nic into the side of the cafeteria, at the end, both Bryce and Nic were bruised and bloody, but the wall stood unaltered.

Suddenly, I heard a series of loud bangs, as if two semi-trucks had collided. The deafening sound was so loud that the hotel windows trembled, and I stepped back, fearing that they might break. I cringed as the noise clashed once again and propelled me from anxious nail biting to panic stricken pulling my hair from the roots. My fingers twisted a thick lock of my curls, as I tapped the polished cherry wood floors with the sole of my foot and bit my lip until the sensitive flesh began to ache.

Guests rushed outside. They were looking for a car accident — they would not find one. After seeing the scene in the alley, I knew that Jonathan and Liam caused the noise. Where were they? Was Jonathan hurt? Better, question, what were they? I had met people throughout my life that I found notably different, including Emma. She is strikingly beautiful. She eats absolutely nothing and manages to keep a killer body there was nothing sickly about her. Emma also has unbelievably cold skin. Those were just things that both she and Jonathan had in common, and while Liam was equally cold, he was ugly. His ugliness permeated from somewhere deep inside, made his features appear harder, meaner, and cold-blooded. I massaged my temple with my free hand, there were too many questions attempting to gain access to the processing section of my brain. My mind was working overtime and if Jonathan did not return soon, I was going to lose it.

The guests returned with confused looks on their faces. Traffic was flowing as usual. I wanted to run up to them and ask if they had seen anything else unusual, like two men knocking down buildings. Their confused looks would change to concern. The poor, crazy American girl, they would conclude. Honestly, if I had not seen it myself, I wouldn't have believed it either.

I took a seat in the hotel lobby and clutched a couch pillow to my chest, kneading the material between my fingers. The clock on the wall seemed to tick slowly, however I forced myself to remain seated. Jonathan would return any second — he had to. I could feel a wave of emotions threatening to surface as thoughts of Liam injuring him plagued my subconscious. Jonathan had warned me never to travel the streets alone, if he were hurt because of me — I shuddered at the thought. A feeling of calmness washed over me, and I went to my feet in time to see Jonathan appear in the doorway. He was safe.

"You're going back to the hotel!" he snapped. I turned to see him standing behind me, completely taken aback as to how he managed that trick. He quickly took my hand. His grip was tight, and his emotions were battling between anger and concern, anger was by far the winner. We rushed down the street in silence, although I was certain he had much that he wanted to say. He continued his silent brooding until I summoned the nerve to speak up.

"Why are you so angry?"

"He was going to do unspeakable things to you!" he yelled. Still, he refused to look at me, just tugged at my arm, ushering me down the street at a faster pace.

"I don't understand." My effort to keep up with him was failing, and it felt more as if he were dragging me behind him.

"That's just it! You don't understand! They crave you!" His words, so harsh tears brimmed my eyes. Jonathan astounded me, and his delivery stung just a little.

"What in the hell does that mean? Damn it, you're confusing me!" "The world is a loathsome, wicked place, with dangerous and evil people that will stop at nothing to destroy all that is innocent and pure! They hunger for it! They hunger for you!" He sounded ominous, and the look in his eyes sent chills down my spine.

I planted my feet hard into the sidewalk and jerked my arm from his grasp. If he refused to cooperate and answer my questions, then I would have to force him.

"I'm not innocent, so please don't treat me like I don't understand what a horrible place this world is! I can be very stubborn and happen to have an extremely bad temper! So, if you know why that man tried to attack me, you should tell me now!" My feet remained firmly in place.

"You have two choices: come with me and I will take you back to the safety of your hotel, or I will carry you. Either way I get the same result." He stood in front of me waiting for my answer. I folded my arms across my chest defiantly. Jonathan shrugged his shoulders before encircling my body with his strong arms and hoisting me over them.

"Put me down!" I squirmed and struggled with his grasp, but my efforts were useless.

"You were given a choice."

"If you put me down, I'll walk with you to the car." Damn it, my plan to force him into telling me the truth had crashed and burned. The fact that I was dangling upside down from his shoulder should have embarrassed me — instead, he pissed me off — he was treating me like a misbehaved toddler.

"You really are a horrible liar." Minutes later, he placed me on the ground and opened the car door to allow me inside. I rolled my eyes, folded my arms, and leaned against the open car door, with my legs crossed in front of me. Okay, now I was behaving like a child, but he started it — what will be next — sticking out my tongue, kicking him in the shin, how far would I carry this. The real question was whether I could recover from a full-blown tantrum. I wanted Jonathan to see me as a woman and that would not happen if I continued down this path.

"You don't even want me in Paris. You are counting down the days 'til I leave. I don't even know why the hell you care what happens to me." I was almost shouting, however held a smidge of control — to prevent that from happening.

"Please, you have done more than enough stalling. Now, get in." Jonathan completely ignored me and reached out to take my hand. I quickly pushed it away. My mind was going one hundred miles a minute as I tried to piece together the events of the past two days.

"Why won't you just tell me? Did he kidnap those girls?" I asked. My anger had begun to dissipate with each passing second. "You said that he was going to do unspeakable things to me, they said the others were eaten alive…" I could not form the horrendous words that Conner had spewed that day in the diner. They were still a rumor; nothing in the news had confirmed that the kidnappers were cannibals.

"Believe me when I say that he had nothing to do with that. You believe those kidnappers are after you. Right now, that is still speculation. That man just attacked you, is an undeniable truth," Jonathan said. "You should leave Paris, Madison," he added a little to matter of fact.

I eased into his car slowly, mulling over his words as he snapped my seat belt in place. Jonathan pulled into the street seconds later.

"Will you at least admit that we share a connection? I'm not sure how or why, but I know you feel it too." I looked intently at him, hoping that he would finally explain everything that I did not understand.

"All that matters is that you're safe." His response was so casual that it frustrated me.

I let out a loud, irritated sigh and closed my eyes for the rest of the ride. When we pulled in front of the hotel, I remained seated. I contemplated locking the doors and holding myself hostage in his car until I got answers. He quickly swung my door open before I had the chance, and slowly leaned over me to unlock my seatbelt. I stepped out of the car, and he walked up the stairs with me to the entrance.

"So, you're not going to tell me why Liam tried to attack me," I looked up at him, wanting nothing more than for him to tell me the truth.

"I understand that things don't make sense right now, the less you know the better." He touched the side of my face as if assuring himself that I was real. He, was so, not going to answer my question. Jonathan left me standing on the top stair, returned to his car, and drove away.

"He's too damn charming for my own good," I trudged all the way to the room.

After securing the locks on the door, I climbed into an extremely hot shower. I reveled in the calming heat as the water cascaded down my back. My sweet day had turned into a nightmare. I put my pajamas on, and wrapped my hair in a towel, before going into the bedroom. A strange feeling came over me, unpleasant, and so cold that it caused me to shiver. I moved toward the corner of the room and grabbed the bedroom phone. I quickly dialed Emma's cell. It rang twice before she answered.

"Are you in the room?" I spoke softly into the phone.

"No, but we're on our way up. What's wrong?"

Suddenly, I heard footsteps. I stayed quiet as I listened. The cabinets in the small kitchen area sounded as if they had been — flung open — heard the rigid wood crack into the wall as the intruder began to rummage through them. Glasses were shattering on the floor, and I could hear the person crunching the pieces as he made his way into the living room. Whoever was in the suite was not trying to hide that they were there. The furniture was shifting around the room, and the bedroom wall shook as the heavy pieces were — hurled into the wall. Then I heard movement in the hallway, outside the bedroom, suddenly everything fell silent. It was as if he had just stopped. My hand was starting to ache, switching hands quickly; pressed my achy hand on the table, hoping the cold marble would ease the throbbing.

"Madi? Are you still there?"

Emma's voice was so loud — too loud. I looked down at the bright red light on the phone's base. My finger had pressed the speaker button.

"Shit!" I cursed quietly, but my whisper turned into a scream just as the wood of the door split and the phone dropped to the floor. Liam broke through the door with ease. He stood in front of me with the same smile he had on the street. I backed up against the window, trying to find the small lock. My mind was racing, but I thought I could back out of the window and climb down the outside stairs. It was no use. Liam was standing over me within seconds, and then threw me over his shoulder as if I were no more than a rag doll.

"Get your hands off me! Put me down!" His grip so tight the pressure inhibited my ability to get the needed air into my lungs; instead, my breathing became small frequent gasps of air. Liam darted across the room and the next thing I knew we were in the hall. He sprinted up the winding stairwell so fast my head began to spin. I screamed as he crashed into the large metal door, and it burst open as if it were paper. Liam raced across the roof with me still swung over his shoulder. He jumped upon the ledge. His arms shifted me in front of him. Knowing I was on the edge of the building's roof, my body went ironing board stiff. His large hand grasped my ankle, and the freak flipped me upside down. He dangled me over the street as if I were nothing. My towel fell from my hair and floated down to the traffic below. As I watched the damp towel twist in the air, and settle eight stories down, I imagined my journey would end far more brutal. "Please forgive me," I cried as my mom's image floated in front of me. She would never forgive herself for leaving me in Nirvana, trusting me, trusting Margaret. I closed my eyes hot tears raced upward into my hair, as I prepared myself for the inevitable.

Just then, the strong undeniable feeling washed through me — I looked over to see Jonathan coming through the now unhinged, steel door. Emma, Austin, and Lucas followed him.

"I didn't realize you were being protected by so many." Liam's voice oozed with bitterness. He looked down at me, and then turned his attention back to the group. "Tell you what," Liam continued, "all I want is the head, and you can keep the rest. Or you can scrape her dead body off the ground."

"Liam, you don't need to do this. She's not who you think she is," Jonathan shouted.

"I know who she is," Liam snarled.

My view of the street became blurry as the blood rushed to my head, causing the bile to rise in my throat. I had never been afraid of heights, but dangling upside down from a rooftop made me question that. I searched Liam for anything to hold onto, and my fingers latched onto the waistband of his jeans, and belt. My knuckles went white from the grip I had on him, but I knew my life depended on it.

I caught a glimpse of Jonathan near the door. The wind began to whirl around us so violently that I struggled to hang on. Liam shifted and was now balancing both of our weight on the tips of his toes. I glanced back at Jonathan again, just as I felt Liam rock back on his heels. Simultaneously, Jonathan lunged toward us, Liam stepped completely off the ledge, and I screamed. Jonathan latched onto Liam's shirt and yanked us back onto the ledge so fast that we both went soaring across the roof. Jonathan caught me before my body crashed into the hard cement. He placed me lightly back onto the ground. I stood there shaking, unable to speak, as Liam's body crashed into Jonathan's. They rolled around the roof, a blizzard of punches from both was so loud that I crouched lower, covering my ears.

"Emma, get her out of here!" Jonathan ordered. Emma grabbed my hand, and we ran down the stairs and back to our room, locking the door behind us.

"Jonathan, we…" my body was shaking badly as I headed back to the door. "We left him." I managed.

"Three against one, not that he needs the help," Emma said, and for the first time I realized that introducing her to Jonathan was no longer necessary. She knew him.

Emma opened the door and Jonathan; Austin and Lucas came strolling through. I backed up to stand in the doorway of my room, still not calming myself.

"Madi, this is my brother, Jonathan." Despite the events that had just taken place, Emma was beaming. I looked at Jonathan.

"Why didn't you tell me you were Emma's brother?"

"I was going to." His answer was borderline dismissive.

"Wait, you know him?" Emma looked back and forth between Jonathan and me. "It all makes perfect sense now." Emma grinned.

"Ok, so we all have a lot of questions…but first let me ask, why the hell did that man come here for me?"

"I explained to you earlier, the less you know the better. We managed the situation." Jonathan's voice remained steady, but there was no mistaking he was angry.

"I need to know what's going on. He followed me here! He says he knows who I am. How did he get into our room? What does he want?" I was becoming frustrated. None of this made sense, and no one was willing to give me answers.

"Don't worry. He's not coming back." Jonathan's words were softer now, reassuring. His soothing voice almost made me forget that someone had just tried to kidnap me, and that he was a liar. That feigning comfort lasted about a second before I snapped again.

"You can't tell me not to worry! That sick freak almost killed me!" I wanted to scream at the top of my lungs. "What did he want from me?" My question directed to Jonathan; however, Lucas spoke up to answer.

"What didn't he want from you?" Lucas shrugged his shoulders, as if his answer were perfectly logical. Jonathan sent Lucas a warning look.

"Eww," I redirected my question to Jonathan, "Why did you tell him I wasn't who he thought I was?" I prayed for the trembling inside me to subside and focused intently on Jonathan as I waited for his response.

"He doesn't, Madison. He thinks he does, but he doesn't. We took care of it and made sure that he'll never bother you again,"

Jonathan said with assurance.

"How can, you be sure?"

"That's easy; we ripped off his head, and then dropped him off the roof. It made this weird crunching sound. You want to see what's left?" Lucas said. For a fraction of a second, I thought he was completely serious, and then he began to laugh. "I'm just kidding. We killed him."

Austin began laughing loudly as he eyed Lucas. "Oh Lucas, don't make jokes like that. I think it's time for us to go, now." Austin ushered Lucas toward the door.

"You are such a buzz kill," Lucas groaned, before blowing me a kiss. "I will see you later, beautiful. Leave a window open." His eyes traveled the length of my body.

"Lucas..." Jonathan began, but he shut the door before Jonathan finished.

He turned his attention to me. "We need to get her out of here, at least until we make certain everything will be safe."

"Wait. What?" I asked, but Emma's eyes were on Jonathan. They were communicating, although neither one spoke a word. She nodded. The next thing I knew Emma was standing in front of me and ushering me into the room.

"You need to dress, quickly." She ordered.

"What's going on? He just said they took care of Liam." I snapped, clearly agitated with all the secrecy.

"Yes, but we need to be sure that he was working alone." Emma said as she tossed me a pair of jeans, and a t-shirt. I jerked them on and stuffed my feet in my sneakers, and went to grab my suitcase, but Emma stopped me.

"We need to leave now," She whispered. I grabbed my cell phone and purse and followed them out of the room. We left the hotel and made our way to Jonathan's car. He held the door open Emma was about to sit in the back, I put my hand in front of her.

"My legs are shorter," I crawled to the back, sitting length wise, knowing that if the space were tight for me, Emma would have had to fold herself to fit back here.

"Are you comfortable?" Jonathan asked. I saw him peering at me through the rear-view window and looked away. He had lied to me. He was Emma's brother. He knew why Liam attacked me. Yet the fact that he wanted me to leave Paris seemed to bother me more than anything else did. I pressed my head against the cold leather seat. My emotions were filled with uncertainty as we traveled through the dark streets of Paris.

CHAPTER FIFTEEN
WINE CELLAR

J onathan's car snaked down a cobbled driveway as if gliding over ice, every movement smooth and effortless; large pine trees created a shadow of darkness, making our journey feel foreboding. Where in the hell were they taking me? That was one of the questions dangling on the tip of my tongue. We had traveled over an hour, and my legs began stiffening. If the ride took any longer, I would fall out of the car due to the lack of blood flowing through my legs. The tips of my toes were tingling a little. I twisted — my face pressed against the back of Emma's seat, as I tried to gauge my surrounding. Unfortunately, the dark tint on Jonathan's windows and the moonless night left me staring into the darkness. I leaned back, glancing at Jonathan through the rearview mirror; his silver eyes met mine for a moment before he lowered them again. There had to be a logical explanation for the past few hours. He would explain everything once we stopped, or at least I wanted to believe he would.

The car eased around the circular driveway, the engine stopped, and Jonathan stepped out. He opened the door for Emma before he folded the seat back for me, and I ungraciously pulled myself from the back seat. The moment his hand touched mine, I felt more at ease. His fingers encircled my wrist as he led me up the steep steps. I glanced up to see identical gargoyles crouched upon massive stone beams. Their twisted faces sent a shiver down my spine, and I quickened my steps until they were in rhythm with Jonathan. Emma was ahead of us. Even in the dead of night, I could see that the home loomed over the trees, a castle formed of stone and brick mortar. The air smelled like a flower garden, and the swamp had merged.

The aroma was much more pungent as I followed them into the cathedral entryway. My mouth dropped open when I saw the double staircase resembling a fancy horseshoe. As far as I could see, there were dark polished wood and white walls. I noticed the furnishings were a deep burgundy, velvet curtains swept the floors, and everything was on a massive scale. The towering bookshelves, enormous paintings, statues, and antique furnishing should be in a museum instead of this home. I quieted my thoughts in time to see Emma glide up the staircase; she gave me a reassuring glance over her shoulder before disappearing.

Then I faced Jonathan, still feeling nervous about my surrounding. The place reminded me of the feeling I get whenever Nic, and I take the shortcut through the graveyard. It feels like a swarm of emotions trying to enter my spirit, all fighting for recognition; right now, fear is winning.

"Where am I?" This one took precedence out of all the questions I could have asked. Yet, I needed to know because the feelings were becoming overwhelming.

"You're at a friend's home," he leaned back against the wall.

"No, I'm in a castle," I snipped.

"Chateau," he corrected, and I suppose he was right. However, the place did have that eerie feeling that I had imagined a spooky castle would — like the one in Dram Stoker's Dracula. The night's events had me on edge. I was thinking about a face-peeling, monstrous creature that stalks young girls. We are in Paris, and I, for the moment, was standing in this dimly lit room with the most handsome man I had ever met. As for the chateau in the morning light, this place would be romantic or at least less creepy. There was no such thing as vampires or monstrous creatures that shift into beasts, which means the vampire theory was a bust — thank goodness. Although this does make the museum curator less perfect, she was downright creepy, judging by her home. The curtain in the living room billowed out, derailing my delusional train of thought. I looked at Jonathan — if he noticed there was no evidence on his perfectly chiseled face. The chateau was eerie, and something was off. However, I could not put my finger on exactly what that was.

"I don't like it here," I whispered to Jonathan, looking around his friend's mansion. The place was dark and gloomy, with heavy drapes blocking any sunlight. The walls were made of rich mahogany, with intricate patterns on the floor. Golden statues stood next to a fireplace that crackled with fire. Above us, a mural covered the ceiling, depicting a gruesome scene of angels and demons fighting for eternity. I wondered how anyone could live with such a horrifying image above their head.

"Come on, Madison, Emma is waiting for us," Jonathan said, pulling me by the hand. He led me up the stairs along a dim corridor, where candles flickered in golden holders. I felt a sense of dread as we approached the door at the end. Emma was supposed to be there, but something told me she wasn't. Jonathan opened the door and pushed me inside. The room was huge, but it felt suffocating. I gasped as I saw what was inside. Emma was nowhere to be found.

The room was huge, but I felt claustrophobic as we entered, and he locked the door behind us.

Was this Emma's way of making the room ready for me? I seriously doubted it. Candlesticks were in every nook, casting eerie shadows on the wooden walls. The room's style was creepy. Giant Persian rugs, bulky wardrobes, and bedside tables were trimmed with gold. The furniture was dark too - not old-fashioned more like ancient. I looked at the massive bed that filled the room. The navy-blue curtains hung from the ceiling and touched the ground. I gulped as I pictured those velvet curtains smothering me – death, by asphyxiation. "You are safe here," Jonathan said, he was surprised by the look of terror on my face.

"I want to go back to the hotel," I muttered, even though I panicked inside.

"You will; Austin and Lucas returned to make certain that

no one followed Liam," his reply brought the Liam questions to my mind.

"Who was he? What was he?" yep, I asked because things were getting stranger by the second. I wanted to ask, 'What the hell are you,' but decided that could wait — at least for now.

"He was the monster that attempted to kill you," his eyes flashed, and his body stiffened. I had hit a nerve.

"I have a right to know! No human is that strong, that fast, and I saw something in him that wasn't right!" I reasoned more to myself than Jonathan.

"Madison, you should rest," he waved me toward the bed, but I folded my arms over my chest.

"You have got to be kidding me!" This entire situation was not settling right in the pit of my gut. Uncle Mike always said, "Listen to your gut; it will never steer you wrong, Madi girl, never." I could almost see him shaking his head in disapproval over my current situation. But, of course, the fact that I was in a scary chateau would be the least of his concerns — I was in Paris, the forbidden city, according to my mom. I had broken more rules than Helen Slater had in The Legend of Billie Jean, except for the whole martyr thing and cutting off my hair.

"Your safety is not a joke to me, Madison. So, to answer your question, no, I am not kidding you," his disapproving tone made me angrier. I could not explain the emotions deep inside me; however, anger was in control.

"I cannot stay here! No, I will not stay in this place!" I would have stomped my foot but simply held my ground instead. My foot tapped the polished wood floor repeatedly, and I placed my hands in the hooks of my jeans, clearly defying any idea of my sleeping in this house or that damn bed.

"You will remain here, and we will talk once you have calmed down," Jonathan said.

"No, I will not! And, 'just so' you know, when you tell me to calm down, it only makes me angrier!" I could almost see the steam billowing over my head.

"Your eyes are glowing." He shook his head before walking out the door. I jumped as it slammed closed, sending a wave of wind through the room, and extinguishing the candles. I raced from the room. As I turned the corner, he disappeared down the stairs. I trailed behind him, taking the stairs three, sometimes four, at a time. Jonathan turned down the narrow hallway instead of returning to the grand room.

There were rooms at the end of the hall. I opened the first door to find an office. A diverse collection of books lined the massive shelves on both sides of the room. The office had the same feel as the bedroom. I was about to slam the door closed when I saw the museum curator — her image enticed me to explore the room further. She was gorgeous in the oil painting hanging above the desk. Her long blonde hair was in ringlets and piled high upon her head. She wore a beautiful vintage silk gown with coordinating gloves that stopped at the crease of her delicately folded arms. A large diamond and sapphire necklace with chandelier earrings accented the gold dress. I wanted to look around more; however, finding Jonathan took precedence over everything else — including the gorgeous curator.

I closed the door before trying the next one, which led to a narrow set of stairs. I followed them below ground to yet another door. The sound of scurrying and something running across my sneakers made the tiny hairs on the back of my neck prickle. I felt the door's resistance as I shook the handle and pressed my hand against the splintered wood. The voice in my head told me to turn around and walk away; however, curiosity got the best of me. I used all my strength to shove the door, but it still refused to budge. I backed up and ran forward, hitting the door so hard that it slammed open. My body kept going. The force sent me headfirst into the cold dark room, and I quickly crashed into a stand before my body hit the floor. I twisted in time to see the extensive structure topple over. My arms went up to protect myself as the thing fell on me, releasing a thick sticky substance. I barely had a chance to catch my breath when gooey liquid began to cover me in a matter of seconds; I was swimming in the sticky goo. Unfortunately, the heavy structure had no give.

The room was cold and completely dark, and I told myself it had to be wine. It was a wine cellar like my parents had in Hatteras. I struggled to push the stand as the metal fixture began to dig into my skin. The damn thing had not budged. Using my hands to grip the slippery floor, I painfully wiggled from beneath the large stand. My entire body was achy and coated in the gooey mixture. I pushed off the floor, slipping four or five times until my ability to walk as a human returned to me.

My eyes struggled to open as the substance weighed on my lids. I used my fingers to clear them and began searching for a light switch. The liquid dripped into my parted lips. It tasted like a mixture of metal, salt, and something else I could not name. This was not wine. My sticky hands ran along the cold stone of the wall. I flicked the light switch. My hands were the first thing I saw. I heard someone screaming so loud that the reverberation caused my ears to throb. My chest was burning, throat felt as if I had swallowed a mouth full of glass. That was when I realized that the screams were coming from me. I was making that terrifying sound. Each piercing cry was louder than the one before. I wanted to stop, but the sight of the room held me in terror. There were rows and rows of metal racks lined with large bags of blood, like a clothesline from hell.

Once my feet decided to move, I ran from the room and sprinted up the stairs and down the hall. Suddenly, I was in the air and, a second later, in Jonathan's arms. My hands beat against his chest as I pleaded for him to let me go as he carried me up the stairs and into a room. The next thing I knew, we were standing in the shower. Jonathan ignored my demand to free me from his hold and the horror of the wine cellar. No, not a wine cellar — that was blood down there — bags and bags of blood.

My body stiffened. I looked at Jonathan as if for the very first time. My jaw dropped as the jagged puzzle pieces came together, and my mind tried to process the picture. Emma, Austin, and Jonathan were family; Lucas was not, yet he felt deathly cold like them. I had never seen any of them eat a single thing. They were all beautiful beyond compare. Jonathan was freakishly strong and fast. Was Liam a vampire too? Could that couple in the lobby of Jonathan's hotel be as well? Did they surround me? I tried to conjure up the specific moments in the past, memories of things I had overlooked or simply chosen not to see clearly.

I looked up at Jonathan, my eyes seeing him clearly. His perfectly sculpted features, those intense eyes that illuminate when he is angry. "I want to hear you say it!" I screamed as my fist landed repeatedly against his chest. "Tell me!" My hand throbbed with every strike that connected with his muscular chest. Until his fingers closed around my wrist, preventing another assault that would fracture the delicate bones in my hand.

"I am a vampire," he said without hesitation.

"You're a vampire! Oh my God, you're a vampire!" I shouted. He turned me toward the water to rinse the blood from my face, which only caused more to seep into my mouth. "You're a vampire!" I yelled again, wiping the liquid from my lips.

"Yes. And yelling that at the top of your lungs won't change that!" Jonathan screamed.

"Take your hands off me!" I demanded. He let go, and I climbed out of the tub, only to slip on the floor. He caught me, but I shoved his hands away, "Take your hands off me!"

"You must understand why I couldn't share this with you, Madison." His voice softened as he stared at me; water droplets dangled from his hair.

"You know what, Jonathan, stay the hell away from me!" I stormed out of the bathroom to find three sets of eyes glued to me. Austin, Lucas, and Emma's gaze traveled from me to the pool of blood collecting on the floor.

"Humph, I guess the joke is on me," I glared at Emma in utter disbelief. She was my best friend, I shared everything about myself with her, and she never said a word. "You're all vampires and Liam?" I sneered.

"Madi, I wanted to tell you," Emma stepped toward me, and I backed away.

"What? That you've been lying to me all this time?" I ran from the room, needing to escape Jonathan, Emma, and this horrible nightmare. My breathing labored as I took the stairs, rushed through the massive wooden door, and down the tree-lined path that led to the driveway. Once I hit the gravel, my footing became slippery, and the weight of the blood-soaked clothes hampered my movements. I flinched as the stone dug into the soles of my feet. The thin rubber was no match for my heavy steps and the jagged rocks. I tried not to imagine the strange creatures lurking inside the thick brush on either side of me and focused on getting back to the hotel. Only the enormous wrought iron gate was, locked. I had no choice; I squeezed my slim frame through — reached the other side and began running again.

Then, I stopped suddenly as a shadowy figure quickly cleared the eight-foot gate. Jonathan landed before me, his body still dripping wet from our shower. Those piercing silver eyes were so intense that they glowed. I turned away, gathering the courage to run from him. Only he was standing in front of me once again. Every time I spun away; he reappeared in front of me.

"I cannot stay here," I cried; all my resolve washed away with that last desperate plea as the sky opened, and I felt the ground shift beneath me — large pelts of warm rain began to cover us both. My entire body shook from the shock of it all, and by all, I mean the man standing before me was a vampire. The man I had come to Paris to save never needed my help.

"Madison, let me take you back to the hotel," he lifted me from the cold pavement and carried me back toward the house before I could say no. He jumped over the gate again, and even with me in his arms, he did not waver.

Jonathan put me down in front of his car, and I glanced up to see Emma in front of me. She held out a large thick towel, which I gladly accepted; as I fluffed the dampness from my tangled locks, she moved closer.

"You should take a real shower and get out of those clothes. You cannot return to the hotel looking like that," Emma started up the stairs, stopping long enough to offer a reassuring smile.

"Do you kill people?" I shouted the question at her and could have sworn she flinched.

"No, although we need blood to survive, we no longer hunt. But Madi, I'm still Emma," her tone was teetering on the verge of sadness.

"What does that mean? Who are you? This morning you were Emma. My obsessive-compulsive, bossy best friend, and now you are Emma the vampire, with vampire brothers and friends that live in a freaking castle, with an entire cellar filled with blood!" I stamped my foot, unable to contain myself, and felt my foot slosh into the soaking-wet sneaker. "You should have told me!"

"Yes, because you dealt with this information so well!" She snapped back as if I had no right to be upset. I stood there studying her in utter disbelief. Emma was gorgeous, had the body of a runway model, was intelligent, articulate, wealthy, and a true fashion diva. She was also my friend — she never treated me like a freak; this secret was too great to share, even among friends. If I were Emma. I would be frightened that she would walk away, which was precisely what I had done.

"Yeah, next time, I will try to take the news a little more calmly. Here, a practice run…." I leaned against the doorframe, ignoring Jonathan's eyes on me. He was watching the exchange with a look of utter confusion. "Oh, Emma, that cellar filled with blood, no biggie, so what if I'm covered in it. The fact that you are a vampire. I could care less. We all have strange eating habits. Oh yeah, 'and so' what if you sleep in a coffin, I used to love sleeping beneath my bed." I smiled sarcastically. "If we agree that I will never become your main course, we can precede as usual." I did a slight curtsy. We both laughed simultaneously. If she had wanted to kill me. I would have been dead and gone.

"That will never be a problem. I prefer my humans without bushy hair and filthy wet clothes, so let's get you cleaned up," She teased, and I had no choice but to smile a little. Jonathan shook his head, and I paused long enough to narrow my eyes before giving him an academy award-winning glare. Emma might be off the hook — he was not. We went upstairs, and she ushered me to the bathroom in her usual bossy fashion. How could it be that so much had changed, and yet so much had remained the same? Emma was still Emma to me. She was still my best friend, and my love for her had not changed.

After showering and changing my clothes, I rode with Jonathan and Emma back to the hotel. Emma and I chatted a little about everything except their being vampires. However, Jonathan remained silent. I could feel him quietly studying me on the elevator up to our room; however, I pretended not to notice. He entered the room before us and came out later to wave me forward. The scene reminded me of a 007 movie if James Bond were a vampire.

Emma followed me into my suite and watched quietly as I dropped onto the bed, curling my feet beneath me. Vampire, my best friend, is a vampire. Wow, it feels surreal. I looked at Emma. "Can I ask you something?"

Emma nodded her head.

"How old are you?" My question was not a complete surprise judging by the perceptive look on her face.

"I've been 18 for 60 years," she admitted, examining my reaction.

"Do you like being a vampire?"

"Yes, I get to live forever. What's not to like," Emma said, although her tone was solemn.

"I would think drinking blood wouldn't be so great."

"Of course, you feel that way; however, for vampires, it's like those chocolate truffles you eat, addictive." Her eyes brightened, and I could have sworn the intensity in her eyes was that of hunger. She looked away uneasily before meeting my eyes again.

"So, how exactly do you become a vampire? I mean, you weren't born one..." I scooted back on the bed and placed the pillow beneath my chin.

"There's only one way to become a vampire; you're bitten," she said.

I waited anxiously for her to continue.

"Vampire bites are venomous. The blood is...drained from

your body, and simultaneously, toxins are released into your veins, destroying all vital organs. Your heart is the very last thing the venom attacks. That process alone is not actually what makes you a vampire, though. You cannot become a vampire until you drink from your creator. That's when the transformation begins. After that, your human body dies a horrific death." Emma's entire body trembled as if recalling the memory had evoked the pain she experienced. Her eyes flashed, her fist formed into tightly cinched balls, and her body stiffened. "When you rise, you are a vampire: young, dangerous, and ready to feed on everything and anything." Emma rushed the final sentence, and I knew that meant she had spent more time on the topic than she felt comfortable with. She stood up, smoothing the folds of her dress. "I promise to answer more of your questions later after I have spoken with Jonathan. You're not the only one that wants answers." Emma left the room without another word, and I fell back on the bed, noticing for the first time they had fixed everything and that nothing was out of place. I flipped over on the bed and dug through my purse to find my phone. There were four missed calls from my mom — they would have to wait. I could not talk to her tonight. Her voice would send me over the edge, and I had to hold my emotions together.

CHAPTER SIXTEEN
FREE FALL

A faint light filtered into the room, urging me to wake up — I refused. Sleep had been impossible. Every time I closed my eyes, Liam's crazed face would appear. I shut my eyes, hoping the images of dangling from the rooftop would dissipate; my headache deepened, and a sharp, throbbing pain surfaced. My hand went to my stomach, pressing the center to calm myself. There were so many unanswered questions. Who was Liam? What was he? And what in the hell did Liam want from me? Who exactly did he think I was? Why was Liam willing to jump off a roof and kill us both? Could he die, or was I the only one at risk?

Emma peeked inside my room, interrupting my thoughts. "Good morning," "Are you alright?" she asked as she came to stand near the window by my bed, fiddling with her bracelet, and I could sense she was uneasy. When our eyes met — she quickly looked away.

"I'm not sure how to answer that." The pounding headache worsened as I tried the seated position. "I don't even know where to start. My entire body aches and I had the strangest nightmare of bathing in blood and learning that you are a vampire. Oh wait, that wasn't a dream."

"You should rest. I'll come back later," Emma said as she turned to leave.

"Hey, I was teasing. But honestly, I get it. You couldn't tell me. The truth is, we all have our secrets." I kicked my legs over the side of the bed, "I hope you can understand that I need to know what happened last night."

"I don't know. I told you as much as I can."

"When we moved to Nirvana, our movers had the same tattoos as Liam," I managed. Unsure if I were more afraid that she wouldn't tell me or that she would. "VHW," I bit my bottom lip and waited for her response.

"If I could…" she turned to stare out the window, "I can't."

"Emma, help me understand. Jonathan's a freaking closed book when it comes to the truth. He knows Liam. Do you know him? Are there others like Liam out there hunting humans? Why did he choose me? How did he find me here?" My tone wasn't angry, but my voice elevated slightly each time I formulated a new question.

Emma looked down at the shoes as if inspecting the red bottoms. "Most vampires hunt humans. I have no idea why Liam came after you. He is a vampire. It could be that simple. There are rules that we must follow. Jonathan revealing our existence to you is not only dangerous for you, but all of us too. Discussing this now is also against our laws," she explained, and strangely I believed every word she spoke.

"This is my *life* we're talking about. I'm not sure if I can deal with all of this!"

"Austin, Lucas, and I were in the lobby. Jonathan arrived right before you called. We followed him up to the roof and found you. Last night was a little crazy; normally, our lives are more boring than you can imagine." she admitted. I watched as her eyes shifted briefly to the floor before they returned to me. She shook her head back and forth slowly.

"What is it?" I asked, curious as to what was going on in that head of hers.

Her mouth slowly formed into a smile as she looked up at me. "I believe Jonathan came here because of you."

"That's another thing I don't understand; how did he know I was in trouble last night or any other time?" My eyes narrowed. "Hey, is that a vampire thing?"

"No, it's not a vampire thing." She snapped. "Anyway, what I meant was I believe Jonathan came back to Paris because of you," Emma said.

"He was already here when I arrived. He didn't come here for me," I tried to explain. "Emma, Jonathan's the reason that I came here."

"You didn't even know him," Emma's brows furrowed. "Jonathan's the man…you know…from my dreams. He needed me, can't explain how I knew he was in trouble."

"He was in Rome. We had been trying to reach him for months. I hadn't seen or spoken to him since you," Emma stopped suddenly and looked away before continuing. "He came here because of you."

"You're wrong; he came here because of his paintings. They are on exhibit at the *Musee d'Orsay*. That must be why he's in Paris," I wanted to say that the gorgeous curator was his motivation; however, I remained silent about her for now.

"You've seen his collection?" Emma asked. She appeared utterly puzzled by my statement.

"No, only private collectors view the paintings. A million reasons could have brought Jonathan here," I began to recall my visit to the museum and the curator who had been talking to Jonathan and the fact that he took me to her freaky château last night. "Or is he here because of that woman?" My heart began to beat rapidly; my stomach looped and tied itself in knots as Emma recognized my uneasiness. "The house with the… wine cellar. Does it belong to the museum curator or her husband?" I asked while silently hoping that she said yes.

"No, she's single," Emma said, her eyes sparkling with mischief and humor.

"Oh, well, she and Jonathan seemed pretty close at the museum…" not to mention he has an all-access pass to her home.

"You have nothing to worry about," Emma assured me.

"Yeah, guess you're right. So, what if she is beautiful, thin, with a radiant complexion, and has long blonde hair."

Emma began shaking her head with amusement. "What?" I

asked, but I already knew the answer. The green-eyed monster had reared its ugly head and refused to back down.

"Annaliese Montgomery is my oldest and closest friend," She put her hand in the air to halt the series of questions now clinging to my tongue. Emma skipped out of the room and returned with her computer in hand. She opened her laptop and found a file named 'Go-Go.'

"That's her!" I said, slightly taken aback by the picture. Emma, Jonathan, and the curator were at a crowded party. The photo was grainy, as if she had scanned it onto her computer. Emma and Annaliese wore bright mini dresses with knee-high white boots. Emma's hair was long like it was now, but instead of being straight, she wore small waves. Jonathan's hair was a little bit longer and hung around his face. He wore a white button-up shirt, black dress pants, and a striped charcoal tie and was as handsome as ever. My admiring smile faded when I noticed the curator's arm over Jonathan's shoulders. I bit my lip and swallowed the jealous lump in my throat.

"When was this taken?" It was challenging to take my eyes off Annaliese and Jonathan; however, I forced myself to look back at Emma.

"We went to a Beetles Concert! They were incredible, Madi!" Emma said excitedly. "We had a blast that day!"

"Looks like it," I tried to hide my irritated expression, but she could tell I was uncomfortable. "So, this woman is a vampire too?"

"Yes, Annaliese is an old friend of the family. Their relationship is completely platonic; nothing for you to be worried about."

"I wasn't implying they weren't friends." I stammered. "Oh," Emma started, shooting me a knowing glare, "maybe, I misunderstood the suspicion in your voice." She walked over to the mirror to examine her hair. I watched as she pulled her hair back into a ponytail. "I'm a little surprised Annaliese is working at the museum," Emma continued, "although I haven't seen her in a while." I stopped her before she could say anything more about the woman.

"I want to talk about last night." I moved to the edge of the bed, and she turned away from the mirror to look at me.

"Oh, like Jonathan staying with you the entire night?" Emma said, giving me a huge grin. Of course, this was not what I meant; however, she quickly changed my focus again. She was good at doing that.

"All night," I lifted a questioning brow.

"All night," She smiled. "He left this morning to take care of a few things."

"I guess he missed you," the fact that Jonathan had stayed the night comforted me a little. She rolled her eyes. "Yeah, because it's not like he has been avoiding me for months," she said sarcastically. I decided to relent — she was right; he stayed here because of me. That thought sounded better each time the words floated through my mind.

"Is this weird for you?"

"What?"

"Jonathan, me, I mean..." I bit my lip, uncertain how to continue. I don't know if anyone has met the person of their dreams, but I have. Emma was still smiling when I looked back at her.

"I'm happy to see both of you happy," Emma chided. "So, does that mean you forgive him?" She asked, more excited than I had seen her in weeks. I shrugged my shoulders as she skipped out of my room. I trailed her steps.

She went directly to her closet and began to sort through her wardrobe. Her closet was packed with designer dresses, stacks of shoes, and small boxes, each holding a delicate piece of jewelry. She sighed with frustration, and I wondered exactly what she was searching for when she practically had a boutique readily available.

"So, you're sure it's not weird?" I asked again.

"I'm certain. On a scale of weird things, I believe that your acceptance of my being a vampire tops the list," she said, tilting her head as if waiting for me to protest. "He smiled when we talked about you last night. I cannot remember the last time I saw him smile. His emotions are normally stuck on bossy," Emma said. Her comment made me laugh hard. "See, you agree with me." Her eyes brightened. "Jonathan's extremely cautious when it comes to you, so he didn't say anything before. In fact, the only person I know he's like that with is me," She added.

"What is he really like?"

"He, um," Emma paused. "He's very protective. He taught me everything I needed to know to survive as a vampire." There was a hesitation in her tone as she spoke. "There is nothing he wouldn't do for me."

"There is something about him that scares me," I admitted. "Not the vampire thing," that comment made her roll her eyes. "The way he makes me feel is difficult to describe; it's as if we're bound to one another. Our connection is undeniable, yet he doesn't seem to agree."

"I wish there were a way to make you feel more at ease. You fell for him, and you're still falling. Jonathan can be as stubborn as you are. The only thing that worries me is that he never settles anywhere. Sometimes it can be months before I receive a phone call. The possibility of him returning with us to Nirvana is slim to none. That means you must decide if these moments with him will be worth the pain it may cause when we leave," She stopped and looked straight at me, "...and he doesn't come with us." Emma had never been more right. Jonathan was becoming more important to me with each passing second. How would I deal with not seeing him again?" Her words silenced me. He had never said that he believed we have something more, and my parents. My parents would never allow us to be together. Phillip would hunt him down.

"Well, not like my parents would allow me to date him anyway." I thought about Phillip's arsenal of weaponry in his locked room being — used on Jonathan, and the notion sent an icy chill down my spine.

"One of the many reasons you can never mention this, Madi!" Emma's voice teetered on demanding. There was something in her eyes that I had never seen before, fear. She was frightened.

"Yeah, I know," their secret would go with me to the grave. Emma quickly turned her attention back to her closet. She threw a couple more dresses across the room and stood up defeated. Her loud voice broke the silence.

"I have absolutely nothing to wear!" She threw her hands in the air as she openly vented her frustration. "I'm going out; you look like you need time to think anyway. We can talk more when I get back," Emma said. She snatched her purse from the table before heading toward the door.

"Oh, I forgot to tell you, the blond came by this morning." She gave me an uneasy look. "Let's say it would be best to keep him and Jonathan apart. The Blond is stupid and temperamental, which could be a dangerous combination with Jonathan. He has a short fuse and little patience."

"You don't think he would hurt Conner, do you?" I asked. I wasn't entirely sure after what I saw last night with Liam.

"Do your best to keep them apart and to answer your question…maybe. I'll see you when I get back." Emma's answer had done nothing to comfort me. I curled up on the sofa the second she left.

My cell phone began vibrating on the table. Margaret's number appeared on the caller ID, and I debated whether to answer. Then, reluctantly, I put the phone to my ear and walked into my bedroom.

"Hello," I whispered.

Margaret's loud angry voice contrasted with mine. "Madi, please tell me that you're on your way back. Beth has called me five times already this morning!" Margaret yelled.

"I need a few more days," the words streamed out before I could stop myself.

"Hell no," she screamed so loud that the phone made an awful screeching sound. "You get your little ass back here, or I will call Beth and tell her exactly how deceitful her precious daughter is," Margaret's threat took me over the edge; I stormed into the bathroom — my reflection in the bathroom confirmed my anger, and if I am being honest, fear did too. I clenched my hand tight around the phone.

"No, if you do that, she won't pay you!"

If Margaret told my mom the truth, my life as I know it would never be the same.

Margaret groaned, and there was a moment of dead silence before I heard a deep guttural cough. The kind that rattled from a lifetime of addiction to cigarettes.

"You look here, Miss High-n-Mighty!" Daniel screamed into the phone. The rattle in his chest caused his words to vibrate. "It's going to be bad if Marge doesn't get her money!" he threatened. Another pause — Margaret was back, thankfully. She was the lesser of the two evils.

"Madi, stop messing with me. Your mom believes you hung the moon. She would be heartbroken if she found out the truth. How could you do this to Beth? She gave up so much for you!" Margaret yelled. I shut my eyes. The bathroom walls felt like they had closed around me. I threw the cell phone as hard as I could. It shattered the bathroom mirror. My eyes glowed in the cracked and distorted glass.

Margaret's phone call reminded me of the risk that I took. She would phone my mom if I stayed in Paris. After a moment, I regained my composure, retrieved the damaged cell phone, and collected the shattered pieces of glass.

I had to leave. I understood that now, as much as I wanted to prove to Jonathan that we should explore this connection, I could not hurt her.

The impatient knock at the door, pulled me out of my stupor and sent me to the door. I didn't bother to ask who it was but was glad to see Jonathan on the other side.

"Are you okay?" he questioned as his eyes scanned the room.

"Yes, everything's fine. Emma had to leave." I walked to the window. It had begun to rain tiny droplets rolled down the windowpane. The tip of my finger trailed down the glass, and I followed its' path.

Jonathan reached for my hand, but I pulled away. He had lied to me, and I knew I should be furious. My anger dissipated as he approached and looked into my eyes. I surrendered to his hug, my head on his chest while he held me tightly. I closed my eyes and nuzzled my face against him.

"What's wrong?" he asked. I reluctantly pulled away, went to the sofa, sat down, and curled my feet beneath me. His eyes narrowed when I tried to fake a smile.

"Madison, if you're still angry with me about," He stopped when I shook my head, I sensed that he wanted to discuss the whole vampire thing. "Would it be okay if I stayed here until Emma returned?" he asked.

"Sure," she would be back soon, and I would still be in my pajamas. I stood to move from the sofa as Jonathan walked toward the door. My confusion peaked as he reached for the doorknob. Had I missed something? Didn't he ask to stay?

"Jonathan." I had barely spoken his name when someone began banging on the door.

"I want to see Madi right now, or I'm calling the police!" Conner demanded.

"Of course, you want to see her," Jonathan responded. "The question is does she want to see you?"

"It's fine," I said.

He swung the door open and allowed Conner inside. Conner looked enraged, based solely on his bright red face and the purple veins in his neck that pulsated as he stormed into my room.

"What's going on?" Conner asked. I didn't say a word, just clamped my mouth shut. Did he know about last night? He glanced at Jonathan, then back at me.

"Um, nothing's going on," I tugged at my bottom lip, "Jonathan, this is Conner Whitman. He's a close friend of mine," dead silence, "Conner, this is Emma's brother, Jonathan Spenser." Okay, the introduction hadn't gone the way I had planned. They eyed each other, but neither said a word.

"Yeah, I met him this morning!" Conner finally said. "He's the creep from the museum!" His eyes flashed, a silent threat in Jonathan's direction.

Jonathan's lips slowly turned up into a smile. He enjoyed

Conner's frustration, even though it didn't seem logical. But then again, nothing was making sense. "Why is he here now? Where's Emma?"

"She's not here. I was going to get ready for the Louvre." I glanced over at the clock. It was already 12:00.

"He was here this morning. Did he stay with you last night?" Conner continued to inquire as he followed me into the bedroom.

"Yeah, he was nice enough to stay here last night," I took one of my new dresses from the closet and placed it on the bed.

"What else was he nice enough to do for you?" His insinuation caused me to glare at him.

"I'm sure it's none of your business who stays in my room, but Jonathan was a perfect gentleman if it makes you feel better." My defense aggravated him more.

"You're telling me he didn't try anything with you?"

"Madison was taken care of," Jonathan taunted as he came to stand next to me.

"Madi can speak for herself, Spenser!" Conner's voice elevated.

"Why are you acting like this?" My frown deepened.

"This guy could be a sick pervert, and you're alone with him in your room. You let him stay with you. There is no way you can be that stupid!"

"Conner! Jonathan is Emma's brother!" My agitation had gone from simmering to a slow boil. He had taken rude to an entirely new level.

"Yeah, like that would change my mind about him," he sneered. "Why aren't you dressed? The tour bus leaves in an hour," Conner continued to pry.

"Kind of hard to get dressed during my inquisition." I snapped at him.

"Jonathan, would you like to come with us?" I felt a little anxious when he gave me a mischievous smile.

"I like it better when I have you all to myself," he said. The seductive look on his face made me flush and in desperate need of water as my eternal thermostat threatened to boil over. Jonathan had a way of sometimes unnerving me with a look, a touch, or everything. The thought of our last kiss sent me to the kitchenette to search for a water bottle. Jonathan followed, and Conner was quick to come behind us. I looked inside the refrigerator and saw the bottle but struggled to open the lid. The top was stuck.

"What the hell does that mean?" Conner yelled. He turned to me and jerked the bottle from my hand. His brows furrowed as his face turned a deeper shade of red. He removed the top with such force that it splashed all over my shirt.

"Thank you," I managed with a frown and quickly grabbed a hand towel to blot the water from my shirt. Then I chugged at least half of the icy cold liquid. When I glanced back at Jonathan, that slow smile had returned. Thank goodness he didn't know the specifics of my thoughts.

"Thirsty?" Jonathan asked as I downed the remaining water.

"A little," my voice peeked with nervousness.

"What the hell does he mean he 'likes you better to himself'?" Conner's tone was mocking and angry. "Have you been seeing him since the museum?" He shifted his focus to Jonathan and then back to me. "You two are a thing," Conner said, only this time not as a question but an acknowledgment. He moved toward Jonathan, and I stepped in between them. Jonathan pulled me behind him.

"Do you have a problem?" Jonathan asked. I remembered how he slammed Liam into that brick wall and recalled Emma's warning.

My fingers grazed Jonathan's forearm, which was, clenched tightly. I leaned forward until my body pressed firmly into his back.

"Jonathan." My voice was barely a whisper. He twisted to look at me. "I need to dress for the Louvre. I'm sorry, he isn't normally so rude," my comment met Conner's glare. Jonathan's body relaxed, and I took a deep breath. He glanced down, and I realized there was no space between us. I stepped back, and he gave me a soft smile.

"I'll let you have your privacy," Jonathan said before he left the room.

"Conner, you can leave now," my unblinking stare met him, "I'll see you at the bus."

"Madi, I'm trying to help," he pleaded.

"No, you were rude!" I crossed my arms over my chest. "You're supposed to be my friend, not the jerk who comes around and makes me miserable."

"Fine, but if he kills you, don't say I didn't warn you!"

"How could I? I'd be dead!" I pointed to the door.

"Fine," Conner shouted. He swung the door open. Jonathan was standing on the other side. "I'm leaving, Spenser, but you better not touch her or else!" Conner threatened. He stood tall with his chest puffed out. Jonathan smirked.

"Only threaten when you are prepared to deliver; I suggest you run along like a good little boy," Jonathan teased. Conner stormed down the hallway.

"You can come back in. I'm so sorry about all of that. I don't understand what's going on in Conner's head."

"You've done nothing wrong," he said. "I'll wait in the sitting area while you get dressed," he walked over to the window.

I looked at the clock and hurried to the bedroom. My shower was quick, and I had to rush to dry my hair. It was still damp when I finally gave up. I tossed on a pair of joggers and my sleeping shirt wrapped my robe tightly around me and stepped out into the living room.

Jonathan was sitting on the couch, flipping through a magazine. He looked up when he saw me."

"Have you heard from Emma?" I asked.

"She's on her way." He was staring at me again with those steely eyes. They seemed to pierce right through me. "It seems Conner's quite fond of you." Jonathan gave me an amused smile.

"He's one of my best friends. My first friend when I moved to Nirvana," I admitted.

Jonathan raised his eyebrows. "There's more than friendship on his mind," he said.

"We're friends," I countered.

"You care about him. Why not take that next step?" His question irritated me. I suppose he wanted to pawn me off on Conner.

"I don't think of him in that way." I pulled the necklace from inside my robe for a moment and rubbed it between my fingers. Jonathan watched me intently. He stared at the key as its diamonds reflected across his face.

I looked back up at him suddenly. "You're close to Annaliese Montgomery. Why haven't you taken the next step, or have you?" Part of me was surprised I asked the question. The other part felt entitled to know the answer.

"You've been talking to Emma, I see." The smirk spread across his face again.

"Are you going to answer the question?" It was hard to sound impatient when he looked so darn good.

"My, you are bossy," Jonathan teased. "Annaliese and I are friends. That was a mutual agreement, unlike your situation. You may not want to be with Conner, but he wants to be with you."

"I might not be an expert on relationships, but I'm sure the feelings must go both ways. Conner is my friend, nothing more."

"Did you come to Paris because of him?" Jonathan asked, "A nice, romantic getaway? No supervision: you kids could have fun here."

My jaw dropped. "No, I'm not sure why you are pushing this narrative, but please stop. He has nothing to do with this." I said, taken aback. The fact that he called me a kid made me angry.

I glared at him and crossed my arms. "You don't know anything about me, or Conner for that fact. We're just classmates who happened to be on the same trip. There's nothing more between us, okay?"

Jonathan raised his eyebrows and smirked. "Sure, sure. Whatever you say. But you must admit, he's cute. And he likes you."

My cheeks began to heat up, "No, he does not, and even if he did, I wouldn't care. I'm not interested in him at all."

Jonathan shrugged and leaned back in his chair. "Fine, fine. Don't get so defensive. I was just teasing you a little. But you know what they say, the lady doth protest too much..." Jonathan's eyes focused behind me. I twisted to see what he was looking at — the damaged mirror had caught his attention. His eyes shifted from the mirror to me and then back to the mirror again.

"I knew something was wrong. What happened?" He stood up and walked toward the bathroom to get a closer look.

"I threw my phone," I said bluntly.

"So, you hate mirrors?" He looked over his shoulder and smiled.

Closing the distance between us, he placed his arms on either side of me in the bathroom doorway.

"Yes, they add at least ten pounds." I ducked because his closeness made it challenging to focus.

"I think that's cameras," he joked. "Oh wait, yes, and mirrors. Mirrors are the worst." His tone was light, almost airy.

I tousled my hair, and he moved closer. He lifted one of my damp curls between his fingers.

"When you're ready to tell me what happened earlier, I will listen." Jonathan's fingers slid through my hair. I lifted myself onto my toes, and our lips touched softly, and then I kissed him. His fingers traveled down me, pressing my body against his. Every touch sent electric sparks through me. I pulled him tighter, kissing him with such urgency that I could hardly breathe.

"Emma is here," he said before taking a step back. "I should go." Before I could argue, he was out the door, and I tilted my head back against the wall in frustration.

Emma entered the living room and tossed two shopping bags onto the sofa. "He's gone," she said. "I asked him to wait, but you know him...stubborn." She rummaged through her bags, and I returned to the bedroom. When I came back out, Emma was inspecting her new shoes.

"How are you feeling?" she asked.

"Oh, much better now," the amused look in Emma's eyes caused me to blush. "Wait, that didn't come out right." My attempt to recover failed as Emma shook her head.

"We're going to be late," I fussed, trying to sideline the subject. "Then I better get dressed," Emma said as she gathered her latest items. She stopped and looked at me, staring me up and down. "Where did you get that dress?"

"It's one of the new ones." I began to tug at the hem. The short, purple dress hugged my curves more than any clothing I had ever worn. "Why is it so tight?

"Relax, it's a nice dress," Emma said. "I wanted to know which boutique."

"Oh, thanks," not entirely convinced by her compliment because this dress was way out of my comfort zone. I pointed to the bags, which were still on the dresser.

"We should stop by that boutique when we leave the Louvre today!" Emma said as she looked through my closet, nodding her approval, "These are the clothes you thought I bought you?" Emma asked.

"Yeah, and I completely forgot to ask Jonathan if he bought them," With everything that happened last night, my clothes had been the least of my worries.

"Hmm, I'll get you some answers," Emma said as she walked back into the living room. She gave me a mischievous smile as she pulled her phone from her purse and placed it to her ear.

"Someone bought Madi an entire new wardrobe at a boutique nearby, and we're not sure who it was," Emma said. I stepped closer to hear the faint sound of Jonathan's voice on the other end of the phone. Emma smiled at me as he continued to talk. "Oh, she wants to thank you personally later," Emma said slyly. My mouth dropped open in shock, and I reached for the phone, but she had already hung up.

"I cannot believe you told him that!" My face reddened. "Sorry," she said, grinning. "Thought that was what you were thinking. You might have a fun night in store." She paused and raised her eyebrows. "You can thank me later."

CHAPTER SEVENTEEN
WALLFLOWER

C onner had convinced me to go with him to a nightclub named *Assetato di Sangue*; one of the tour guides told him the club was to die for, and, knowing my luck, he might be right. He reminded me that we only had four days left in Paris and then refused to take no for an answer. Therefore, I reluctantly agreed to go with him.

Around 9:30, I started to get ready. After shuffling through the dresses Jonathan had bought, I chose the coral-colored V-cut dress in the front, which revealed way more than I expected. The sparkles created a light display across the rise of my breast, drawing more attention to them. But I shook off my reservations about the dress and searched for a pair of shoes. Unless the club allowed sneakers or flip-flops, I would need to borrow a pair of Emma's. The meticulously aligned shoes made my browsing effortless, and I quickly chose a pair of strappy sandals.

I would have stayed in my warm, comfortable bed, reading a book, or watching a movie. But Blake had already persuaded me on the phone that Conner knew what he was talking about. He said I couldn't miss the opportunity to explore Paris's vibrant and glamorous nightlife, the city of lights. Blake also made me agree to not be a wallflower in the club — he went so far as to dare me to dance. And, of course, I decided to accept his challenge. Still, I refused to give him the satisfaction of knowing he had gotten under my skin. He was in

Australia having the time of his life, and I was debating whether to toss my pajamas back on. "Take some chances, Madi," was the last thing Blake said to me. Well, that is precisely what I'm going to do.

"Wow, Madi, you look, ah, great," Conner exclaimed when I joined him in the lobby.

"Thanks," there was an awkward silence between us, making every second feel like minutes. Conner was staring at my breast, granted I had put them on display to refute Blake's suggestion that I was boring and had no idea how to have fun. However, he did believe that my wallflower status was my choice. Blake was right; I wanted to remain unnoticed and hidden from the world. Then, no one would ever discover the level of my freakiness. Being a wallflower is a form of self-preservation but also incredibly lonely.

Shifting away from Conner's unblinking stare, I searched the lobby for the rest of the group. "The Queen B" was missing. "Where is Lauren?"

"Oh, yeah, she's not coming. She's still hungover. We hit a pub after the Louvre." Conner said and shrugged. "Braden and Ashley are coming. They should be down soon."

A taxi pulled up to the front of the hotel, and Conner motioned for me to follow him out. Shortly after, Braden and Ashley joined us. Braden sat in the front seat while Ashley slid into the back beside me.

"Poor Lauren, she's still so sick. You should stay and take care of her," Ashley suggested to Conner. "And then Madi could sit in her room by herself like usual." Ashley gave me a wicked smile before looking at Conner.

"Lauren will live. Madi needs to experience the Paris nightlife; let's face it, I'm the nightlife expert," Conner said as he leaned closer to me. "With you in that dress, I might have to show you some other things I'm an expert at," he whispered. My eyes widened as I turned toward him quickly. He lifted his eyebrows in that "what do you say" look.

"I'm telling Ms. Betty!" I yelled between my teeth while pretending to search for my phone.

"You're bluffing," he elbowed me in the side. I laughed, "See, you're enjoying yourself already, and you haven't even seen me on the dance floor," Conner lifted his shirt and began rolling his belly. My sides were aching from laughing so hard. Ashley shot us a weird look.

The taxi driver hit a bump, causing me to adjust in the seat, only to find myself pinned against Conner as he took a sharp right, pushing Ashley against me. He dipped down a narrow back street and weaved in and out of lanes. I surveyed the scenery. Yellow-tinted streetlights cast eerie shadows on the grey buildings. The deep ache in the pit of my stomach told me that something was off; we shouldn't be here.

"What kind of club is *Assetato di Sangue*?" I asked. No one answered my question as the taxi stopped at the club entrance. My eyes settled on the large, crimson-colored door. The bright red paint contrasted with the dull grey buildings.

"Sure, you want to party here?" the taxi driver asked. He turned to face me — beady dark eyes now wide with fear my caution flags were waving frantically.

"Hell yeah," Braden shouted, to both of our dismay.

"Conner, maybe we shouldn't," I tried to pull back, but his grip on my arm was too firm. He dragged me out of the taxi and pushed me towards the club.

"Come on, don't be such a buzzkill!" Conner said. I looked around for Braden and Ashley, hoping they would back me up. But they were already at the door, talking to the bouncer. He was a massive guy with pale skin and dark hair and didn't look too friendly.

"Relax; you're going to have fun!" Conner chided. I could convince Braden and Ashley this was a bad idea; however, they were already heading to the entrance. The bouncer, a tall man with milky white skin and jet-black hair, stopped them at once.

"Members only," the bouncer said without even looking at them. A young man and woman pushed past Conner, Braden, and Ashley. The bouncer allowed them inside. Conner refused to move, and the man's eyes flashed with anger. I joined the group quickly.

"Please forgive my friend," my eyes met his, and I knew he was a vampire. "We're leaving," instinctively, my fingers gripped Conner's hand to lead him away from the bouncer and back to the taxi. Only to discover that the cab was gone, unsure what to do. I looked at the bouncer again.

"You look familiar," he said smoothly. He was waiting on my response, and when I did not produce a single word, he gave me a stiff grin. "Are they with you," the bouncer asked me in French. His stare was frightening.

"Yes, yes, but I'm okay." My voice trembled, "We didn't realize this club was for members only. Sorry, we bothered you," I explained.

"No, forgive my rudeness and consider yourself formally invited," the bouncer said. My eyes went to Conner's before traveling back to the man. The lump in my throat was now the size of a boulder, "You can bring your friends inside with you." He opened the door and kissed the back of my hand. His lips were much colder than expected as they touched my heated skin. There was recognition in his eyes when they met mine.

"You are sweet; innocence is a rare and beautiful quality." He whispered.

"Thank you." I eased my hand away and tucked them behind me.

"The pleasure is mine," he said in French. I noted the faint hint of a smile, although he quickly masked his delight with his earlier stoic demeanor.

Our group hurried inside the dimly lit club. Scantily clothed people stood along the walls; however, they made up for their lack of clothing with heavy perfume and cologne. We moved closer to the bar, the scent changed, and I decided the smell of beer and liquor were the lesser of two evils. The music blared loudly from all corners of the club. The ear-shattering surround sound reminded me of the Mega Cinema, about forty minutes from Hatteras. Like the cinema, this place was so loud that I could barely hear myself think.

This was my first time in a nightclub, but I could tell this was elaborate. The plush, red velvet sofas and chairs arranged throughout the room. The seating was peculiar — small groups and couples positioned to face one another but away from others. I suppose they wanted everyone to have privacy; that thought caused another caution flag to wave frantically. Ignoring my better judgment, which was screaming get the hell out of this place — I scanned the room instead. People were dancing on an elevated dance floor. Others were in cages that dangled from the lofty ceilings. Their naked bodies moved seductively against the poles.

We found a table near the bar, and a waitress appeared before we could sit. Her tightly fitted dress looked painful, but she didn't seem to have any problem breathing. She introduced herself as Zara. She was stunning.

"The gentleman would like to buy you and your friends a drink," Zara said as she pointed across the room. "Order whatever your sweet little heart desires." Her words were like liquid as they poured from her crimson lips. I looked past her to the man sitting in the corner. The whites of his eyes were all I could see. "What will you have, beautiful?" Zara asked as her cold hand grazed my arm to get my attention. My discomfort grew when she licked her lips.

"Nothing, thank you," I pulled my arm away, slanting my eyes at her. She was vampire too.

"You would not want to offend him," Zara's gaze lingered on me. "We'll have two rum and Cokes," Braden said as he ordered his and Ashley's drinks. "And four shots of tequila," he added. I looked at Braden, wondering who would take the fourth shot. "If you don't drink it, more for me," his tone dripped with arrogance. Zara looked at all of us before focusing her attention on Conner. Hopefully, she wasn't a human hunter — and she had a wine cellar filled with donated blood like Emma and Jonathan.

"I'll have a Red Bull and vodka," Conner ordered. "Madi, try something," he pleaded, turning toward me.

"A Coke will be fine," I decided not to make a fuss — fitting in was the best course to take here. Zara gave me a quick smile before gliding toward the bar. Conner shook his head in disappointment. "Thought you had to stay in shape for football camp. If I'm not mistaken, there is no drug or alcohol tolerance for you to remain on the team." Conner shrugged me off.

"Damn, Madi, chill," Braden responded. "He'll have the rest of the summer to get back in shape."

Zara returned with our drinks. "Here, sweetie," she placed my soda before me. "Let me know if there's anything else you need." Braden passed out the tequila shots, leaving mine in the center of the table.

"To Paris," he said, holding up the shot glass. All three threw back their shots. Conner finished first and quickly grabbed the one in the middle. Before Braden could object, he drank that one too.

"Oh, come on," Braden complained.

"See, Madi, I've still got my speed," Conner joked.

Zara should have worn skates instead of the six-inch stilettos that would have made her trips to our table easier as Braden and Conner competed to confirm who could consume their shots the quickest.

"Here you go, boys," Zara said as she sat down the eighth round of drinks. She looked at me with the same hunger I saw in Liam's eyes. I covered the pulsating vein in my neck with the palm of my hand because my throat piqued her interest.

"She likes you," Conner said. His breath smelled like liquor. "The woman has good taste."

"Your opinion is somewhat hazy," I pushed him lightly as Braden signaled for another round. Zara returned quickly with a platter of mixed drinks. There were three tall glasses with steam rising from the tops.

"I think you will like these," she said, winking at Conner. She turned to me after she placed the drinks down. "Sure, you don't want anything else?" Her icy hand touched my shoulder — traveling quickly across my collarbone.

"Yeah," I brushed her hand aside and lifted my brow as if to say, "Back the hell off." Zara's crimson lips turned downward as I slid closer to Conner. If she thought for one second that I would become her after-hour snack, she could not be more wrong. She continued to stare at me. Her eyes dared me to flinch. I refused to back down, and she broke eye contact.

"Too bad we would have had a really nice time," she whispered. Okay, one of two things was happening here; she wanted to kill or sleep with me, and I chose neither. Zara straightened her long shapely frame, licked her lips slowly, and then sauntered back to the bar.

"Man, I thought we would see a little girl-on-girl action!" Braden yelled before he passed Conner a drink.

"We still can if you make out with her," Conner teased. Ashley and Braden scowled, but I was thankful for Conner's joke. Conner and I continued laughing, "You would make a pretty girl," Conner added; Braden shoved him and grabbed Ashley's hand, and the two stumbled toward the dance floor.

A stunning older woman came over to our table. She wore a tight, black leather dress that looked painted on. "Would you like to dance?" her words dripped with seduction. She looked at Conner as if they were alone in the club. Conner smiled at me, raised his eyebrows, and allowed the woman to lead him to the dance floor — leaving me alone at the table.

My jaw dropped when an overly exposed woman breezed past me and climbed inside one of the dangling cages. Her body moved rhythmically to the music as she removed her clothes. The fact that the woman was stripping appeared to be acceptable behavior. Once I scanned the room again, I understood the reason for her risqué behavior. Everyone in the club was drinking, dancing, or making out on the plush lounge chairs and sofas. "Is this some sort of vampire sex club?" I reasoned, tossing around other possibilities until a familiar feeling washed over me.

Jonathan was here. The club had so many shadowy spaces I knew I would only find him if he wanted me to. Was he here with a girl — a vampire girl? The beautiful museum curator, vampire girl. The thought sent a wave of heat through me, traveling upward from my toes and peaking at the roots of my hair. I caught a glimpse of my eyes in the glass and forced them closed until the feeling evaporated. When I opened them again, they were as close to normal as they ever would be.

My cell phone was causing my purse to vibrate on the table, retrieving it quickly to see a missed call from my mom. I scooted away from the table and hurried toward the entrance answering the phone once I was outside.

"Madison!" Her voice was frantic, concerned, and a little angry.

"Mom, sorry I forgot to call you back," I bit my lip hard, glancing around to see the bouncer staring at me suspiciously. I cupped the phone in my hand, afraid to move further down the street; no telling what was lurking in the dark alleys between the buildings.

"Madison, I called you at least five times; you talked to your father but refused to answer my calls!" wait, what? "I'm happy that the two of you are getting along better," again, words fail me. "I know you're angry about my leaving you there," she sniffled.

"Mom, I'm not upset. Things have been crazy, that's all; sorry for not checking in more."

"I know I'm being silly, you called your father, and that should be enough."

"Mom, it's hard talking to you over the phone. I hate saying...."

"I know, and I miss you too; see you soon. We should be home no later than Tuesday."

"That's great!" I wondered if she could sense that her daughter had become a liar.

"Madison, please be careful; I love you."

"Love you too." I closed the phone, brushed away the weight of the lie from my shoulders, and composed myself before entering the club again.

The lip-locked Braden and Ashley barely noticed me when I plopped down in the chair until I cleared my throat. Ashley looked me up and down as she wiped Braden's saliva from her mouth. "Thought you left," her concern would have been believable without the scowl on her stupid face. "Oops, meant to say I hoped you left!" Ashley laughed, and Braden did the same. However, his rude behavior could be the liquor; Ashley's was indicative of the Pink Squad. "Why are you here?" She quipped with an air of disdain that rubbed me the wrong way.

"How can you speak with your head so far up Lauren's ass!" I snapped and leaned back in my chair. I wanted her to give me a reason to knock the crap out of her. "Braden, did you hear what she said to me?" Ashley cried.

Conner chuckled and almost fell into my lap, saying, "I found what she said amusing because Madi can take care of herself, so it's best to leave her alone." Ashley quickly grabbed Braden, and they both went to the bar.

"Come on, let's dance!" Conner said, and I nodded. He draped his arm over my shoulders as we pushed through the crowded dance floor. We squeezed through to find a small area. Conner smiled down at me. His eyes could barely stay open as his body moved to the music. His hands moved down to the small of my back. I grasped both and forced them up a little higher. "I'm surprised you're a good dancer...," he teased.

"I'm not sure if that's a compliment," I managed, still trying to push images of Jonathan and his vampire girlfriend out of my head.

"You're supposed to be chill tonight... no worries, okay?" Conner leaned in and kissed my cheek. "You're so pretty, Madi. I love y...," he slurred as his hand slid over my bottom, and I pushed him away.

"That's the alcohol talking. You should consider 'saying no,'" I said, but Conner smiled.

The song ended, and he made a beeline to the bar to take another shot. I tried to lead him back to our table, but he latched his arms around my waist, molding my body to his.

"Conner, stop it," his hands didn't move, "Seriously, before I kick you where it hurts!" Yeah, he heard nothing. The little jerk made me pry his fingers off me. "You've had more than enough to drink!" If he were sober, I would have popped him upside the head.

Braden stumbled up to us and grabbed Conner's arm. "Chill, Madi, he's fine. You should get a drink; it'll help you relax a little bit," Braden said. Ignoring Braden, I hurried back to the table. Honestly, this scene was not for me, and catching a taxi and returning to the hotel was becoming more appealing.

"I hope you and your friends enjoyed the drinks. Would you like to dance?" someone asked. I looked up to see a tall man staring down at me. He wore all black and looked like he was attending a funeral. As I studied him further, I realized his black hair and pale skin elevated him to 'undertaker' status.

"No, thank you," the man's eyes flashed as he processed my response.

"Then perhaps there are other things you would rather do?" the man offered.

"The answer is most definitely no," I glanced around the area for Jonathan, hoping he would come to rescue me from the creeper. My nose wrinkled as I caught a whiff of the man's scent. He smelled different and reminded me of the woods after it had been raining for a couple of days when everything smelled like earthworms...quite unpleasant.

"You know it's considered a great insult to refuse an invitation." The man's sharp eyes traveled down the entire length of my body.

"I already said my answer is no! So do us both a favor and find someone else to bother!" I had barely gotten the words out of my mouth when two imposing men approached the table.

"You heard the lady," the larger of the two said to the man. The man scowled but turned and walked away.

After expressing my gratitude, I leaned back in my chair, feeling more at ease now that we had space between us.

"We need you to come with us," they both said in unison. "Why?" The two bouncers towered over me as I looked up at them.

"You're invited to the VIP section. This is not an invitation you can decline," the large one added. My eyes skimmed over the crowd again, this time for either Jonathan or Conner — hell, I would take Braden's presence right now. However, seeing none of them, I slowly pushed away from the table and followed the men. Their presence not only alarmed me but the entire club. Without a word, people shifted aside when they saw the men coming. As we passed the elevated dance floor, I noticed the base was a large, caged area. My stomach dropped when my eyes met the wild-eyed stares of the people inside. These cages were not like the ones that the women were dancing in. Instead, the people's bodies contorted in peculiar positions. Something told me they could not refuse their invitation either.

CHAPTER EIGHTEEN
VIP

The men led me through a set of black curtains near the back of the club. The small area lit by black lights, creating a fluorescent glow on every white object in the room. We glided between the illuminated tables draped in white tablecloths. There were people seated in the room, all engrossed in one another. I found it interesting that the whites of their eyes did not illuminate. Strangely, the trivial things gain my attention instead of the larger picture, such as allowing these men to lead me out of sight to meet someone I did not know. The men suddenly stopped, and I nearly bumped into the smaller one. He shifted quickly to prevent us from touching. I somehow found comfort that he did not want to touch me. "Sit down," the larger of the two men instructed me. He pointed to a seat beside an incredibly handsome man. His skin was radiant. I imagined it would feel like porcelain or marble, smooth, cold, and deadly. Instead, he lifted my hand and pressed his lips against my fingers. They were frigid, and I was not surprised. A nervous knot returned to my stomach as the two men exited.

He was young, late twenties, tall, lean, with neatly cropped wavy brown hair. His eyes were the color of what I imagined the sun would be a bright golden hue. Although they darkened to more of a honey brown as I moved closer.

"I'm pleased you came to see me. I'm Roberto," he said in a captivating tone.

"Well, your bodyguards didn't really give me a choice," I confessed, slightly irritated by my compliance.

"They have a way with words. Don't be hard on yourself; you made a smart move." Roberto spoke as if he could read my mind.

"Look, I think you have mistaken me for someone else," I said, hoping that he would rectify his mistake and allow me to leave. The last thing I wanted to do was create a scene.

"No mistake Madison," Roberto said. He appeared entertained by my discomfort. "You are Elizabeth's daughter," the smoothness of his voice continued to lull me. I relaxed in the chair, overwhelmed with the sense that everything was ok, and that Roberto would not harm me. Even though I had no idea why. "It's astounding. You could be her twin."

"I've heard that all my life, and I still believe it's one of the nicest compliments anyone could give me. How do you know my mom?"

"Elizabeth is a special woman. She cared for my family when we needed help. I could never repay her for the repeated thoughtfulness she showed to our kind," he admitted.

"What does that mean?"

"Spaniards," he said and then laughed as if there were a joke only, he was privy to.

"A small part of me wanted to say, "No a-hole vampires," except there was no way that I could utter the words. My knowledge of vampires' existence will go with me to my grave and beyond.

"Elizabeth does not know that you have come here. She vowed to never allow you to visit this place," he said with a certainty that bothered me.

"She knows I'm here," I lied. He didn't need to know that I reasoned. This was self-preservation I told myself.

Roberto leaned in. "Lying does not come easy to you." His eyes lightened or flashed; I couldn't be sure. "Elizabeth understands that this place is dangerous for you. She is determined to keep you out of this country…and with good reason. Anyone who sees you will know whose child you are." Roberto's boldness continued to push my buttons.

"Why would anyone want to hurt me because of her? My mom is the nicest person I know!" I screamed at him, feeling tears well up in my eyes.

"Elizabeth is the angel that married the devil." He shook his head. "They will see you and know that you are Elizabeth's daughter, which means they will also know that you are Phillips. They will kill you slowly to drag out your agony. To avenge the lives that Phillip has destroyed."

"I'm sure there may be times when he must kill to protect innocent people." Phillip and I did not have the typical father-daughter relationship but calling him a devil took it too far. Besides, he had covered for me with my mom. Although I could only assume he wanted to prolong their life without the "Wild Child." Whatever the reason, I appreciated the help.

"What does that make me?" I asked.

"Your mother's daughter," he said as if reading my mind.

"Why do you hate Phillip?"

"Business and personal reasons that I refuse to bore you with," His eyes flashed with anger, and I would swear that every muscle in his body constricted. "Phillip continues to make enemies. I hope Elizabeth will not pay for his deeds or you, dear Madison. If you're not careful, this city will devour you," Roberto said ominously.

"Imagine, for a moment, that you are an incredible piece of cheese in a room filled with rats. The smell alone would drive them mad. They would gnaw their own tails off to get to you. Not because they are hungry — they will do so because they have no other choice. Instinctually they have a desire to own rare and beautiful things." His eyes slanted, and his confidence unnerved me.

"Why?" I leaned into the conversation, "None of this makes any sense! Why do they want me?" I closed my eyes as images of those girls raced through my subconscious. Their curly hair, light eyes, and honey-colored skin are like mine. My world was turning upside down.

"I have explained this to you."

"That was a very cryptic load of bull!" I bit my bottom lip to prevent myself from angering this man.

"Madison, Paris is crawling with rats, one might say infested. They want you. They will find you. Ultimately…they will destroy you." "Because I'm Phillip's daughter, they think of me as a piece of cheese." My sarcasm annoyed him only slightly. "Well, thanks for the help. I need to go." I finally meet one of my mom's friends that I feel comfortable talking to, and he is crazier than a loon—cheese, yeah, right.

"I share this information with you out of respect for Elizabeth. Have you never asked yourself why she refused to bring you here? Why would she not share this beautiful place with you? Elizabeth knows that Paris is not only the most romantic place in the world, but it can also be the deadliest. Therefore, she would not want you here." Roberto paused before continuing. He clasped his hands together and looked forcefully at me. "My advice is simple — leave this place and never return." His voice had an eerie tone that shivered through every fiber of my being. "They will come after you again," he warned.

"Again," I whispered under my breath. "There is no way that he could know about Liam."

"Madison, there are also rats in America; they are messy little beasts leaving behind droppings as they devour anything in their path. Although you already know this," his eyes rolled as if he were growing bored with our conversation.

"They all look like me," a single hot tear slid down my cheek.

"No, not you." He said with such certainty that I clung to his words anxiously. "They are hunting for the girl that looks like Elizabeth, not you," when he stopped- I told myself to breathe.

That would explain their brown eyes. They were searching for someone that looked like my mom. Phillips daughter. They wanted to get revenge by murdering me.

"Until you came here, they could only guess. Nothing will stop them from finding you once they know what you look like." Roberto said. I looked up at him, studying his face, wondering if he was right.

There was no reason to lie. Besides, he told me what everyone else refused to tell me. All those girls died because of my family. Roberto said that my mom was the angel that married the devil — he left out that she had also procreated with him. What had he done? Could he be the reason for all of this?

I slid closer to him. "Who are they? Why would they want to hurt me over something Phillip did?" my question was more of a plea.

"Phillip, my dear, is a bad man. He is responsible, for hundreds of deaths. No one has forgotten what he did, nor will they forgive. Unfortunately for you, there is a heavy debt, and Phillip is far too difficult a target. The next logical choice would be to kill his only child. Your blood could quench their thirst," Roberto explained.

I was returning to Earth and thought silently, 'In what universe would that be considered normal?' Had I given this man too much credit? "Phillip's responsible for the deaths of hundreds? Yeah, I mean, he hunted down serial killers. They may have died, but it was to protect innocent people. Phillip saved lives. He's been working for the FBI for years," I argued.

Roberto shook his head and chuckled to himself. He made me feel naïve because I was clueless about my parents, and he knew everything.

"Elizabeth vowed to keep you safe no matter the cost. She may have done more harm than good by shielding you from the truth." He was being honest I could see it in his eyes.

"If there's ever anything I can do for you, please let me know." He handed me a card with the name Roberto De' Leon scrawled across it. "Don't be afraid to call me," he continued.

"There is something you can help me with; what is the VHW," I started to say, but Roberto stopped me mid-sentence with a look so intense that my hands began to tremble.

"You must never speak of such things where others can hear you! Come with me!" he barked. The two men rushed back into the VIP room as if they knew I had angered Roberto. They ushered me through a doorway, where we went up a narrow stairwell. At the top, Roberto opened the door to a dim-lit room and allowed me inside.

He followed me in and directed the two men to stand at the door before closing it. A large window captured my attention. I could see the entire club and wondered if they could see me too.

"No one can see you," Roberto said as if he could hear my thoughts.

"Did your parents speak to you about the VHW?" he asked. I shook my head and swallowed a lump in my throat.

"I wouldn't have thought that to be the case. However, I must caution you never to speak those words aloud again. The council is one thing that holds us all bound," Roberto said.

"If the council is so dangerous, why would they allow Phillip to kill?" I questioned.

"They were unaware of what Phillip was doing. The council refuses to believe that someone under their control would dare to go against them. Arrogance, stupidity, they have underestimated him."

"How did he get involved in this VHW council? What does my mom have to do with all of this?"

"You have asked questions that I cannot answer, Madison. You should forget about the council. Understanding it is not an important matter. He can only protect you from so much. There is nothing but death waiting if you succeed in your search for the truth."

"He? You said that he can only protect me from so much."

"Who are you talking about?" I asked. Roberto looked out the window to the crowded club and extended his finger.

"Jonathan Spenser," he said. Jonathan stood directly below. His gaze burrowed holes into the large window. I moved away, afraid that Roberto had been wrong about them being unable to see through the glass. "We had all but written him off. But he's back... and you, my dear, are the reason," he continued.

"You're wrong," I said.

"Madison, nothing is as it seems. Jonathan has not visited this club for years. It is not a coincidence that we also have the honor of his presence the one night you're here." Roberto shook his head. "It is a hopeless feat that he strives to overcome." He leaned against the glass window. "The moment he met you, it was already too late." My mind was full of questions I may never have the answers to. As if I can walk up to my parents and say, "So I hear you work for a secret organization, killed tons of people, and now they want to kill me," however that explains the reason she went all psycho on Phillip that night, and drastically reduced the amount of fine China we owned. I needed time to process all the information he had given me, and I had to talk to Jonathan.

"I'm not sure I agree with you, but thank you for answering my questions; well, some of them," I said.

"You have my number," he said, nodding toward the card in my hand. "I shall await your call." Then, he returned his attention to the crowd below. "You should leave now. Your friend needs you," Roberto said nonchalantly, although his eyes were deadly serious as he pointed toward Conner.

His oversized bodyguards moved to let me out of the room. I hurried down the narrow stairs and through the curtains of the VIP section. The crowded, dark room made it difficult to find Conner. Finally, I spotted him on his way into the bathroom. The older woman he had danced with earlier was practically carrying him inside. It took me minutes to push through the crowd to get to the bathroom. When I swung open the door, buttons scattered across the floor, and Conner's shirt ripped open. His pants were at his ankles, and the woman was on her knees in front of him. This was much more of his sex life than I should have seen.

"Take your hands off of him!" I shouted. My voice was so strong that it surprised me. The woman whipped her head around to look at me. Her skin was the color of coffee, and her eyes were darker than night. She moved quickly; she stood at least six feet tall in heels. Her long fingers slid over the tight, black dress that clung to every curve.

"The boy is mine! We were in the middle of something. Either join us or get out!" Her threat only angered me more.

"You're disgusting, and I won't tell you again...leave him alone!" I yelled.

The woman reached for me. I spun away from her before she could latch onto my dress and grabbed Conner's hand, thankful that he had enough sense to fix his jeans. We ran out the door, but the woman was behind us. Her fingers locked onto a handful of my hair. Conner fell to the floor as she slammed me into the wall. The hallway was dark except for the flashing strobe lights from the dance floor. The woman went after him again. I searched blindly for something to use as a weapon. My hand touched a cold, iron pole as I felt around. The thing was stuck in a statue — one hard tug caused the figure to topple over. I lifted the rod high.

"Leave him alone, or I'm going to ram this through what should be your heart!"

The woman turned to look at me — the whites of her eyes were gone — replaced with darkness. Tiny veins prickled her once flawless face, and her coffee complexion was now ashen.

"She's with me." Jonathan suddenly appeared beside me. The woman's eyes continued to burn holes in me. The woman growled at me, but Jonathan took a step forward, and she surprisingly backed down. "She is also a guest of Roberto's. You would find it best to remember that" Jonathan added. He spoke with such authority that he forced the woman to halt her attack.

"Don't come here again, princess!" The woman warned. Her face flashed with anger as if she were about to pounce again.

"Touch her, and you will be nothing but a memory," Jonathan threatened. It worked, and I watched as she turned quickly and disappeared around the corner. Jonathan followed behind her without saying a single word to me.

I raced over to Conner; thankful he was back on his feet.

The wall supported him as he used it to hold himself up.

"We need to get out of here before she comes back," I said. My body was still angry as I looked over my shoulder to see Braden and Ashley walking toward us.

"What happened to him? Did he get sick?" Braden asked. I wanted to snap but bit my lip to avoid an unnecessary argument.

"We need to go," I insisted, guiding Conner to the door. Luckily, two taxis were waiting at the curb. Braden helped me get Conner into the backseat. I scanned the outside of the club once to see if Jonathan had followed us out. Although I knew that, he was still inside. I could feel his presence in the distance. Conner began to groan, and I slid in next to him so we could hurry back to the hotel.

"Lightweight…" Braden mumbled. He laughed before turning around to look at Conner.

"Please feel free to pretend- you care," I yelled at Braden. He shook his head and laughed to himself. My frustration was boiling. Of course, he was clueless about what happened to Conner in the bathroom, and I could not tell him.

The taxi had to pull over twice. First, Conner threw up, and then Ashley threw up after seeing Conner get sick. Once we arrived at the hotel, I helped Conner to his room. As soon as the door swung open, he ran for the bathroom.

"So, you let him get drunk? Impressive. Was that your plan? Get him drunk so you could take advantage of him?" Lauren shrieked. She had been sitting on the edge of the bed, waiting for him to return. I think she had been waiting for this exact confrontation, any excuse to fight with me.

Lauren pushed past me to join Conner in the bathroom. I picked up the trashcan and placed it next to his bed. When Lauren returned to the bedroom, Conner was still heaving over the porcelain bowl. Her arms crossed — mouth pulled tightly into a scowl.

"I'm not in the mood for stupid tonight, so go ahead, say one more word!" I snapped before she could even open her mouth.

"Conner is my boyfriend!" Lauren spat the words back at me.

"If you're going to stay with him and make sure he's ok, I'll leave," I retorted, "because it's taking everything inside of me not to slap the hell out of you right now!"

"You think I'm stupid enough to leave you alone with him all night," she barked.

"No, Lauren, I think you're stupid because you confirm that fact every time you open your mouth!"

I slammed the door closed and leaned back against the wall. My body heaved with anger, skin flushed, and eyes stung. I squeezed them closed, counted backward from ten until my body cooled to my regular hundred and one degrees, and my eyes no longer stung. The stress from tonight had bubbled to the surface, and it took everything inside me not to crumble to the floor. When I finally opened them, I saw Jonathan. His narrowed eyes laser focused on me.

I approached my door as I fished through my purse for the key. Jonathan had not spoken to me at the club, so many thoughts raced through my head I felt unsure how to start a conversation with him. My hands shook as I tried to unlock the door. The damn key would not stay still long enough for me to swipe the card.

"Allow me." Jonathan took the key and opened the door. I sat down on the arm of the sofa and allowed my purse to slide off my shoulder and onto the floor.

"Madison, why were you at *Assetato di Sangue*?" His words were as harsh as the frustrated look he directed my way.

"We went there to have fun," I admitted.

"Did you?" His anger caught me off guard again. "How can I protect you when it seems you're hell-bent on finding trouble?" he said with clenched teeth.

Jonathan's tone surprised me. His voice had the same anger I saw in Roberto's eyes tonight when I mentioned the VHW and Liam's eyes that night on the street. His brows were tense, his jaw clenched, and his coldness sent a chill down my spine. So much had happened tonight that an argument with Jonathan could leave me undone. Before I questioned Jonathan, I needed time to figure out everything Roberto told me. He watched as I crossed the room, opened the door, and motioned for him to leave.

"Someone should have told you; trouble has always been a close friend of mine!" I snapped.

"You think this is a joke? They would have killed all of you." He had softened his voice, although his anger remained undeniable.

"She attacked my friend! I'm not exactly laughing, but right now, I'm going to bed…" I opened the door wider.

"How do you know Roberto?" he asked quickly.

"How do you?" My retort caught him off guard.

"Tell me," Jonathan's demand came with a bright flash of his silver eyes.

"Roberto said he's a friend of my mom's," My response angered him more.

"So, you don't know him. You have no idea how dangerous he can be or what could have happened to you. You blindly went with him to his office?" Jonathan's tension continued to build. His voice rose, and I would swear that the crystal glasses rattled.

"I'm not a child. How would I ever meet anyone if I didn't talk to strangers?"

"This is different. First, you had to know that place wasn't safe."

"I had a feeling," I paused for a minute as I replayed the night's events. "But if I hadn't gone, I wouldn't have met Roberto. He knows things about my parents that I'm still trying to process." I managed. "He said it has to do with Phillip, ah my father and his involvement in a secret organization, the VHW."

Jonathan turned away as I slowly shut the door before walking toward him.

"Do you know anything about the VHW?" I asked. He refused to look at me. "So that's a yes on the VHW?"

"What exactly did Roberto say?" Jonathan demanded without looking at me. His avoidance was beginning to piss me off.

"You know something, don't you?" I moved in front of him so I could see his face.

"I know you should have never gone to Assetato di Sangue."

"Conner thought it was a cool place to hang out. I went along. And besides, Roberto gave me more information than you have," I defended my decision once again.

"You went because of him? If, he's the reason you came on the trip, why don't you leave? You know that people are after you, and you are willing to risk your safety for him." Jonathan argued, so quickly that it caused my head to ache.

"What are you talking about? How are any of these questions relevant to the conversation?"

"Don't insult my intelligence," he responded firmly.

"Ok, seriously, either tell me what you're talking about or leave my room!" I folded my arms over my chest and bit my lip slightly.

"The blond...with his damn hands all over you tonight," Jonathan's eyes flashed.

"You're angry because of Conner?" My eyes narrowed, and I had to stop my jaw from dropping.

Jonathan threw his hands in the air. "You're the one that tried to convince me that he's your friend. Deny it all you want, Madison. How you defended him tonight proves that you care for him!" He took two steps backward, slowly moving away from me.

"I never told you I didn't care about him. If you knew me, you would know I would have done the same thing for anyone," tears collected in my eyes.

"You two seemed pretty close tonight," his words were colder than ice.

"We are close!" I tapped my foot against the floor. Each tap held a louder thump than — the one before.

"He's the reason you're in Paris," Jonathan said. His assumption was the final straw.

"Conner's not the reason I'm here! He's not," I shouted. "Jonathan, I came here because of you!"

My confession came with mixed emotions; fear of his reaction overwhelmed me. However, I no longer cared. I released the truth and that felt good- it felt right. I looked hard at him and waited for the tension in his body to relax and hoped that this would finally lead to his realization of our connection.

"You would say anything to hide the fact that you care for him," Jonathan snapped. "Why are you so afraid to be honest?" His response aggravated and frustrated me simultaneously; it was hard not to laugh from sheer exhaustion.

"Ok, you want the truth. Here it is! My coming to Paris will not be without consequences. This was not a fun school trip for me. I could lose the one person that loves me most, but I came anyway! I'm not sure if it was a vision or a dream, but I know that it was you. I saw you on the ledge of *The Concorde la Fayette*. You wanted to let go!"

Jonathan didn't say a word as I looked directly at him and continued.

"I can still feel it…your sadness. The pain is so deep that even you sometimes forget it's there. That is until a scent, a memory, a vision sends it all back. You're drowning in the misery of your own existence. You tell yourself that you're strong enough to make it alone. Because you believe that if you never love anyone, you will never have to lose them. You run from your family and your friends, but mostly from yourself. You're afraid of the connection we share. You might think I'm crazy, but our connection is why I'm in Paris and how I knew you were in that club. It's what brought you there tonight and why you're in my room now!"

There was silence. I searched Jonathan's eyes for his response. "You have no idea what you're talking about!" he shouted.

"Is that why you're trembling?"

Jonathan squeezed his fists tighter, but I could still see them slightly shaking. "Stay away from the club and take Roberto's advice; leave Paris." His words were suddenly calm. I stood there, unable to speak. The air in the room had vanished and taken away my ability to breathe when he turned and walked toward the door.

"If I leave, will you come with me?"

"I don't deserve," he stopped mid-sentence, but I knew.

"You're a good person! If you could only see what I do!"

"You know what I am! You know, and you still believe that there is good in me! Madison, that tells me how naive you are."

"I may not have a wealth of wisdom, but I have the power to connect with people both living and dead and take on their pain as if it's my burden to bear. It's not something I can turn off. So, I know that you are lying. And I also want you to know it's okay not to share with me, but please, I need you to find a reason to keep going. Any reason," I sobbed, barely able to finish. There was only one other person that knew this about me, and he had left me too. He left the room, without a look back and slammed the door closed. All my resolve melted as I stood in the empty room.

CHAPTER NINETEEN
OMG

The tour bus eased toward the Eiffel Tower. Traffic had been brutal, which had turned the thirty-minute drive into two hours of torture. The interweaved streets of the city created an illusion that the infamous tower was around the corner. I should have canceled, although there was no way I could leave Paris without a tour of the Eiffel Tower. So, I came with them. Lauren glanced at me every time the bus stopped but remained quiet. She had to sense that my current state of mind was not to be- played with, not today. She would get smacked or punched in the throat if she tried me. I grimaced when the bus hit another pothole — every part of my body ached from the uncomfortable seat.

I peeked out the window as the tower finally came into full view and sighed in relief. Lauren and Conner had seats in front of me. I had overheard their arguments but chose not to add any of that information to my already overwhelmed mind.

Lauren stood quickly and moved to sit with Ashley. He shook his head before he dropped into the seat beside me.

"You sure are quiet. I thought you would be excited about this," Conner exclaimed.

"Yeah, it's going to be great." I had feigned excitement for the better half of the day but now felt resolved to be miserable.

"Madi, it's not the end of the world. So, what if Spenser stays here? That will be one less freak in Nirvana, and besides, you barely know the creep."

I turned away from him. And I decided to focus on the reasons Jonathan, and I should be together. He makes me feel — he makes me feel alive. But he wants me to move on. How can I? How can I return to a life that does not include him? I squeezed my eyes closed and gripped my skeleton key.

"Okay, change of subject," Conner said, and jolted me back into the conversation. He jabbed me in the side with his elbow. "Have you talked to your mom? I swear my mom calls at least five times a day! She's all Conner; remember your sunscreen, wear your sunglasses, and don't talk to strangers," He laughed, and I did too.

"Actually, I talked to my mom last night."

She was happy that Phillip and I had become close and talked every other day. He continued to cover for me, although I had no idea why. And my mom said they planned to return to Nirvana on Tuesday. All were signs that my time here would end. I had booked my flight — the earliest was tomorrow night. The person I told of my plans was Blake. He and Bria had returned to Nirvana yesterday, so he agreed to pick me up at the airport. He would also be there to support me when I confronted Margaret. I knew she would be mad, and I felt a witness might smooth the reunion. Phillip was another story; witness or not, I would have to feel his wrath.

"I checked over my shoulder sometimes to make sure my mom's not hiding behind a bush," Conner laughed and slapped me on the leg, he found more humor in his jabs at Ms. Betty than I did.

My attention shifted to the tour guide as his voice came over the loudspeaker. He was explaining a significant landmark to us. His monotone voice reminded me of Mr. Brambleton. Everything he said was ridiculous, mumbling. We stopped, and I peered through the window at the flashing indigo lights. At least four police cars were alongside the bus. Margaret, no, she wouldn't, would she?

Two starchy officers boarded the bus. Their heavy boots thumped loudly as the bus became silent. Everyone looked as wide-eyed and confused as I did. The tour guide greeted the officers. His forehead creased as the officers gave him stern directions.

"Listen! We will need to see your passports. This is a standard procedure," one of the French officers explained.

"You will remain in your seats until instructed to move down the aisle. An officer will meet you once you exit the bus. But first, we must confirm your passports," the shorter of the two officers said. "I ask that you remain silent until you've been cleared to continue." His colleague exited the bus after he tapped the first set of people on the shoulder. Their steps were apprehensive; however, they followed along as instructed.

Lauren tapped the aisle with her foot to get Conner's attention.

Conner signaled that she needed to relax. Lauren was still looking at Conner when the officer tapped her shoulder. His assertive touch caused her to jump. She gathered her things and left the bus with Ashley. Braden and another student followed behind them. Conner and I were next to last. I rummaged through my bag in search of my passport as the officer herded us down the aisle.

"Oh, my God! I don't have it!" I cried, a little panicked. "Madi, stop playing," Conner jested as we waited beside the bus. He seemed oblivious to my distress as I continued to search. I watched as the officer checked Conner's documents and allowed him to rejoin the group.

Damn! It's in the suite, I remembered. I could picture my new black purse on the nightstand. My passport is inside the zipped inner pocket. The officer aligned himself before me and extended his hand as I searched for an escape route. My eyes returned to the bus as I devised a quick, hopefully effective, plan.

"Your documents, Madame!" the officer snapped. His eyes flashed, and I felt a sudden wave of nausea, "Madame!"

"I left it on the bus," I said smoothly, so smoothly that I surprised myself — uncertain when I became such a good liar.

"You were asked to bring all your things," he said.

"Sorry," I felt the simpler my responses, the better.

"Your name?" he demanded. His eyes sparked and then glowed,

before they returned to normal. I watched as he lifted his hand and gestured to a man near the cleared group. My eyes widened when I saw his tattoo. "What the hell is the VHW? "Why do they seem to be everywhere?" He moved without haste toward us, and I tapped my foot nervously.

"You're Phillip and Elizabeth's daughter, aren't you?" the man asked, his raspy voice matched his unpolished demeanor. He was a short, scruffy and if I am honest, awful man. I noticed the contrast between his gold eyes and brown, ashen skin. His long fingers slid slowly through tight, black curls as he smirked. I turned to go back toward the bus — he followed behind me. "I asked if you are Phillip and Elizabeth's daughter. We need to question you down at the police department," he spoke harshly in French. I twisted to face him when something strange happened- I could see the darkness inside of him. He had done such horrible things that I felt an icy chill travel down my spine.

"I believe it is her," the officer said. The two men gave each other a look of confirmation, and I bolted. My eyes fixated on the wooded area to our left. I raced through the field, pushed myself harder, when I noticed a woman in my peripheral as she raced toward me. The woman stopped so close I had to step back to prevent us from colliding. A strange smell permeated from her, and my stomach began to twist in knots. The scent nearly caused my knees to buckle. Her yellow eyes were aglow, and saliva dripped from the corner of her mouth. I gagged when she wiped it off with the back of her hand. The woman's nails were — sharpened to a point, and the hunger in her eyes was now a look I found disturbingly familiar. She came closer, and I took another step back, but right into the arms of the officer from earlier.

"And now that I have your attention tell me who your parents are!" The man snarled as he yanked me around. His fingers looped the chain of my necklace until it snapped before he shoved me to the ground. I jumped back to my feet quicker than I had ever moved before.

"Yeah, that's not going to happen! You are creepy! You and your girlfriend should take care of those major personal hygiene issues. It's not healthy, and seriously, the drooling, major disgusting!" I snatched my necklace from his hand and pushed it deep inside my pocket.

"She's Elizabeth's daughter! We can take her," the woman barked.

"Like hell, you will! She's not going anywhere with you!" Conner yelled as he raced to my side. Their deviant scowls caused my fists to clench tighter.

"Isn't that precious? The boy wants to protect her." They laughed while circling us.

"Stop harassing tourists and take care of that problem we discussed!" After that, I must have lost my mind because I felt completely unafraid.

"We tried for years to convince your mom to join us. But you must admit it is ironic that we end up with a younger, stronger version. We've been searching for you for over a year, but it seems all we had to do was wait and allow you to come to us," the man sneered.

"You should leave us alone...now." My voice remained steady. "Maybe you shouldn't threaten them," Conner whispered. "The boy doesn't know about you. Well, he's in for a real treat," the man said. He smiled as the woman leaped toward me. My hand went up, and she crashed into a large tree near the edge of the woods. Conner's eyes met mine a second later — he was as confused as I was when the woman hit the large trunk and fell to the ground. Did I do that? No, there is no way that I could have. Only, I had. I looked back at the woman again as she stumbled to her feet.

"Oh My God!" I screamed and shoved Conner back toward the bus as she came at us. My hand shot out and I leveled her again in the damp grass.

I continued to push Conner forward — stopped only when I felt Jonathan nearby. A moment later, he was in front of me.

"Conner, take her back to the bus!" Jonathan commanded without a single glance in my direction.

"No, I'm not going to leave you here. I can help!" I argued, ready to use the freaky little trick with my hands again. His silver eyes flashed.

"If you don't want to see anything happen to her, you will listen to me!" Jonathan demanded. I looked past him to see three scruffy men on the run and headed in our direction. Jonathan lifted me and pushed me into Conner's arms. When I refused to move, Jonathan changed his approach.

"Madison, you remember what happened at the club. This will pale in comparison. You take your friend and return to the damn bus!"

I gave him a hard-determined look before I grabbed Conner's hand and raced away.

The trees cracked, and the earth shook. I started back, but it was too late. Conner grabbed me and carried me in his arms. He sprinted to the bus and threw me on a seat. Then he fell next to me, panting and sweating.

I rubbed my eyes and tried to calm myself as they continued to sting. "Don't cry. It was too dangerous back there," Conner said in a voice that could only comfort a child. "Let Spenser deal with his problems, sick freak!" Conner's words rang loud in my ears.

"I'm not crying, and he was protecting me. Those people wanted me! It has something to do with my parents." I glanced at the window again, thankful my eyes had finally dimmed. When I looked at Conner, he appeared unaffected.

"Oh, man! Did you lose your necklace?" he asked.

"No." I tapped my pocket to assure myself that it was still there. "Spenser will be fine," Conner said before he mumbled "unfortunately" under his breath. "Hand me your necklace."

I pulled the broken chain from my pocket and handed it to him. My eyes focused on the field. I waited for Jonathan would come into view. My anxiety had peaked, it was dark now- still no sight of Jonathan or the police officers. Well, if they were police officers. The group began to pour back onto the bus, and I stood to get off. Conner pushed me back into the seat. The bus waited for ten more minutes as stragglers continued to board. I tried once more about to lose it, as the bus pulled out of the lot. My phone started to vibrate seconds later, and I saw Emma's picture appear.

"Where are you? Have you talked to Jonathan? Is he okay?" My questions poured out of my mouth quickly.

"Yes, I've talked to him. Everything is fine. We will both see you back at the hotel," Emma said.

I breathed a huge sigh of relief and found it impossible not to smile. "So, Jonathan wasn't hurt?" I struggled to find the words.

"No, he's fine. How are you?" Emma asked.

"I'm okay. Conner held me, prisoner. Other than that, I'm wonderful," I said.

"Can you pass the phone to your friend?" She sounded reluctant to ask. I placed the cell phone in Conner's hand. You would have thought I had offered him poison by the disgusted look on his face.

"I don't talk to creepy chicks," he said before he slammed the phone shut. The already damaged cell phone crumbled. He gave it back to me in pieces. "Yeah, I can't repair that, but your necklace is fixed!" He placed the chain over my head. I stared down at the pieces that were once my cell phone.

"I'm sleepy," I said through a yawn, suddenly exhausted. My lids felt heavy, and I struggled to keep them open. The motion of the bus lulled me, and I drifted off.

"Madison!" Someone yelled, "You have to wake up!"

My eyes shot open as the bus screeched to a stop. Everyone slammed into the seat in front of them, Conner and I included. He mumbled something inaudible. I adjusted and peeked over the seat to see two men near the bus driver. Something was wrong. One of the men said my name, and I tried to slide down into the seat. Only my necklace caught on the end of the cracked vinyl. I yanked it gently, thankful that it was still intact. I quickly shoved it into my pocket.

I crawled to the back exit, but they guarded that door too, which left me no choice but to hide, so I wedged my body between the seats. The loud footsteps caused the floor to vibrate, and I held my breath when everything went silent. Time felt as though it stood still as I waited for them to leave.

"She's not on here. I thought you said she got on this bus!" one of the men barked.

"Madi," Conner said. The urgency in his voice caused me to flinch.

"That's the girl's name! He knows her. We'll take the boy, and she can find us," the men reasoned.

"Hey, take your damn hands off me!" Conner screamed. The sound of his sneakers raked down the aisle and Lauren's screams pushed me from my spot.

"Wait!" I shouted as I climbed from beneath the seat. A man's strong fingers latched onto my wrist.

"See? That wasn't so bad. Now we just need to talk to you for a bit. You don't want any trouble for these folks, right?" He sneered at me as I walked down the aisle. I saw people cowering under their seats or clinging to each other. Lauren held onto Conner's shirt like a lifeline.

"Let go of her!" Conner demanded. I pushed him into Lauren, but he grabbed my arm.

"Stop! This is about Phillip. I need you to call Emma at the hotel. Tell her what happened, okay?" I whispered.

"I'm not going to let them take you!" Conner shouted.

"This will all be straightened out, and I will see you back at the hotel," I lied. The people on the bus were innocent, and they would only be safe if I left with these me.

"Move!" the abrasive man yelled as he tore me from Conner's grip. We moved silently from the bus. He stopped in front of a police car. Bright blue lights flashed on and off quickly. I caught a glimpse of the bus as it rushed down the street. The largest of the men shoved me to the ground. I fell hard on my stomach before I slid across the slick grass. The mud was thick and clunky, which sealed me to the grass as I tried to back away, only to dig myself in deeper.

"What, what do you want?" I gasped for air as the men dropped to the ground beside me. Their large hands locked around my wrists and ankles.

"We want you! Your father will follow where you are or that sweet Elizabeth," one said. They all laughed as tears fell from my eyes.

"Go to hell, you stupid bastards!" I spat the words at them as the anger built inside me.

"Oh, you hear that, boys? She thinks we're stupid bastards!" he cackled. "We've had to wait too long for this moment."

"Had ourselves a good old time along the way, right boys?" another shouted.

"They were all so delicious!" someone chimed in.

"She smells better than the others; I want to keep her," I felt something wet brush across my cheek and knew that the rough ridge was one of their tongues.

"Man, she's so soft," he grabbed my chest and squeezed until I cried out, then cackled.

"I wonder if you're as sweet as you smell!" the one closest to me said, his saliva dripped on the ground beside me.

"GET YOUR DAMN HANDS-OFF ME!" My voice thundered. The invisible vibration caused the men to fall away. I leapt to my feet to wait on their next move.

"They said she wouldn't be able to fight back!" one man said.

"That's okay, I like my prey feisty!" another man thundered.

"Leave me alone, and no one has to get hurt," I reasoned as the men continued to come at me from all sides. My hand pushed outward and forced them back again. "Please don't make me do this!" I screamed, but they would not stop.

I extended my arms toward the sky. The wind rushed around me, and I pushed outward again. My hair billowed out as the air circled around me. My body felt as if it were fire; a charge of heat rushed through my entire being. The energy shielded me as the outward force began to strip the flesh from their bodies. They cried in pain as my movements left them suspended high in the air. I could feel myself absorb the energy around me, and the air became stronger, ripped, and tore away large sections of their body. Suddenly, the wind stopped, and the men crashed down to the ground. I walked over to the one that grabbed my breast, placed my hand on his chest — felt him vibrate against the muddy grass. He pleaded with me to stop, but all I could see was the faces of those girls — this one had done unspeakable things to them. A fraction of a second later, the man exploded. His remains were all over me.

I looked around in horror at what I'd done to them. Pieces of tattered clothing flesh, and blood covered everything.

I moved in slow motion away from the grizzly scene. My tears blinded me as I stumbled down the dark road, unable to understand all that had happened. Their blood dripped from my hands, yet my tears were for those girls. I couldn't believe what I had done. All those girls suffered because of my family. The rain began to pour, saturating my heated skin with the cool liquid and rinsing away the traces of blood. But it couldn't wash away my guilt or my pain.

"Madison." I heard Jonathan's voice. I continued to concentrate on each step. "Madison." He reached for me, and I flinched, drawing myself away.

"Please, stay away from me. I'm a horrible person," his eyes examined me, and then I felt the coolness of his hand smooth my hair back.

"If something had happened to you..." his voice hesitated, eyes softened, and his hand trembled against my cheek. He lifted me into his arms.

"I killed those men. I'm SOOO sorry. They wouldn't stop!" I cried.

"You didn't kill them. They were still alive when I arrived- weak but alive." His words softened by the sound of the rain on our skin.

"I have him on me!" I looked down at my hands and clothes, still saturated with blood. "Were they alive?" I stuttered, but knew no matter what Jonathan said, at least one died at my hands.

"I'm the one who killed them, not you. You must believe me. I'll do whatever it takes to find the one who got away and keep you safe," Jonathan said with urgency.

"I don't want anyone else to die because of me," I cried.

"They have a choice. We must always respect their choice," Jonathan said, his voice steady. "You will only be free when every one of them is gone," he said softly. I cried until my eyes closed, "And Madison... I will make them pay."

CHAPTER TWENTY
LIAR

I felt a surge of energy in my fingers, and my heartbeat quickened. It was like I had been asleep too long. Then, I heard whispers in my ear, "Please wake up. Madi, I need you to wake up." I shook off the fog and realized the voice belonged to Emma.

"I told you she's still asleep. I've tried everything I can to wake her up," Emma said with a frustrated sigh.

I groaned and tossed in the bed, feverish and weak. The blanket was too heavy on my body, and I kicked it off with a sigh.

When my eyes finally opened, I saw Emma and Conner. They both looked at me with a combination of concern and relief. Emma came closer and helped me sit up while Conner watched.

"You scared us," he said. "You need to see a doctor, or at least let us call your parents. You were barely breathing when Spenser brought you back here." Conner gawked from a distance.

"My head hurts," I managed to say when Emma shoved large pillow behind me, peeled the blankets away and smoothed out the sheet. She tucked it beneath my arms and fluffed the pillows on the bed.

"Do you need anything?" Emma eased me back down.

"Are you okay? I told them we should call your parents Madi," he paused, searched for the words, although they failed him. "I thought you were in a coma," Conner stammered.

"I'm a little hungry and thirsty," my voice was dry, scratchy, and desperate for a toothbrush.

Emma left the room and returned with bottles of water. She opened the bottle and handed it to me, which I gladly accepted. I had downed over half the bottle before I could lift my eyes to meet them. They smiled simultaneously. I wanted to laugh, but I feared that my head would split into pieces. The water helped, so I finished the first bottle and reached for another. When I went for the third one, Emma stopped me.

"You should eat something first," She reached into her wallet and placed money on the nightstand.

"Why don't you get her something to eat?" she suggested to Conner.

"Do it yourself!" he huffed. I flinched as Conner knocked the Euros onto the floor.

"I would, but Madi needs a bath, and as much as you would love to help her with that, I'm almost positive she would not," Emma snapped. Conner ripped the Euros from the floor and stormed from the room. He slammed the door behind him.

"More water, please," I managed.

"Sure, I will grab a couple more; promise me you will eat something too," there was undeniable concern in her voice. Emma breezed from the room and returned a second later with more water. She placed them on the nightstand while I downed the third bottle.

"I can't seem to move," I said, struggling to get my legs off the bed. "What happened? I feel like someone hit me with a bus." Emma helped me to the edge of the bed, and the feeling slowly returned to my limbs.

"You don't remember?" she questioned.

"The last thing I recall was tucking this in my pocket." I glanced down and lifted the skeleton key from my chest.

"Let me run your bath," Emma chided.

The short journey to the bathroom proved difficult because my legs felt weak and shaky.

"Do you know what happened last night," I asked breathlessly; everything took more effort than my body could supply.

"I'm not sure. Jonathan carried you back here. He hasn't spoken a word since he arrived except to say that he will remain in Paris," Emma said.

My attempt to smile fell short, and my heart sank.

I had missed the opportunity to convince Jonathan to come with us. My hands began to tremble — I tucked them behind me, afraid my eyes had already revealed too much.

"Oh, okay," my brows narrowed as I tried to recall last night's events. There were only fragments, a puzzle with missing pieces or a book with the pages ripped out. I glanced over at the clock 11:30 still had time to pack and speak with Jonathan before I left for the airport.

The bathtub slowly filled with bubbles, and I told myself not to think about Jonathan or last night, at least not until I had a chance to talk to him.

"I'm right outside the door if you need anything," Emma offered before she closed the door.

"Thank you," I tugged the gown over my head, lifting the necklace; I placed it on top of the heap, sunk into the heated water, and began feeling better with each passing second.

My mind continued to race as I scooted further inside the tub, allowing my feet to rest upon the faucet. I felt better and refreshed once the water covered my face and my energy returned. I sat up, shampooed the questionable smell from my hair, and scrubbed tinges of dried blood from my limbs. My skin tingled from the vigorous cleaning. However, I still had to pursue my mission. Something inside me compelled me to wash — to remove the residue from last night. I inspected my limbs, satisfied. I climbed from the bathtub and slid into one of the hotel robes. Then I tried to untangle my curls and secured the messy bun with a band — pleased with my handy work, I stepped out of the bathroom.

Jonathan was in the living room; he stood up when our eyes met. "Are you feeling better?" He approached me slowly.

"Can you stay here? We need to talk," I nibbled at my lip, and waited for him to respond.

"Of course," he left the room while I watched him walk away like a crazy stalker. He turned quick — too quick and flashed me a smile. I prayed my body would evaporate into the atmosphere. "Did you need something?" Jonathan asked with a slight tilt of his head.

I almost said, "Yeah, take your shirt off and walk away again... only slower this time."

He appeared in front of me so fast that I gasped. "You should finish getting dressed," he said teasingly.

I nodded my head and hurried to wash my face in the hope that my thoughts of Jonathan would return to 'PG' status. Silently I wondered if one hundred 'Hail Marys' would be enough for such impure thoughts and thanked my mom for never forcing me to choose a religion. If I were Catholic, the confessional would be my second home, and 'Hail Marys' would be the extent of my vocabulary. Well, at least since I met Jonathan. His presence consumed me, and I wanted to know him in every way.

"Madi, hurry before your food gets cold," Conner yelled from the other room, his voice catapulted me from images of Jonathan.

I rewashed my face, dressed quickly, and headed to the living room.

Austin, Lucas, Emma, and Jonathan stood near the window while Conner shoveled fries into his mouth. I sat in the chair next to him — he pushed my food closer. My eyes remained focused on Jonathan, while I unwrapped the burger.

His back was to me, although his reflection in the glass pane revealed he was watching me too. I took a large bite of the burger — then another. "So, a bath was all it took to get you back on your feet," Conner teased.

"Yeah, our moms were right when they said dirt can make you sick." I sunk my teeth into the burger once again. My eyes widened when my teeth hit something crispy and salty. I grabbed a napkin, frantically brushing the remnants off my tongue, but it was too late.

Tears filled my eyes as a fragmented picture of a defenseless pig filled my subconscious.

I could see the animal lying on a bed of greens, with a large apple shoved deep into its mouth. The memory always evoked sadness within me. I wished my mind would cooperate and reveal the rest of that night. My mom said it was one of Phillip's business parties, although she would not elaborate further.

"Oh, my bad, you must have mine," Conner said as he pulled the burger in front of him. "Stop crying; you barely took a bite. I'm telling you, Madi, your lack of respect for bacon is un-American. We might not let you back in the country."

My eyes traveled down to the burger as the bile rose in my throat.

"Look, it's mind over matter," Conner tried.

"You know how I feel," I snapped, more frustrated with my broken memories than I was about the bacon cheeseburger.

He shrugged his shoulders and stuffed more of the burger into his mouth.

"What's wrong?

You don't like the food?" Emma asked.

"No, it's fine, lost my appetite," I shoved my fries toward Conner, knowing the human vacuum would gobble them up too.

"She can't eat bacon, some kind of phobia or childhood trauma… can't remember." His mouth was full of the cheeseburger. It obviously meant nothing to him because he took another bite; swear, he could eat a burger in four bites.

I left the room and headed straight to the bathroom to brush my teeth again.

"Was it a childhood trauma?" Jonathan asked from the doorway. I put the toothbrush back in its case and wiped the water from my face.

"It's a long story."

"Can I get you something else?" he offered.

"No, I'm not hungry anymore. Jonathan, what happened to me? I can't remember anything about last night."

"The only thing that matters is that you're safe now." He said dismissively and looked toward the door.

"Am I keeping you from something?" My hands trembled so; I shoved them in my pockets.

"I wanted to tell you goodbye." There was only a hint of regret in his voice.

Goodbye, funny how the finality of that single word made me feel sick, "No," I managed. "I won't accept your goodbye," my voice faltered. "I'm not going to say it." I cried. The phone rang, and I glanced over when Jonathan did. That was strange. No one ever called the room. Finally, the ringing stopped, and he again gave me his attention.

"I'm not going to Nirvana. You'll be fine there without me," he said as if we were discussing the weather. There wasn't an ounce of emotion as he looked down at me.

"You know something is happening between us... you don't want to see where this will lead?" My eyes welled up with tears, and I twisted away from him. I prayed that he would change his mind.

"There can never be an us. Even if I return to Nirvana, we could not be together," he said with such coldness that I flinched.

"You're not that much older than me. I'll be eighteen soon," well, a year and four months. Jonathan's stoic expression stopped my thoughts dead in their tracks.

"Technically, I'm nineteen, but I've experienced much more life than you could imagine." Jonathan's coldness sent my eyes to the floor. The phone rang again, and he started towards the door.

"I don't believe you. You're afraid of us," I wanted to scream, but my words came out as a whisper.

"I never meant to hurt you. I thought you understood that we were having fun, and I had hoped we could still be friends," he added. I stepped back. "You have my number. Call me if you need anything." That was the first thing he said that had emotion.

"Madison," he began but stopped short.

"This is for the best; you will find someone that deserves you,"

Jonathan said as if any amount of reasoning would make this moment easier.

"I'm sorry for all the trouble I caused." My voice cracked, and I wondered if he could hear my heart breaking. My eyes met his once more, and then I heard a loud knock on the door. He looked at me with such regret that I was slightly confused.

"Madison, please forgive me," he whispered as the door opened. Phillip's towering presence encompassed the doorframe. Conner rushed to greet him, quickly engaging him in conversation.

"You called Phillip," I trembled and looked at Jonathan through tear-filled eyes.

"Conner, give me a few minutes with my daughter," Phillip said. And I slid back until I hit the wall.

Once Conner left the room, Phillip turned his attention toward me, and I lowered my eyes.

He stormed into the suite, and I heard a click — my eyes widened, and a scream tore from me so loud that it shook my frame. I leapt through the room — too late; Jonathan was on the floor, blood oozing from his chest.

He wasn't moving.

"Jonathan," I screamed, pounding his chest. Emma and Austin rushed to his side. Austin reached into Jonathan's chest and removed the wooden bullet. Jonathan jerked upward — rushed Phillip. I'm unsure how he missed him, but Jonathan hit the wall and the floor.

"Stay away from my daughter, or my next shot will end your existence!" Phillip thundered, "That goes for all of you!" His anger directed at Emma. I could see her skin darken, the tiny veins in her face thickened, and she let out a growl. They were vampires, yet they were backing down to Phillip; a second later, I understood their reasoning. The room filled with a wild bunch of men, all bearing the VHW tattoo, their eyes bright and yellow, salivating, and the muscles in their bodies pulsated.

Considering the high voltage of anger in the room, the walls should have exploded.

"What are you doing?" I asked, stumbling to my feet. "Why are all these people here? "You shot him!" My eyes widened with anger. "You shot him!" I shook my head back and forth. He crossed the room and backhanded me, which sent me into the wall.

Jonathan caught me — I brushed his hand away.

"Hit her again, and I will detach your hand," Jonathan threatened. "Madi, if you want your friends to live, get your things, and let's go!" Phillip said, ignoring Jonathan's threat. I gathered my purse and checked to see if my passport was inside.

My face was throbbing, and my head felt like it would explode. I looked down at the lighthouse Jonathan bought me, reached for it, and tossed it in the trash. Jonathan had betrayed me and called Phillip. Why would he do that? I was planning to leave today anyway. Was he trying to protect me or trying to get rid of me?

I pressed the button for the elevator, utterly unaware that Phillip had followed me until he reached for my hand; yanking it away, I turned angry eyes on him.

"Who are you?" I yelled as his posse gathered behind him. Phillip shoved me into the elevator. His entire body was tense with anger, and I knew that he was debating whether to direct that anger toward me. Phillip held out his hand. I placed my purse in his large palm and watched as he riffled through my belongings and returned with my busted cell phone. He closed his hand around it, grinding the metal into fine dust, and twisted to look at me.

"You will never see any of them again! They are monsters!" Phillip yanked me off the elevator when the door opened to the lobby.

He practically dragged me out of the hotel and onto the busy street. I waited silently while Philip hailed a taxi. Only he knew the driver. I thought when I noticed the tattoo on the man's arm. We climbed inside, and he removed the gun he had shot Jonathan with from his waist. He dismantled the weapon in seconds, ground the wooden bullets into dust, and reached beneath the passenger seat. Where he removed a small duffle bag, placed the gun inside, and shoved the bag back into its hiding place.

"What are you?" I stammered.

He yanked my chin up and eyed me with such disgust that

tears trickled down my face. "Why did you shoot him? He didn't do anything wrong."

Phillip lowered his voice and gripped my chin tighter. "I don't know what you mean," he managed to say as he spread his fingers across my face and squeezed harder.

"But I want to know if you let him touch you," His voice boomed in the confined space of the taxi.

"No, I…" my fingers clawed at his hand. It felt as though he wanted to grind the bones in my face- the same way he had my phone. "Let me go!"

"Phillip, she's still innocent," I heard the driver say, wondering how he knew. "Remember, we can detect those things." The man shouted over the radio static. His words seemed to resonate with Phillip because he removed his claw-like grip from my face.

"Madi, I would have killed you if you had been with him," Phillip said as if his reasoning made perfect sense. "Your mother can never know that you came to Paris. I fear that her worrying over you could compromise the pregnancy."

"Maybe this one will be deserving," the news of my mom's pregnancy saddened me.

Because I knew that the kid would toe the line or suffer the consequences of disappointing Phillip.

"This child will change everything," he said more to himself. He glanced down at his gold wedding band before settling back in the seat.

The plane ride to Nirvana was unpleasant, to say the least. Phillip refused to talk to me, well, except to bark orders. He reminded me of his threat to 'destroy my vampire friends.' His words, not mine. In addition, he avoided my questions about what he was; however, if Roberto was right, he was a killer. Something told me that the men at the hotel were affiliated with the VHW and were murderers. I remembered Tobias, the other movers, Liam, that couple at the Eiffel Tower, the police officers that wanted to check my passport, the men at the hotel, and the taxi driver.

I wanted to ask him about them, but he gave me a sideways glance that told me to walk faster — I did.

We parked in front of Margaret's house an hour later — he stopped short of knocking and reached into his phone to call my mom. He asked if she was feeling okay, and I heard the happiness in her voice as she talked about her latest sonogram. The embryo is thriving, and she should only need a couple more weeks of bed rest. My mom asked about me, and Phillip handed me the phone.

"Madison," my mom said with undeniable excitement.

"Mom," I cried, "So good to hear your voice."

"Did your father tell you the good news? You're going to have a little brother or sister soon," she gushed.

"Yes, he told me. I'm happy for you," I said, choosing my words carefully.

"I heard that the two of you had a wonderful weekend. I could not ask for more," there was a break in my mom's voice, and I knew she was crying.

"Mom, I have to go; love you," I handed Phillip the phone quickly before the past few weeks spilled out, and I broke her heart. Phillip told her to rest and that he would see her later tonight.

I went to knock on the door, but he stopped me. "Did you hear how happy she is?" he asked. "She wants this; stress could cause harm to both her and the baby. You will keep your mouth shut about Paris! You will not go around those monsters! Your mother carrying our baby to term is all that matters. You will dedicate all your free time to caring for your mother!" He took a step toward me when I didn't answer.

"Yes, of course," I stammered, moving out of his reach, or so I thought. But he grabbed the collar of my t-shirt and dragged me to the door, knocking loudly. I felt a surge of panic as I realized he would force me to stay here. I struggled to free myself from his grip, but he was too strong. He looked at me with a twisted smile."

Margaret answered with her hands resting on her boney hips. "If she so much as crosses the frame of this door, you will have me to answer too!" He shouted, and I swore he had grown at least five inches because he had to duck when he entered Margaret's house.

"The girl doesn't listen!" Margaret said in defense.

"Madi understands the consequences if she disobeys me!"

"We will take care of her," Margaret's voice quivered.

"Yes, you will," he handed her an envelope filled with cash. "She can spend time with Conner, no one else. He was the only person that had sense enough to call me." Phillip snapped.

I went to the Pepto room after listening to an hour-long rant from Margaret; truthfully, I had not heard a single word she spoke. But the cadence of her voice was like two pieces of metal grinding together, making my head pound. Jonathan consumed my thoughts — he never called Phillip; Conner unknowingly had.

Jonathan and I could still find a way to be together, and I would find my way back to him.

CHAPTER TWENTY-ONE
BITELY

Summer break was over, and classes had resumed. My mom and Phillip should have been home weeks ago, but the doctor insisted that she not travel for six weeks due to a complication and the risk to her pregnancy. But I received a call from her today and had a silent celebration in my head. She phoned this morning to say they were on the road and should be home no later than tomorrow night. Phillip didn't want to take any chances with my mom's pregnancy, so they drove. They planned to drop my mom off and continue to Traverse City, where another girl had disappeared. There was a search team already on the ground. I could not wait to see her. Honestly, I was excited about being back home. I missed my mom, and my room — oh God, how I missed my room. At least at home I felt safe.

Margaret and Daniel had become a little scary. Margaret was short tempered and yelled about everything, she worked all the time, and her idea of a well-balanced meal was a frozen microwave dinner. Daniel watched every move I made, and I knew he had rummaged through my things the other day. Although he denied it, there could be no other explanation. If I'm being honest the thing that disturbed me the most was the way, he lounged around the house in his boxers. The image of his gangly legs and hairy chest made my stomach churn.

Since Phillip, left strict orders with Margaret about who I could hang-out with, Conner was my pardon. He didn't seem to mind. I locked the door, and headed to Braden's car, but paused, because they seemed preoccupied with something in the trees.

"What's wrong?" I questioned when I climbed inside, and we drove slowly down the street.

"Braden thought he saw something run into the forest," Conner said.

"What did you see?" I asked, looking back toward the house.

"I'm not sure; it looked like a group of guys were standing by the side of the road, then they were gone, weird, right?" Braden said, glancing over at Conner before focusing straight ahead.

"Maybe they were hikers?" I reasoned. My words did not sound believable. I knew there might still be people searching for me. The abductions had continued when I was in Paris, with the most recent being a week ago, in Traverse City. That fact alone had everyone on edge. Something was off and I could feel it deep in the pit of my stomach. Suddenly, the car went sliding across the street, and then came to an abrupt stop. Thankfully, my seatbelt was firmly in place. I stopped short of hitting the back of Conner's seat.

"What the hell was that?" Conner yelled.

"I don't know, a deer or something," Braden offered nervously. My eyes traveled to the forest, narrowing when I saw a pair of glowing eyes. I felt a familiar coldness, and watched as the trees rustled, seconds later the feeling dissipated.

"Okay, that was crazy!" Braden exclaimed as he sped off. He continued talking with Conner about the incident, but I was — consumed in my own thoughts about what could have been in the woods. We stopped in front of the school and Braden slammed the door, which jolted me back to reality.

"I'll see you in class," Conner said once I climbed out of the backseat. He walked over to join Braden, who was now standing with a group of guys near the edge of the building. I went to sit on the table and tried to calm the queasiness that nearly toppled me. I jumped to my feet and grimaced when the tardy bell rang.

When I walked inside, Emma and Bria were in deep conversation, and for a second, I wondered if I had entered the twilight zone. "Bria was aggravating," Emma's words, although I agreed. When I joined them, Bria stopped talking to Emma; she never acknowledged my presence. Instead, she turned and walked down the hallway. I looked at Emma, only her focus was on Bria as Peyton, Blake, as others stepped into the corridor to join her. The small group exchanged knowing looks as they sniffed the air simultaneously.

"What's going on?" I asked Emma, but her eyes remained focused on the growing group.

"You're late for class. We can talk later." Emma said. Her eyes flashed when Bria walked toward the door. I watched as the entourage followed closely behind her, and my mouth dropped when Emma raced to join them. I thought that it was a gathering for the beautiful people.

I waited until they were out the door before, I trailed their footsteps. When I stepped outside, the group had assembled in the courtyard near the forest edge. I strained to hear their conversation, but the sound of splintered trees or branches deep in the woods caught my attention. And then I noticed the trees- they trembled. The group shifted their attention toward the forest. I crouched behind one of the picnic tables and peered over the bench. Emma and Bria sniffed the air, and I did the same that smell was familiar- musky, dark and dangerous. My eyes widened as the ground began to shake beneath me. The disturbance and that smell was coming from the forest, and whatever it was, it was getting closer.

"Why aren't you in class?" Emma was suddenly beside the table, she bent down to look at me. When I didn't move, she grabbed my hand and helped me up, then urged me to go back inside the school. I was about to demand that Emma tell me what was going on when my mom shouted for me from across the school grounds.

"What are you doing here?" I yelled. I stood there stunned that she was at my school when they weren't due until tomorrow.

"Madison!" she shouted, and moved, quickly toward us. "Hurry, we have to leave right now!" My mom cried. I began running with her, and then stopped when I realized Emma headed back toward the group.

"No, wait, you have to come with us!" I screamed at Emma. My mom was here; there was no way I could deny that something bad was about to happen.

"You go; I'll be okay," Emma said, her voice calmer than it should have been. I jumped, as ear shattering screams saturated the air.

"Emma, she's not going to go without you! I must get her in this car now!" My mom yelled, and Emma finally agreed. We sprinted to the car and jumped inside.

"You are so damn stubborn!" Emma fumed as we tore from the parking lot.

"Wait, what about everyone else?" I asked. I had forgotten about the other students in my attempt to get Emma to safety. "Mom, what's wrong? Why are we leaving?" I needed to understand, but I could not make sense of anything.

"I'm not sure what's going on; I know I need to get you to safety," she responded, as her small foot hit the gas pedal, plastering my back to the seat.

"We can't leave them back there!" I turned to look at Emma, but she was on the phone. She must have felt my eyes on her because she mumbled something and hung up.

"Madison, we have no other choice," my mom said as we left hundreds of innocent people behind.

"What is going on?" I asked, only to be ignored again.

"Buckle up, because we need to move a little faster," my mom instructed. The speedometer was already in the red. She buzzed past the other cars as we headed down south Kings Highway.

"I don't understand! Why won't you tell me?" I shouted as I grabbed the sleeve of her shirt, and pleaded for to tell me, something, anything. The car swerved and her eyes flashed.

"Stop it now!" she demanded. Her eyes pooled with tears. "I don't like this anymore than you, but you're going to have to trust me." She glanced in the rearview mirror, and I could see the distress in her eyes. "I tried to stop this," she added as she ran her fingers through her hair in frustration.

"That's all any of us can do," Emma joined, as if she knew what my mom was referring to. Her eyes saddened for a moment before they met my confused stare.

"Where is Phillip? Where is Uncle Mike?" I demanded.

"They are at the school," my mom said.

We continued to break all sort of speeding limits for another 20 minutes. No one said anything. The silence was driving was making me angry. I looked from my mom to Emma. My mom kept her eyes glued on the road wiping away a steady stream of silent tears.

I put the window down, the car felt too small, and I felt nauseous. I could not shake off the feeling that since Phillip was involved people were going to die. Those people running in the woods and the ones at the school I would bet they all had something to do with the VHW.

I shook my head, when I saw the 'Welcome to Bitely, Michigan' sign. This entire situation was unbelievable. I closed my eyes and tried my best to process the events of the day when my mom's phone began to ring.

'Hubby' popped up on the screen. She pulled over to the side of the road. She hopped out of the car and moved quickly out of hearing range, although the distress on her face told me things were not okay. My mom slid back inside minutes later and looked over at me, "we can go back now." She turned the car in the direction of Nirvana, only we were moving much slower.

"We're going back?" I asked.

"Yes, it's safe now," her voice was shaky; "Phillip said it's safe to return."

"What happened at the school?"

"I'm not sure of the details," she was lying; I could hear it in her voice. I continued to ask questions the rest of the car ride, but she refused to answer. Instead, she suggested we listen to the radio to relax. I rolled my eyes, knowing her intention was to drown me out.

"Please stop the car. I will walk home," Emma interjected. Her house was only ten minutes away; it would have been easy for us to drive her home.

"We can take you," I offered.

"Please, stop the car," she insisted. My mom stopped the car on the side of the road. I watched as Emma disappeared into the forest without faltering in her five-inch heels.

"Do you think she'll be okay?" I asked my mom.

"Yes, I'm certain that she can take care of herself."

We were getting close to the school because I could hear the blaring sirens, but she drove right by the turn and continued toward our house.

My phone vibrated; I answered quickly, relieved to hear Conner's voice on the other end. He sounded as shaky as I felt, but he told me that he was okay, however, Bria, and Lindsey died. Conner said that the police found them along with four more bodies behind the school. Phillip said it was a shooter.

The sheriff said Bria died trying to help Lindsey. Phillip and Uncle Mike had ushered everyone into the gym until they killed the shooter. He sounded almost excited as he described the horrific scene in vivid detail. Bria and Lindsey had been horrible, but I would have never wished this on them, or anyone. Conner was still talking, but I had stopped listening, as he continued to describe the ghastly scene.

It had begun to rain, and the huge raindrops hitting the car's roof sounded more like drums.

"Who was that?" My mom asked as we stopped in front of our house. I stepped out of the car, but my feet did not move in the direction of the house. They felt so heavy, I thought to myself as tears slowly streamed down my face.

"Wait, you said Phillip was tracking the killers to Traverse City. Why did they come here? You knew they were coming; that's why you came for me! You were going to let Emma stay there! He killed them, or he allowed that to happen. Bria and Lindsey are dead! Instead of helping, we ran!" I screamed. I was so confused and angry; I could barely get my words out.

"Madison, you're the only person in this world that matters," My mom said as she began to cry. The realization of what happened sucked the air from my chest. "I've been so busy protecting others that I allowed my daughter to be placed in harm's way, but never again!" she sobbed.

"This whole time you knew they were after me. That's why we moved here! All those girls died! You made me leave my home and any chance of ever seeing Nic again!" I couldn't stop myself there were far too many secrets. I turned to face her, "You knew, and you let people die, you and Phillip!"

She tried to wrap her arms around me, but I moved away. "They wanted to kill me! You should have let them!"

The town held a candlelight vigil to remember Bria, Lindsey and two others killed in the attack. Out of respect, I attended with Emma. Blake had stopped, talking to me. I couldn't blame him, because although the town believed the lie about the shooter — he knew the truth, and so did I.

CHAPTER TWENTY-TWO
FORSAKEN

Emma and I had planned a day away from the fallout of the shooting. A month had passed, and we were still on edge. I would not allow Emma to pick me up or drop me off at my house for fear of Phillip. My parents were out of town because of my mom's follow-up appointment with the fertility specialist. I planned to take full advantage of their absence. Emma decided that a beach trip was in order, and who was I to disagree. I stared up at the lighthouse, and my mind traveled to Jonathan. I had been back in Nirvana for three months and still had not heard from him.

Therefore, her idea of a day at the beach was perfect, except that Austin and Lucas had decided to tag along. I enjoyed being with Austin. However, he reminded me so much of Jonathan that I often stared at him. Austin didn't seem to notice, or at least was polite enough not to embarrass me. Lucas, however, did not. He had pointed out my preoccupation with Austin every time the opportunity presented itself, which was every time I saw him. The ride to the beach was no different. I thought to myself that Lucas should have been the one that stayed in Paris.

My feet sunk a little deeper into the wet sand with every step. I giggled as the cool water caressed my legs. The feeling was delightful. I continued walking until a sudden rush of icy water hit my back. I screamed from the shock.

"You looked like you could use a little cooling off," Lucas said.

My eyes narrowed when he began to laugh. Austin came out of nowhere and tackled him. I couldn't help but enjoy the spectacle they were making. Emma waved me forward, and I walked around the two men, although they behaved more like teenagers.

"Sorry about Lucas," Emma said as I joined her on the blanket. She glided her sunglasses back to hold her hair in place. The wind had whipped the strands all around her.

"He's fine," I began, "Okay. So, I'm learning that Lucas is Lucas." I glanced back to see Austin lift Lucas above his head and toss him as if he weighed nothing. Lucas landed with a large splash. I sat up.

"Austin's, strong," I managed.

"He's a showoff," Emma huffed. She leaned back and stared upward. There was something strange in her eyes as she looked up at the cloud-ridden sky.

"I know, for once, it would be great to feel a little sun," I said before flipping onto my back.

"No, this is a perfect day," Emma said. "We are allergic to direct sunlight."

"Oh, what would happen?"

"Burst into flames and cease to exist."

"Wow, I didn't think about that," I admitted. My relationship with the sun was simple; I had never experienced a sunrise or sunset. Only cloudy and overcast skies, I wondered if I, too, would burst into flames under the sun's glare — then smiled at the craziness of my thoughts.

"I wonder what it feels like," I said more to myself than to Emma.

"What?"

"The sun."

"Are you joking?"

"No, I have never seen the sun. This is all I know." I pointed up to the sky, and the grayish colored clouds.

"Hey, one more thing we have in common," she had a giant

smile on her face, but it quickly turned upside down when droplets of water splashed across us.

"If another drop hits me," she began.

"You're going to do what?" Austin teased. His eyes filled with mischief; I found that delightful. Emma sat up with a daring look on her face. I started to laugh because I knew this was going to end badly. Austin scooped her up so fast that if I had blinked, I would have missed it. He ran down the beach with Emma over his shoulder.

"Put me down!" Emma screamed. Her demand was too late. Austin tossed her into the water. Emma disappeared beneath the waves, and I waited for her to resurface. She didn't. I raced down the beach but found myself lifted off the sand. Lucas had me firmly in his arms, and I joined Emma a second later.

I dove deeper in search of her. My eyes adjusted to the salty water. She had her finger over her lips, signaling me to remain quiet. I saw a pair of legs and then another walking toward us. She snatched them both, pulling Austin and Lucas under. Emma and I came to the surface simultaneously. She hurried from the water, and I followed behind her. Austin and Lucas remained in the crashing waves. They wanted to gauge whether Emma was mad. That was a wise choice.

"He's such a bully," Emma fumed. She gathered her things and placed them inside her bag.

"You're his little sister. I thought big brothers were supposed to torture you." I put on my flip-flops and wrung out my shirt. The blue jean shorts were now stuck to me, and I felt gross.

"I guess." She looked back at them before we started the walk to the car. She placed a towel in both seats for us to sit on. "We can stop by my house to shower and change." Emma began to back out of the parking lot.

"Uh, you're leaving them here?" I twisted in my seat in time to see both men standing on the beach, their arms tossed in the air.

"Yep, payback's a bitch. And so am I." Emma laughed. She shifted gears, and we sped down the road. I almost felt sorry for Austin and Lucas.

Emma loaned me a sundress and let me use the guest room

to shower, and change. I headed down the winding staircase. Emma was in the great room talking to Austin and Lucas. The conversation stopped when I walked into the room.

"Glad to see you made it back," I said to Austin. "You, not so much," I commented to Lucas.

"Sorry about today. We got a little carried away." Austin's apology seemed legitimate. He stared at me with his familiar silver eyes, and I had no choice but to forgive him. But, truthfully, today was more fun than I would openly admit.

"Speak for yourself," Lucas said. "Today was fun as hell!" His voice faded as he left the room.

"Are you ready?" Emma asked.

"Yeah," I slid the strap of my bag over my shoulder. "See you later, Austin."

"So, we're good?" Austin asked.

"Of course," I said as I waited for her in the foyer. "Are we on speaking terms again?" Austin asked Emma. "We're even," she said. "My hair is a mess," she scoffed.

Emma opened the door and allowed me outside first. I slowly descended the stairs of her porch.

"Would you mind stopping by the mailbox at the corner?" I asked her as we opened the car doors.

She bit her lip knowingly. "Sure."

I slid into the seat and lightly patted my bag before placing it beside my legs.

"So, I don't even get to see what it says?" Emma asked.

I felt a strange urge to write to Jonathan, maybe because I was too scared to call him. For two weeks, I had been thinking about doing that. After looking at the phone for a long time, I finally wrote the letter last night. Emma told me to just text him, which wouldn't be personal. Jonathan would understand what the letter meant. He would see that I cared about him more than a text.

I gave Emma a chiding look.

"Fine, I won't ask," Emma said before smiling. She swerved the car to the right and shifted the gear into the park. The mailbox was on the sidewalk, only steps away. My heart pounded as I removed the letter from my bag. I sat there, staring at the large blue box. Emma was trying her best to be patient.

"Hello? Madi? Earth to Madi!" She teased. I looked back at her and bit my lip nervously. She threw her hands up from the steering wheel. "The girl who wanders aimlessly through the woods and travels halfway across the globe because of a dream is afraid to mail a letter?" She opened the door and crossed in front of the car. My eyes followed her as she flung my door open. "You've got to do this," she said.

She linked arms with me and forced me to quicken my pace as she walked me toward the mailbox. It's okay, I told myself. I gathered the strength to open the door and dropped the letter in before I could stop myself.

My fate sealed when the cream-colored envelope slid from my fingers into the blue steel box. I swallowed the large lump in my throat before releasing the handle. As the mailbox closed, I tried to retrieve the letter at the last second. Emma stopped me.

"That would be a federal offense," She warned. The Thelma and Louise thing would so not work for us. You are far too pretty for prison, and I detest those orange jumpsuits." She laughed as she ushered me away. I was half-tempted to take my chances with the federal government. Still, as we drove away, I had to accept that my destiny now rested in the bottom of the mailbox.

"Thanks for the ride," I said as she pulled to a stop down the road from my house. I hesitated before leaving her car. "See you tomorrow."

"You're welcome. Should I go back and padlock that mailbox?" Emma teased.

"No, maybe, I don't know," I debated before heading up the sidewalk.

"I better not receive a phone call to bail you out of jail," Emma joked before she sped down the street.

Between my nightmares and my aching stomach, sleep evaded

me. I grabbed the pink bottle of medicine from the cabinet. Thankfully, they left me with Uncle Mike this time instead of the couple from hell, A.K.A., Margaret, and Daniel.

The doorbell chimed through the house. Before I could get to the door, it rang four more times. "Can I help you?" I questioned, staring blankly at the sheriff. I had met him once before when we arrived in Nirvana and had seen him on the news. I tried to rationalize why he would be standing at my door.

"Yes, I'm Sheriff Hilton. Is this the home of Mr. Phillip and Elizabeth Ryan?"

"Yes, this is their home. I'm sorry my parents aren't here right now, but they should return tomorrow," I responded, still confused about his visit.

"Is there an adult here I can speak with?" he asked slowly. I had seen this look before…during the press conference after the attack at school.

"My uncle is here, but I think he's asleep. Is there anything I can help you with?"

"I need you to wake him up; this is important," the sheriff insisted.

My curiosity was starting to grow. I wondered if there had been another incident in town. "Okay, please come in," I stepped aside to show the Sheriff to the sofa.

I knocked on the guest bedroom door, "Uncle Mike, the sheriff, is at the door. He needs to speak with you." Feeling anxious, I wiped my sweaty palms against my thin pajama pants.

"I'm coming," he called from inside, sounding thick and crackly. I knew how rude it was to leave guests unattended, but I didn't want to return there alone. Something was unsettling about him, so I sat beside the door and propped my feet against the wall. I jumped up seconds later when Uncle Mike opened the door, stubbing his toe and uttering his favorite curse words before he noticed I was there.

"What's going on?" he grumbled, rubbing his eyes with his enormous fists as he stumbled through the door.

"I don't know; he said he wanted to speak with an adult," I replied, following him down the hall.

When we entered the living room, Uncle Mike turned around. "Madi, will you grab me a glass of water? I'm a little thirsty," he said. I wanted to go with him but followed his request.

With the glass full of water, I joined them in the room. The sheriff whispered, and I strained to hear what he said. Uncle Mike was pulling his hand through his hair; I could tell this meant something was wrong. The last time I saw him with that look was when his wife left. A lump began to rise in my throat. It wasn't until tears welled up in his eyes and he began to sob that the world seemed to stop spinning on its axis. The glass hit the floor, breaking into pieces, and the water pooled around my feet. He walked over to me and pulled me close.

"What's wrong?" I cried, pushing against his chest. When he looked at me, I could see a fresh wave of tears streaming down his face as he tried desperately to compose himself.

All his words came out jumbled. "Madi, your parents..." he started, struggling to continue. I stared up at him.

"What's wrong with my parents?" I demanded, getting ready to lose it if he didn't start speaking at once.

"There was an accident last night." He wrung his hands now, "I'm sorry, Madi, but they didn't make it."

"What? No! Why are you saying this to me?" I demanded and then stormed from the room, searching frantically for the cordless phone as I knocked the phone book off the table. I couldn't find it, so I ran into the kitchen to use Uncle Mike's cell.

My hands trembled as I picked up the phone. My mom's cell went straight to voicemail. My heart felt like it would explode when Phillip's phone went to voicemail too. This had to be a horrible mistake; it had to be they would return soon. My mom promised to come right home after the appointment. She had never broken a promise before, and there was no reason for me to believe she would start now.

On my way back into the living room, I stopped at the door

and watched the sheriff hand Uncle Mike a small plastic bag. He poured the contents on the table, and two gold rings spun around before clinging to a stop. I told myself the wedding band could have belonged to anyone, eyeing the simple, circular piece. Uncle Mike held up the second ring; intricate carvings and two triangular sapphire gems surrounded the round diamond. It glistened in the light as he rolled it between his thumb and forefinger. He shook his head solemnly as tears began to blur my eyes. I tried to convince myself that someone else had one like hers. Uncle Mike placed it in my hand. I dropped it on the floor; it felt like fire against my skin. Throughout my entire life, I had twisted that ring around my mom's finger. I knew every flaw. The band was an old family heirloom passed down from mother to daughter. My eyes squeezed closed, forcing the tears back.

"Madi, can I get you anything?" Uncle Mike asked as his warm hand touched my shoulder. The moisture from his hand crept through my shirt. When I opened my eyes, the watery film made it hard to see. I stared down at the ring that belonged to my mom; the gold seemed to have lost its shine. I bent over to pick it up. My heart felt like it would stop, and I gasped for air. Leaning on the wall for stability, I slid the gold ring on my finger. I pressed it against my lips. Silent tears began to fall down my face because I knew she would never have taken it off.

"Madi," Uncle Mike said, sending my mind crashing back to reality. I looked up through a veil of tears and saw her standing in front of me, and suddenly, her image disappeared. "You should sit down," he offered. I twisted away too quickly from his grasp, and the room spun. My head hit the floor with a resounding thud that vibrated in my ears. I tried to open my eyes, but the darkness was unyielding.

Suddenly my senses were — overcome with a God-awful smell. I tried to move my head away, but something held me there. The unpleasant scent forced my eyes open. Uncle Mike was sitting on the floor beside me, and the sheriff was waving a small glass bottle of a white, crystallized substance in front of me. The strong ammonia smell stung my nostrils and caused my eyes to sting. I pushed it away.

"We should take you to the hospital. You may be going into shock," Uncle Mike suggested.

"Please, let me rest a little longer," I cried.

"Yes, of course, you can," he replied as he carried me to the sofa and placed the quilt my mom had made for me over my legs. She used it more than I did, and it smelled like her. I pulled my knees to my chest and buried my face in the soft material. As I inhaled her scent, I tried to stifle the gut-wrenching sobs.

The next few days, I was no more than a ghost watching as the world passed me. This must be someone else's life, I told myself. People I hadn't seen in years suddenly professed undying love and devotion for my parents. Uncle Mike said they flew in for the funeral and urged me to try my best to appreciate it. They offered me things like food, clothes, and a shoulder. Older women were going through my mom's things. Emma stopped me from bashing one woman's head in with Phillip's wooden bat. Uncle Mike later told me that I should be ashamed of myself because she was from the funeral home and needed a dress for my mom in case her body was — found.

I could not understand going through life feeling this way, being alive but not living. The bile began to rise in my throat. I grabbed my stomach as another wave sent me, heaving over the porcelain seat. The cool tiles on the bathroom floor seemed to soothe my overly warm body.

"Do you need help getting dressed, sweetheart?" Ms. Betty asked as she peered inside. I shook my head and crawled from the floor. "Now, sweetheart, I have your dress lying across your bed, and I laid your 'delicates' there," she fussed before closing the bathroom door.

Once I picked myself up, I showered and brushed my teeth.

I stared in the mirror, searching for any feature that would remind me of my mom. I never wanted to resemble her more than now, so I could see her face again. My normal caramel-colored skin was now pale, almost ashen, and dark circles surrounded my eyes from lack of sleep. I blow-dried and flat-ironed my hair, so the strands now rested below my waist. Emma had been kind enough to buy the jasmine and daisy flower arrangements. I tucked one of the blossoms between my fingers; the smell reminded me of her.

My eyes traveled to the black dress my mom had bought me weeks ago. My fingers trailed across the material. I put the dress on but tossed the stockings in the trash. I never did see any need for such things. Then I slid my feet into the high-heeled shoes that belonged to her only days ago. Uncle Mike came to the door, and I looked at him with tear-clouded eyes.

"We need to leave now," he said, his eyes filling with regret as I nodded. I followed him down the hall, stopping at my parent's bedroom for a second. Uncle Mike took my hand and led me out the door. The rain was cold and felt good against my skin. As I slid into the back of the limousine, the reality of where we were going set in, and a new stream of tears flowed down my face.

I made it through the funeral but refused to entertain the guests. Instead, I went to my room, needing to escape from all the people who had migrated into my home. After I shrugged off the dress, I lay across the bed to stare out the window. When a shadow passed, I stepped outside on the roof, only to find no one was out there. I peered over the edge, looking for any sign that someone had been nearby. A knock at the door startled me, and I nearly fell. I grabbed the overhanging branch to balance myself and then steadily made my way back inside. I locked the window and closed the drapes before grabbing my robe and putting it on.

"I know you're still awake; it's me," Uncle Mike called through the door.

"Come in, it's open," I yelled, picking the dress up and placing it with the clothes that needed to be, dry-cleaned.

"I wanted to make sure you're okay," Uncle Mike said, wringing his hands.

"Yes, I'm fine." The lies were coming easier these days.

"Okay, then I'll see you in the morning. I love you," Uncle Mike said before he left.

Seven days after my parent's funeral, I woke up surprised I had made it through another night. My mom was gone, and I felt as if I were too. Had I survived? How would I continue to exist in a world where she didn't? My head was throbbing, and I felt squeamish, so I went downstairs; I saw Uncle Mike sitting on the sofa. His eyes were puffy from crying, and he motioned for me to sit beside him. He appeared nervous as tiny beads of sweat formed on his brow.

He cleared his throat and said, "I have something important to tell you. It's about your mom and dad." Then, he paused and looked away as if he couldn't bear to face me.

"I don't know how to tell you this, Madi," he finally managed. 'What else could he possibly have to tell me?' I asked myself, beginning to feel anxious. My fingers gripped the cushions of the sofa. I needed to touch something tangible.

"We need to discuss the arrangements your parents made for you. Since we received the news, I have reviewed your parents' last will and testament, probing for loopholes. There is no way around it," he muttered as his eyes focused on the floor. My stomach began to churn as the bile rose in my throat.

"Loopholes for," I asked impatiently.

"According to their will, your mother's best friend, Margaret, now has custody of you and a small portion of your sizable inheritance." He pulled his hands through his hair. "I've spoken to Margaret, and she won't consider you staying here with me. The house was paid-in-full, and it now belongs to you. But, of course, you cannot take ownership until you turn eighteen. Your father's Porsche, his truck, and the beach house in Hatteras are yours as well. Beth made sure you'll never want for anything," Uncle Mike explained.

I sat there with a dumbfounded look, unable to understand why he was saying these things to me.

"She will be here in the morning," Uncle Mike added, and my heart dropped. My gaze quickly went back to his face, hoping this was a cruel joke. "I didn't know how to tell you. If Margaret had agreed, I would have kept you here with me," he continued, seeing the confused look on my face.

"This can't be happening!" I screamed, jumping to my feet.

"Madi," he grabbed my hand as tears consumed his tired eyes and revealed his anguish. "She will be your legal guardian until the day after your 18th birthday. Besides, you're going to college next fall," Uncle Mike reasoned.

"No!" This time the words echoed throughout the room. "I won't be eighteen for another year. Why can't I stay with you?" I pleaded.

"It's going to be all right. I know it doesn't feel like it right now, but it will be, you'll see," Uncle Mike said to reassure me.

"No, everything's not all right, not even close! It will never be all right again, and I wish people would stop trying to convince me that it will be! You're standing here telling me I'm the only one with no say about where I will live! Why would they send me to live with Margaret? None of this makes sense!" I shouted back at him. My nervous energy sent me pacing back and forth in front of the fireplace. I had never been so angry; my eyes burned as they illuminated. "First, I'm told my parents are dead, and if that's not enough to make me want to jump off a cliff, you throw this news at me and expect me to back away from the ledge and be okay." The words rolled off my tongue like angry daggers. "You don't want me, so why not send me away so I'll be out of your hair forever!" I wanted nothing more than to die.

"Madi!" he thundered, "Stop this at once; this is what your

parents wanted!" His long legs crossed the room quickly, and he grabbed my arm, holding me close. "I know it doesn't feel like it right now, but you will survive this! I'm not sure why they chose Margaret to take care of you. We both have questions that will remain unanswered," Uncle Mike said, his voice softening. My knees went weak, and I grabbed my chest, trying to hold together the millions of pieces my heart had broken into.

The following day, I packed my entire life into brown cardboard boxes. Margaret only allowed me to bring five boxes into her home; the rest is in storage. She said Daniel did not like clutter. Mike was gone before I even woke up. He lost the title of uncle when his only goodbye was — scrawled across a piece of paper.

CHAPTER TWENTY-THREE
INVITATION

The following year was a complete blur; days blended into one another. My senior year, graduation, holidays, and birthday all felt like I was watching someone else's life. Life with Margaret and Daniel was intolerable. I'm not sure how I survived.

Although my job helped keep me busy. I'm officially the newest employee at the Grandin Theater, thanks to Margaret. She had been hard at work finding a job for me. She pulled a couple favors with Tommy, the manager. The theater was the local hangout, and it stayed busy. Life in Nirvana began and ended at the Grandin. People were either coming or going to the movies.

Margaret drove me to work the first day in Phillip's Porsche, which I thought had been in storage. "It was collecting dust," she had snapped. "You're a child! What difference does it make? I had listened as she rambled off a string of excuses.

Once inside the house, I removed my load of laundry from the dryer and trekked to the kitchen. It was relaxing to see that Margaret and Daniel were not home. I shuffled through the envelopes on the counter, bills, and delinquent payment notices. I was sure I'd hear about how the past-due payment was my fault. According to Margaret, she had lost a series of checks that totaled $20,000. She believed I had taken them.

I went to my room, kicked my sneakers off, and grabbed my

book from the nightstand. After reading the first chapter, all the words began to blur as I drifted to sleep.

The past week the Grandin had been busier than usual. The latest H. P. movie had drawn in huge crowds. So, I was glad to have a day off from work.

"WAKE UP!" the terrified voice demanded.

The feeling of hot breath on my skin was heavy, and it smelled like a mixture of beer and cigarettes. Something wet brushed against the side of my face. My eyes shot open, and I jumped from the bed, stunned to see Daniel there. His beady, brown eyes traveled down the length of my body. I folded my arms over my chest, and he finally made eye contact.

"Margaret found herself a real winner when she married the pervert from hell," I mumbled before wiping away the slimy substance his tongue left behind. "What do you want?" I asked. My voice was shakier than intended, and I wondered if he could hear my sheer uneasiness.

"Oh, yeah, Marge wants you to come down for dinner," he said, wringing his dirty hands.

"I'll be down in a sec." I felt sicker by the second.

When he left, I rushed to the bathroom to wash my face. I reprimanded myself for making such a stupid mistake. How could I have fallen asleep without locking the door? My face burned as I desperately scrubbed the slimy residue Daniel had left behind. Although, his touch, no matter how hard I scrubbed, could not be — removed. I paced the room, thinking of ways to avoid dinner with the couple from hell.

"Madi, don't make me come up there again!" Daniel yelled up the stairs. Reluctantly, I trudged downstairs to join them.

When I sat down, Margaret came around the table and dropped a plate before me. She seemed proud that she had cooked. Wait, Margaret cooked. I thought to myself. She had never prepared a single meal. This had to mean one of two things. Either she had lost complete grip on reality, or the food had been — poisoned. Regardless, I wasn't eating. I took my fork and moved the concoction back and forth across my plate. The sloppy mess looked like overdone spaghetti noodles, although they were so mushy it was difficult to tell. There was meat clumped on the sauce and scattered pieces of burnt tomatoes. My eyes followed a meatball as the glob slid across the plate, and I wondered if it was still alive. I shook my head.

My eyes tightened when Margaret cleared her throat. She passed the parmesan cheese to me, and I tried to empty the bottle, hoping to help its appearance.

"We need to discuss the missing checks," she said. I had no clue where the checks were. "If you give them back to me, no questions will be asked," Margaret offered. She held her hand as if I had the phantom checks in my pocket.

"I'm not sure what you want me to say. I would help you search," I said. My eyes traveled down to the uneaten plate of food that had begun to congeal.

"She's lying, Marge!" Daniel argued. "You never listen to me!" Daniel sounded like a child. His hand slammed on the table and caused it to vibrate. My eyes scanned the small room for the quickest exit.

"She's going to get us the damn checks!" Margaret spat the words at him before focusing on me again. "I want my money no later than Friday! Have I made myself clear?" Margaret planted her hands firmly on the table. Yep. That's the Margaret I had grown to despise. She is consistent. I looked back at her. She was a prime example that growing old doesn't always make you wiser. Because she was dumb as hell. "Madi, if you think I'm playing games with you, you'll be in for a rude awakening!" Margaret continued. My eyes examined the greedy woman with her perverse husband. He rubbed his hand over his unshaven face. The stubble was patchy in areas, which made him look even more unpleasant. Yep, my opinion had not changed about Daniel; he was the ugliest man I'd ever met. "You know what? Go to your room. You can forget about dinner! You don't deserve to eat!" Margaret yelled as she snatched the plate of untouched food. I cringed as the lumpy forms of meat, mushy noodles, and burnt sauce slid into the trash can. There was a thick, greasy residue left behind on the plate.

"Thank God!" I said, quickly moving from the table. I was glad to be free of them.

"What did you say?" she asked as if I would answer her. I went upstairs and locked the door.

I sat in my mom's chair and let the cool breeze float through the window.

"Jonathan." I breathed the word. To speak his name aloud often brought me comfort. I closed my eyes as a tear slowly traveled down my cheek.

I finally pulled myself from the chair and went to bed.

My eyes squinted to see the shadowy forms down the street. I forced myself to remain hidden in the thick layer of fog. My body was perfectly still as their cloaked heads twitched from left to right. The coldness of the damp wall caused me to shiver. I held my breath when a set of yellow, glowing eyes met mine. Suddenly, all eyes were staring in my direction. I started to run. My feet hit the pavement quickly as I descended the cobblestone street. The sound of their heavy footsteps was close behind. I ran faster. The muscles in my legs began to tighten as I pushed myself to move quicker.

I turned down the dark alley and raced deep to the back. There was no escape. I looked behind me to see the four cloaked figures closing in.

The ground shook beneath my feet, and I found myself speechless as a pair of silver eyes appeared, then twisted to face my pursuers. Jonathan's arm came around me protectively. The smell of sweet honeysuckle and sandalwood intermingled with the alley's dampness. Jonathan slid me behind him and leaped toward the cloaked strangers. I screamed.

My heart pounded deep in my chest as I sat up in bed. Once I could calm my rapid pulse, I laid back down. I couldn't help but smile as I recalled the sweet scent of honeysuckle and sandalwood. I could smell Jonathan in my room. I buried my face in the pillow, lost in thoughts of him.

The alarm went off, and I dragged myself out of bed. I went to my closet and dressed for work. My uniform consisted of a T-shirt, a fitted cap, and a pair of black jeans. I made my bed and sat down at the desk. I got ready quickly. There was enough time for me to write Jonathan. Twelve days had passed since I had sent him the last letter, and he still had not responded. I was impatient and hoped that he might write me back this time.

> Dear Jonathan,
>
> I hope you are doing well. This letter will be brief, as the previous one was closer to a novella. I have been waiting for your reply since my last letter. Did it get lost in the mail? Or did you forget about me? If that's the case, I don't blame you because you are all I think about. I never answered your offer of friendship, so let me tell you now: I want to be your friend.
>
> Although, there is only one question that haunts me: Why did you stay in Paris?

I placed the letter in the cream-colored envelope and tucked it inside my bag. Conner had offered to drive me to work. I would have asked him to drop by the mailbox, although that would have annoyed him.

Conner was waiting by the car, dressed in a t-shirt and sweats for football practice. We could only see each other when he picked me up for work due to our conflicting schedules. I decided that was for the best since he seemed hell-bent on arguing whenever we were together.

We got in the car, and Conner focused on my breakfast bar. I sighed before handing it to him.

"Thanks for the ride," I said before taking a huge bite of my apple.

"No problem. Thanks for the food," Conner said, lifting the half-eaten bar. "We won't have to drive so far when classes start."

I groaned; thinking about the prospect of spending another four years in school, not to mention another three and half months at Margarets,' only made matters worse.

"You don't seem excited. I thought you'd be happy. You'll finally be able to get out of that house. So, where's the enthusiasm?" he questioned jokingly.

"I don't have a dorm room. MCU has a large class coming in, and unfortunately not enough housing. They tried to contact me. The students they could contact were — offered housing near the campus. Margaret told the admissions department that a dorm room wasn't necessary. Of course, she wants to pocket my room and board money for herself. She forgot that I have no way to get to campus since she won't allow me to drive my car," I vented.

"Why didn't I have any problems with my room?" Conner reasoned.

"Because you're a football player and far superior," I said with a hint of sarcasm.

"Oh, yeah, I am superior." He slapped the side of my leg softly. "There should be someone in admissions you can talk to," Conner said. His tone changed, and he seemed concerned.

"Yeah, tried that. But, unfortunately, the feisty redhead behind the desk was no help." It was impossible to hide the defeat in my voice.

"No worries. You can sleep over at my dorm any time you like.

Well, I would have to sneak you in." He offered — with a wink.

"I've heard your idea of sleepovers and adamantly choose to decline." I had heard the sounds coming from his room in Paris, and I wanted no part of it. I wrinkled my nose.

"There are about a hundred things that I'm dying to say right now, but they would only cause your entire face to turn red," Conner teased.

"So, what's your plan? You should be able to get a dorm by the spring semester or, better yet, an apartment. Then you could invite me over," he said as the grin widened on his face.

"Honestly, I'm debating whether to take a year off to travel." My eyes brightened as my mind carried me across the Atlantic Ocean.

"Let me guess. Paris would be your first destination," Conner snapped. His voice intruded into my moment of solitude. The temperature in the car went from hot to steaming in seconds.

"Yeah, I've considered going back. I'll be eighteen soon, and no one can stop me." I said, suddenly regretting my honesty. Conner slammed on the brakes, and my hands went to the dashboard. The wheels of the car came to a screeching stop.

"Madi, if he cared about you, he would be here. Has he called or even acknowledged that you exist since we've been back?" He shook his head. "Did he bother to call you when your parents died?"

Any chance he got, he tried to dismantle my feelings for Jonathan.

"What is with you? How can you be so gullible? There are guys around here that would love the chance to date you. But you're stuck on the guy who has made it clear that he doesn't," Conner said.

"What I know is that something has changed between us. You're different. I'm not sure when you became this person that's always negative, but I have enough to deal with. We need to spend time away from each other," I reasoned.

Conner didn't say anything. Instead, his eyes remained firmly on the road.

He reached over and turned the radio on. "You're mad that I think you deserve better," he mumbled.

"No, I'm mad because you think it's your decision!" I shook my head. "I think we need a break from each other." I leaned down and turned the radio up to end the argument.

I felt Conner's eyes on me every few seconds. So, I twisted in the seat to face the window.

"Hey, I'll try harder not to be so negative." His voice softened as we pulled in front of the theater. I sadly found myself relieved to be out of his car.

"I will find a ride to work until that happens."

"I said I would try harder," he explained.

"When you succeed, give me a call."

He looked at me but said nothing. I moved away from the car, and he sped off; the sad thing was, the further away he drove, the better I felt. Negative energy had a way of draining me.

CHAPTER TWENTY-FOUR
UNREST

The cool, thick mist surrounded me as I raced away from the sound of footsteps. My eyes strained to see the distance that separated me from the cloaked pursuers. They were getting closer, despite my effort to run at top speed. I turned down the damp, poorly lit alleyway. My feet sloshed quickly through puddles that reeked of earthworms, urine, and garbage. When I reached the dead-end and found myself stricken with panic. Jonathan wasn't there. He had always been there. "Jonathan!" I screamed. My chest was pounding, and my anxiety soared as I searched the alley's shadows. "Jonathan!" I shouted once more. Suddenly one of the men grabbed me by the arm.

"Jonathan!" I screamed as I awoke. A quick look around the dark room brought a fresh wave of tears. My sobs muffled as I buried my head deep into the pillow.

I awoke with knots in the pit of my stomach. My eyes were swollen, and I felt like last night's dinner might resurface. I placed my hands over my mouth and dashed toward the bathroom. My sudden movement caused the feelings to intensify, and I had to latch onto the windowsill as my knees buckled. The bathroom was only steps away, but I couldn't move. I tried to pry the window open as tiny beads of moisture gathered on my brow. Suddenly I stopped because, for a second, I thought that someone was standing outside. The large shadowy form was near the edge of the forest, but from my hunched-over position, I could not be — certain. I labored into a standing position, but no one was there. Thankfully, the strange feeling dissipated, and I could move again. I went to the bathroom and splashed freezing water on my face.

"Must have been something I ate," I rationalized before brushing my teeth. I made a vow to never eat at that pizzeria again.

Emma and I agreed to meet at Nirvana's history museum following my shift. Before leaving the theater, I rushed into the bathroom to change and fix my hair.

The museum was a half mile from the theater, so I hurried down the street.

"The rumors are true. Madi's working for a living," a familiar voice said. My eyes came to rest upon Blake.

"Hey," I said cautiously. I hadn't talked to Blake since before the shooting, and it was not a pleasant conversation as I remembered.

"I took a trip to Rio de Janeiro. I had to leave this place before I went crazy," Blake offered. He approached me slowly, and I stopped beside one of the overhanging trees that bordered the sidewalk.

"I know the feeling," I said with an uneasiness that I was almost sure he heard.

"I hope you found peace. My time in Rio helped me put things back in perspective." Blake's eyes held a mischievous glow, although I dared not ask why.

"Yeah, I found peace, just like me to lose it again," I said glumly. He placed his hand on the tree over my head and stared down at me. My head tilted upward, and I silently thought Blake's demeanor had changed. He seemed much more relaxed. He looked as if he had walked off the beach. His khaki pants were — cuffed, and he wore a white unbuttoned cotton shirt. I glanced down to see he had on a pair of tan flip-flops.

"I want to apologize for how I treated you," Blake paused, "after Bria died. I shouldn't have taken my anger out on you." His apology made me feel worse. I would have almost preferred the anger.

"You had every right to be mad at me. We could have helped or at least tried," I said.

"Stop," his long finger shushed me. "We can't change what

happened. All we can do is move on. I miss Bria, but none of us are meant to live forever. They didn't have to die that way; I wasn't prepared for that," Blake admitted. "But I don't blame you." He appeared to have made peace with his loss.

"I'm glad that you're feeling better. I need to meet Emma now. See you around." I started to walk off but felt Blake grip my shoulder and hold me in place.

"Madi, I want to make sure that we're cool."

"Of course, we're fine," I admitted.

"I'd like to get together soon if we can," Blake said.

I looked at my watch. "Sounds good." I gave him a quick head nod and raced to the museum.

My day went by quickly, and I returned to Margaret's house. Daniel opened the door before I even had a chance to pull my keys from my bag. I didn't say a word to him. Only he followed me with his eyes as I headed toward the stairs. I jumped when he slammed the door closed. The vibration caused the windows to rattle loudly.

"Where have you been?" His mouth turned upward. I prepared to run full speed up the stairs, but Daniel darted and grabbed my shoulders firmly. He slammed my back into the wall, pinning me. I pushed against him with all my might, but he used his leg to brace me harder.

"Where have you been, Madi?" Daniel screamed the question in my ear. I refused to make eye contact with him. "Maybe you didn't hear me." He squeezed his fingers deeper into my shoulders. His skin smelled like hot garlic.

"Take your hands off me!" I screamed. The feeling of sheer terror coursed through my body. "I'm going to call the police if you don't get your disgusting hands off me!" My attempt to push his sweaty body away failed miserably. I cringed as my fingers glided over a thick film of moisture that had collected upon his chest.

"Go ahead, call! I went to school with them! Who do you think they'll believe?" He slid his hands off my shoulders and grabbed me by the arms. I groaned as his fingernails dug into my skin. "Besides, I'm not the one you should be worried about! You had a visitor today.

He's pissed about what you and your friends did to his family in Paris!" Daniel yelled into my ear. "I lied, told him you were still in Paris, but I don't think he believed me. He won't stop until he finds you," Daniel said with an eerie undertone that caused me to tremble.

"I don't know what you're talking about! I didn't do anything!" I shouted.

"Well, he's convinced you were involved!" His voice was so loud that I recoiled. "You better stay close to home because they aren't paying me enough to deal with this shit!" Daniel warned. I winced as spit flew from his mouth. The distinct smell of alcohol was on his breath.

"Mike will send the checks. He'll give you more money," I blurted out, hoping to appease the disgusting freak.

"You think I'm talking about Mike? No, sweetheart, the VHW has been footing the bill for my services." His words caused my eyes to widen.

"What do you know about the VHW?"

"Well, they've been paying me to keep track of you. A special assignment, and you sure are special." Daniel smirked. I gritted my teeth, pushing against him again. He didn't budge and had the nerve to laugh at my attempt. "That daddy of yours screwed people over. So, I've been thinking that I should return the favor." He licked his lips greedily.

"Let go of me!" The sick freak ignored me. Thankfully, the screen door creaked open. Daniel released his hold on me. I rubbed my arms. They still stung from Daniel's hands. Margaret stumbled inside, weighed down by the bags of groceries in her arms. She looked from me to Daniel before placing the bags on the table.

"Hey, Marge, I caught her in here with Betty's son," he eased over and coiled himself around her.

"You know the rules! No boys in my house!" the witch commanded.

"He's a disgusting liar! He touched..." Margaret approached me, stopping inches away from my face.

"That's a damn lie! We take you into our home, and you lie on my husband! You had better not be telling your uncle that shit!" she yelled. "I don't know what happened here, but it better not happen again!" Margaret screamed at Daniel. "That girl's money is our ticket out of this damn place!"

"Marge, the girl's lying. You believe me, don't you?" Daniel pleaded.

I used Daniel's whining to make my escape. As fast as I could, I ran into the forest. I didn't stop until the house was entirely out of sight. My fingers ached to call Emma as I held the new cell phone, but I reluctantly dialed Blake's number instead.

We decided to meet in the school parking lot. He was leaning against the side of his car, texting, when I arrived.

"Hey," I said slowly. I examined Blake's face as a million thoughts and questions ran through my mind. Where was I supposed to start? There was something calming about Blake's face. His eyes. I hadn't noticed before, but they reminded me of my mom's eyes. The bright flecks of amber contrasted with the warm chestnut irises.

"Hey..." Blake said before pausing. A wave of embarrassment washed over me.

"Sorry," I said, lowering my lashes.

"Why were you staring at me like that?" Blake asked. I had hoped he would let me off the hook.

"It's your eyes; they are almost identical to my mom's. Sorry, I haven't been myself."

"Oh, I was like, whoa, I don't want to hurt your feelings, but" "No, no, no, definitely not."

I rolled my eyes.

"I don't see..." he said but stopped mid-sentence.

"Blake, you're attractive! But I'm not attracted to you! Not at all, not even a little." My voice held an air of uneasiness. "Sorry, that didn't come out right." My discomfort increased.

"No, I feel the same way," he said with a shrug. "So, you sounded pretty frantic on the phone."

"Yeah, I was thinking about what you said., about the school shooting," I interjected.

Blake scoffed. "Yeah, school shooting," he said sarcastically.

"That's what I mean! I don't understand." I was practically shouting.

"There was no school shooting," Blake replied.

My voice cracked. "I figured out that the men that killed that girl in Traverse City. The ones responsible for the kidnappings. They came to Nirvana for Phillip or for me. And my parents covered this up." My eyes went back to the ground.

"That was a lie too. Don't you see your parent's not only lied to the public, but they also lied to you?" Blake's eyes flashed. He leaned close to me and rested his hands, on my shoulders. His palms were hot and caused my temperature to rise. I eased backward as moisture gathered beneath my shirt where his hands had been.

"They lied to me about what?" I lifted my hair off my neck. "God, your hands are like fire." They were hotter than mine were, I thought, but I didn't dare speak the words aloud.

"Your parents lied about everything," he said.

"I don't understand..."

"Your dad 'working for the FBI..." Blake said. He used air quotes when he said, 'working for the FBI.' "Your dad used the FBI as his cover. He contracted his 'services' to them. My grandfather," he started with a hint of hostility, "told me the truth after Bria and Lindsey were killed." Blake stopped to gauge my reaction, but I had none. "I started, digging around. The murders in Hatteras were identical to the ones that happened nearby. Don't you see? The killers followed you here. He knew they were coming. He helped them, and I watched him shoot Bria, with a high-tech bow-n-arrow. He twisted the story when the reporter came that day." He paused before continuing, his words cautious. "Your dad didn't try to save them, Madi. And, I kept thinking, what if you were there when they arrived? How could he risk you being killed? That's the part that I don't understand. And I know for fact that they were searching for Emma, but she was with you." Blake glanced down at his vibrating cell phone.

"Wait, I figured out that Phillip was involved. Based on what I learned in Paris. I met someone there and he knew about my parents.

He told me that Phillip murdered those people were searching for me." I stopped, my mind bringing all the pieces together, "there must be two groups. The people in Paris and the group that had been with Phillip," I continued to mull over this explanation in my head.

"Ah, shit." He slammed the screen closed. "I must go. We can talk more later. There is something that I must do," He didn't wait for my response, and I didn't have one. I felt numb.

Did Phillip help them? Had he led them to Nirvana? I had blamed myself for so long, but he was at fault. My mind replayed Blake's words: "He contracted his 'services' to the FBI." If Phillip hadn't worked for the FBI, then he must also be a part of the VHW, otherwise why would they join forces to target a high school. A part of me wanted to uncover the extent of his deception; however, another part wanted the truth. No, I deserved the truth.

I snuck back into the house, hoping that Margaret and Daniel would not even realize I had returned. On my way up the stairs, I noticed a stack of letters rubber-banded together on the table. On top were letters addressed to my parents. I crept up the stairs, closed and locked my bedroom door, and plopped down in the chair. I skimmed through the return addresses before my eyes rested on a vanilla-colored envelope. A Paris postage stamp and my hands began to shake.

Hello Ms. Ryan,

It's great to hear from you. I'm sorry for the late reply. Your letters were lovely, and I enjoyed reading them. Emma told me that Nirvana has been getting an abundance of rain lately. I hope you're not feeling unhappy because of me. I'm still in Paris due my work obligations.

You wondered if I had forgotten about you, and I want you to know that's impossible. Madison Ryan, you are unforgettable.

Always,
Jonathan

I pressed the letter to my chest before taking out a sheet of stationery. The pen was still shaking as I pressed the tip against the paper.

> *Dear Jonathan,*
>
> *I'm relieved you're okay, so I can now be okay too. I dreamt of you last night, but my dream was different this time. We walked together on the beach, only there wasn't a star in sight. The two of us swam together until I could go no further. You slipped from my grasp, and the waves pulled me under. I cried out for you, but the water engulfed me. As I was about to let go, a beacon of light appeared and guided me to the safety of the shore. Only now, I don't think it was so much a dream as it was a premonition. That light came in the form of this letter. I received it when I needed it most.*
>
> *Yours truly,*
> *Madison*

I placed the folded letter into a pale blue envelope and sealed it closed as tears streamed down my face. And I tucked it beneath my pillow and crawled into bed.

The second Margaret and Daniel left for work, I went outside and lost myself in the forest. I sat by the river beneath a large maple tree. This had become my favorite getaway. The sound of rain upon the branches quieted the turmoil buried inside me. When the sky began to darken, I headed back to the house. My rain boots sloshed in the soaking wet ground. It had been raining nonstop for two days, and last night, it poured so hard that Margaret said there were flood warnings. I thought the riverbank had been high as I followed the slippery trail.

I paused for a moment as my fingers encircled the doorknob. The deep ache in the pit of my stomach had returned. I twisted around and searched the darkness for anything out of place but saw nothing. "You're going to drive yourself crazy," I told myself. Daniel was trying to frighten me. I glanced back once more before ducking inside.

My eyes widened with fear when I saw the entire living room torn apart. I stepped inside, and the wind blew the door shut. There was a puddle of what looked like blood on the floor and bloody handprints smeared across the walls. The lump in my throat continued to grow. I turned to leave when I heard heavily placed footsteps and twisted to look behind me. I examined the intruder.

His dark, angry eyes watched me silently. My body felt like cement.

"Welcome home," the intruder said. His voice was raspy and thick. "I've been waiting on you." I tried not to react as drops of blood dripped from his thick hands. When I looked back up, our eyes met. "Daniel lied to me. I hate liars. His deceit fit the punishment, a crushed bone or two, or three," the intruder sneered. "You should keep that in mind." Working up all my energy and strength, I reached behind me to ease my hand around the doorknob again.

"That would be a bad decision on your part." He didn't raise his voice, but his threat was clear. I cupped my hands in front of me.

"I want to know who helped you kill my pack?" he bellowed.

"Your pack?" I managed.

"Who helped you?" His anger continued to heighten.

"I don't know what you're talking about."

"I'm not going to ask you again," the intruder said. I backed up against the door, wishing there were more distance between us.

"I don't…" I saw movement and then heard a gushing sound. The palm of his hand landed against the side of my face with so much force it lifted me off the floor. My head hit the wall, and a streak of blood trickled from my mouth. He tossed me across the room with little effort. I fell to the floor, and his boot landed in my stomach. His large hands hit me repeatedly.

"I don't know anything!" I kicked and scratched, but he seemed unaffected. "Take your damn hands off me!" I cried as he dragged me toward the stairs.

"You are going to tell me who helped you!" he screamed. I kicked him hard between the legs when he leaned down to grab me again. He went to his knees, and I raced toward the door. My fingers fumbled with the lock. I threw the door open and stood there in complete shock when my eyes met flashes of silver.

"Jonathan," I stammered in disbelief.

"Invite me inside, Madison!" Jonathan demanded. "Madison, invite me inside!" Jonathan screamed so loud that his voice resonated in my ear.

"Come in," I managed. I watched as Jonathan sent the large man flying across the room. He appeared back in front of me as if he hadn't moved. I groaned as he lifted me into his arms.

"Get her out of here!" Jonathan said as he placed me carefully in Austin's arms. But unfortunately, the rain obstructed my view. I watched in horror as Jonathan returned inside and closed the door behind him.

"No! Help him!" I heard something that sounded like a scream. "Put me down!" My hands beat against his face and chest until the pain shot through my side. "Why won't you help him?" I cried out as he placed me gently inside a car.

In seconds, we were in motion and traveling down the street. "Austin, please take me back! I cannot lose him too! You don't understand!" My eyes fluttered closed.

I shifted in the bed; my head and face were throbbing. I pressed deeper into the pillow, and everything faded to black.

"Madison." Jonathan's face came into view, only to disappear again. He brushed the hair back from my face, but I could only see a hazy version of him.

"Madison," Jonathan said as his cool fingers touched the side of my swollen face.

My eyes finally could focus again. "It's you? You're not hurt, are you?" My voice was barely a whisper as I struggled to clear the cloudiness from my head.

"No, I'm not hurt, but you didn't fare as well."

"I told Austin not to leave you there." I looked past Jonathan to glare at Austin. He was standing in the corner of the room.

"I'll get you something to eat."

"No, please don't go," I managed. Jonathan's eyes filled with regret as he returned and sat beside me.

"You rest, and I will stay." His offer brought a smile to my face, and I noticed the tenderness in his voice. He sat with me for a while before getting me something to eat.

"Annaliese's here," Austin said. He went to the door as if he knew someone was on the other side. He opened it, and I was awestruck when the curator entered the room. She was even more beautiful than I remembered. Her skin was radiant, with soft emerald eyes, and her long blonde hair flowed loosely around her perfectly sculpted face. The yellow sundress made her skin appear luminous. I couldn't help but feel jealous.

"The curator," I said softly.

"Hello, my name is Annaliese. I have been eager to meet you, although not under these circumstances, of course." Her green eyes filled with warmth as she smiled down at me. "I'm going to examine you if that's alright?" I wanted to refuse.

"You're the curator at the museum, *Musee d'Orsay*. Are you a nurse too?" I questioned.

"I have experience in many occupations," she said warmly. "You're afraid; that is more than understandable. I'm here because Jonathan said you needed me. However, the choice is yours." She sat down on the bed beside me. I looked past her in search of Austin, who had already disappeared.

"I can help you," she offered. The level of comfort she gave me was strange, as if we'd known each other for years. "Would you like my help, Madi?" Annaliese questioned again.

"Yes, thank you, but I'm fine," I'm not sure how long she sat there with me or why it felt okay to talk to her. She listened without judgment. I told her about my parents' death, Nic and Mike disappearing from my life, Margaret and Daniel, and the man that attacked me last night.

When I finished, what seemed like the story of my life, I pushed the covers back so that she could examine me. Her fingers touched my side, and it took everything in me not to scream.

She removed my necklace and placed it on the nightstand and applied an icepack to my face; apart from a small bruise, I was fine — I told her as much. I put my necklace back on and eased back on the pillow.

"How is she doing?" Jonathan whispered. His voice was like the sweetest lullaby.

"There are bruises everywhere. The salve will help them heal faster. Madi's a strong girl and should be fine, although she does need to rest. To think that we are known as the violent ones," Annaliese said.

"He attacked her." There was a pause. "I should have come here when she asked me," Jonathan whispered.

"How could you have known this would happen? Don't blame yourself for what he did to her. She's already carrying the weight of the world on her shoulders. Your guilt would only add to her burden." There was an extended pause. "Jonathan, I understand your need to keep her safe. How can anyone look into those eyes and not see that she's worth protecting?"

"That, my dear Annaliese, is an understatement," he replied before their voices faded.

My eyes slowly fluttered open. I stared up at the ceiling. So many unanswered questions rattled around inside my head that I found it difficult to focus.

"I'm glad to see you're awake. How are you feeling?" Jonathan asked when he entered the room. He smiled, but it didn't reach his eyes, and I wondered why he could be so upset.

"Better now." I looked down at the comforter. "Why are you here?" I questioned and silently waited for his answer.

"There was a layover; I thought I'd stop by to say hi," he

said jokingly. "You needed me, and I needed to be here for you," he admitted. His fingers feathered across the back of my hand. My eyes traveled upward and stopped when they reached his.

"Annaliese said you need to eat something." He flashed a genuine smile as he lifted the lid to reveal a large, steamy bowl of soup and crackers. "If this isn't okay, I will get you something else." He held it up for me.

"Thank you." The creamy liquid stung as it slid down the back of my throat. I sipped another spoonful and then handed it back to him.

"Did this happen because you came to Paris? Are these the consequences you spoke of?" His question caused me to look away.

"No," I admitted. Jonathan eased off the bed as if afraid the movement would cause me pain. My eyes went to the ceiling, and I slid into the comforter. "What am I going to do?" I wanted to bite my bottom lip, but it was too — swollen.

"You're going to rest," Jonathan said over his shoulder.

"When are you leaving?" My voice cracked as the words caught in my throat. I wasn't sure if I wanted to hear the answer.

"I'm going to stay here for a while." His eyes narrowed as he came back over and sat in the chair next to the bed. I sat up quickly to embrace him but found myself collapsing back to the bed in pain. "You are supposed to remain still." He placed a kiss on the top of my head. His fingers smoothed the hair away from my face. "Just because I'm staying in Nirvana doesn't mean things change between us."

"I'm happy that you're here. I only wish..." I sighed and snuggled back into the pillow.

"Goodnight, Madison," he whispered.

I awakened to discover Jonathan sitting in the chair beside the bed. His sketchpad balanced upon his lap. I watched as his pencil moved effortlessly across the paper. The second that I shifted; he looked up. His eyes cautiously examined my face. I folded the comforter back. My skin was a little damp from the insulated heat of my body. Jonathan stood to adjust the room's thermostat before returning to sit beside me. I positioned myself higher in the bed.

"How are you feeling?" Jonathan inspected the dark bruises that ran down the length of my arm.

"Better, much better," I admitted.

"You didn't eat anything." His eyes went to the covered platter on the bedside table. He lifted the covering, and my stomach squirmed. A poached egg, sliced ham, toast, pancakes, and fruit were on the plate. Yep, eating was out of the question.

"I honestly don't think I can keep anything down." I fanned my fingers through my hair to remove the tangles. Jonathan went to the bathroom and returned with a brush, which I gladly accepted. He leaned back in the chair and returned to sketching as I brushed my hair until the bristles ran freely.

"What are you drawing?" I tried to lean forward; he lifted the sketch pad out of my reach.

"You," Jonathan said nonchalantly.

"Why would you? I look horrible." I yanked the covers over my head.

"You could never look horrible." The pressure of his weight on the bed forced me to pull the covers back down. He placed the sketchpad in front of me. I dared a quick look — surprised by what he had done. The sketch was of me, but I was sitting in the grass on a blanket in Parc des Buttes Chaumont. My smile widened until the sides of my mouth began to ache.

"You must have a photographic memory." I tilted my head to examine his incredible skill.

"You, Madison Ryan, are unforgettable," Jonathan repeated his written words verbatim. I leaned against him as I stifled a couple yawns. "You should get some rest." He went to move, but I placed my hand on his arm.

"Please stay for a little while." My fingers relaxed their hold on his arm and shifted to grip the covers. I wasn't sure why I believed my grabbing him was okay — something about Jonathan made rational behavior impossible. He eased his arm behind me instead. My head rested upon the hardness of his chest, and I closed my eyes once more.

To say the time, we spent between those four walls was

enjoyable would be an understatement. Jonathan had been different here, less guarded. We talked about the letters, my parent's death, and having to move in with Margaret and Daniel. Our favorite places and our favorite books. He left me speechless when he recited a couple of love letters verbatim. Next, he gave me vivid accounts of his travels and asked where I would like to go. My reply was simple. I want to see as much of the world as possible.

Jonathan explained that Paris was the one place I should forever cross off my list. But he also said that Paris wasn't the same without me. There had been no one to laugh at his ridiculous jokes or engage him in the art of arguing.

His eyes narrowed when I told him I was now a working member of society. I let him know that although Margaret played a role in securing my job, earning my own income gave me a sense of independence. Hearing this, he appeared more comfortable.

I must have fallen asleep because the next thing I knew, the clock read 2:30. Jonathan had not returned, but I knew without a doubt that he was near. I slid out of the large bed thankful that my body was beginning to feel normal again. When I opened the balcony door, the wind-swept droplets of rain through the large door, and onto the long white gown. I closed my eyes as the cool light rain caressed my heated skin.

"Are you alright?" Jonathan asked as he came to stand next to me.

"I, ah…" I stopped myself.

"Madison, you know that you can tell me."

"Are you leaving? I mean, once things settle down, are you planning to stay, or will you return to Paris?" I brushed away a tear. "I missed you."

"Hey, he cupped my face in his hands, "I missed you too, and to answer your question. I plan to stay in Nirvana," He admitted as he gathered me in his arms; ignoring the rain, Jonathan kissed me. This time, instead of pulling away, he pulled me closer.

PRELUDE

My legs ached, and my lungs pleaded for air as I raced down the murky streets. "Run or die! Run or die!" I chanted to myself, urging my limbs to continue. The adrenaline-induced sweat collected and was now dripping from my body. I could feel them behind me. They wanted to kill me. They would kill me. "Run or die!" My inner voice screamed once more. The graveled cobblestone tore at my bare feet, each step more painful than the one before. They were getting closer. The sound of their footsteps was so loud my eardrums pulsated. I glanced back and saw the four hooded shapes gaining on me. "It's now or never!" I shouted. "Run or die!"

The men were on my heels, compelling me to move even faster. I turned down a narrow alley. The next turn left me at the forest perimeter. I looked back as my pursuers raced down the path. "Run or die!" My subconscious urged. I plunged into the blackness of the forest. My heart-pounding so hard that I thought it would burst. The trees ensnared my gown, ripping the gauzy fabric and supplying a trail for my pursuers. Something, no, someone hit me from behind, and I fell hard, too hard, forcing the air from my lungs. "Run or die!" I could not. One of the cloaked men was on top of me. All I could see were the whites of his eyes, but I could feel the sheer hate radiating from him.

"Fight or die!" My subconscious thundered, and as a sudden wave of energy soared through and assembled within my hands, they began to exude a blinding light. I placed them on his chest and pushed him, although my arms never moved. The wind started to swarm around him, nipping

275

and tearing at the dark cloak, removing large fragments of his flesh. His body twisted violently, constricted, and then he lay motionless.

"Fight or die," I heard the voice say, only this time with such clarity that it tugged me out of my paralyzed state. My heart lurched forward as she stepped from between the trees. The voice that had urged me to fight had not belonged to me.

"Mom," I reached for her, but she lifted her hand to prevent me from moving forward.

"Madison, there are more," My mom finally spoke, "They are searching for you even as I speak." I went to my feet and then stumbled over. "They will stop at nothing to destroy you," She leaned over the motionless figure, "You must first kill the body so that you can destroy the soul," my mom explained as she peeled the tattered cloak back.

"It was the man that attacked me at Margaret's house. I screamed. My mom disappeared a second later, and the three remaining pursuers descended upon me.

"NOOOO!" My body jerked upright in the bed.

ACKNOWLEDGEMENTS

My husband, Darrice Price, for his unwavering support throughout the process of writing and publishing Madison Ryan's Kismet.

Deep gratitude to Linda, Kelly, Laura, Jennifer, and Tynisha for your red pens and words of wisdom that guided me through the writing process. To my focus group - Tierra, Nikqua, Natesha, Tiffany, Jennifer, and Cyndi - your feedback and encouragement were pivotal in capturing the essence of the narratives that inspired this work.

My children, Dante, Troy, Shamia, Tre'Vaughn, Tierra, Sophia, and Ahleeya- your presence in my life has been the greatest blessing. The opportunity to love and nurture you all has been the most profound responsibility and joy. Thank you for allowing me to be a part of your journey. My grandsons Javion, Dante Jr., and Kyler - you are my heart's joy and my inspiration's source. Mom, your lessons in kindness have shaped not only my life but also the pages of this book. To Tanya, Charles, Mica, Odell, Beth, Michelle, Sean, Tim, Rhonda, Zeddie, and Tiffany - your support has been a gift that has kept on giving throughout this writing adventure.

A special nod to Najla, Qamber Designs for a cover that resonates with the book's core message of overcoming adversity.

Nada Qamber's talent in interior design and formatting has given life to the words within these pages.

This book is dedicated with love and remembrance to my daughter Shamia Aisha Wilson and son Troy Maurice Wilson "Reese". Your lives were the spark that ignited this journey of storytelling and continue to illuminate my path and those that continue to love you.

ABOUT THE AUTHOR

DEBORAH PRICE'S passion for Greek mythology and her fascination with the timeless realm of vampires serve as the ideal setting for her novel, "Kismet." An accomplished author, Deborah has penned the heartwarming "How Big is Your Love?" as well as the delightful adventure "Mila's Super Duper Scared," both of which are cherished children's books. Away from the written word, Deborah's creative spirit finds joy in dancing and singing alongside her lively ten-year-old twin daughters. Born in Roanoke, Virginia, Deborah now embraces the warmth of Arizona where she resides with her loving husband and children.

Made in the USA
Monee, IL
30 December 2024

72487973R00164